The Du Rose Prophecy

The Hana Du Rose Mysteries

K T BOWES

Copyright © 2013 by K T Bowes

All rights reserved.

No portion of this book may be reproduced in any form without written permission from the publisher or author.

This novel is a work of fiction. All characters, events and locations are either derived from the author's imagination or used fictitiously. Any resemblance to actual events, locations, businesses, organisations or persons, living or dead is entirely coincidental.

The genealogy of Logan Du Rose is entirely made up, as are some details relating to the Waikato Wars during the 1800's.

Would you like to be part of it?

I'm a believer in 'try before you buy.'
There's nothing worse than forking out your hard earned cash on a doozy and regretting it.
I don't want stinky reviews. I want you to love my work and feel like you got value for money.

If you'd like 4 free eBooks, then you can join my mailing list at ktbowes.com
I will take care of your email address and won't be sharing it or spamming you.
You can unsubscribe at any time. I promise not to send Rohan Andreyev after you…maybe.

Acknowledgement

For the real David Allen - who will always be my hero.

Special Thanks

Credit for the weapons expertise and the combat moves goes to Haydn Holdsworth for his knowledge and advice on all things soldiering.

Chapter One

The grounds of the Waikato Presbyterian School for Boys were silent and calm, just as the man liked it best. Holidays and weekends carried a different atmosphere for him, when the whole place felt like his own. No noisy students or aggravating teachers; just peace and solitude, as if the land was asleep. Time to finally think straight.

He sighed and ran a hand through his curly hair, feeling the glossy blond locks under his palm. Vanity momentarily distracted him as he caught sight of his smart figure in a reflection from one of the expensive framed watercolours, donated by a past student who was now incredibly famous and sought after. "Nice," he chuckled to himself, remembering how he coerced the poor man into parting with it. "The painting, not you. Mind you, you're not bad either, you old bugger," he said to his reflection, adjusting the angle of the toupee to his particular satisfaction. He surveyed his empire from the upstairs landing in the main building. The heavy bannister rail under his palms shone in the light from the high, stained glass windows. "This school wouldn't cope without me," he muttered under his breath, running his hand over the kauri wood beneath his fingers. He had always loved this staircase. He blew at an imaginary speck and wiped at it with his sleeve.

Even in a hurry, dashing from class to class or simply storming about, catching out errant boys and staff in equal measure - the man always stopped there. The stairs swept away from him on either side, completely identical, cascading downwards at a steep angle for a school. The health inspectors raised concern over it every year. One hundred and thirty years of existence and yet they wrung their hands with the imagined fear of some lump of a boy, falling down it and breaking his neck. At the bottom, each staircase curved around to greet the parquet floor of the administration corridor, like a pair of arms rushing to enfold it in a loving embrace, the antique wood intricately carved and delicate. He never knew until he reached this spot, which of the staircases he would descend to the ground floor. It was enlivening - that moment of choice. Life hadn't allowed him many choices, not since the day his heart was broken. "*No, don't go there,*" he chastised himself, straightening his spine and clicking his heels together.

Someone with a good business head would have rented the building out for weddings at weekends and in the holidays, making a fortune. The bride could have swept down either staircase of her choosing, gliding elegantly into the Great Hall at the end of the corridor to make her grand entrance. The building was filled with stained glass windows, beamed apex ceilings and all manner of expensive heritage, left to the city by Hamilton's founding fathers. It was one of the few places preserved in this throw-away-culture.

The man turned once again, checking his shiny hair in the reflection of the delicate brush strokes of a watermill scene, before choosing the staircase to the left. In truth, it was his favourite. He loved the stained glass window on that side, glinting at him from above. The Virgin Mary smiled down on him with gentle, tender eyes, offering him absolution. The window on the other side depicted a sword wielding Christ, which filled the man with fear and regret. Still, when he walked down his favourite staircase he was careful only to look at Mary's face and no other part of the picture window; especially not the bouncing baby boy in her arms. The child's eyes could drill into his conscience with terrifying astuteness if the sun was at the right angle. Yet it remained the better route. He only chose the other staircase periodically to tease himself. "If you get what you want all the time, you don't properly appreciate it," he muttered, a familiar, time-worn mantra.

He teetered on the top step, the toes of his shiny black shoes poking over the uppermost tread. It was the staircase designated for staff. Boys used the other one, which is why the teacher occasionally deviated to it. He loved the way the adolescent males surged out of his way in both directions, irritated, but too afraid of him to display it openly as he forced himself right through the middle of the narrow space and caused a bottleneck. They hated it. He loved it. *Power.*

Listening to the silence was calming but perplexing, because it shouldn't be silent at all. The intruder alarm should be clanging out into the surrounding area with deafening peals of distress. The school nestled into a suburb on one side with gully and fields the other. The Waikato Presbyterian School for Boys existed first, out in the countryside for years until the city encroached on its sanctuary, bringing arterial roads and ugly modern housing.

The phone call came early, as he washed his car and enjoyed the peace of a Saturday morning. "One of the local residents reported the alarm sounding. Want us to check it out?" the alarm company co-ordinator asked, making a horrid slapping sound into the phone with whatever he noisily chewed.

"Don't bother!" the teacher snapped. "Not at your prices for a callout." He finished smoothing the paintwork with a leather cloth and told his wife where he was going.

On the top step he listened for a moment, still hearing nothing. "Thanks for the wasted trip!" he spat. "*Idiots!*"

His body jerked as a sound from behind made him turn sharply, almost overbalancing and pitching down the staircase.

The faithful bannister helped him right himself, grappling to hold onto the smooth wood at the last minute. The experience left him shaky and disquieted.

"Well, hello." The man's eyes widened and he whipped around to face the speaker, the last of the colour draining from his face as cold eyes regarded him, shrouded in a characteristic smugness.

"You!" He gulped, forgot where he was and took a foolish step backwards. The last thing he saw was the flash of silver in the visitor's hand as sunlight glinted through the stained glass window and reflected a myriad of prism colours, enticingly beautiful. But it was a hated thing, the cursed metallic object, and it caused a deep frown to cross his features as his flailing body hit the first of many hard-edged wooden steps.

The seasoned oak did not yield, but the teacher's fifty-eight year old body did. By the time he rolled awkwardly down the final, curved embrace of his beloved staircase; he was already unconscious.

The teacher might have survived if the visitor cared enough to ring for help. The bang to his brain from the sharp edge of the newel post would ensure a different kind of life, but he would have lived to labour it.

With a small smile of satisfaction and a casual, "Oops," the visitor slipped stealthily away, thoroughly delighted with the unexpected outcome of the not-so-chance-meeting.

Chapter Two

"Come on, Phoe, please don't be difficult!" the child's father complained through gritted teeth, fighting impatience as his long fingers struggled to fit little booties over her socks. The baby whinged and kicked her legs, causing one knitted object to slip off while the other pinged from her father's hand and landed somewhere near the lounge door. He sighed and sank onto the battered red leather sofa next to her, putting his head into his hands in a picture of despondence. "I can't do this."

The little girl beamed a gummy smile. Seven months old with dark wavy hair and a light olive face, she bore the same piercing grey eyes as her daddy. Their combined Māori genealogy screamed out in waves of inherited *mana*. She sighed, her head touching the back of the sofa and her legs dangling over the edge of the seat cushion as she rooted for her thumb. Turning sideways, she eyed her father with uncanny wisdom, waiting for his next move. His hair was overlong and wavy and he hadn't shaved for three days or slept properly. Not since the *terrible thing* happened. He pinched his fingers over the bridge of his nose and willed the headache away. The child extended her legs over towards him and pitched into the crease between the two seats, making a cute gurgling noise over her thumb and smiling broadly.

Logan Du Rose looked down at his baby, her grey eyes crinkled at the edges in an almond shape as she looked at him with mischief. Her dexterous fingers snatched up an offending bootie from behind her head and she flapped it around in front of her face, her pupils dilating with pleasure. Logan exhaled and smiled at her. "I don't think you need those, do you?" He sighed. "I don't know how the hell they fit on anyway. That's Mama's job. How does she do these silky ties with you wriggling around?" A tightness gripped his chest and fear settled again. He pushed it away. *Give me a difficult brood mare any day, over a pair of woolly shoes!* "Let's go find *Whaea* Leslie," he said out loud, standing and lifting Phoenix onto his hip. He stooped to retrieve the dirty nappy and the other bootie, hurling the nappy into the roaring fire as he left the room and shoving the woolly article into his tight jeans pocket.

"I hope youse dint throw that nappy on the *ahi!*" the Māori housekeeper chided him as Logan pushed open the door to the family dining room. He looked guilty and the brown skinned old woman growled at him, hefting the baby against her huge bosoms. "Youse keep doin' that!" she complained. "It just cooks it and makes the room stink of *roke!*"

Logan shrugged. Shit was the least of his problems. "Stop, woman!"

"Your mama wouldn't do that, would she?" Leslie asked the infant, degenerating into baby talk as the child fixed her with a hopeful gaze at the mention of her mother. The woman looked at the child with sympathy, deliberately avoiding the eyes of her employer. She pressed her lips against the baby's soft olive forehead, neatly avoiding the inquisitive hand which shot out to grab a long, black plait resting temptingly on the old woman's shoulder.

Logan kissed his daughter on the side of her face and tousled her hair with his big hand. She turned her face to him, offering a knowing smile that made him feel stronger.

"Youse go see the missus." Leslie smiled at him, "We're all praying for her."

Logan nodded once and turned to leave, almost bowled over in the doorway by a group of women who pushed inside roughly. The front girl froze on the spot, causing the other three to run into each other behind her. "Bloody hell!" he spat, grey eyes flashing and his face hard.

"Sorry, Mr Logan." They shifted nervously in the doorway, fear creating a haze around them. Devastatingly good looking, he was a hard businessman, not afraid of a fight. Two of the women looked at the ground, knowing even if Logan said nothing else, they would get it from the housekeeper later. The other two looked up at the six foot four inch man through their eyelashes, betraying the lifetime crush each of them nurtured since they were all teenagers together. Logan knitted his brow and moved aside for them to pass, hating the way they sized him up like a piece of muscular meat.

He left with a wave at his daughter and a pause to allow her to wave back, her little hand twisting on the wrist as though she wiped an invisible window. The heels of his cowboy boots clicked on the tiled hallway of the old hotel as he strode towards the lobby. He still heard Leslie explode.

"This is a hotel!" Her voice boomed. "Not a bloody playground! Go clear up the dining room and start on the bedrooms. Youse will be the death of me, *heahea* girls!"

Logan unlocked the silver Honda CRV in the staff area of the hotel car park. The sweet scent of his wife's perfume hit him in a heady cloud of longing and his chest hurt with fear. He pushed his emotions aside as always and climbed in. The weather was crisp and the mountains rose up around the gothic style house his great-great-grandfather built, over a century and a half ago. Sometimes the hotel felt like a blessing, the hundreds of acres of bush and pasture, thousands of prime quality beef stock and the horse stud. Other times it felt like a millstone hanging around his forty-one-year-old neck. The responsibility dragged him down when he least needed the added complications.

Logan adjusted the rear view mirror as he started the engine, noticing another line of grey hairs beginning in his sideburns, peppering their jet black companions. He exhaled and pulled out of the gravel car park, hitting the five kilometre tarmac driveway at a dangerous speed and almost piling into a campervan lumbering through the huge wrought iron gates.

The driver wound his window down. "Is the campsite round here?"

Logan nodded. "You should have gone off to the right after the last bend, but it's fine. Go down past the motel units and say Logan Du Rose sent you that way. They'll have to open the barrier for you."

The English driver rolled his eyes in relief, not wanting to brave the breakneck road again for a wrong turn. Logan nodded and sped away, desperate to get to the private hospital in Auckland where Hana was. His phone trilled and he juggled it onto the cradle and pressed the speaker button. "Du Rose. What?"

"Your *wahine matua* texted last night but reception is bad again so I only just saw it. She wants to see Phoenix. Will you come back for her?" Leslie's voice sounded crackly on the line.

"No, I'm not!" Logan snapped. He disconnected, rudely avoiding the housekeeper's tirade. He felt split, knowing his wife wanted to keep breast feeding but was physically unable to cope with the distress. The previous day she struggled against the pain of four incisions in her chest from the heart surgery as the little girl fed. *The child coped well with cow's milk and a feeder cup that morning*, Logan reasoned, knowing he was kidding himself. "She'll kill me."

Pulling out onto State Highway 1 and heading north towards Auckland, Logan tried to concentrate more on his driving, noticing the cop car hanging around on the hard shoulder touting for business. He touched his brake lights as he approached it, cursing himself for the futile moment of weakness which would show in the radar gun. He indicated and overtook a slower vehicle, maintaining his speed at a steady hundred kilometres per hour until the motorway turnoff to the hospital.

It was after nine o'clock and he missed the rush hour traffic deliberately, although Phoenix made him later than intended. Even though she wouldn't complain, he knew Hana would be waiting hopefully for his face to appear around the door. *And her daughter's.* The thought of her disappointment cut into him and he considered driving all the way back for the baby. *Don't be stupid*, he convinced himself; *you're almost there now*.

The private Monty Lassiter Hospital or the 'Monty' in medical circles was both expensive and fortunately covered by Logan's medical insurance. Taken ill at Rangiriri Pa, between Huntly and Auckland, the the air ambulance flew Hana straight to Auckland General Hospital, for the lifesaving surgery. A genetic fault led to a thickening and blocking of her aortic valve, slow and deadly. The tear was almost fatal, leading to a massive heart attack. Her brother's expert compressions dragged her back from oblivion until help arrived. A happy family picnic quickly degenerated into chaos, misery and disbelief as history repeated itself and the Creator attempted to snatch back Logan's wife, just as he had her mother twenty-six years earlier.

Logan ran a shaking hand over his face, trying not to relive the awful afternoon. It came back to him when he laid his head on the pillow, making him avoid their comfy double bed. He blamed himself, as did her brother. "She's forty-six years old!" Mark shouted angrily in the hospital corridor as they waited for news of Hana. "She's just had a baby! How the hell did you miss the fact she repeatedly fainted during her pregnancy? I can't believe you allowed her to brush it off so casually!" The gifted surgeon was livid. "I suppose you'll tell me you didn't know about the other episodes either?"

"I didn't!" Logan kept his teeth gritted. "You're the surgeon, not me!"

"Yeah well I checked her over a few weeks ago and told her to see her own doctor. I knew something was wrong!" Mark's anger switched to himself and he worked to deflect it back onto the handsome Māori pacing the linoleum floor. "Didn't you notice how tired she got and the weight loss, breathlessness under stress, pains in her upper abdomen and chest...geez man. Don't you care about her at all?"

Logan balled his fists in fury, wisely keeping his mouth shut but only for Hana's sake. He didn't think he had ever felt so helpless or guilty as he did that terrible afternoon, waiting for the emergency surgery to finish. At the *pa*, Logan and Mark almost came to blows over who went in the helicopter with Hana, but her father, Robert stepped in and insisted Hana's husband went. "Mark!" he quietly chastised his son, his Scots accent failing to disguise the terrified wobble. "Let her husband go with her. It's what she would want."

Mark followed them to the hospital by car and a tense standoff between the men ensued as somehow they both ended up feeling guilty and pushed out.

Logan paced along the corridor to his wife's room, his boots making no sound on the plush, expensive carpet of the private hospital. He felt the familiar skip of his heart at the thought of seeing her. He loved the wisps of red hair hanging around her face and the shy smile she kept only for him. She was the only person in his life who ever made him feel needed and it completed him. *Please be ok, Hana,* he begged an unseen God.

Hana's bedroom was immaculately spotless, not a trace of her remaining. The high bed was stripped and lifeless, the room empty. Logan panicked. He ran back to the nurse's station with long strides, arriving with a face of dismay and confusion. His grey eyes were the colour of grit and his tanned skin paled horribly.

"It's ok, Mr Du Rose," the young nurse said with kindness in her face. "Your wife's waiting for you in the day room. I'll show you where it is." She came around the side of the desk in soft soled shoes which made a dull squeak on the carpet. They entered a room which looked as though it could feature in a *Homes and Gardens* magazine.

Hana Du Rose sat in a high-backed chair watching television without registering anything happening on the screen. She was rake thin and her clothes hung off her like curtains. The usually pretty face was colourless. Her emerald green eyes were listless and had temporarily lost their twinkle. Curly auburn hair was pulled away from her face in a loose ponytail, which Logan could tell someone else did for her. Tendrils escaped and hung around her face like a curly halo.

At the sound of the nurse, Hana turned to face her with a serene smile that didn't reach her eyes. But when she saw her husband, it lit up like sunshine on a mirror and she was beautiful. She struggled to her feet and he half-ran to her, frightened to grip her in his usual firm embrace. Instead, he held her as though she was fragile china, feeling the bones through her fleece and chastising himself for his neglect yet again. "I'm sorry," he breathed. He used his thumbs to brush the hair gently off her forehead and kissed her there, keeping his lips pressed to her skin for as long as he dared with the nurse still looking.

Hearing the attendant's shoes squeaking as she left the room, he moved his lips onto Hana's, enjoying the familiar taste and feel of her. He drew her into him, trying hard not to hurt her against his body, but needing to show her how much he needed her. Logan breathed in the scent of her hair and the accustomed smell of her skin, centring himself and trying to regain some semblance of security, realising his nerves were frayed and jangling. The underlying scent of disinfectant and cleaning fluid ruined it.

Hana let him hold and kiss her, needing the physical contact. Her husband felt so strong and invincible, it gave her a needed sense of safety. Every incision or needle mark on her paper thin skin hurt, leaving a continuing ache which wore her out. "Where's Phoe?" she asked. "I need to feed her." Hana's chest hitched at the unexpected relief of finding Logan alone and guilt made her tone rough.

"At home," Logan's voice was muffled through Hana's hair. "It was too hard yesterday. Everything will be all right, but we need to be patient."

"Yeah, it was hard. She waved her arms around, grabbing hold of anything within reach," Hana acknowledged. It was exhausting, trying to feed the seven month old baby and keep the tiny hands away from the stitches, the drip wire and everything else of interest. In the end, Logan swaddled the baby in a blanket to pin her down and the little free spirit had not enjoyed the experience.

Hana sighed, laying her cheek against Logan's chest. She slipped a hand up the back of his tee shirt and savoured the feel of his smooth skin under her palm. He smelled like he always did, of fresh hay and summer sunshine. It gave her comfort and peace which translated into a long relaxing exhale.

Logan misread it, stiffening in panic and dropping so he could catch his wife behind her knees and lift her bodily off the ground. His strong biceps tensed and her lightness terrified him. Hana stifled the groan which almost escaped as the stitches pulled in her chest. She snuggled her face into his soft neck. His hair tickled her nose and made her want to sneeze. "I want to go home, Logan," she begged plaintively. "Please take me home?"

Logan spun on the spot, trying to find somewhere to put his wife down so he could talk sense into her. Finding nowhere instantly appealing, he plonked himself down in a comfy armchair and snuggled her into his lap. Hana resisted, as though taking part in a silent protest and Logan relaxed and drew her into him, savouring the normality of the embrace despite the distinctly abnormal surroundings. He stroked Hana's hair and kissed the top of her head numerous times, his brain practicing sentences of negation.

"The doctor said I could go," Hana persisted. "I've got a discharge notice with instructions and a prescription for pills. Please can I come with you?"

"I'm not sure," her husband answered truthfully. "We're a long way out if something goes wrong and it's not the easiest place to land a chopper."

Hana sat up and looked at him in dismay, betrayal in her green eyes. "You don't want me to come home." Anger and astonishment curled her upper lip in a pout. She shoved herself off his knees and stalked away, her slender back rigid and her ponytail swinging. "If you don't have faith in me, then what's left?"

Hana saw only personal rejection. She had accepted the discharge notice, convinced rest and familiar surroundings would aid her recuperation. The insurance company wanted her out, her room had been reallocated, and her few belongings were behind the nurses' station. Now she had nowhere to go. Hana went to the immaculate bathroom half-way down the corridor, shut herself in and sat on the top of the toilet seat in tears. If Logan wouldn't take her back to his hotel in the mountains, she would need to find an alternative destination. "Because I'm not staying here!" she sobbed.

Hana contemplated her options, which were limited. They included getting a taxi to her house in Ngaruawahia, or even back to the staff unit at the Waikato Presbyterian School for Boys where she lived during term time with her teacher-husband and baby. The major flaw in the plan centred on her heart attack and emergency airlift not including her purse or handbag. "I'll call Tama then," she chuntered stubbornly to the empty bathroom. "He'll fetch me." Her chest hurt with the realisation that if she dragged her nephew into the miserable situation; it had the potential to fracture his relationship with Logan and they would both blame her. Besides which, she couldn't go anywhere without Phoenix.

Hana continued to run through her list of friends and possible rides out of the hospital, counting them off on her fingers. Her daughter, Izzie was in Invercargill at the opposite end of the country with her three young children, but her son was an hour and a half away in Hamilton. Their relationship was not the best, but he might be willing to drive up and get her if she begged him. "No house keys!" Hana wailed to herself, hearing her pathetic voice echoing back to her from the wall tiles.

"Mrs Du Rose, are you all right?" asked a soft voice through the door after the owner of it knocked gently. Hana recognised the nurse who cared for her over the last few days.

"I'm fine," she sniffed, blowing her nose loudly and not wanting the nurse to open the door on her.

"Your husband's here. He's concerned about you. Could you please open the door?"

"No," Hana said sullenly, blowing her nose again. "Tell him it's fine, he can go. I'm organising a lift for myself. I need to find a way to get my daughter off him and then I'll be sorted."

Hana heard whispering outside the door and ignored it. She enjoyed the rare power self-pity fuelled for her after four days of being constantly under someone else's control. She leaned sideways on the toilet seat and looked at her face in the mirror. "*Ugh!*" It was blotchy and pinched-looking with a smattering of tears on her drawn cheeks. She squeezed a few more out easily and looked again. She already felt like a geriatric and now she looked like a pathetic one as well. *A sad geriatric whose husband won't give me a ride home from hospital*. Hana hiccoughed and the tears ran freely then at her pitiful situation. She tugged at the roll of toilet paper and the last three sheets detached themselves, leaving an empty cardboard cylinder dangling from the metal hook.

The whispering outside the door stopped and the handle turned and clicked. Hana watched as it opened slowly and Logan appeared in the doorway. She screwed her face up in exasperation; forgetting his ability to break in anywhere. "Get lost!" Exhaling crossly, Hana turned away, swivelling on the toilet seat and hearing the hinges emit a dreadful creak. The nurse looked in at her through the gap between Logan's arm and the door, satisfying herself the patient hadn't collapsed. Hana pressed the fragile squares of tissue against her eyes and tried to mop herself up, hearing the door click shut again. She wondered if her husband had gone away but couldn't peek, as one of the tissue pieces had stuck to her eyelid.

Standing up, Hana felt for the sink, only able to see through one eye. The water was cold as she splashed it over her face and she spluttered as some of it went up her nose. A paper towel dispenser hung on the wall to her right and she reached out and snatched towels from it, rubbing the hard material over her face. When she looked at herself in the mirror again, she was pleasantly surprised to find the cold water had reduced the puffiness of her eyes and the frantic rubbing had given her cheeks colour. Her husband's grey irises met her refection as he stood watching patiently for his wife to finish her ablutions. "I'm organising a lift," she said facetiously at him. "You can go now."

The livid scar underneath Logan's right eye twitched slightly as Hana stared at its reflection in the mirror. It was back to front and looked wrong. Without removing his gaze, Logan leaned back against the smooth wall and put the sole of his boot against it, bending his knee and settling in for a long wait. Hana's nerve began to leave her, knowing she would inevitably lose this game. She wanted to get out of her claustrophobic self-imposed prison, feeling trapped by the giant male blocking the doorway, his muscles bulging through the white tee shirt. Logan studied his wife with interest as he settled into a comfortable position. *Stalemate.* A tiny smirk lifted the corner of his lips and he folded his arms.

The battle of wills began and it was familiar and safe, re-establishing their dynamic as a couple. Hana's fragility terrified her husband. He fell in love with a feisty redhead and very much wanted her back, regretting the foolish doubts he shared out loud. It was selfish and possibly a little cruel. He was ready to say sorry, but wasn't sure if Hana was ready to hear it. She unnerved him and so he waited, treating her like a horse he was in the process of breaking, exercising his never-ending patience and inviting her to test his iron will for herself. Hana huffed and puffed and sat back down on the toilet seat, determined not to give him the satisfaction of beating her. Again. *Deadlock.*

The sound of shuffling made them both look round as an elderly man pushed the door open. Dressed in a fluffy green dressing gown, he walked with difficulty, pushing along a metal walking frame. He looked uncomfortable. "Oh, terribly sorry," he said seeing Logan standing to the right of the door and Hana sitting on the toilet. "There's a problem with my ensuite and the other one's engaged." He tried to turn his walking frame and almost toppled sideways, saved by Logan shooting out his strong forearm.

Hana rose from the toilet lid, her face laced with guilt and called after the retreating white hair, "It's fine. I'm done here. You can have this one."

Logan helped the old man shuffle through the toilet door, listing like a stricken tanker. "Thanks so much." He looked grateful, "I don't think I'd have made it."

Hana bolted, hoping to escape the bathroom before her husband but wasn't nearly quick enough. Clamping his big hands around her upper arms from behind, he pushed her in front of him towards a cupboard door on the opposite side of the corridor. Finding it unlocked, he forced her in one-handed and shut the door behind him. Hana opened her mouth to speak, the metal shelves digging into her back but Logan put a finger over her mouth to stop her. "Firstly, I never said you couldn't come home. You jumped to conclusions. I have valid reasons for being worried, but I've talked to the doctor now and I'm fine about it. They've given me an emergency number to call and an advice line I can access if you get sick again."

Logan leaned in close to Hana and placed his right hand against the shelving unit above her. He towered over her and she felt tiny in comparison, looking at his shirt buttons at close range to avoid the penetrating grey eyes reading her like an open book. One of the little buttons was coming adrift, its cotton threads protruding dangerously. They fluttered comically in her breath.

"So how do we play this?" Logan asked, sounding tired of Hana's amateur dramatics. She shrugged like a sullen teenager and shook her head. "Will you stop being difficult and get in the car with me, or do I carry you out kicking and screaming?"

Hana smirked, relieved he hadn't suggested leaving her there to fend for herself. She felt grateful it wasn't even on the list of options. She hung her head and feigned contrition. Logan ran his fingers down her damp cheek and lifted her head to look at him. "What am I going to do with you?" he whispered, his voice laden with emotion. His mouth was warm and luscious against Hana's dry lips and she drank in the kiss with enthusiasm. The wounds on her chest ached as the familiar feeling plummeted through her stomach, desire and lust reviving her tired body. She pushed her hands under his shirt and felt the solid muscles either side of his spine and the tautness of his body, wanting more. Clattering in the corridor disturbed them and Logan pulled away first, indicating the door with a jerk of his head. "Stop being an egg and get your *nono* in that car!"

Hana slipped out from under Logan's arm and scooted, rattled by the loud beating of her heart in her ears. Logan stirred something latent within her and the new pacemaker responded, channelling the heightened blood flow caused by passion. Hana hoped it would be able to cope with the responses the beautiful Māori invoked, every time his feather light touch dusted her porcelain skin.

Chapter Three

Hana wept bitter tears in her room for half an hour after her father; Robert McIntyre left for the airport and his arduous flight back to England. She cried over the twenty- six wasted years, having truly believed he hated her for her accidental teenage pregnancy. The Scotsman found her in McDonald's in Hamilton, of all places on the earth and the reunion was eventually healing. But the parting was bittersweet, her heart attack robbing them of further precious hours in his short visit. The sight of her strong father in tears at their good-bye was something Hana knew would haunt her until her dying day.

The melodramatic side of her nature told her she would never get over it, while the rational, sensible side wrestled and argued and urged her not to be silly. It was enough to set her off crying again, conjuring up that image in her mind of his steady blue eyes fighting the terrible inner pain of leaving his daughter. *Especially now.* She recalled his trembling hand waving up at her on the balcony as Logan stuffed his belongings into the boot of the Honda. *What if I never see him again?*

Robert had been so brave, holding it all in until the last minute, but that final look up at her had done it for them both.

Tears coursed down his crinkled face like a burst dam and he struggled for control, knowing he was upsetting her further. Even from the distance between them, Hana saw the glassiness of his eyes and the emotions there. His soul seemed to cry out to her, *I don't want to leave* and hers answered painfully, *then don't*.

Elaine, his second wife, belted him into the back seat like a child as Tama climbed into the front. Robert wiped his eyes on the back of his hand and waved in the general direction of the balcony, but he couldn't look at Hana again. Another glance at her agony on display would break him open for sure. Even Logan didn't look at his wife as he backed the car out and drove towards the gates and Hana felt unacknowledged and invisible.

She stood watching for a long time after the sound of the wheels on the driveway dulled to nothing and the Honda treacherously bore her parent away from her. The wind got up and caused Hana's red hair to stream out behind her, buffeting her thin frame relentlessly and making her feel even more of a victim. Her life felt like a bad movie; one where everything went wrong for the heroine and while the innocent cinema goers waited patiently for a happy ending, the credits rolled and the heroine stayed dead or alone. A sick feeling rose up in her chest and she struggled to name it so she could send it away, but it refused to be called by any label that might help. So she stayed feeling sick, unsettled and lost.

"I want to come with you," Hana wept to Logan the night before. "I need to say goodbye."

Logan shook his head and denied her. "No way, Hana. The journey here was too much for you. I'm not taking you to the airport. Stay here and rest."

Hana was inconsolable, crying before daybreak at the injustice of it all. Surely at the very least, they could have let her squish in the back between her father and his wife and not denied her that last hour of comfort. "Why's Tama going?" she had sobbed.

"He's signing his contract at the Fire Department headquarters in Auckland." Logan was resolute and immovable and Hana pouted at the memory of his strong jaw and the determined set of his shoulders. He held her while she cried and protested, unmoved by the enormous tears that ran down his shirt and speckled his arms.

"I hate you," she wailed and he had laughed at her then.

"No you don't."

Hana regretted all the wasted hours when she could have sought her father out and made the most of his presence on her side of the world. She should have hugged him, kissed him and told him she loved him until he knew for sure she meant it. She should have stopped him going sightseeing, made him stay in her company the whole time and not told him he deserved a holiday. She should have been selfish and kept him all to herself.

Even as she worked through those feelings, Hana knew they were irrational and childish. Robert McIntyre knew his daughter loved him. The greatest resentment in Hana's muddled emotional shopping list was that the heart attack and subsequent surgery robbed her of precious time with her dad. It forced her to sleep often and seem tired and unenthusiastic in these last days. She hated her body for subjecting her to that. And therein lay a huge part of the problem. She no longer trusted her body. She was forty-six years old, not ninety-six and yet it hobbled her as thoroughly as if she was. The cuts on her chest and the invasive pacemaker were a constant reminder of her own mortality, her inability to predict anything about her life, not even the next heartbeat.

Anger bubbled up inside the woman like an ugly thing. Hana daren't even go to the family dining room, where she knew Leslie looked after her baby. *Even Phoenix doesn't need you or your milk anymore,* a spiteful voice whispered in her head and she finally named the thing that ate at her soul. It was a spirit of *abandonment.*

Hana ran from the bedroom and down the spiral staircase to the ground floor. The rush of adrenaline caused her to grab at her chest, terrified she might cause the object next to her collarbone to administer the promised shock the consultant described for her. She didn't want to be jabbed like a kick to the chest and felt an overwhelming urge to rip the hideous thing out herself. *Nobody asked if I wanted it, no-one consulted me!* The dreadful sadness morphed into something terrible inside, reeking with the stench of self-pity and powerlessness. Hana caught the reflection of ingratitude in a hallway mirror and it was not attractive.

She needed to get away, to be high up out of reach and look down on her situation from a different vantage point. Hana craved the wind in her face and the sense of freedom which illness robbed her of. The isolation of Logan's new house in the mountains called to her with a recognisable voice, shouting to her on the wind to come, feel its enfolding grace and find herself again. The doctors told her not to drive, not until her condition was settled and her local specialist signed the documentation. Nobody banned her from horse riding.

Hana kicked off her slippers in the mudroom at the back of the hotel where the stockmen kept the riding boots and broken tack. Digging around, she found her sister-in-law's, boots and chaps and fitted them on over her jeans, clamping Miriam's hat down over her hair. She felt a flicker of sadness for her dead mother-in-law and buried it, knowing her fragile courage would fail in the face of overthinking. Even the short walk to the stable yard seemed endless. A lot of things did nowadays.

As she neared the sound of clattering buckets, Hana tried to get her story straight for Jack, the ancient stable manager. He might be deaf but he missed absolutely nothing and he wouldn't let her ride out on her own without talking to Logan first. She felt momentarily relieved at her husband's absence and then teared up at the thought of the airport run which took him away. Getting her tale ready and fortifying herself for an argument or abject refusal, Hana took deep breaths and forced herself to saunter casually into the yard.

Jack's old Jeep was noticeably absent from its space at the entrance to the lunge arena gate and Hana experienced instant relief. An urgent neigh came from a row of stalls facing east, the brick work bathed in sunlight. Turning, Hana found herself face to face with Sacha, Logan's temperamental mare. The beast jerked her regal white face upwards as though in greeting and Hana lifted her hand to wave, feeling suddenly stupid and putting it back by her side. "Hi," she said instead, feeling a fool.

The yard seemed empty of humans and Hana considered her options. Sacha's tack rested on a wooden stand outside her stable door and she contemplated struggling to tack the horse up, discounting it instantly. If the effort of lifting the heavy tan stock saddle didn't kill her, then the angry mare probably would within the confines of her stall. Sacha's mean reputation preceded her although Hana had ridden her successfully once, much to everyone's astonishment.

Sacha stretched her neck out for a pat and scraped her shod front foot against the concrete floor of her stall. Hana reached out a nervous hand and stroked the elegant forehead gently. The horse shook her head from side to side and closed her eyes. Hana got closer, convinced at some point the mare would take her revenge for stealing Logan's affections away and bite, but she didn't. The woman stood and caressed the white forelock and stroked the rounded Anglo-Arab nose tenderly. "I want to go up to the new house," Hana whispered, "but I know they won't let me. My dad left and they wouldn't let me go. They didn't want a scene at the airport. Logan said it was for my benefit but it was really for his. And while I've been in hospital, they've been feeding my baby cow's milk so she isn't bothered about me that much anymore. She always preferred her daddy, so that proves it. I guess you know what that's like; your colt must be getting big now."

Hana faltered, unable to describe the emotions raging through her mind. She lay her forehead against the mare's and closed tired green eyes. The horse stayed still and all Hana could hear was the sound of snuffled breathing from the huge lungs.

The clatter of footsteps on the concrete behind made them both jump away guiltily. A young man in his early twenties approached with a bucket and a yard broom. He was dark skinned and black haired with a confident stride. Despite the winter chill, he wore jeans but no tee shirt, his shoulders and ribs swathed in tattoos denoting his *whakapapa*, lineage. He stopped abruptly, staring at Hana. "Miss, I'd watch that beast. She's a nasty mare. Real up herself, she is."

Edging closer, his eyes widened in surprise at Hana's proximity to the horse, cradling the whiskery chin in her cupped hand. The mare's eyes were closed in pleasure, but she opened one of them to give the man a wicked, white rimmed eyeball. He pulled a face and stepped back.

"Where's Jack?" Hana asked, forcing politeness in the hope of assistance.

"He's gone to the township for some stuff. He'll be back soon though."

Hana hissed through her teeth. She needed to get away before Jack returned. Otherwise, she wouldn't get away at all. She decided to risk it. Leaning close into Sacha, she whispered, "-*Please help me*," and unlocked the top and bottom bolts on the stable door. The horse put her head up obligingly as Hana took hold of her halter and pulled her forwards through the door, intending to lead her over to the tacking area. The young man stepped in front of her, shaking his head, his face disbelieving.

"No, Miss, that's Mr Du Rose's beast, you can't take her. You wouldn't want to. Wait till Jack gets back and he'll sort you out something else. Are you a guest from the hotel? I've got other mounts and if you wait, I'll take you on a ride through the lower slopes."

Hana continued walking, Sacha following meekly at her side. "Please could you bring her tack?" Hana asked with quiet authority.

The inexperienced young man groaned. He looked increasingly awkward and his strong hands fluttered by his sides. "Miss, I'm new here. I'm apprenticed to the best horseman in the central North Island and it's all about to come to a skidding halt. You'll get me fired, Miss."

He bit at a ragged thumbnail, confusion blemishing his handsome features. Relief coursed across his face as another man entered the yard, head down, his hat covering his eyes. "Toby, can you help me mate?" he begged. "This lady..."

The new comer stopped at the sight of the pretty redhead leading the usually ferocious mare. "Hey Mrs Du Rose," he said and touched the brim of his cowboy hat lightly. "You feeling better now?"

"Yes thanks, Toby," Hana replied, smiling at Logan's head stockman. "Please can you help me tack Sacha up? I can't lift the saddle; it's too heavy."

Toby was conflicted but only for a second. "You rode her before, aye?"

Hana nodded. "Yes, she's fine with me."

Toby nodded once and then shrugged. He looked across at the statue of a stable hand, hopping from foot to foot like an idiot. He beckoned him over, his voice sharp. "Rawhiti will help, if that's ok? I'm taking the quad up to the forty-first to move some stock and I should get going."

On cue, his radio chirped and an impatient voice crackled through like a disjointed universe calling. A string of swear words followed as somebody somewhere reached the end of their patience. Toby looked apologetically at Hana and beckoned the young man again. "Geez man, you made of salt or what?" he asked angrily, "Help the missus will you?"

He looked back as he strode over to the huge equipment shed, pleased to see the man finally come to life. Toby paused to watch Rawhiti bring the saddle and bridle across the yard, gingerly avoiding the mare's back legs. The stockman fired up the bike with a roar and shot out of the shed, making them all jump.

"How do I say your name?" Hana asked kindly as the man put the saddle pad onto the shiny white body with care. "Rawhiti, Miss," he answered politely, pronouncing the '*wh*' at the centre of his name as an '*f*'. Hana repeated it a few times until she got it right and the man nodded, pleased at the trouble she took. "Most *Pākehā.* just call me *bro*," he said sadly. He fitted the saddle onto the ridged spine and jumped once when the horse turned to look at him. He hissed with exasperation. "I've worked with horses since I could walk and this mare is one b..." he bit back the swear word, remembering who he was talking to. "Are you Logan Du Rose's wife? The boss man?"

Hana smiled serenely. "Yes, I am. And Sacha's playing with you," she said, stroking the long shaggy forelock out of the mare's eyes.

Rawhiti raised his eyebrows as he tightened up the girth, watching the back leg come slightly off the floor in warning and readying himself to dodge it. He got the bridle on without incident but could swear the mare narrowed her eyes at him as she took the metal bit behind her front teeth. "Evil, just evil," he muttered. "Want help up?" He offered Hana his cupped hands for a leg up, but she shook her head and led the mare over to the mounting block.

The horse stood meek as a lamb while the woman settled herself in the saddle. But Rawhiti caught a flash of pain in her pale face as she swung her leg across the broad back and clambered on. "You sure you're all right, Miss?" he asked. Something hammered in his brain about the missus having not been well, but he couldn't recall what important detail clamoured to make itself known. As Hana clattered sedately out of the yard, he went back to his sweeping, hoping he hadn't made a bad first impression.

"Which way, Sach?" Hana asked the horse quietly as they left the pristine stable yard. "I don't think I'm in any fit state to open gates today." The mare snorted and turned left, making for the steep track put in for the construction vehicles in the house building process. It would later become the five kilometre driveway. At the moment, it was hard-core packed down with bright orange sand and safe for the shod feet to walk on, provided they stayed in the middle. "I hope we don't meet any big lorries," Hana said, observing the dense bush on one side and the perilous drop on the other. "There's nowhere to wait."

Hana relaxed into the saddle and enjoyed the freedom of being alone. It had become a rarity in the last week for the woman to be left by herself. In the hospital, nurses and doctors checked her constantly, waking her to do their various tests. Once at the hotel it was Logan or Leslie, Mark, Tama or her father who peered over her anxiously. She was tired of waking up with a start to find a worried face above her line of vision, checking her for signs of life.

The wind gusted and threatened to steal Miriam's hat off her head. Hana took it off and reached inside, finding the elasticated cord and pulling it down over her chin. It was too precious to lose. Irreplaceable. As the driveway progressed underneath the canopy of the bush, it grew more shaded from the elements and the rule of nature took over. It didn't seem to matter what man did; the bush would retain its fierce hold on life as long as it was able, defying the odds and springing back up even after a bush fire.

They walked along making decent progress on the incline, Sacha walking with lengthened reins and her head down, seeming to examine the ground underfoot with interest. Hana let her pick her own footing and sat heavily, allowing herself to breathe deeply and consider the events of the past week with objectivity.

She had felt the cold fingers of death exactly a week ago, knotting eagerly around her heart. The pain was far more frightening than dying itself, something Hana had never considered. It made her think of her late husband, Vikram Johal. He died in a horrific car accident on the Kaimai Ranges, ploughed into head-on by a speeding articulated lorry which ran out of control on a bad downhill bend. Vik, coming up the mountain, didn't stand a chance and the coroner said he died on impact. Hana hoped so. Her heart attack was so unbearable, she didn't want to think of Vik's premature death being one of hopelessness and agony.

"Perhaps my experience would have more purpose," she told the plodding mare, "if I could stand up in church and claim an out-of-body moment or a meeting with Jesus." But she couldn't. It had been as terrifying as it was pointless. Hana felt as though she learned nothing, except perhaps not to trust her body. Neither she nor her poor husband needed showing how fragile life was. Surely they had lost more than enough between them already.

Hana felt the tightness of the stitches in her chest and shoulder as Sacha negotiated a piece of disturbed ground and she reached up gingerly to touch the outside of her shirt. Her fingers strayed inside, to touch the object underneath her left collar bone. It wasn't huge, hardly noticeable. They said that she would get used to it. It felt odd. Hana sighed heavily and Sacha lifted her head and flicked her ears back and forth. The woman leaned forward and patted the velvety neck with gratitude. "You're uncannily perceptive. Perhaps that's why my husband keeps you."

The gate to the top site was wide open; so different to the coveted, protected piece of land Logan first introduced Hana to. She was his girlfriend then, tentatively taking her first steps into a new relationship and terrified of being hurt. She hadn't known he was obsessed by her and had been for almost three decades. Right from the age of fourteen when he first saw her on a London tube train, pregnant, unmarried and tearful, Logan Du Rose made it his life's work to find and possess the affections of the stunning redhead.

Hana doubted if Logan would ever have taken 'no' for an answer. He hadn't needed to. She fell in love with him almost straight away after a chance at the school she worked at. Then circumstance forced them together, far quicker than if they were left to their own devices.

Sacha nosed her way through the gate and stood patiently waiting for instructions. Hana neglected to bring the halter or lead rope and now she was here, didn't fancy the jolt which a dismount would cause her sore scars. "I don't know how to do this, Sach," she said, looking around her with a returning sense of hopelessness.

The mare, sensing her anticipated discomfort, wandered slowly over to a picnic table the builders used for their lunch breaks and lined herself carefully up next to it. Hana was grateful for her equine thoughtfulness and dismounted onto the table top, leaning on Sacha's neck to get herself down without overbalancing it. "You're pretty amazing, do you know that?" Hana kissed the side of the furry face.

Logan usually untacked the animals and put halters on them now the paddock was a building site, tying them up to the nearest fence. Hana doubted if she would be able to lift the saddle back and if she didn't, the mare might roll and hurt herself or damage the saddle. It seemed as though having made the journey up here, Hana would be unable to look around the house. "I don't know what to do now," she said to the horse, sounding pitiful and Sacha snuffed gently into her hand. Hana lay her cheek against the soft furry forehead and closed her eyes, wondering what to do. Finally, she unclipped the reins from the bridle and loosened the girth a little. "Please don't roll on Logan's saddle because after he's killed me, he'll be coming for you. You can eat the grass and I'll wash your bit when we get back."

The horse snorted grass seed and proceeded to graze, lifting her head once as Hana added, "Oh and please could you come when I call you? I don't think I can chase you home anymore. I've got enough problems."

Sacha appeared to nod in her direction and carried on grazing, despite the metal snaffle in her mouth.

Hana wandered around the site looking at the familiar landmarks now incorporated into her new home. At the end of the driveway before it plunged steeply down the mountain, stood the old kauri tree. It stood there forever. Hana lifted her arms and tried to reach fully around its huge girth, finding she didn't even get half-way around its smooth, knotless bark. With her cheek pressed against the cool wood, she fancied she heard its steady heartbeat drawn from the gentle motion of the earth turning on its axis. Looking up she read the names of Logan's family. The beautiful script began with the Frenchman, Du Rose, who settled on the land in the 1800's. It stretched through the family, a rich tapestry of names interlocked in swirling graphics and ended with her own baby's name, *Phoenix*.

Hana wondered how Logan got up there to do that last carving, figuring he must have climbed the tree. He would tell her off for hugging the sacred object. It had great *mana* in his family, his own and his daughter's afterbirth buried at the bottom in the dusty earth. She should wash her hands to get rid of the *tapu*, but rebelled and didn't even bother looking for water. "What else can go wrong?" she mocked Logan's ancestors. "Kill me? Too late!"

Hana raked the ground with her eyes and a sense of growing distaste. She thought of the night of Phoenix's birth and the sound of Logan burying the placenta in the hard ground with the heel of his boot, the mountain noises and the cackle of the tui who fluttered in the trees, watching instead of settling in his nest for the night.

Hana skirted the outside of the house. The almost-finished-brickwork looked beautiful, exactly the kind of thing Logan would build, classical and visually pleasing. He had fostered the design in his mind's eye since the age of five, when his grandmother bequeathed him the land in her will. Along with the gift came the cryptic message to *'build a new house'*. The matriarch meant a new legacy, an untainted household, not a building. Logan was trying to do both and this structure was the physical representation of that.

Hana thought about the original Phoenix Du Rose, Logan's paternal grandmother. She was well aware of Logan's heritage, sired by one of her sons yet raised by the other. The forty year old feud, which split the family down its core and banished one branch to a small section of the property nearby, had been down to Logan's birth. It was the best kept family secret of all time and

Logan's devastation at his revealed heritage was catastrophic, just a few months earlier.

Hana mooched around, looking through windows as the builder's debris made it impossible for her to enter the house. She pulled up short on the far west corner as she came face to face with the electricity generator powering the work and eventually, the house. Clapping her hand over the pacemaker, Hana backed away, her eyes wide with fear. It was one of the details she remembered from the consultant's visit on the last day in hospital. "*Stay away from magnets and generators.*"

"How far do I have to be?" Hana cried out into the empty landscape. The futility of it all hit her in a tsunami-like wave of despair. "Logan's building me a house I can never live in!" Hana backed away from the machine and the structure housing it, not looking where she was going and finding herself flat up against the wooden balustrade of the porch. Her feet grappled in sand and debris and she stumbled forwards, falling onto her hands and knees with the leather reins still clutched in her fingers. The pain was excruciating, not in her chest but on her knees as they took the brunt of her fall. She felt grit and sharp stones through the cloth of her jeans and the heels of both hands were grazed and dirty when she turned them over.

Like the motherless child she was, Hana cried without control, feeling her life unravel in front of her and powerless to stop its collapse. She forced herself off the dirty floor and staggered around the building to open ground, picking her way over discarded polystyrene and bricks, metal piping and used cardboard. Logan's neat-freak tendency would send him crazy and the builders would be thrown off the job if he saw it. Hana stumbled like a drunkard to safety, hopelessness shrouding her like a sorry veil.

The cliff edge at the back of the house was steep and treacherous, masking a drop of hundreds of metres and Hana sank down on the precipice, her feet dangling dangerously over the lip. Logan promised the house was built into the rock, drilled down securely so it would be safe from heave and slip, certified by countless engineers. Suddenly she didn't care anymore. Her chest hurt, her head ached and she felt tiredness wash over her like a blanket descending over her head.

Hana lay on her right side facing the distant Port Waikato. Her husband drove her to the tiny town once as curiosity got the better of her. "It seems silly," she had argued on the drive there, "to live on a mountain looking down on a town you've never visited."

There was nothing there. Port Waikato was a shop, a few houses and a café that was closed. Logan tried to warn her, but Hana was convinced he was wrong, making him drive up and down countless dead ends and roads to nowhere. The Mighty Waikato River terminated there, joining the Tasman Sea in a beautiful estuary which went largely ignored. Logan found a deserted area with sand dunes and made love to her, the bump from her pregnancy getting in the way and reducing Hana to giggles. They got sand in their underwear and Hana remembered how beautiful her husband looked, the breeze tousling his dark hair and the sex appeal present even in the way he bit his lip. She sighed and squeezed her eyes shut against the difference in her life after the heart attack, wishing he would ravish her that reckless way again instead of fearing she might break in his fingers.

In England, a port would be marketed as a tourist destination, visited by coach loads of holiday makers with cameras and picnics. In New Zealand, nature went about its business unhindered, the biggest, longest and most treacherous river in the North Island sacrificing itself into the sea unnoticed. Hana felt the soft green grass underneath her ragged hands. It tickled and stung at the same time.

Sacha stayed nearby, snuffing and munching, seeking out the sweetest shoots with her surprisingly adept lips, wrapping them around the blades and tugging them free. The presence of the mare was comforting and Hana sniffed and wiped at her eyes and nose. She streaked her face with dirt and blood from her hands and caught her cheek with the leather reins, still clutched in her fingers. Sleep and exhaustion took her from there, casting her off into a cloudy peace, the warmth of the winter sun beating down on her shoulder. At some point, the elastic under her chin became restrictive, pushed away by her sleepy hands. When she awoke, the hat had tumbled off and lay on the ground near her face. Reaching forward to touch its leather brim, Hana saw the familiar tan cowboy boots of her husband and knew from his stance; she was in big trouble.

Chapter Four

"Just leave us at the drop off point," Robert said, his voice sounding strained as he mopped at his eyes with a clean handkerchief. "Don't come in. I can't bear it."

"I don't mind," Logan began but Hana's father shook his head. Robert looked like a broken man and Logan felt genuinely sorry for him as he pulled up outside the departures terminal of Auckland Airport.

"Please look after my daughter," Robert asked the tall Māori tearfully and Logan nodded and allowed the Scotsman to pull him into an awkward embrace. "Tell her children I'll see them next time we come," Robert begged, eyeing his wife hopefully and she nodded and smiled at him. Relieved, he seized the handle of his suitcase and wheeled it along behind him, casting desperate looks over his shoulder at his son-in-law before the departure doors slid closed. Logan stood for a moment, leaned against the front wing of the Honda and wondered if he would ever see the gentle man again. He hoped so.

"I like him," Tama mused thoughtfully.

"Yeah," Logan replied. "Robert McIntyre has grown on me over the last month." The old man had worked particularly hard to repair the damage with Hana, overwriting the rash words of a bitter argument with heartfelt encouragement and admiration for what she had achieved during the years of separation.

"Does he have to go back for his cancer treatment?" Tama asked and Logan shook his head.

"Hopefully just check-ups." Logan felt sad for his wife. She wanted this last week with her father to be special, up at the hotel together. After twenty-six years without contact, it was meant to be a time of healing and reconnection. The heart surgery robbed her of that and Logan didn't think he would ever forget the ashen look on the old man's face as Hana sank to the ground at the redoubt in agony. *"Not again,"* Robert had sobbed. *"Not like her mother."*

As Hana's handsome husband leaned against the car with his arms folded, thinking about his beautiful but fragile wife, a security guard approached with raised eyebrows. "Move your car, sir. Now!"

Logan gave him a hard stare before turning slowly and folding his tall frame back into the vehicle, the man's attitude towards the colour of his skin prickling something antagonistic in the Māori. The guard turned away, muttering to himself. "Bloody Māori's. Think they can do what they like."

Both Logan and Tama were silent on the way back to the hotel, their minds occupied by their own personal thoughts. Tama clutched his precious offer of employment from the Fire Service headquarters in eager, excited hands. He signed it in reception after Logan checked it over. They both knew he would have signed it anyway, but his uncle drove him all the way there and it seemed churlish not to ask for his help. The main office was only open until midday on a Saturday and it was a rush to get there after the airport run.

"Thanks for all your support, Uncle Logan." Tama shook hands with him in the hotel car park. Logan smiled tiredly and they went indoors, Tama to raid the chiller for his lunch whilst dodging the sharp tongue of Leslie and the kitchen girls and Logan to check on his wife.

He discovered their room empty, the ranch slider still open wide and the temperature cool. Logan closed the doors and stayed long enough to wash his face and then sought out his wife downstairs, expecting to find her either in the family room or the dining room next to the huge industrial kitchen. She wasn't in either place. His daughter slept soundly in her pram in a corner of the dining room while Leslie bustled around next door, giving orders to the kitchen women and chopping up kumara like a maniac. "I thought you changed youse mind!" she hollered at her employer. "Din't she go with you? I ain't seen her."

Logan brushed a curl out of Phoenix's face and sensed how deeply she slept. He touched her tiny fingers and she didn't even stir.

"I ain't seen her," Leslie told him again as she flipped a tea-towel at Tama's backside for snatching some chicken off a serving platter.

The kitchen girls shook their heads. "No, sir. We ain't seen her today."

With a horrid foreboding in his heart, Logan went in search of his wife with more urgency. In the stable yard, he hit pay dirt. Jack emptied sacks of feed into the huge wooden bins in the feed shed, lifting them effortlessly onto his stooped, broad shoulders. Chaffage and seed covered his face, hair and hat, drifting into the air in the process. He was an elderly man of indeterminate age who had worked for the Du Roses forever. Deaf from birth, he ran the stables since before Logan's birth. Jack read Logan's lips as the younger man asked him if he had seen Hana and where his horse was. He shrugged at where Hana might be, but looked genuinely bemused at the question about Sacha. He pointed frantically to the stall where he put her that morning, banging his chest to make a point. It was empty. The stand which formerly held Sacha's tack was mysteriously back inside and bare.

Rawhiti appeared and Jack waved his arms and grunted at him, leaving the poor stable hand feeling as though he was living in some alternate reality.

"Have you seen Sacha?" Logan asked him quietly.

Rawhiti's answer caused a mixture of anger and terror to cross his new employer's face. Jack read the young man's lips as he haltingly betrayed the beautiful woman. The old man slapped him forcefully on the upper arm, grabbing at his own chest and trying to explain why she shouldn't have gone off on her own. Logan saw the confusion in the young man's face but didn't have time to waste in lengthy answers. He spun around, assessing the situation with his usual brand of competency.

There were four horses tethered by the tacking area, none of them particularly dynamic. They were already tacked, but for a party of guests who arrived at that moment for a trek, expecting Rawhiti to take them up into the bush and give them a taste of rural New Zealand. Jack's Jeep sat idle at the end of the stable yard, but Logan was too impatient to drive to where he needed to be, especially when he knew there were quicker ways. Beyond the vehicle was a gate into a lunge arena, where a young grey speckled appaloosa colt grazed quietly. He was a two year old that Toby was having trouble breaking in and stock training. Logan helped him whenever Hana had a nap and Phoenix was with Leslie. It took his mind off his own problems for a few hours a day. Hana's father had watched him working with the large, determined colt a few times and taken photos, impressed by the man's skill and endless patience.

Logan sized up the animal, certain of his own ability but doubtful of the colt's. He didn't feel as though he had much choice. "Open the end gate," he told Rawhiti with authority.

The young man faltered, plainly having the worst day of his life. Jack nudged him and pointed towards the far gate at the end of the stable yard, nodding his head emphatically towards it. Rawhiti walked towards it slowly, not understanding what was going to happen. Logan stepped into the arena, greeted enthusiastically by the colt. It nosed into him trustingly, used to his presence and gentle voiced demands. It was excited by this rider's domination of its muscular body and relished another go at getting him off. Sensing the tension in the air, the three female guest riders stopped trying to guess which of the four horses would be theirs and fell silent. They also ceased loudly attempting to squash their hair tidily into borrowed riding hats and stood watching the men. "Ooh, what's happening?" one said a little too loudly, ignored by her friends who stood raptly staring at the handsome Māori with the death wish.

Logan took a rope from the wooden fence and clipped it to the metal ring at the side of the colt's halter. He waited a moment, moving round to both sides of the animal's face, needing to be seen by both dark brown eyes and acknowledged. "*Mārū tamaiti tāne*," he whispered, soothing the flicking ears and watching the white rims around suspicious eyeballs.

It seemed as though the man spent long wasted moments putting the colt through its paces, but it was only a waste if he never intended to make it to where he was going in one piece. Finally Logan ran his hands gently over the animal's back, neck to tail, then he bounced once and landed neatly behind his withers. The horse looked surprised but had been ridden a number of times bare back in the arena, so kept his cool. *For now*.

Logan urged him out through the arena gate and the colt faltered and shied at the metal rungs, the sensory overload threatening an explosion of hysterics. Logan pushed forwards gently, not wanting to fall off on concrete in front of such a captive audience. He wasn't sure which would be worse, the pain or humiliation. The colt was afraid, his ears lying flat against his head as he registered unfamiliarity and didn't like it. Logan felt the power bunching power into the muscular shoulders and knew what was coming. He couldn't either pair of dinner plate hooves come together or he would be flat on his back and unable to get to Hana. He knew with an unfailing conviction exactly where she was. After all, it was where he went to think, to rage or just to be still.

"On you go, boy. Steady now *tamaiti tāne*," Logan said, keeping his voice light and his body devoid of tension. He pushed the beast with his heels, keeping those hooves moving. The animal stepped high, picking its feet up and dancing on the spot. Logan felt its back arch and pushed him in the direction of the end gate, seeing with dismay Rawhiti staring at him open mouthed and the gate still closed. Logan's heart sank. He couldn't afford a bad fall; his haemophilia was barely manageable as it was and he needed to be mobile and fit for his family. "Open the bloody gate!" he roared at Rawhiti, who still stood there.

Jack flapped his arms like a frustrated, flightless bird, grunting and looking comical. Logan didn't know whether to laugh or cry. There was no way he would get the terrified horse through the small gap from the courtyard of the hotel. The gate was the only exit. His shout finished off the horse's nerve once and for all and he took off, recognising for himself the only way to freedom. Unshod hooves scrabbled on the concrete and they were off and running, gathering speed across the stable yard even as Rawhiti grappled with the gate latch. Logan had no reins and no bit, holding onto mane and lead rope as the colt took off into the air. It cleared the metre-high gate with room to spare, galloping flat out into the paddock beyond, increasing speed even as it climbed steeply uphill.

Rawhiti managed to duck just in time, feeling the air shift as the half-ton animal moved above his head. He looked fearfully at Jack expecting a reprimand, but all he saw in the old man's face was speculation and surprise. Looking over at Rawhiti he smiled, showing the gaps in his mouth where teeth were missing and indicated with his hand the motion of a jumping horse, followed by a shrug and a palms-open movement. Evidently nobody realised the colt's particular talent.

Bred from stock horses with a legacy of rounding up cattle and covering heavy terrain, the young, green animal's ability to jump an obstacle with such precision and confidence under stress, was a rare thing indeed. Jack was impressed. "Geez!"

Rawhiti breathed and wiped his sweaty forehead on his forearm. He was a competent rider. Plonked into the saddle by his father before he could walk, even he would have struggled to ride a barely broken, ungelded colt over a solid obstacle and stay seated bare back. He was filled with admiration for his employer. A collective gasp behind him from the visitors caused him to look back at the horse and rider, now disappearing into the bush line. They had cleared the next gate flat out and after a series of hefty bucks ran into the canopy and were lost from sight, Logan still sat firmly on board.

"That was amazing!" the visitors agreed, exhilarated by the free show of horsemanship on display. They were oblivious to Logan's panic, nurtured by Rawhiti's offhand comment that Hana left over four hours ago.

The female riders secured their own hats and each other's, proceeding towards the docile horses in the tacking area. Jack helped them to mount and sort out their stirrups, girths and other paraphernalia. By the time they set off up the track into the bush following Logan's deep hoof marks, the company was increasingly jolly. Especially as Jack obligingly opened the gate for them and they weren't expected to jump it. They jogged uphill, hoping very much to see the handsome rider on the fiery horse again on their travels through the bush. "Will we see that hot guy at the top?" one of them called. Rawhiti shifted uncomfortably in his saddle.

"Sorry, ladies. You'll have to make do with me."

The colt had bent itself to Logan's will by the time they reached the top paddock. Jack taught Logan as a boy that a beast might be one hundred times mightier than him, but his will needed to be stronger. As long as he set his will immovably, he could defeat any living thing. He never forgot that lesson and it served him well during his lifetime, especially as it worked on school boys and other adults similarly. He was never again beaten by anyone or anything. The incident in which his two older half-brothers chased his eleven year old ass through the bush and cut him open with a machete, was put firmly behind him and never to be repeated. Logan despised his childish self for the weakness and misplaced trust in his blood relatives.

Jack was sickened and disgusted by the older boys' jealous behaviour, especially as Logan remained unaware of the reasons behind their hatred. His bastard parentage was not his fault. The scar was wretched and ugly, made worse by the difficult healing of a haemophiliac and marked Logan forever, a rubbled road of flesh running from under his armpit to his hip. The old man taught the gangly boy the 'principle of wills' and knew he would use it. Jack loved Logan more than any other child, for reasons he would never share.

Unfortunately for Logan Du Rose, the only person the principle inexplicably never worked on, was his wife. It was a source of continual bafflement for him. The harder he set his will at Hana, the more likely she was to rebel or run. When she gave in to him in the laundry room at the hospital, he was surprised.

Logan stood over his wife, watching her sleep and wondering how to get her back from the edge of the cliff without causing her to pitch over it. She looked like a small child curled up on the grass and his heart ached for her, not understanding her pain but acknowledging its presence. His big colt made a bee line for Sacha, seeking out comfort with a dominant, lustful air and the dignified mare turned her backside on him and put him in his place. He moped along behind her, experiencing the most perplexing of days - beaten by a man and rejected by a woman - the sweat drying on his coat and making it sticky and dull.

Hana stirred and rubbed her eyes and Logan tensed, ready to catch her if she reacted badly and went the wrong way. She had been crying and her eyes were swollen, her eyelashes beaded with tears. Tracks in the muck on her face betrayed her further. The tell-tale hitch in her chest caused by uncontrollable sobbing bothered Logan and saddened him beyond belief.

Logan stayed still but as Hana woke further and saw his feet, she panicked and thrashed and he had no choice. He seized her under the armpits and pulled her away from the cliff edge.

Hana cried out in pain as the action lifted her left shoulder and disturbed the scar and the foreign object under her skin. When Logan let go, she was enraged and frightened, irrationally convinced the leads inserted directly into her heart might have been dislodged. "You shouldn't have done that!" she raged. She lay on her back in the grass for a moment, waiting for the fear to subside. When her husband's face appeared above her looking concerned, she raised her right hand quickly and tried to slap him. He caught her wrist easily and held on, sinking down next to her in the grass and not letting go. His grip was like a vice and Hana knew from experience that struggling was futile.

Exhaling loudly in exasperation, she lay back and stared at the sky above her. Clouds scudded across the cold blue expanse as though being herded, responding to the push of the wind as cattle might to a stockman's whip. Logan lay down next to her; his fingers warm on her cool wrist as he balanced on his elbow and watched her. Hana tried to pick out shapes in the fluffy white objects but they moved too quickly, merging and distorting without settling in any particular pattern. It was frustrating, but Hana persevered, desperately avoiding her husband's gaze whilst knowing she was wasting her time. He wouldn't give up. He never did. He would lay there and stare at her until it grew dark and she froze in position, but he wouldn't back down and look away.

The trouble was, Hana hadn't really worked out how to deal with things yet. She knew what was wrong, but not how to cope with it.

Logan let go of her wrist, gently laying her hand on her stomach and reaching for a lock of her long red hair. He twisted it in his fingers, examining it like a priceless artifact, admiring how it caught the light. Hana felt the movement and sneaked a look at him, dismayed to find him staring straight at her. She looked away quickly, but not before she caught the smirk in his eyes at her weakness. He exhaled and there was a laugh caught up in it as he moved closer to his wife so their bodies touched. "Go away!" Hana snapped.

Logan shifted slowly, as though dealing with a frightened or unpredictable horse, inch by inch imperceptibly until he leaned over Hana and obscured her view of the sky. Reluctantly she looked up at him, resisting the urge to slap him again or burst out laughing. He kept his grey eyes fixed on hers, his pupils as intense as black holes. His lashes brushed his cheeks and caused his fringe to bounce as it got caught up on them. He brushed her chin gently with his thumb and Hana felt like crying at the raw compassion in his face. "I was scared for you," he whispered.

"Sorry, if I worried you," Hana replied, her voice laced with sarcasm.

Logan kissed her dirty face with such tenderness it felt like the start of something. He brushed his lips gently over hers. "I wasn't bothered about you. You stole my bloody horse." There was a twinkle in his eyes as he waited for Hana's reaction. It didn't come. She didn't fight him or argue. She yawned and ran her hand over her face, feeling dust and sticky dirt under her fingers. Hana reached up with her left hand and ran her forefinger down the ugly scar on the right side of her husband's face, a dubious injury from a brawl after a 'friendly' soccer game. Her grandson, Jas said it made him look like Action Man. The thought made her smile and Logan looked relieved. "I thought you might be here," he said and kissed her neck.

Hana shifted underneath him guiltily. "I can't live here, Loge," she said sadly and he started in surprise. "The generator. I'm meant to stay away from them. They might damage the 'thing' and I wouldn't realise until it failed and I was dead."

"Ok," he said, so easily Hana was astounded. He pushed his right hand behind her head and up into her hair, stroking the back of her neck and she closed her eyes under the spell of his caress. He made everything feel so much better, as though nothing was a problem; everything could be sorted.

Logan didn't seem interested in anything except his wife, keen to re-establish their relationship on a more secure footing. He undid the buttons on her blouse and kissed the ridge of the pacemaker, not once breaking eye contact with her.

By the time his lips sought hers, hot and intense, Hana had forgotten everything except her husband. Logan wouldn't let her talk anymore, keeping her there on the grass amongst the building debris and flying polystyrene, which danced around them carelessly in the grip of the wind.

Chapter Five

Hana brushed the dirt from her hair, pulling a face as leaves and bits of grass tumbled free every time she ran her fingers through the red tresses. It seemed endless. "I hate having a shower at the moment," she grumbled.

Logan nodded with understanding. "It's because it forces you to face your body's flaws and the fact that it failed you at the worst of times." He flicked at a piece of polystyrene and tutted. "Bloody builders."

Hana gulped and bit her lip, forced to acknowledge Logan's easily spoken truth. She didn't know if she would ever forgive her body. "If I was a broken-down-car, I'd get rid of myself," she complained.

Logan watched her out of the corner of his eye as he pulled his clothes on. He understood her better than she could have imagined, knowing what it was to detest his own body for letting him down – *for being faulty*. "Want me to help you wash your hair when we get back?" he asked Hana with a gentle smile in his grey eyes.

"Yes please. I can't keep my arms above my head for very long at the moment. I couldn't even do a ponytail after you left this morning."

Logan looked at her her long hair hanging loose down her back to her waist, instead of sensibly under control. He reached over and pulled polystyrene out of her fringe. "It's more robust than you think," he said and Hana looked at him in surprise.

"Polystyrene?"

"No, the pacemaker. It's quite robust and banging yourself won't detach the wires. When I pulled you back from the cliff, you panicked."

Hana looked away, immediately irritated. "Are you going to give me the 'lots-of-people-have-them-all-the-time' speech? Because if so, I don't want to hear it. Those people are old people, who don't have any choice. I'm not old!"

Logan looked off into the distance, narrowing his eyes to watch a coil of smoke rising from a chimney down in the tiny town Hana had once made him drive for an hour to see. There was nothing there, but she refused to believe him. He didn't know why he was bothering now. She infuriated him with her dogged refusal to hear the truth. He wisely kept quiet, but Hana felt aggressive at the thought of the long ride back down the mountain, dreading it. It made her spoil for a fight. "Go on then. I know you're dying to put me straight," she said, deliberately making herself sound bored and adding a fake yawn for good measure.

Logan fixed his wife with a hard stare, sighing and using his hands to push himself off the grass. "I'm not dying to do anything, Hana. You, on the other hand, you were just plain *dying*."

He strode away on his long legs, snatching the discarded leather reins up from the ground and issuing a low whistle through his teeth. Sacha appeared at a run, closely followed by the strong colt.

Hana clambered up awkwardly from the ground, feeling the soreness of her hands and knees from her fall. The scabs had dried and stuck to her jeans. She didn't fancy bending her legs to sit in the saddle, knowing it would unleash yet more pain and she had surely endured enough recently. While Logan sorted out the horses, Hana wandered around the outside of the house looking in the windows, clambering over the loose bricks onto the porch.

All the glass was in place and the internal fittings began to make the rooms take shape. Hana pressed her nose to the glass, saddened at the thought she wouldn't be able to live there, knowing she desperately wanted to. The wooden panelled front door was a replica of the one at the hotel and Hana stroked it with her hand, feeling the smoothness of the grain under her fingers. The frontage of the building faced the bush, away from the cruel weather which came off the sea to the west. The partially constructed wrap-around porch would eventually protect the house from the elements, giving it a buffer and allowing for outside living whatever the weather.

Her body language oozed despondency as Hana turned away from the beautiful house and walked slowly over to Logan. Sacha's reins were back on her bridle and Logan leaned heavily against the fence waiting, his eyes boring holes in Hana's nerves. His legs were loosely crossed in front of him, his arms folded and the white horse snuffed lazily at his shirt. Hana felt like one of his Year 9 students doing a walk of shame after some random misdemeanour. She felt sorry for the boys, suffering under the glare of those dark grey eyes. It was debilitating. The colt grazed, his lead rope lying slack over the fence. Hana walked slowly up to her husband, close enough to lay her cheek against his broad chest and mutter a 'sorry' into his shirt. He sighed and wrapped his arms around her tightly. "It'll all be fine," he promised, kissing the top of her head and hoping he would be able to make good on it.

Hana believed him. They stood close together for a while, but the dropping temperature made Hana shiver. Logan led Sacha to the fence so Hana could climb onto the top rung and clamber into the saddle. The horse stood as meek as a lamb in the company of her favourite human and her increasingly second-favourite one. The colt however, danced with a glint of unpredictability in his eyes and took some persuasion to allow Logan onto his back. As always the man won and vaulted quickly up, gathering the halter rope in his left hand and moving off as soon as he was settled to prevent the colt bucking him off.

"Where's your gear?" Hana asked.

Logan raised an eyebrow. "My wife's using it!"

Hana looked down at the exorbitantly expensive stock saddle under her and the leather reins she held in her cut hands. "Sorry," she sighed.

Logan winked at her as the colt jogged on the spot. "It's ok. He's not great with the saddle yet and we haven't tried him with a bit. I might not bother actually. He's got a nice soft mouth and responds well to my seat. I need to get him to stop deciding he wants me off though."

"How can you do that?" Hana asked, interested as she followed the youngster's bouncing rump down the track. Sacha picked up speed but offered no threat of behaving like the colt.

"Be gentle and patient with him." Logan threw his answer over his shoulder. "Give him lots of work he can manage and encourage him to enjoy being around other working horses and part of a crew. I've discovered he's got a really intelligent jump, so once Toby gets working him properly, it might be that we don't use him for stock anyway. I'm not sure yet. We've never bred a jumper. He's still full of surprises." Logan led the way down the mountain, hoping the surprises didn't involve him sitting on his backside on a rocky outcrop and walking home. Sacha's presence eventually seemed to have a calming effect on the younger horse and he carried Logan back to the hotel without incident. In the stable yard he exacted his revenge, putting on a show for the guest riders arriving back from their trek.

Jack didn't make Hana shower or groom her horse like last time, but she felt indebted to Sacha for her kindness and rubbed her down with a curry comb. Her brush strokes were tired and feckless, but the mare appreciated the sentiment, nuzzling the woman's shirt gently and flicking her ears back and forth in response to Hana's efforts. Jack waved his arms and took the brush from Hana's hand, forcing her to leave the mare alone. Hana kissed Sacha gently on the nose and thanked her with an apple she found in the feed store, hoping she hadn't just pilfered Rawhiti's afternoon tea. "Good girl, Sach," she whispered. "Thank you."

Logan put his arm possessively around his wife, scotching the hopes of the women riders as he led her into the mud room at the back of the hotel. Bending down he helped Hana get her boots off and she rested her sore palms on his shoulders like a small child. Her feet dragged as they went to the kitchen and Leslie took one look at the horse hair all over Logan's jeans from his bare back ride and waved them away. "Get youse arse out of my kitchen, man! You want the health inspector to shut youse down?"

Phoenix did her cute wave at them from the high chair by the dining table, where she fed herself squares of toast and jam. Hana ached to hold her and stole a kiss and cuddle while Leslie dealt with the dinner mayhem in the kitchen next door. "I love you, baby," Hana whispered, rewarded with a blob of jam in her hair.

Hana's brother, Mark had reappeared and sat next to his niece, feeding her the little squares one at a time. "Mum and Dad get off alright?" he asked his brother-in-law as Logan leaned against the door frame. Logan nodded once in reply, looking nervously at Hana who praised her baby for her grown up eating and didn't register the question. "I covered those two shifts for my colleague and then one of the other surgeons became available to do the rest of the weekend. I hope it's ok to come back up?" Mark looked at Logan for confirmation and the owner of the hotel nodded, relieved he would have a capable doctor on hand in case Hana needed one again urgently.

Hana kissed her baby once more on her perfect little head, heavily chastised as Leslie came in and caught her. "Get out of my kitchen! Look at all youse dirt and muck goin' everywhere. Bloody hell!"

The couple went in the shower together. Logan washed Hana's hair and smoothed conditioner through her curls with his fingers. He tried hard not to snag the frequent tangles, loving the way it cascaded over Hana's shoulders and down her back like a red sheet. The warm water was enticing and it was tempting to stay in there all day, buffeted by the clear fresh spring water on their backs and heads. "I might try and feed Phoe again later," Hana said, her cheek resting against Logan's chest. He rubbed soap into her back and nodded, hoping that it was more successful today than previously. "Maybe if I leave it until her bedtime, I can swaddle her up tightly and hold her. What do you think?" Hana looked up at him and got a face full of shower water from the overhead nozzle. She coughed and spluttered and it forced her to get out.

"It's a great idea," her husband replied, washing the soap off his muscular body, "I'll help if you want." His olive skin shone with the slick soap and his height made him imposing, even unclothed.

Hana pulled a bath towel off the warm rail and wrapped it around herself, nuzzling into the fabric. "Loge, I keep seeing your face," she said softly.

Logan turned the shower off and Hana passed him a towel. He resisted the urge to be glib. "What do you mean?"

Hana pushed her face into the fluffy white towel, hiding her mouth as she spoke. "At the redoubt, when it happened, before I lost consciousness I saw you running towards me. I keep seeing that whenever I shut my eyes. I think it's why I can't sleep properly and why I'm so tired. I relive it over and over, on a loop."

Logan stepped out of the shower, holding a towel around his waist as he struggled to tuck it in with shaking fingers. He pulled Hana into him and held her tightly. His skin was tacky and warm against her soft cheek. "What about it bothers you most?" he asked, not sure he wanted to hear the answer.

"Death," she whispered, "you had death in your face. It was like all your hope disappeared and your eyes looked so empty. I was frightened for you."

"For me?" he asked in surprise. "Weren't you scared for yourself? Why on earth would you be frightened for me?"

Hana paused. Now she had started, she needed to finish. She had to tell her husband the reason she lay awake at night, looking back into the memory of his dulled eyes and seeing the nothingness there. "I wasn't scared for me, because I knew where I was going - it wouldn't hurt anymore, but I was afraid for you because you couldn't follow me there."

Logan's arms dropped from around Hana and she felt instantly cast off. She regretted even starting this conversation. Her husband reacted badly. "So, are you saying I'm going to Hell?" he spat, affronted. Hana closed her eyes and sought help from her God. She had to trust he provided it because she didn't feel any wisdom arrive in her brain.

"No, I'm not saying that," she placated, "I saw in your face, if I died then you died too, but in your soul not your body."

Logan looked poleaxed, his brow knitting and his lips parting. That was exactly how he felt. He saw himself dump Phoenix on Tama, running towards his wife as she sank to her knees clutching her chest. He knew instinctively it was bad and he had missed the signs. He had dismissed weeks of warning symptoms and the fact was like a guilty knife burying itself in his own chest. He knew what was happening to her as he reached her prone body and he stared Death full in the face and acknowledged he was powerless. Hana was right. He also knew his life would be over and he would never recover.

Logan's face was ashen as the memory and emotions flooded back over him. He worked hard this last week to stave them off and avoid facing the shock still trying to work its way out of him. His back slid down the bathroom wall and he squatted with his elbows on his knees feeling sick. Hana knelt on the bath mat next to him and put her arms around his neck, pushing her face into his hair. The towel pressed on her sore knees, the cuts and grazes burning against the fibres, but she switched the pain off and focussed on her husband. "I never felt good enough for you and now this makes me feel even less worthy." Hana sniffed into the bony ridge along Logan's shoulder. "I'm sorry, it must have been horrific to watch," she whispered.

"Yeah." Logan gulped and rubbed at his eyes with a hand made into a fist. Hana had never seen him so broken, not even when his mother ran into the fire to burn with her lover and Logan couldn't save her. So much had happened in their year together and three times, Hana woke up in the hospital with some injury to find her husband's worried face looking into hers. When she woke after the heart surgery, it was different. It wasn't a worried face which greeted her but a devastated one, belonging to a man who had plumbed unfamiliar depths and got decompression sickness of the soul coming back up again. "You know one of us will have to go through it at some point don't you?" Hana said gently. "One of us will die and leave the other one alone. It's a fact of life."

"Maybe we could go together," Logan said quietly. "Get matching concrete gumboots and jump off a bridge."

Hana smiled into his hair, smelling the hay and sunshine that was him, underneath the scent of her girly shampoo. Logan stirred and ran his hand over his face. "I've never felt so dependent on anyone before. I've been my own person all this time, just existing. Sometimes I hate how loving you has changed me."

Hana nodded, making a swishing sound with her hair against his smooth shoulder. "I know," she replied, "I guess we've both learned things about ourselves. And there but for the grace of God, go I. I've realised I can't just will myself to stay alive and hope for the best. It doesn't matter if I eat well, exercise properly and do all the right things. If my time is up, then it's up. I'm so frightened of this stupid thing in my chest, so fixated on not disturbing it or causing it to go off, I've forgotten how lucky I am to still be alive. It's perspective I suppose. I lost mine temporarily."

Hana let the towel slip from above her breasts and rubbed her finger over the raised area where the pacemaker sat under her collarbone. She would get used to it and if it went off, she would deal with it. "Surely the shock of it kicking in can't possibly be worse than the awful feeling of being unable to breathe or function properly? It will save me from that at least."

Logan's fingers joined Hana's in stroking the ridge under her skin and he bit his lip. "The problem is, it's like sitting in a chair while a nurse prepares an injection, having told me it's going to hurt. I just don't feel ready."

Hana watched her husband's tense face as he gritted his teeth. *Everyone lives on borrowed time,* she thought to herself. *I just need to use mine more wisely from now on.*

Logan looked down onto the bleached tiles as though expecting to find some stunning revelation there. When he stood, he was pensive and confused and Hana didn't know if he'd listened to anything she said. But his question caused her to dig more deeply into herself and find the thing she lacked; *peace*. Now all she had to do was hang onto it and forget everything else.

Logan's back was warm and smooth as Hana laid her cheek against it, feeling strong muscles rise up either side of his spine. She traced the *ta moko* tattoo on his shoulder, following the delicate genealogical lines with her forefinger, round and around, the images and symbols which meant something deep and personal to her husband. "I think I'd like a tattoo," she said dreamily and Logan turned and looked down at her as he loaded his brush with shaving cream.

"What would you have?" he asked.

Hana thought for a moment and smiled up at him, satisfied. "I'd have a tramp-stamp just above my bum. And it would say '*Made in Great Britain*' in really nice italics."

Logan put his head back and laughed and it was a perfect sound. Hana realised she hadn't heard it for a while and missed it. She smirked up at him, teasing him and wanting him to dare her to do it. He shook his head and reached for his razor, sniggering to himself periodically as he shaved off the hard dark stubble from his face and washed away the week's awful events into the drainage system. He felt their hold on him loosen as the suds entered the large septic tank out in the hotel grounds.

Logan dressed and went downstairs to fetch his daughter, returning eventually with a grizzling, tired baby on his hip. "Mark's gone off to do one of the bush walks with Alfred before dinner," he commented, unable to hide the surprise in his voice. "The old man's seen Phoe regularly since we came here and now he's playing nice with your brother. I guess I should be grateful for that, at least."

"Just give it time, babe. There's been a lot of hurt."

"Yeah!" The hardness leaked from Logan's heart into his words. "He raises me for forty years knowing I'm his brother's bastard and then once both my birth parents are dead, he figures now's a great time to cut me loose. There's been a lot of hurt alright and it's mainly mine."

Hana bathed her baby in the sink in the ensuite, allowing her to splash and enjoy herself while Logan moved around behind her putting towels down on the floor to prevent her slipping. Then he stood next to his wife and they both played silly games with the child, enjoying the deep belly laughs the little girl produced and the easy way she soaked up their combined attention. She played with a bar of soap, squeezing it between her tiny palms and giggling when it shot out the top and slithered into the water.

Phoenix shrieked with glee when Hana pulled the plug out and the water drained through her legs, but when it was all gone she became grumpy and the bottom lip shot out. Hana tried to pick her up in a soft towel, but the little girl wriggled and began a feeble tantrum. Logan stepped in quickly, seeing how hard it was for Hana to even lift her. "No, Phoe! None of that," he said with firmness. Young as she was, Phoenix looked contrite and kept the bottom lip out for good effect as Logan carried her into the bedroom and laid her on the bed. She kept the sad lip on display as Logan dried, powdered and dressed her in a baby suit with little fluffy clouds and teddy bears. "Drama queen," he chastised her but she pouted more and looked like she might cry.

Hana sank onto the bed, laying on her back and fixing her gaze on the ceiling. She felt exhausted. Phoenix reached a hand out sideways as her father did up the poppers on the front of her suit and rested her little hand on her mother's shoulder. When Hana looked at her, she smiled and Hana smiled back.

"Don't let her push you around, Han," Logan said quietly as he lifted the baby over his shoulder. He didn't want to point out he had no intention of ending up with a replica of Hana's demanding policeman-son, Bodie, who manipulated his mother on far too many occasions to list.

"I don't usually," she sighed in reply. "I'm strict about some things, like staying in the pram without a fuss when I put her there and feeding and stuff. I feel a bit physically weak and so when she wriggles about, it's hard." Hana turned on her side. "I feel disconnected from her at the moment. One minute I was breastfeeding her all the time and cuddling her a lot and now I don't seem to do much of either. It makes me feel sad."

Logan held his spare hand out to his wife and helped her up. Phoenix copied him and held her hand out too and Hana had to pretend to be hauled up by them both. They cuddled together as a little crowd and Phoenix wrapped an arm around each parent. "Let's go down to the family room," Logan suggested. "I'll stoke the fire and you can feed her there."

They went into the hallway, clicking the bedroom door shut behind them. Hana made for the lift, but Logan forced her to walk down the back spiral staircase to the level below. "The doctor said you should get gentle exercise daily."

"I just rode your horse!" she complained.

"Yeah and now you're walking down the stairs. Clever girl."

The ride was good for Hana, although exhausting. The previous few days she did little more than stroll in the gardens, arm in arm with Robert and Elaine. "I don't want you to fester indoors for the next week, now Robert's gone. We need to get you moving and back up to full health quickly." Hana heard the urgency in his tone and resented the reason. Logan was due back at the school boarding house the following Sunday night for a duty and the next day it would be back into the third term of school for his English department. "I'm worrying about leaving you alone when I'm on night duty. I wonder if Tama wants to come back to the staff accommodation with us, before he leaves for his fire brigade training. What do you think?"

Hana pulled a face and shrugged. "I'd be happy not to go back there at all," she sulked.

In the family room, Logan settled Hana on the battered leather sofa which sat in the room since his grandmother's time as matriarchal queen of all she surveyed. The original Phoenix Du Rose ruled with a rod of iron clamped in her tiny, genteel fist, while her male offspring wreaked havoc in their personal lives. The television in the corner was ancient and probably needed throwing away, but nobody ever watched it with Miriam gone so it was more ornamental than functional. Logan put the stereo on low, his parents' old music crooning out; Glen Campbell ballads and some ancient Kenny Rogers making a peaceful atmosphere in the room.

He swaddled his daughter up tightly and lay her on Hana's knee, watching as his wife lifted her tee shirt and undid one side of her bra. Instead of wriggling and complaining this time, Phoenix gave her father a penetrating look with her inherited striking grey eyes and latched on obediently, suckling until her eyelids closed in sleep. "Thank goodness for that!" he whispered, sitting next to Hana and stroking his daughter's forehead.

"Yeah, she's much more content." Hana smiled and exhaled with satisfaction.

Logan nodded. "Well, it helped that I snatched her away from Leslie as she heated up a feeder cup of cow's milk," he said. "It might be good to get back to Hamilton and try and grab back some normality for all of us."

"Leslie's been brilliant though," Hana conceded and Logan agreed, leaning against the cushions and fixing his arm around his wife. The housekeeper had been helpful, especially this last week, but was appropriating his daughter as her own which wasn't good for Hana. Logan was grateful for the look of contentment on his wife's face as she cuddled her baby, her head leaned back against his arm. The next battle was to get her to eat properly.

He left his girls in the room together and went to the industrial hotel kitchen, managing to get into the chiller while the staff served guests in the dining room. The only person in the room was a man from the township, who came in on daily shifts to load the dishwasher and hand wash the huge pots and pans in the big Belfast sink under the window. He was willing and competent at his job; happy to be in employment.

Benaiah was Polynesian and had Down Syndrome, like Hana's eldest granddaughter. He laughed good humouredly as Logan emerged from the huge chiller armed with two plates of left overs. "Leslie's gonna kill you," Benaiah snickered to himself. Logan shoved the plates into the microwave one at a time, heating up the covered portions of chicken casserole.

"I'm starving," Logan commented. "I missed lunch to go and find Hana." He spotted a block of cheese sat temptingly on the work surface where someone was grating it and got called away. Seizing the knife, he cut a slab off one corner and popped it into his mouth.

Benaiah let out a huge belly laugh. "You're naughty!" he shrieked. "Leslie gonna shout."

Logan pulled a face and shrugged, the only male not scared of the large Māori woman. The relationship between Logan and Leslie was strained for reasons Logan kept to himself, but he willed the microwave to hurry up. He cut off another slab and offered it to Benaiah, who opened his mouth like a little bird and took it, his hands deep in the sudsy water of the sink in their yellow rubber gloves. "Now we're both guilty," Logan said deviously and Benaiah chuckled again, not understanding.

Logan knew he would tell Leslie as soon as she reappeared, oblivious of his complicity in the crime or the cheese crumbs around his lips.

The microwave pinged and Logan grabbed the second plate out, shoving it on a tray with the first and seizing cutlery wrapped in serviettes from the container on the table. Calling a hurried goodbye to Benaiah, he fled, racing down the corridor and making a sharp left turn as Leslie's voice was heard coming out of the dining room. *This is ridiculous*, he told himself. *I've owned this place outright since I was twenty-five and I'm being told what to do by a woman who beds stupid old men!*

Phoenix was finished and fast asleep but stayed latched on, moving her lips periodically as she disturbed. Hana smiled at her husband as he struggled through the door with the tray of food. "All good?" he asked, his eyebrows raised hopefully as he set the tray down on the wooden coffee table.

Hana smiled and nodded, feeling like she had begun the journey of taking back her family and her life. Logan took the baby gently, laying her carefully sideways on the other sofa after making a nest with cushions and throws. She wriggled slightly until he released one of her tiny hands and a little thumb found its way into her mouth. Then she was out for the count and her father covered her with a blanket.

Logan gave Hana her plate of casserole and cutlery, watching her as she picked at it gingerly. He tucked into his and was finished before she ate even a quarter. "Did you take your aspirin?" Logan asked and she nodded, touching the top of her stomach with her thumb and making him curious. "Hana, what's wrong? You haven't eaten properly since the operation. What's the matter?"

Hana leaned forward and laid her tray on the table. "I don't know," she replied, "it's a bit scary. Before the heart attack, I kept thinking I had indigestion and it put me off eating. Now when I eat, it happens again and makes me think it's my heart."

"Where does it hurt?" Logan asked, masking his fear. His appetite abandoned him and he knelt in front of his wife on the wooden floor. Hana moved her hand over the centre of her body, just under her sternum and pressed, wincing. "Is it the same place as before?" he questioned. Hana shook her head.

"Not really. It was higher up, more in my chest. It doesn't even feel the same if I think about it. The whole thing has been so...I...every little twinge makes me panic. Sorry, I don't want to worry you."

Logan picked her hand up and pressed his lips to her skin, wishing he could take it all away from her, the pain, the memory, the lasting fear. He looked at her hard, his grey eyes soft and comforting. "I think aspirin can affect your stomach. Maybe you should take antacids as well, to help. We'll mention it to the cardiologist at your next appointment, see what he says. Yeah?"

Hana nodded and sighed, leaning forward until her forehead touched Logan's shoulder. He put his arms around her and stroked her back, shaking his head and shushing her when she tried to say sorry again. Logan left Hana curled up on the sofa watching Phoenix, the stereo playing softly in the background and returned the tray to the kitchen. Leslie bustled around orchestrating the waitresses to deliver desserts to the dining room, complaining about the slowness of one of the newer girls. She was truly formidable, like a river in full flood. Logan put the tray on the side and began to unload the dirty dishes but Benaiah pushed him out of the way. "No, my job!" He flapped at him with his hands.

Logan felt a moment of irritation as he suppressed the urge to remind everyone in the room, he owned everything in the damn place and they shouldn't forget it. But they ran the property competently in his absence and had done for years, albeit with Alfred and his mother at the helm before. It was the reason he was able to live in England for years, searching for Hana in the crowds. *They* were the reason he could live and work at the boys' school, exercising his gift for teaching.

He stood in a corner over by the chiller, his backside resting against the work surface casually as he waited for Leslie to finish her latest tirade and let the women go. They filed out of the kitchen door, eyeing each other warily, not liking it at all that the big boss hung around. "Don't you put your backside where you put your *kai!*" Leslie squawked at him, noticing his butt against the edge of her pristine worktop. Logan fixed her with a dark glare and she recoiled as though slapped. She had known him all his life, from boy to man and understood the warning signs. The old lady modified her tone slightly and asked him with careful politeness, "How can I help you?"

"I need something from the hotel stores," he explained. "Mum kept a stock of toiletries and sundries in her office. I'm guessing you've got the key?"

Leslie nodded and fingered the bunch of brass keys in her apron pocket. "Come," she said. "We'll look in her old cabinet."

They walked to the front of the building, to Miriam's office next to the reception desk. Logan let Leslie walk on ahead, thinking mean thoughts about the voluptuous backside that got his father into so much trouble recently. He huffed angrily at the old man's indiscretion and saw Leslie's back stiffen.

The evening shift receptionist smiled happily at them as she sorted out a wireless internet query with a guest. Leslie unlocked the office and led Logan inside, like the headmaster admitting entrance to a pupil. The fading scent of his late mother overwhelmed him with grief and unasked questions. Her betrayal was like a knife in his chest and he clenched his hands into fists. Unaware,

Leslie opened a filing cabinet and extracted a bag of items, fossicking around inside it on the desk. Out spilled unopened packs of condoms, tampons, individual sanitary towels, packaged toothbrushes, small tubes of toothpaste and a bottle of what looked like mascara. Logan spotted some antacids lying at the bottom of the bag and snatched them up, turning on his heel to leave.

"Hey, that'll be five bucks please," Leslie said starchily and Logan turned back to stare at her in amazement. His eyes widened and his jaw dropped. He took a step towards her, his grey eyes flashing like granite.

"A few months ago you were sleeping on a cold floor in an empty house in the township, only eating when there were left overs at my table!" he spat. "Me and the boys sorted out the debt collectors and I gave you my mother's old apartment. My wife wanted that for you, *my wife!*" Hana was in pain and this ungrateful *employee*, challenged him to pay cash for something he funded in the first place.

Leslie took a step back and gulped, knowing immediately she had gone too far. Logan's mother had been dead less than eight months. Although Miriam kept Reuben Du Rose as her lover during her marriage to his brother, Alfred jumped so easily into Leslie's bed it made her wonder if either of them ever had any scruples. She knew the women complained about her, moaning that her sex life gave her assumed airs and graces; getting above herself. Leslie saw exactly what they meant as she made the grave mistake of treating her employer as if he was her step-son. *Which he wasn't*.

Logan treated her with the feigned deference he was raised to give the strong women of his household. It was the Du Rose way, acknowledging the women's organisational superiority within the domain of the hotel whilst retaining ultimate control. The old woman knew abruptly that her power was an illusion, nothing more than a disappointing smoke screen as it faded in front of her eyes.

Logan walked close to where she stood, towering above her with a terrifying look in his eyes. Without taking his eyes off her face, he dug around in his tight jeans pocket and retrieved a handful of notes and coins which he flung onto her desk without checking it. Then he leaned in close to Leslie's quaking face and hissed, "*Taihoa koe ka kite i te hē o tāu mahi!*" He whirled around in his socks and was gone. The door slammed hard behind him, making the receptionist jump.

Leslie put her hand to her chest, waiting for her heart to calm and feeling a complete fool. "You stupid old woman," she chastised herself. "You will see the error of what you've done, just like he says." She pushed the money around on her desk, noticing with dismay Logan left over twenty dollars on its shiny wooden surface. Her heart sank, knowing she would have to find a way of getting it all back to him somehow.

Leslie's mood didn't improve any as she reached the kitchen, greeted by an upset Benaiah. "The Missus didn't eat her dinner," he started to cry. "She's sick." He adored Hana and the penny dropped as Leslie recognised Logan's errand of mercy on her behalf. The antacids were for Hana.

The housekeeper was quiet and subdued for the rest of service and the kitchen girls and waitresses were relieved. The receptionist gossiped that Logan went into the office with Leslie and slammed the door on his way out.

"I wonder if he's finally put her in her place," they pondered.

"I don't know. There wasn't any shouting," the receptionist concluded and they all sighed.

"Mind you," one of the older women said slyly, "Mr Reuben never needed to shout to let you know when he was pissed at you. Logan's a carbon copy of him!"

The women turned their attention instead to talking about the terrible Christmas Eve revelation which devastated their employer and outed the best kept secret on the mountain.

Logan grabbed a pair of his old cowboy boots from the mud room and went outside to cool off in the cold wintry evening. The frost was already laying on the grass and hanging in the air as freezing mist. He snatched a packet of chewing gum from his jeans pocket, hearing a coin fall in the darkness. Kicking wildly at the ground, he heard it ping off into the gravel somewhere. "Who gives a crap?" he hissed into the darkness. He put a stick of gum into his mouth and chewed, feeling the peppermint seep out and finding it calming. The Māori walked around the grounds slowly, intending to go back to his wife and knock on the French doors into the family room where he left her.

A gnawing ache bit at his soul at the loss of his mother. The scent of her in the office had assailed his nostrils and caused him physical pain. "I miss you, Mum," he whispered. "You sure knew how to make life hard for me." Miriam Du Rose had been blood. She wasn't a great mother by any standards, but she was *his* mother. Logan had so many questions he needed to ask her, but her suicide prevented him, leaving behind an unbearable legacy of lies and causing him to wonder who he really was. She denied him truth in life and continued her stance in death.

Logan called in at the stable yard, finding Jack had sent all but the grey appaloosa colt out into the paddocks to graze. The horse wore a rug against the winter chill which was a new event for the animal and meant Toby had done more work with him. The colt ceased his grazing as Logan leaned his forearms on the top of the gate and after some deliberation, came over and snuffed at him, smelling the mint on his breath with curiosity. "Hey," the man said gently, allowing the animal to scent him thoroughly, tasting his mood and demeanour through his exhalations. The colt sighed loudly and itched a spot on his girth. "Exactly," Logan replied, as though they shared a two-way conversation, "Life sucks big time." The colt put its big head up so that Logan could scratch the spot between his ears, moving his head up and down to get the most from the action. "At least I know why you're crap at stock work," Logan mused. "I think you need to be somewhere different, don't you?"

The big colt nodded his head as if in agreement and sauntered off to continue his ruminating. Logan watched him in the darkness, the glint from the metal buckles on his rug reflecting the moonlight. "Maybe I should be somewhere different," Logan whispered. He stood for a while, trying to put his problems into order. The year before, his birth father managed to get Alfred to sign over a key section of the property to him, effectively defrauding Logan out of land his grandmother bequeathed to him. Developers moved in, putting in the start of the road up to the top paddock, until Logan called time on it and involved lawyers. The developers were enraged, having heavily invested and accepted deposits on the expensive lifestyle blocks they intended to build and sell for a small fortune. They hounded Logan by mail, through his solicitor and in person, stonewalled at every turn.

After the fire which killed Reuben accidentally and Miriam deliberately, the family next door decided not to rebuild in the same place, moving down the mountain and nearer to the township. Logan snapped up the land, determined not to let the developers get any foothold. But they continued to hound and wear him down, trying to persuade him to let go of some of the precious acreage, keen to salvage something of their reputation amongst the big Auckland players. Until recently. Lately they had gone suspiciously quiet.

Logan grew increasingly tired of everything nowadays. Alfred had run the stock and stud, after Phoenix Du Rose's untimely death, foolishly and systematically ruining the family empire from the inside. Reuben Du Rose was the business head of the family and Logan had unwittingly inherited his genius. But Reuben was powerless to help, banished to the other side of the mountain for his affair with Miriam and the fathering of his illegitimate son. Alfred continued wreaking devastation on a thriving stock business, running it into the ground with little effort until bankruptcy loomed.

In his twenties, Logan Du Rose salvaged what was left, buying the business out gradually and taking over the reins, dictating from afar and rebuilding the legacy from the bottom upwards. Miriam ran the hotel, effective and efficient for most of the year, unless her Bi-polar disease reared its ugly head and drove her upstairs to her apartment to nurse her confused mind. Then Leslie would step up and take over and Logan would quietly increase her wages for the duration. Until this year.

Miriam's death heralded the end of life as they all knew it and Alfred effectively retired - from work, from life and definitely from the man who grew up believing he was his son. Logan watched the flickering lights on the lower slopes from the campsite and resisted the urge to kick something in order to exorcise his agonies. Ironically, Logan's empire thrived as an unintended tribute to Reuben.

"Hey." Toby's low greeting dragged Logan from his musing. "I'm going back to the bunkhouse now. The green quad's knackered and I can't get the bloody thing going."

"Is that what you've been doing?" Logan looked at his watch and saw the hands nestling against eight o'clock. "Just call a mechanic."

"He won't touch it anymore. He said to scrap it last time." Toby took his cowboy hat off and scratched his fingers through his wavy hair. He caught Logan's eye and smiled. "Trouble, boss?"

Logan shook his head and rested his right foot on the bottom rung of the fence. He balanced his chin on his forearms. "Order a new quad tomorrow but don't ditch the old one, hey? I've always liked it." He ran his lips over his wrist.

"Yeah sure, whatever you think." Toby looked up at the lights from the camp and nodded his head. "That campsite on the lower slopes is a roaring success, aye? Near enough to Auckland to be a weekend getaway during the summer. And I heard the bush walks, trekking and mountain views are drawing international tourists, even now despite the cold."

"Yeah, it's all turning over ok."

"You've done great with this place, boss," Toby said, replacing his hat. "Why don't you stay up here? You don't need to teach or run some boarding house for snotty *Pākehā* boys to survive financially."

"Na, I do it because I want to, because I'm not ready to move back here permanently. And I'm good at it. And they aren't all white there, idiot!"

"But your missus likes it up here, doesn't she?"

Logan nodded. His first tentative suggestions to Hana about moving back just after they married were met with dismay. But after a year of being together, she increasingly wanted to be here rather than anywhere else. His safe place had inadvertently and gratifyingly become hers too. Logan ran his hands through his hair and leaned his elbows on the gate. "Yeah, Hana likes it here."

"Boss," Toby began, getting to the real reason he sought Logan out. "Some of the boys are hearing whispers about the developers getting ready to buy the mountain. They're worrying about their jobs. I told them you wouldn't sell, not while you had breath in your body but I'm wondering, why would you turn down millions to take this kind of crap every day?" Toby sought Logan's eyes in the darkness. "Do I keep telling them that, boss, or are you gonna make a liar out of me?"

Logan pinched the bridge of his nose and closed his eyes. *Why am I holding onto all of this?* His heart ached in his chest. He could go anywhere and do anything, so why was he stood there with the weight of the world on his shoulders, when it would be so easy to sell up and move on? He almost heard his grandmother's anguish from the otherworld at the suggestion.

"Boss?" Toby pressed him, dicing with danger but willing to take the risk.

Logan heaved out a huge sigh. "I dunno sometimes, mate. The old lady would drop lightning bolts on my head if I sold up, wouldn't she?"

Toby laughed and nodded his head, knowing Phoenix Du Rose only through stories and gossip. She died when Logan was five. They went for a ride up into the bush, arriving at the top as the sun was setting, Logan riding his pony bareback and his grandmother on her strong mare, Sacha's great grand dam. They made the trip often, paying homage to the huge kauri tree at the top, where his *whakapapa* was scored into the wood for generations – literally - the family tree.

They sat together on the cliff edge and she told him again the story of the invading English, driving the Māori off their land. They seized it mercilessly, not caring who they left for dead on their rampage through *Aotearoa*. Logan was entranced with the repeated story, seeing the bloodshed at Rangiriri Pa and hearing the deafening musket shot in the eyes and ears of his vivid imagination. Phoenix Du Rose's story was always the same. It never varied in the telling;

"The English soldiers came to the family home that day with their muskets and their threats, mob handedly driving Māori off their land and forcing the tribes away in the name of colonisation. Seeing the brown skinned whānau children who greeted them with fear and curiosity, the soldiers postured and threatened, intending to seize the dwelling. They hadn't counted on the Frenchman who was head of the family and who appeared from the bush wielding a musket of his own. His genealogy defeated their claim instantly. He was a prominent French entrepreneur and they had heard of him.

His Māori wife, Hinga, was related to the Ngapuhi chief by birth and she stood aside her husband bravely as he cursed the Englishmen and held his ground. Du Rose kept his gun barrel aimed at their Captain's face as he refused them hospitality even after they capitulated to his claim on the land. The soldiers were exhausted and hungry, dragging their injured who were wounded at Rangiriri Pa. They progressed no further west that day but turned at the gates of the original homestead, moving back towards the Waikato River and their warships."

Phoenix Du Rose's mother was one of the little brown children, watching her French father drive away an army all by himself. Legend had it that the fleeing Māori king was hidden out back in one of the barns. The white historians who followed, repeatedly refused to believe the story but Māori history was communicated verbally from generation to generation and the tribes were satisfied with its legitimacy. That was all that ever mattered. Screw the English with their fountain pens and written fabrications.

More of the French family arrived over time, mingling their blood with Māori and forging their own dynasty. The colourful lineage wound its way around Logan's upper arm in his *ta moko*, the tattoo twisting and dividing as the branches of the family split, reuniting and dividing again. Logan's tattoo followed Alfred's side of the Du Rose family, trailing off to the left and allowing a wider line to truncate above it. *It was wrong*. Logan rubbed a hand over it and released a frustrated sigh. Toby took it as irritation at him and tapped Logan's forearm. "Night, boss," he said, disappointment in his voice.

"Night," Logan replied, his mind agonising over his tattoo. Logan was Reuben's son and his genealogy should have followed the other line. As a remedy to the anguish the indelible error caused him, Logan had his tattoo artist inscribe Phoenix and Hana's names underneath in beautiful italics. On a whim, he added Tama's too, feeling as though the boy was as much a son to him. It gratified Tama more than words could ever have expressed, to feel the uncustomary sense of belonging. Like Logan, Tama had grew up on the wrong side of the fence, raised as another man's cuckoo. It was as though history repeated itself over and over again down the generations, taunting, eroding and destroying their peace. *No more*, Logan thought as he gritted his teeth against the relentless march of time and history. *I'm done, it's over!*

Always there was the promise of the *new house* prophesied, something clean, new and founded on honesty and integrity. It bound Logan to the land; to *tangata whenua*. He single-handedly held back the progress of the developers, refusing to let them scar the landscape with their neat brick houses and picket fences. With his tattooed, muscular arm held out over the land, the black ink denoting his slewed *whakapapa*, Logan Du Rose prevented the reign of the wealthy. They commuted to their plush offices in Auckland and their SUV driving wives took their brats to school. They wanted to go home to luxurious homes in the Du Rose native bush and he was all that stood in their way. In reality, not much had changed since the Frenchman took his stand generations before. "What the hell am I gonna do?" Logan raged at the mountain.

Chapter Six

Hana dozed on the sofa, comforted by the sound of her daughter's steady breathing on the red leather seat opposite. She felt at peace for the first time in ages and sighed with contentment. Her dreams took her back to the tennis court at school, practicing with the blond haired stranger. Hana returned his serves with confidence and he laughed and encouraged her. *"Awesome, Hana. Squat into your shots more and give it some power."*

Sounds encroached into her sleep-pictures, dispersing the man's face and causing him to disappear like white mist. Hana's dream-self stood in the centre of the court knowing he would go. When she looked down, even the racquet was gone from her outstretched hand. He did the same thing the night she told her husband and the policemen she played tennis with a blond stranger whose name she didn't know. She felt ridiculed and humiliated by their silent disbelief. The tennis player hadn't been seen since and Hana knew they thought her crazy. Her dream-self stamped with annoyance. It wasn't just that the blond man had disappeared. She was winning at the time. Hana turned onto her side and tried to manufacture the scene in her head. The blond man laughed and served a hard ball straight towards her outstretched racquet.

There was a knock at the family room door and the click of buttons being pushed into the keypad to unlock it. Irritation filtered into Hana's waking at the loss of the pleasurable tennis game. In real-time, her body felt leaden and sore. She didn't think she could walk up a flight of stairs, let alone spar with a decent tennis partner. Hana stayed where she was, assuming it was Logan coming back from the kitchen and bumping the door by accident.

Leslie's brown face appeared in the gap, surprising Hana. "You awake, Mrs Du Rose?" she said formally.

Hana sat up. "Oh, hi. I nodded off. Sorry. Come in."

It wasn't like the housekeeper to be so reticent or stand on ceremony and it acted as a warning to Hana. She shifted her position, realising her legs were numb underneath her. She swung them down onto the floor, feeling the dreadful tingling begin as she pulled the throw around her cold knees. She felt exhausted and the absence of a fire in the grate made the room chilly. "Logan said he would light a fire," Hana muttered, rubbing her hand over her face. Leslie came right into the room and hovered there uncertainly in front of Hana. She had a dullness about her that was perplexing. "I thought Mr Du Rose was here, Miss," she said carefully and Hana felt sad that something had made her revert back to the 'miss' again. She liked being 'Hana'.

"He nipped off to get me some antacids, but that was a while ago. I think I might go to bed." Hana folded the throw blanket neatly into a rectangle, "Actually, please would you be able to carry Phoe upstairs for me? Loge's been gone ages and I'm too tired to sit here any longer."

Leslie glanced towards the doorway and Hana caught sight of a pair of legs waiting outside. They looked to belong to a very tall man. The angle of the door obscured the rest of the body. Leslie pursed her lips looking exceedingly troubled and it bothered Hana. "Come in," Hana called to the person in the hallway, wondering why the visitor unsettled the housekeeper so much.

Neville Du Rose's tall frame walked into the family room. He had removed his boots and stood in his socks, jeans and a warm Swazi shirt. He looked like a hunter. He probably was. Hana tried to smile at him nicely, but Leslie's agitated behaviour made the situation intense and difficult. In the end, Hana took charge. "Leslie, would you mind taking Phoe upstairs and waiting with her, please? Send someone to look for Logan and I'll be up shortly."

Leslie nodded and lifted the sleeping child into her arms, glad of an excuse to escape. Her employer was definitely going to fire her - for her behaviour earlier and now for leaving his wife alone with one of his unpredictable half-brothers. "I might as well get to cuddle my *moko* for a while, before your daddy throws Leslie out on her ear," she whispered to the sleeping infant. She climbed the spiral staircase, feeling more miserable than she had for a long time.

"Please sit down," Hana said to the man stood awkwardly by the empty fire grate. She indicated the seat Phoenix had vacated and Neville sat with some degree of nervousness at being in the presence of a woman whom he had only seen a few times before.

"I remember you from my dad's funeral," Neville said, his voice soft. "And the fight between Kane and Logan."

Hana cringed. The scrap between Neville's brother, Kane and Logan looked set to end an age old battle. It would have ended in bloodshed. Hana had walked into the middle, all tiny body and flaming red hair. She punched Kane in the face and yelled at both the fighters and spectators, including Neville.

"I'm not sure how I feel about being alone in a room with you," he joked. "You look harmless enough now, but I know you pack a punch." He heard on the grapevine she nearly died. It wasn't that he was afraid of *her*, but Logan Du Rose was funny about his woman and Nev didn't want to be caught in his bad books. Nothing was worth that.

"I don't think we've been properly introduced," Hana said politely, sounding so English gentry it made Nev hide his laugh behind a cough. He could imagine pulling her into a *hongi*, pressing his forehead against hers in greeting and having her husband walk through the door and pound him into next month. He didn't even dare shake her hand, so he nodded once and introduced himself.

"I'm Nev. I'm Logan's cousin...well, half-brother really..." he trailed off. It was too messy to explain.

"I know," she replied. "I should probably apologise for my behaviour last time we met. I shouldn't have hit your brother, Kane. I'm sorry."

Neville Du Rose sat for a moment in surprise and looked hard at the woman before him. Hana observed him in return. She wondered if she dare speak freely with him. There was so much she was curious about and couldn't ask Logan. "You and Logan are so similar to look at. It's freaky."

Nev put his head down and nodded sadly. "Alfred and Reuben were brothers. Miriam and Antoinette, his mother and mine were sisters. All cousins. That's probably why. Same father and sibling mothers." Hana nodded, intrigued at the new piece of information. Nev continued, "All that 'keeping it in the family', there's no wonder so many of them are crazy. We take more care with inseminating our livestock, so there's no surprise it's all a big mess." He laughed dully at his own joke and Hana watched him fascinated, his penetrating grey eyes, the little mannerisms and the way he spoke. It was all Logan.

Nev felt Hana's eyes on him and stopped speaking, feeling self-conscious. Hana realised she was ill-mannered for staring, but there was so much the same about the men and yet something different too. At first she couldn't work out what it was and then it came to her. Logan had what the Māori called *mana*, but Nev didn't have it in such huge proportions. The English would call it the 'x' factor. The older man was handsome and would turn female heads in any situation, but he didn't have that added spark. "I met Reuben Du Rose once,"

Hana said and Nev's eyes widened. "He was very handsome. You're both carbon copies of him."

"Where did you meet him?" Neville looked confused.

"He sought me out here, in the hotel. He wanted to meet me. I knew instantly who he was." Hana sighed. "I understood why you all hated Logan then. Reuben obviously loved him. It must have been hard for you." Logan really did inherit everything and what he hadn't inherited, he bank-rolled. It made for an intense soup of broiling emotions, fuelled by jealousy and directed at an unsuspecting child, boy and eventually, man. Nev was right; it was a big mess.

"For the record, I personally don't hate Logan and never have. He and I have always gotten along just fine. But I probably shouldn't have come," Nev said and Hana pulled herself back into the present, shaking her head slightly to clear her confusion. "The developers want an answer and I can't keep putting them off. It's not fair on my wife or my children. If we're moving into the new house, then we need to get on and do it, but if we're going, then for their sake, we need to go."

"I'm sorry; I'm really not understanding. Please could you run that by me again?" Hana asked, making more of an effort to listen to her husband's half-brother.

Nev looked impatient, but obligingly started again. "Logan bought the land at the top of the hill, where the...where Dad's old house was. And we were going to start again in a new house near the bottom and keep running the land that was ours. But now Kane's gone south, I'm on my own. Logan gets all the good labourers so I get what's left and I'm tired of it. My wife wants us to stay, but I must admit, I've had enough. I've had a gutsful of this land, this family and this life. I want out. The way I see it, I have two choices. The developers Dad got involved with still want their pound of flesh. They've made me a very attractive offer that might just clear all the debt. I can happily stand back and watch them put a housing estate right on your boundary and believe me, it wouldn't keep me awake at night - not if the money was good enough." Nev ran his hands through his hair, leaving his black fringe sticking up at the front and Hana almost giggled with the similarity between his habits and Logan's. He didn't notice, forging on with his tale – and his proposition.

"The other alternative is that Logan buys me out. Lock, stock and barrel. I loved my grandmother...Hana..." He faltered. She had introduced herself by name and it seemed ridiculous calling her Mrs Du Rose, but there was something almost improper about it. The redhead smiled at him encouragingly and didn't bat an eyelid. He continued, suddenly glad he was dealing with her and not his half-brother after all. "I loved *Kuia* Phoenix and I know she loved me. She banished my father but she knew I loved the land and that's why she left him that side of the mountain. Oh, I know it wasn't the best land - but it was generous enough and more than he deserved. Dad never had any interest in making anything of it, but I did. I just had no power to do it properly. Now he's gone and I don't have the capital to put in or the energy to make it happen. The money Logan paid for the upper section all went on paying off debts. I can't stay, so I have to go somewhere. If I sell, I can divide the money up between my family and...Caroline...and start again."

He saw Hana's eyes flash at the mention of his foster sister. She had caused Logan so much trouble over the years and even more recently, been absolutely hell bent on wrecking his marriage to Hana. She was the ex-fiancé from hell and Hana wrinkled her nose. But Reuben's *whānau* grew up together and Nev clearly felt he should be honourable. "It's only right." Hana's reaction made him feel as though he had to defend himself. "She and Kane got married down in Christchurch a few weeks ago. All the years Caroline drove my older brother mad for her and now, she's let go of her fantasies for Logan and married Kane. He's happier than I've ever seen him. And sober too."

"What do you want from me?" Hana asked bluntly and Nev faltered, not having expected her to be so forthright.

"I don't know," he replied honestly. "I actually came to see Logan and tell him all this but I figure I got a better deal, seeing you. Will you speak to him for me? I think he'll tell me to sod off. The word with the developers is that he's weakening. They think he's tired of fighting and they're getting ready to carve up the whole mountain, make it into a new suburb of the city. They're rubbing their hands together as we speak."

Hana looked surprised. She couldn't imagine it but maybe Logan wasn't being honest with her. It wouldn't be the first time. "Ok, I'll talk to him," she said quietly. "How will I get hold of you when I have?"

Nev scratched his head and thought for a moment. "Get Leslie to send me a message. She knows what to do."

"What do you mean?" Hana asked, curious about Leslie's relationship with the 'other' Du Roses.

Nev's face dropped and his complexion paled as he realised his blunder. He began to stutter; another trait of Logan's when under extreme pressure and Hana was on red alert. She stood up and straightened her back, looking at the man expectantly. The quiet, demure woman morphed again into the formidable force who cut his brother's face open with a neat punch and gouged out a layer of skin from his shin with the sole of her shoe. Nev rubbed his hand over his face – another Logan stress-tell. *These guys should never play poker*, Hana thought to herself, knowing she had gotten to him, but wondering if she wanted to know the terrible thing he worked so hard to conceal. "Why would Leslie know how to reach you so easily? What does our housekeeper have to do with you?"

Nev swore and having stood up, sat down again, knowing he had unleashed a whole heap of trouble. He sweated uncomfortably in the cold room and a wet patch spread out from under his armpits. "After my mother died and Dad and Miriam started their affair, we still all lived in the same house. Leslie was on the staff, long before it was ever a hotel and she was also Miriam's friend. When Logan was born and we all got kicked out of here and had to move over the fence, Miriam and Dad...they carried on. It was a bit on and off. They would go for long periods without seeing each other. But Leslie would carry messages between them, mainly about how Logan was doing. She never got found out. I shouldn't have said anything, I'm sorry. Just phone me, get Logan to text me, whatever. I don't want any more games. Let's be open and honest and above board on all of it. Don't let old news get Leslie into trouble now, please? She was a good friend to Miriam all those years, it's not worth it. The damage is done. They're all...gone."

Nev stood up again and drew his hand across his face. Hana stood speechless in the middle of the room, standing her ground as she tried to process this last bombshell. *Leslie!* The tall man held his hand out for Hana to shake and she took it, surprising him with the strength of her grip. Then he strode from the room, still in his socks.

Hana faced the door as it closed firmly behind him, knowing she needed to go upstairs to her baby but unsure what to say to the woman looking after her. Not now she knew the damaging secret. Leslie had been sleeping with Alfred for months, if the rumour mill could be believed. What Miriam had or hadn't done was her own business, but to find out for certain she and Rueben had been lovers for over four decades almost continuously was a shock. But now it put Hana in a dreadful position with Alfred, a man she still liked immensely.

The question was, did he know the woman he periodically shared his bed with had facilitated the continuance of his wife's affair with his brother? Somehow, Hana very much doubted it. She ran her hand through her hair, pushing her fringe back from her forehead. Then she heard a gentle tap on the outer door. The curtains hadn't been drawn and the outside lights were off. Hana peered out into the darkness. She took the key from its peg underneath the curtain and unlocked the door. "What are you doing out there?" she asked Logan. "It's freezing."

He came in gratefully, shivering in the cold and kicking his boots off on the doormat. Hana locked the door and hung the key back up, pulling the curtains closed. "You only went for antacids. Couldn't you find any?" Hana smiled at him and pressed her hand to her stomach. "It's eased off now."

"Let's go to bed," Logan said gruffly, not looking at his wife. Hana felt suddenly cold to the bone. He hadn't asked where Phoenix was and that was unusual, unless...

"Sweetheart," she said softly, catching hold of his wrist as he passed her carrying his boots in his other hand. Logan stopped dead and Hana kept a tight grip on his frozen flesh, pulling the boots out of his grasp and dropping them carelessly onto the rug in front of the sofa. She looked up into eyes that he tried to shield from her with his lashes, failing miserably. Desolation cried out to her from the grey depths.

Hana ran her hand up Logan's dark, rough cheek, feeling the stubble pushing its way back through his skin again. She forced his head up so she could look into his face properly, knowing he could react at any moment and lock her out of his soul. His irises were pale and dull as though bleached and wrung out. He looked like he had been kicked in the guts.

"You heard?" she asked him in a whisper and his forehead furrowed as he dropped his head with a nod. "All of it?" Logan nodded once, an almost imperceptible movement that made Hana's heart want to break. "I'm so sorry," she whispered.

Hana reached backwards with one leg and clambered up onto the squashy, ancient red sofa and pulled Logan into her breast. She wanted to be higher than her tall husband, to hold onto him around the neck hard and somehow enfold him and make him feel safe. She wrapped him up tightly, pulling her big cardigan up around both their heads and making a tent of grief around them. His life seemed like one endless betrayal and Hana didn't know how to take the pain away.

"I'm so sick of them all," Logan raged into her hair. "They can all go to hell. I'm gonna sell the whole sodding lot and let them live with it. I hate this family and this bloody small-minded, disloyal township. I hope it collapses when this place gets bulldozed for housing. I've had enough, Hana. I'm out of here."

Hana stopped him from speaking, kissing his lips, face and neck. He was livid and for a change, it wasn't with her. She wanted to make it all better. Hana felt only momentarily guilty about Leslie, up in their bedroom babysitting and probably wanting to go to bed herself. But the pang faded as Hana undressed her husband and herself and distracted him with her body. It was exciting. Logan was so pent up and dangerous it was a different kind of loving, which left them both frayed and unsettled afterwards.

"You go and put your boots back in the mud room." Hana kissed him lightly on the lips, avoiding his determined hands as she struggled to get off the rug. He swiped at one of her feet and Hana giggled, breaking free and letting her tee shirt slither seductively over her breasts.

"Get back here," Logan growled and she shook her head, her eyes full of promise. Hana dashed from the room, still pulling her clothes on. She had to get upstairs to their bedroom and send Leslie away before Logan got back.

The housekeeper sat in a chair by the ranch slider watching TV and Phoenix slept soundly in the travel cot. The only light came from the bedside lamp and it was easy to thank the older woman and let her go without her noticing Hana's dishevelled state. Hana badly wanted to ask Leslie some questions but needed her to leave quickly. The housekeeper's behaviour was odd and unusually untalkative. Hana wondered if she had guessed that Neville would out her, but Hana felt certain he hadn't done it on purpose. Why would he? He could have done it a million times before now. It made no sense when he wanted and needed Logan on side.

Logan came up to the bedroom via the private spiral staircase and bumped into his housekeeper as she turned to close the door up to her apartment. He hesitated. Leslie stared him down hard, wondering if he was still mad about earlier in the office. She opened her mouth to apologise and then stopped. There was something else in his eyes and it foxed her. Logan's grey eyes flickered dangerously and she instinctively knew it was about more than just her officious behaviour. She waited for him to speak, to take her down a peg or two or perhaps fire her. He said nothing, holding her gaze with latent hatred. Then his eyes flicked once to her apartment door, to the stairs leading up to his parents' marital home. There was a spark of misery and then stony, grey accusation. It dawned on the old woman as surely as a sunrise, with the dreadful realisation. He knew.

Leslie put her hand up to her mouth and closed her eyes but when she opened them again, Logan had gone. After locking her door, the old woman climbed her staircase, shaking all over her body. Alfred was up there waiting for her, but she didn't want to see him tonight. "No, old man, I want to be by myself," she told him, not caring it left him feeling hurt and rejected.

Alfred slunk back to Jack's house behind the bunkhouse, hearing the stockmen laughing at something on the TV and the clank of beer bottles. He couldn't have disturbed his deaf flat mate even if he wanted to and he crawled into bed, feeling the loneliness of a failed fifty-year marriage descend onto him once again.

Chapter Seven

Logan's appearance in the bedroom was accompanied by even more pent up frustration and anger than he exhibited downstairs and he paced the room, trying to regain control. "Bloody woman!" he snapped.

"Don't think about Leslie, think about me," Hana sulked, enticing him into bed. "I fancy more of what I had downstairs, please." She smirked as Logan shed his clothes and pushed his muscular body onto the sheets next to her. Hana ran her cold hands over his torso making him shiver and slipped on top of him. "I love you, Logan Du Rose," she whispered, running her tongue lightly across the underside of his top lip.

Logan's hands strayed under Hana's tee shirt and his fingers wound their way between her panties and the soft skin of her bum. He moaned and opened his mouth to her eager kisses, happy to be distracted from his present misery.

They woke in the middle of the night, freezing cold and naked on top of the covers. "When did you pull your tee shirt over us?" Hana asked, sitting up. "It's not covering very much."

She pulled herself into her nightshirt and they snuggled down in the bed but Hana couldn't get back to sleep, mulling things over in her head too much to nod off. It probably didn't help that she had allowed herself to get physically over-taxed. She felt shattered and harried the next morning, not helped by her husband's reluctance to let her out of bed. "I need you," he sighed into her hair and pulled roughly at her night shirt. A couple of buttons made a horrid popping sound as the stitching gave and they pinged onto the sheets.

"Are you always this insatiable when you're upset?" Hana ran her hands over his strong back and smirked at his answering growl. "I'm just enjoying you being mad at someone other than me."

Logan looked up at her, his dark hair mussed and sexy. His eyes burned hot and passionate in his face and his kiss was insistent. "Stop talking," he said roughly, "you're just trying to put me off." He yanked her shirt over her shoulders and pressed his lips to her bare skin, his chest rumbling with the ecstasy of the prospect of satiated desire.

Escaping some time later, puffed and physically exhausted, Hana plucked her baby out of the cot. "Pooh, you're smelly," she said, pulling a face. "Daddy would love a cuddle with a bugle bum. I think you're the perfect thing to cool his ardour!" She put Phoenix in bed with Logan and they snuggled down together, the little girl periodically giggling heartily when Logan tickled her feet through her baby suit. Hana showered quickly and dressed, putting some makeup on for the first time in days and feeling much better for it.

Back in the bedroom, Logan had reluctantly dealt with the stinker and climbed back under the duvet. Hana sat in the chair by the window feeding her daughter. She sighed. "Phoe seems to have settled back into breastfeeding again, doesn't she? It's such a relief. It's stopped me feeling like a spare part." Hana caressed the tiny outstretched fingers and enjoyed the closeness it gave her. "Loge," she said thoughtfully, seeing the top of Logan's dark head pop out of the covers and hearing a grunt she assumed meant, 'yes.' "What will you do?"

The top half of him appeared with a look of confusion on his face. His olive skin was darker against the white sheets and his St.

Christopher necklace hung sexily to one side across his muscular chest. His hair was tousled and Hana felt something stir in the pit of her stomach as he smiled at her. "Do about what, babe?" he asked, looking gorgeous as he ran his hand through his hair to push it back from his face. Grey highlights peppered their way through his sideburns, making him look distinguished and even more devastating. Hana smiled covetously and he beckoned her back to bed, trying to entice her in. She pointed at the suckling child, who failed to help her as she drifted peacefully off to sleep, satisfied with her old brand of milk.

"About what Nev wants. What are you going to do? Last night you wanted to jack it all in and sell up. Do you still feel the same way today?" Hana studied her husband, waiting for his reply. "I've learned to love it up here. If I'm honest, I don't want you to cash in your heritage. I know it wasn't given. You earned it through pure hard work and savvy entrepreneurialism." Hana sighed. "Ah, look. It's yours to do with as you please. It's technically none of my business."

Logan lay back on the pillows and put his arms up behind his head. Hana lifted Phoenix carefully and laid her back in the cot, hoping she would sleep for another hour. Then she climbed onto the covers next to her husband and waited for his answer. It didn't come, possibly because at that moment, he didn't honestly have one.

Logan turned on his side and took his wife's left hand in his, seeing her wince in anticipation, even though he would never deliberately hurt her. He turned it over, looking hard at the livid pink scar which ran up her wrist from the heel of her hand. It was ridged and obvious, betraying the afternoon of horror she suffered as a hostage a few months ago. "Still hurts?" he asked softly.

"Yeah. Mark says there's still a piece of the whiskey glass in it. It's bizarre really, isn't it? I don't see my brother for twenty-six years and then discover later how he spent the night trying to save my life."

Logan's brow knitted. It had been traumatic. He thought about what it would mean to lose this woman. What made him any different from her kidnapper? Laval was all about money and status and always had been, even at school. He mistakenly assumed Logan's family had money and sought friendship with the Du Rose brothers. The irony was they were all at the grammar school on scholarships. Logan's family home belied an illusion which once rang with the sound of extended *whānau*. When he brought Michael Laval home for the weekend it was empty, deteriorating before his eyes without explanation. *Now he knew why.* His birth was the catalyst for the *whānau's* detonation, brother betraying brother in an act of adultery which divided the family. "Am I so different from him?" Logan asked softly, turning Hana's hand back over so he couldn't see the damage which offended him daily. Hana cocked her head inquisitively and the name was out of Logan's mouth before he could take it back. "Laval."

Hana snatched her hand back in an instant, a disturbed look on her face. "Why are you thinking about him?" she asked, her eyes flashing and her jaw clenched.

Logan lay back on the pillows, disconnecting from his wife while she calmed down, knowing he would only make things worse if he tried to hold her. He didn't want it to turn into a fight. "Just thinking," he said casually. "Forget it."

Hana saw the walls crash down over his soul and sensed herself firmly left on the outside again. Regret pierced her heart. "I'm sorry. Tell me, please?" she begged, climbing fully dressed under the sheets and putting her cold hands onto Logan's warm body. He groaned and cringed as her icy fingers touched his firm stomach, laughing and seizing her hands in his warm ones. "Please?" she said again and kissed him on the mouth, pulling back as he tried to get serious, staying safely out of range for now.

"I was wondering what the difference was between me and...Laval." Logan tried to explain. "We were good friends at school, right up until Year 11 when his dad showed up and corrupted him. We were both academic, both sporty and had a similar business head. We both created empires but his went one way and mine steered a more middle course, not straight, but better than his. When it came down to it, he couldn't care less about family, about his dad or the impact his business would have on his mother. His mum was a nice lady - I remember her. So I was wondering what he would do in my situation. That's all."

Hana lay her head on her husband's shoulder and snuggled in tightly. "Easy," she said, surprising Logan with the surety in her voice. "He'd sell them all down the river for a fast buck. Even I know that!"

Logan lay with his arms around his wife; his baby daughter snoring loudly on her back in the cot and thought about Hana's assumption. She was right. Laval only cared about his own comfort. He came after Logan purely out of revenge, making it look as though he wanted to stop Hana testifying against his father but ultimately, he hadn't cared less about the old man. He wanted to hurt Hana to get back at Logan. He dragged it out and made an art form out of his psychotic need for violence. Logan shuddered involuntarily and tried to wipe the man's face from his mind, pulling Hana into his body. "You're right," he said with certainty. "I won't sell. This mountain belongs to the Du Roses and I won't give it up. *Mana tangata whenua* will keep us here as long as we're physically able."

"What should I tell Nev?" Hana asked quietly. "He's desperate for an answer. It cost him dearly having to admit his financial mess to me."

Logan kissed the side of her head. "I'll buy him out," he answered, "but I've got an idea about that. We'll arrange to meet him somewhere else to talk about it. Ok?"

Hana felt happy at her husband's inclusion of her in his business dealings. It felt good. He tried once before. A disastrous trip to Auckland to meet with the Chinese Triads ended in misery for her and almost finished their marriage, but they had come a long way since then. Hana snuggled down feeling gratified. "I love you Mr Du Rose," she sighed.

But she had unwittingly crept into the tiger's lair again and was kept there, despite her protestations. Logan was passionate and impossible to refuse. He undressed her slowly, never taking his eyes away from hers. There was a pop as another button hit the mattress and she sighed resignedly at her horny husband. The lips which covered hers were smiling. With very little effort, he always managed to get her to the same place and she never grew tired of him.

The rain hammered down outside and Hana went down to breakfast, leaving Logan in bed to watch mindless TV programmes while Phoenix snoozed in her cot. The forecast promised it would clear up by lunchtime. Mark read the newspaper and sipped a cup of black tea at a table in the guest dining room and Hana plonked herself down opposite, pulling a face at the weather outside. "It was such a hard frost last night, I felt sure it would be a nice day," she grumbled, ordering a pot of tea from the waitress with a smile. "How come you're eating in here?"

Mark shrugged and laid his paper down on the pristine white tablecloth. "The housekeeper shooed me in here and treats me like a lord. It really is quite unnerving."

Hana smiled and tried not to think bitchy thoughts about Leslie's attempts to make amends. "How was your bush walk with Alfred last night?" she asked him, watching from under her eyelashes.

"Awesome," Mark replied with genuine enthusiasm. "He's very proud of your husband's achievements. He took me all over the property, showed me the camp-ground, the motel rooms, the stables and then we went back to his for a few beers. I called in to see you last night but couldn't get any answer. I wasn't sure if you were out or asleep."

"I think we were in the family room around the back," Hana said guiltily. "Sorry. This place is like a maze. I should have shown it to you before. We go there to chill out. Otherwise, we have a tendency to come here for a break and stay trapped in the bedroom with the baby."

"Yes, I can imagine that would be easy to do. I'm sure it'll be better when you have your own house to move into. At least then it'll be a proper family home, especially when your little girl is toddling."

Something made Hana ask, "Have you been up to our new place then?" surprised when Mark replied with enthusiasm.

"Alfred took me up there in a vehicle. It's a long way up that driveway, isn't it? He was proud of everything his son's achieved. He's excited about the house and you all living here much more."

Hana looked at him, her face screwed up in disbelief. "Alfred?" she asked. "Tall, skinny man. Thinning white hair, grey eyes and a bit of a stoop? Are you sure we're talking about the same person?"

Mark laughed and nodded, confirming it was indeed the same Alfred. Hana shook her head, bemused. She brushed away Mark's enquiry, not wanting to gossip or besmirch the old man's character even though he made little attempt to see Logan of late. He could have been of help and comfort to him in his distress over Hana's illness, but he hadn't bothered. The pretty redhead sat at the table and decided she would never understand the complicated Du Rose men, no matter how long she lived.

Without warning, Mark, ever the surgeon, grabbed Hana's wrist and turned her hand over so he could look at it carefully. He looked sadly at his ruined work and she tried to pull her hand away. "I wish I knew what the problem was with this," he said thoughtfully. "I've been thinking about it a lot. I even spoke to one of the radiographers about it. Would you let me open it up and take a look inside? I could probably do it with a camera and..."

"No!" Hana answered and risked the pain, pulling her hand away roughly. "I've had enough!"

Other guests in the dining room looked their way in alarm and Hana caught hold of her flaring temper. The waitress had evidently rushed to get Leslie because the housekeeper appeared next to their table, still looking subdued as she asked

Hana if everything was alright. Hana nodded sombrely and flustered, requested more tea. Then she forced herself to calm down. "What would you like to do today?" she asked Mark, determined not to let their relationship be damaged by trivia. He looked pensive.

"I'm heading off early tomorrow. I've got a shift starting at two in the afternoon. So, whatever you like really. I'd like to explore here more, as opposed to driving around anywhere else. What do you suggest?"

"Did Alfred, your friendly local tour guide, take you up to the memorial site?" Hana asked him, sarcasm leaking through her voice. "I bet he didn't."

"No. Where's that?" Mark shook his head and looked enthusiastic. Hana told him a little of the history of the site, shivering as she recounted the night of the fire, her child's birth and the subsequent clearing of the charred cedar wood house.

"Logan's half-brother couldn't face building on the same site so he persuaded the insurance company to use land at the bottom of the mountain. The memorial gardens are being constructed on the site of Reuben's charred house. The remains of the building are gone now and the garden will eventually be a maze."

"That sounds fantastic."

Hana raised her eyebrows. "Yeah, it's an appropriate tribute to the chaotic sense of lost-ness that seems to surround Logan's birth parents. Elaine helped plan it with me and Dad. She did some drawings which were pretty amazing."

Mark seemed keen to take a drive up there. "Let's meet after lunch," Hana suggested and Mark agreed, freeing him up to do some journal writing for a few hours. He mentioned he had some serious thinking to do, but didn't seem to want to expand.

Outside the dining room, they dodged a big group of latecomers who stayed up drinking the night before and staggered around with the classic hung over air. Hana dragged her brother into the industrial kitchen to grab a tray with two bowls of porridge for her husband and daughter. She put more sugar on one than the other. Mark helpfully took the tray while Hana wrestled with the heavy door. "Dad and Elaine have arrived in Singapore fine. They're taking in the sights for a few days."

"Such a waste of time," Hana said wistfully as she wound her arm through his and led him to the spiral staircase. It had 'Private' posted on it and was only used by staff and family. Mark bristled with an irrational sense of privilege as other guests watched him with curiosity.

"Oh, I think it's rather a nice city actually," he said, sounding very English.

"I'm sure it is. I was referring to the wasted twenty-six years while we all thought badly of each other and got on with our own lives, packed full of regret and longing."

"I totally agree," Mark said, squeezing her arm and then letting go so she could lead the way up the narrow spiral staircase. "Don't you think it's silly though," he said from behind her, "that you and I get on better now we know we're actually cousins, than we did when we were brought up as brother and sister?"

"I don't think that's the reason," Hana called down to him. "I think we're both too old for arguments and posturing. We've each realised what's important. Which reminds me, you put your number into my mobile phone that day at the hospital, as 'Aarsehole' and I should probably change it."

Mark threw his greying head back and laughed loudly as they reached the first floor of the hotel, the bowls clanking gently with each step. "No leave it," he said, still chuckling. "It's how I felt and it can be my penance for what happened. I shouldn't have treated you the way I did back then. Everyone makes mistakes – teenage pregnancies are commonplace now. Looking back with hindsight, it's actually humorous."

Hana jerked her head around to look at him, her face unreadable but tending towards disbelief. Mark held his spare hand up to placate her. He observed a flash of the redheaded fire that burned in her as a child and which he delighted in igniting as often as possible. It was still there - veiled but still there. "Not the bit where I called you names, or where I hit ...Vik, that isn't humorous. Just the part where my eighteen-year-old sister turns up at our nice, respectable Anglican home in the racist 1990's and tells her vicar-father she's knocked up by a brown man. Meanwhile her imperfect brother, who is really her adopted cousin, spawn of a young, unmarried aunt is sitting in the kitchen about to lose his wife and two sons because of his own ineptitude."

Mark's mouth was smiling but his eyes weren't. Hana shook her head and walked the few steps back to him, putting her arms around his waist and forcing him to raise the tray above her head. "Still not getting it," she said, muffled by his woolly jumper, "still can't see the funny side."

"Perhaps there isn't one then," Mark said, holding her tightly one handed and kissing the top of her head. "Did Dad tell you how much like your mother, Judith you are?" He felt her nod against his clothing and sighed. "She was the most beautiful woman I have ever known, not only her looks, but her incredible nature. I often think of her."

"Me too," Hana replied. "I missed her especially when I had Phoenix that night up on the mountain. I wished she was there – she would have known what to do. I seem to blunder through life making a complete hash of things. A little bit of maternal wisdom would make all the difference sometimes. I crave it, like feeling thirsty or something."

They walked down the hallway to Hana's room. "I know what you mean," Mark said sadly and Hana looked at him, a strange jealousy burning behind her green eyes.

"But you have Aunty Elaine. She's your mother and although I've only known that a few weeks, you've known it for years."

"I agree. I do have Elaine, Hana. But the real fact is; she isn't Judith. Our parents were always up front about my adoption, but not about my parentage. When Elaine dropped her bombshell that time, it detonated a lot of things in my life. It's not a great feeling knowing your father was a sailor who put into port only once, in more ways than one. Elaine is not Judith; and she and I both know it."

Hana looked up at him, as he balanced the tray against his shoulder like a waiter. He stared back at her and his eyes crinkled in genuine mirth as he threatened her good naturedly. "Don't!"

"I can't help it," Hana sniggered. "A sailor. Now *that's* funny. My grandson has an obsession with Popeye's muscles..." She squealed as Mark jabbed her in the ribs one-handed, balancing the tray gingerly to stop the porridge slopping over the edge of the bowls. Hana invited him into her room, but he declined and they agreed to meet outside the main doors at one o'clock, provided the rain stopped.

As he turned to go, Mark leaned in close to Hana and gave her some doctorly advice, "Go steady on the bedroom antics at the moment. It's quite obvious, you know." He pointed to a red mark on her neck and smirked. Hana flushed with embarrassment.

Mark raised his eyebrows at her and smiled, striding away down the hall and round the corner without looking back. Hana felt both smug and embarrassed. She negotiated her tray through the door and discovered her husband and baby on the bedroom floor. Logan's hair was damp and sticking up. He wore jeans but no socks or tee shirt and the baby was dressed, her hair poking up in a wet tuft, like a large dark Mohawk. Phoenix sat on the floor with Logan laid on his stomach, in front of her. "Come on girlie," he encouraged her, "do it again."

"What's she doing?" Hana asked curiously, putting the tray down on the neatly made bed.

"She's trying to crawl," Logan said, sounding delighted and the baby grinned and flapped her arms.

Phoenix spotted Hana and smelled the porridge and didn't want to play anymore. She flapped her arms again but her mirth turned to a grizzle as her father gave up his cajoling and stood, scooping the little girl up in one easy movement.

"Now I've brought this up here, I'm not sure how to do it," Hana said, indicating the messy mixture and the arm waving baby. "Maybe you should sit in the chair with her on your knee and I can feed you both," she suggested hopefully.

"Yeah...na!" Logan answered bluntly. "You hold and I'll feed."

Hana tutted and fetched a bath towel from the ensuite, wrapping the little girl up like a sausage. Then she sat on the bed and held her. Logan scoffed his own bowl of food at the same time as pushing spoonfuls into the baby. She didn't like being squished in the towel much but put up with it for the sake of food. Logan polished his off quickly and Phoenix made it through half as much as him, which added up to an enormous portion. Every single mouthful went into the slot and nothing came out, making the towel slightly redundant. Phoenix began to nod off in Hana's arms but when Logan stopped filling the teaspoon, she kicked her legs angrily and opened her mouth like a baby bird, wanting more. "I'll give her a quick breastfeed and then put her down for a nap," Hana whispered.

"Just one more," Logan insisted. He put more porridge onto the spoon and pushed it into the child's mouth. It seemed to stay there, teetering on the edge of her lips before being sucked in. He looked satisfied and was about to get off his knees when the child did an enormous sneeze. Porridge shot out of her mouth in every direction, adding up to far more than a teaspoon's worth. It had multiplied into a grey, slurry-like mixture that shot down the front of the towel, narrowly missing Hana's hand and jeans and splattered over her father's face and hair with gusto. Logan said a hideous swearword his wife hadn't even heard the stockmen use and she chastised him.

"Duh, children present!" She ruined the effect with a snort. Hana tried to contain her laughter at the sight of her mortified husband but her body shuddered with the effort. Detaching the baby from the towel and finding her fast asleep, Hana laid her in the travel cot at the foot of their bed. Her husband stayed on his knees, using the remaining clean bits of towel to wipe his face.

He swore again. "It looks like chuck!" he said, disgusted. "I'm off porridge for life now!"

Hana dissolved into hysterics and couldn't control herself, especially when she noticed a blob of it on the door handle, a few metres away. Logan stripped his jeans and boxer shorts off and got back into the shower for another hair wash, scrubbing at his face with shower gel and infuriating himself by getting it in his eyes. Hana calmed down and went in to clean her teeth. "I got chatting to Mark and forgot to eat breakfast, she commented. The grey plops of porridge in the shower tray danced as they disappeared down the drain around Logan's feet and Hana pulled a face. "I don't fancy anything now. It actually does look like sick."

"I've got soap in my eyes now!" Logan sounded fed up, running his head under the water to clear it. He rubbed at his face and made funny watery noises as the torrent cascaded down onto his head.

Hana dried her mouth and turned to leave the small room, alarmed as the shower door flew open in front of her and a large, strong hand grabbed her upper arm. "No!" she squeaked in annoyance as her husband pulled her fully clothed into the shower and shut the door again. "Logan!"

As the water poured onto her hair and her gorgeous husband kissed her neck and undid her shirt, she wondered if it was true that you couldn't get pregnant if you did it standing up.

Chapter Eight

The rain eased off mid-morning and Mark drove Hana and Phoenix up to the memorial site in Jack's old red Jeep. "It's not fair," Hana moaned for the tenth time. "How long do I have to wait until I can drive again?"

"Until you've been checked out by your specialist and he's happy with your progress," Mark replied patiently. "And I'm not saying it again!"

"What if my specialist turns out to be a woman? You said, 'he' so what if it's a woman?"

"It won't be," Mark's patience began to fray. "Most of the cardio surgeons in this region are men."

"Well, that's just sexist," Hana complained and Mark raised his eyes to a crack in the top of the windscreen, glad the journey was almost over.

The new driveway forked a few kilometres in and went off left to Logan's new house at the top of the mountain, but Hana instructed Mark to keep going round to the right. The developers had swept the driveway around the back of what had been Reuben's old house, taking it further up the mountain to the area of land where they intended to put their houses. Interestingly, Reuben only ever gave them right of access through his property and hadn't sold the driveway to them as a titled section. "I feel sure Reuben knew what he was doing," Hana mused. "I think it was always his intention to pull the plug on the development at some point and leave them high and dry."

"Why?" Mark asked.

"The developers were so desperate to get their hands on the land, they were sloppy in their checks and ignored the usual investigations. They handed large amounts of deposit money to the wily old man, probably in cash from what I've heard about Reuben Du Rose. Nobody knows where that money went. Logan's land wasn't Reuben's to sell and although the developers didn't hold complete title, they forged ahead, putting in the road and doing other earthworks. Logan got wind of it last year and the developers panicked as the whole thing tumbled down like a pack of cards in the legal system."

"But can't they sue Reuben's estate for fraud or something?" Mark put the handbrake on, feeling the vehicle slump backwards against the slope.

"They've tried, but there's no proof they paid Reuben anything. You'd think they'd know better, wouldn't you?"

"So what was it all about?" Mark asked, confused.

"Logan," Hana replied simply. "They denied Reuben his son for forty years and he'd had enough. They wouldn't let him near Logan and Reuben promised his mother faithfully he wouldn't tell him the secret. That promise bound him. So he hatched this elaborate plan to get Logan's attention. He stole the land and knew Logan would come after it. But he didn't expect Logan to do it legally. He imagined some great showdown, or that someone would crack and tell Logan the truth. Nobody did. Logan sent in the lawyers and ruined his own father. It was a mess."

"Do they think the fire was deliberate?" Mark's voice was low and sad.

"The fire investigators said not. It was some dodgy Christmas tree lights which shorted out and the wiring was old and coated in that flammable rubber stuff. It just seems like a dreadful coincidence. But when Logan's mother ran into that fire, she knew exactly what she was doing." Hana shivered. "We shouldn't have come here. Their deaths still hang over this place like a vibe of senselessness.

"We'll be fine." Mark's fingers snaked through Hana's tenderly, securing her in the company of the living. "How has it all been left now? Is Logan still fighting the developers?"

Hana shook her head. "No. They were stung for an out-of-court-settlement, paid to Logan for damage to his property, removal of fencing, acquisition of planning permission on land not belonging to them and lots of other stuff." She sighed, "The worst part and the most heart-breaking are all the families who paid deposits on flash mountain villas. We had lots of visits right after the funeral, these angry businessmen turning up to challenge Logan. They held him personally responsible for devastating their dreams and most of them haven't got their deposits back. Logan had to take an injunction out against one guy."

"That's terrible."

"Logan was teaching a Year 12 English class at the time and wasn't best pleased by all the frantic calls to his mobile about a madman wreaking havoc up here. The hotel staff called the cops and apparently it was a real sideshow outside the dining room windows."

"I think you need to watch your stress levels at the moment." Mark squeezed his sister's fingers. "Maybe cut back on the sex a bit while your heart settles down too. They did a fair bit of work in that operation."

Hana was indignant. "I might not be having sex! You don't know what I'm doing." Her pretty porcelain face flushed pink.

Mark laughed. "Then tell that stud of a husband to stop giving you love-bites on your neck and I'll stop worrying about your blood pressure."

Hana bit her lip and looked out of the side window, a smirk fleeting across her face. She moved so she could see her neck in the cracked wing mirror. The red mark peeked out of her sweatshirt like an accusation. "Oh that. That's not a..." Mark was already laughing and he gave her a pointed look. Hana conceded. "Logan was upset and I just..."

Mark raised his hand. "I don't particularly want details, thanks, interesting as I'm sure they are. If that was him *upset,* I'd hate to see what he does when he's pleased. Just go steady and whatever you do, don't get pregnant!"

Hana got the pram out of the boot and slotted the baby into it with a frown. *Pregnant! I'm a granny for goodness sake!* Phoenix was wide awake and happy, enjoying being swaddled in her blankets and able to look up at the huge sky. Loud bird noise high up in the canopy made Phoenix turn her head to see the maker of it. She caught sight of a flicker of movement in one of the tall kauri trees on the boundary between Reuben's old place and Logan's and squealed with delight. Hana looked up and saw the tui, smiling to herself at its continual presence around her and the baby. "Tui," she told her daughter. "He was up at daddy's new house yesterday." It hadn't disturbed her but she knew it was there, watching. It was with her when Phoenix was born, calling and cackling as she struggled to birth her baby. A New Zealand native, the tui grew rarer with each encroachment on the bush, but this one was safe, for now. Its black body glistened in the white of the sky, making its feathers appear shot with electric blue and it wore its fluffy white bib at its throat with pride. Hana whistled to the tui and it cocked its head and fixed her with one beady black eye. Phoenix squawked and did her funny little wrist wave from the pram, delighted when it mimicked her call.

As Mark walked around examining the site, Hana remembered the visit with her father, missing him with a familiar ache. He had blessed the site with oil, driving off the spirit of death and catastrophe and bringing his and Hana's God into the miserable place. He also blessed Hana, anointing her, ironically a few hours before her heart attack. She tried hard not to think about the sincerity on his face and the seriousness with which he approached his task and the fact it was God's favour which saved her.

"What's this?" Mark asked, indicating a pole, hammered into the ground on one corner of the site. Hana pushed the pram over to look. It was a tree branch, white like bone where the bark was stripped bare. Wording graced its surface, burned there by some kind of hot iron before the whole thing was plunged into the ground. It felt immovable when Hana touched it. She stroked the wood gently with her finger, tracing the Māori words and then she stepped back suddenly, causing Mark to jump. "What? What's the matter?"

"It's a *pou rāhui*," Hana said, moving away. She shooed him back, pushing the pram to one side but staying close enough to read the words. "It declares a *rāhui* over an area, making it *tapu* – sacred. Sometimes Māori will do it for a recent death or to conserve something precious. It's a prohibited area. Reuben and Miriam died months ago now and this looks new. I don't know what it means but Logan knew we were coming here and didn't mention we shouldn't. It's been placed here by someone who has *mana* or standing within the Māori community. The only person who could do it would be Logan himself or a *kaumātua* and the local man came at the time of the fire. He was lovely actually." Hana thought back to the knowing in the man's face as she hid her labour pains from everyone else.

"What do the words say?" Mark asked curiously, pushing a pair of wire glasses onto his nose from a case in his pocket. Hana read the words haltingly, having to follow the carving as it wound its way around the pole, her voice stumbling as she struggled to make the words sound like they should.

"E kore hoki te tokotoko a te whakaarokore e waiho tonu i runga i te wahi o te hunga tika: kei totoro te ringa o te hunga tika ki te kino." She turned to look at Mark's baffled face, realisation dawning on her. "It's Psalm 125 verse 3."

"How do you know?" he asked her, clearly impressed. Hana pointed to where it was written, to where the last word wound its way around. She recited it for him from memory in English, the Sunday school lessons of her youth seemingly paying off.

"The sceptre of the wicked will not remain over the land allotted to the righteous, for then the righteous might use their hands to do evil."

Mark looked at her curiously. "Is your husband a Christian?"

"I sometimes wonder," Hana mused quietly as she recalled the rest of the scripture out loud. *"As the mountains surround Jerusalem, so the Lord surrounds his people, from this time forth and forevermore."*

Mark walked around the rahui pole carefully, taking in the beautiful italic carving on its surface, wondering who produced such a wonderful object with their hands. They moved on towards the area marked out for the maze. Elaine and Robert designed it on paper and then supervised the physical roping out, during the hours when Hana needed to sleep after the operation. She knew what they were doing during their absence, but actually seeing what they produced with their dedicated hands made her chest feel tight.

"So this is what they were doing," Mark said amused. "I worried about them feeling abandoned when I was called back to work the day after you got out of hospital. Plainly they were having a ball up here in the mountains."

Hana nodded, feeling choked as she pushed the pram around the site. Over in one corner was a huge collection of leylandii trees, tiny little things intended for use as the maze walls. They would be quick growing, although Logan conceded someone would have to be employed to trim them regularly to stop them getting overgrown and out of hand, especially in the New Zealand bush where everything grew like wild fire. "Why were you called back?" Hana asked, trying to distract herself from the threatening sadness of thinking about Robert's shaking hands, laying out string and hammering in small stakes. *All for her.*

"Singh broke his leg," Mark said calmly, poking around in the small trees.

"Oh no!" Hana said, genuinely upset for the kind Sikh doctor who removed Logan's spleen the previous year, after a cowardly attack from behind with a crow bar.

"Sorry, I forgot you knew him. He was skiing with his family and had to be airlifted off Ruapehu. I don't think he's a particularly good patient. Ironically there aren't many doctors who are!"

Hana looked into the pram where Phoenix sucked heartily on her thumb, her eyes drooping gently. It must be so wonderful to be able to lie down all warm and snuggly, with a full belly, a clean bottom and enjoy the motion of being pushed around. Not a care in the world.

"This child sleeps a lot," Hana remarked to her brother. He came and peered into the pram at the bobble-hatted head and the healthy flushed cheeks.

"She's having a growth spurt probably. She certainly eats like a horse! Also the mountain air must be so refreshing, a bit like the English going to the seaside for a constitutional." He went back to poking around in the pots of conifers, popping his head up to ask, "Hey, I don't suppose you fancy doing a spot of planting with me, do you? I feel like I need to be busy."

Hana looked at the site. "It's already marked out," she mused. Small threads were placed along the string at even distances, presumably denoting where individual plants should go. Logan was so precise and ordered. "Logan probably agonised over the distances." Hana imagined her husband with a ruler, measuring out the gaps and starting again if he wasn't entirely convinced it was perfect. She sniggered. "I'm not sure." She sounded doubtful. "What if we do it wrong and Loge has a fit and rips it all up again?"

"Would he?" Mark asked fearfully, his brow knitting and making him look older.

Hana shrugged. "He doesn't tend to overreact like that actually," she conceded. "He'd come back up here and start from scratch and do it all again without telling anyone."

"Is he compulsive?" the doctor asked.

"Very." Hana admitted, "But bizarrely it's one of the things I love about him. I suspect he gets more frustrated with me than I do with him. He never leaves his stuff lying around, the house is always spotless and he does everything properly. You'd think it caused problems with doing things quickly, but he's expert at thinking on his feet and following through."

"You make him sound like he's perfect," Mark said and Hana smiled, her face taking on the serenity of one who is loved and loves in return.

"He is." Hana creased her brow as Mark dropped his gaze, looking piqued and she relented, regretting his loneliness. "Come on then, let's give it a go."

Hana put the brake securely on the pram and pulled the blankets up around her sleeping baby. Then she and her brother started work, fetching the little trees from the stack and lining them up where they were supposed to go. While Hana did the fetching, Mark started digging little holes with a trowel he found amongst a stack of tools. He popped the plants from their plastic pots and sank them neatly into the loamy soil. Hana found bags of compost stacked up behind the plants and dragged one of them over to her brother. They had fun trying to open the hefty plastic bag with their fingers, laughing and giggling at their failed effort as Mark pulled at a tiny opening and ended up sitting on his rear end in the dirt. "Ah, car key," Mark smirked, pleased with his clever idea. He stabbed Jack's Jeep key through the plastic to make a tear big enough to get the trowel in.

"No wonder you messed my wrist up," Hana teased. "I bet you did surgery with a rusty craft knife and a car key."

Mark snorted and dished out a scoop of the dry compost to each of the trees he had planted. "Yep. That must be why." He grunted with the effort of moving the bag along. "I kinda had my money on it being the embroidery thread I found to stitch you up."

Hana felt invigorated by the creative activity, although she pushed her luck one time too many as she pulled the heavy bag along the ground in an attempt to help Mark. It caused her chest to tug and feel uncomfortable, the sudden reminder of the pacemaker an unwelcome jolt back to reality. She sat down for a moment on the ground, catching her breath and pretending to admire the first line of tiny trees. Mark looked at her in alarm as Hana's breath contained an unhealthy catch. "Oh no," she puffed. "What if they were doing different coloured ones in between or something? We've probably mucked everything up!"

"What?" Mark stood up and the head fell off the trowel, landing with a dull thunk on the baked earth.

Hana lay back on in the dirt and snorted with laughter. "Gosh, your face was funny then. Imagine it though. We'll spend the rest of our lives hiding photos of the maze from Dad and Elaine so they're not offended. And I'll spend the next thirty years shadowing my husband to stop him coming up to look!" She shrieked with laughter, made all the more incongruous by the fact it wasn't funny, but Mark's face descended into a festival of grumpiness. He observed Hana with a scientist's calculated stare, eventually conceding a dainty giggle and wiping his dirty hands on his jumper.

His lips curled up in a smile on one side. "You nearly had me there. There are no other colours, you idiot!"

Hana grinned and squinted up at the sky, watching the clouds hurry over the mountain. Her hair splayed out behind her in a vibrant red carpet and her brother seemed uncharacteristically agitated as he sat down next to her. "Hana" he said, abruptly serious. The moment of hilarity died in an instant. She sighed. She had an idea what was coming and wasn't sure she wanted the moment ruined. "How would you feel if I asked your friend, Anka out?"

Hana exhaled slowly, not sure how to answer. "You only met her once," she said, hearing the whine in her voice. "How could you be thinking along those lines already?" She grimaced at the memory of the shared coffee and the obvious attraction Mark harboured for Hana's dangerous friend.

"I don't know," he replied with honesty. "I felt a connection and wondered if it would be ok if I pursued it."

"I can't stop you," Hana said and her voice sounded frail and disconnected. "You do what you like."

"But I'm not going to, not without your blessing." Mark's eyes fixed on Hana's face, demanding an answer with the intensity of his emerald gaze.

"Fine!" she said crossly, feeling under immense pressure. "But be careful."

Mark cocked his head at her, curious, asking 'why' with his eyes. But Hana pursed her lips. "If Anka wants to tell you her story then that's up to her. I'm not going to betray her, but I need you to know you can't bring her around Logan. They don't get on and for good reasons, so please don't meddle with that. I'm friends with her again but I respect my husband's feelings and I don't mix my marriage with that particular friendship. Anka and my family have to be kept separate, especially her and Ta..."

Hana had already said too much. *You can't forgive someone-*, she chided herself, *and then beat them over the head with something they've apologised for.* That wasn't forgiveness at all. Anka apologised for her affair with Tama and consequently lost her marriage, her job and her children over it. But Mark's revelation stood to complicate matters horribly.

Hana sat up, dirt and leaves in her hair, brushing away the feeling of foreboding as she reacted to the veiled smell of lingering charcoal. "I don't want to talk about it anymore." Her voice sounded strained and Mark's eyes narrowed with guilt.

"Do you not feel well?" He studied her like a laboratory specimen, half interest, half concern.

"Just tired." The sound of a familiar snort on the breeze interrupted, making Hana look up towards the high bank between the two properties. She tried not to allow the vision of her pregnant-self to impede on her present consciousness but it was pointless. The image of her cut fingers hauling herself up the bank, scrambling awkwardly up its slippery surface, cut a sorry figure in her waking nightmares. Even though Robert blessed the bank and Logan's *rahui* pole declared spiritual wholeness, the memory of that dreadful night still encroached on Hana's sensibility as a ghoulish roll of film in the back of her inner vision.

Hana shaded her eyes with her forearm as Mark resumed his digging, knees bent and back arched. A horseman sat high up on the bank, his face in shadow from the brim of his hat. His body was strong and tensed on the majestic white mare as he watched the scene below. Hana ached for the feel of his strong arms around her and she wanted to cry out for him to come to her. All the bending and stretching made her feel exhausted, as though her energy had been slowly robbed through the back of her head without her noticing. She tried to get up, having a couple of attempts before succeeding. Standing unnoticed by her brother, she reached with her arms outstretched towards the horseman, like a desperate child begging to be cradled. She willed him to know and understand.

With a bounce and a spring, the silhouette turned towards the steep bank, plunging down it with force, bringing soil and weeds after in its wake. The noise was like the beginning of an avalanche and caused Mark to turn from his work in fear. Sacha crashed into the area, tossing her head and hurrying forward, her huge dinner plate hooves dancing on the charred ground and her beautiful mane flowing as her tack clinked and jangled.

Logan dismounted with a thud and was next to Hana, lifting her up around the waist and letting her wind her arms around his neck. Her sore shoulder felt tight and under pressure but she held on for as long as she could. Mark shook his head perplexed and eyed the dappled-white beast with the wild eyes nervously, the trowel still guiltily in his hand and the head of it held on by his thumb and forefinger. Logan set Hana down and turned to admire their work, keeping an arm around her shoulders, the fingers massaging her arm through her shirt.

"I hope you don't mind," Mark said with uncharacteristic awkwardness. Hana cocked her head as he resembled the sixteen-year-old brother she remembered, uncertain of himself and uncomfortable with his own body. She looked up to him as a little girl and worshiped him like an idol, hanging off his every word and loving him despite his obvious animosity towards her, the irritating sister he never wanted. Hana's damaged heart softened towards him, seeing the conflict and loneliness in his eyes and the desperate need for acceptance. He wanted to be loved just like everyone else; the great Dr Mark McIntyre was flawed.

"No, it needed doing. Good on ya." Logan held Hana's hand while Sacha snuffed in the grass at the edges of the plateau where Reuben once grew vegetables. He walked down the line of planting, seeming relieved they obeyed the neatly tied threads. "It's going to be beautiful when it's all grown into a maze. Very fitting for Mum and...him. You've done well," Logan concluded, running his hand over his face. One wonky conifer offended his eye and he chose to ignore its imperfect placement, knowing realistically over time they would bend and twist under an unseen hand, individual and at the same time uniform; a bit like the schoolboys, he taught. Logan held onto Hana's hand, enjoying her dependence on him.

"How will we water up?" Mark asked, brushing his hands down his trousers and looking around him.

"We're putting a rainwater tank up here tomorrow when the guys are back at the building site. It makes sense if we're planting stuff. I shouldn't worry about these though." Logan indicated the deep green plants with his outstretched hand. "They grow like weeds so they'll be fine for today. The rain is on its way in from the west."

Mark looked up at the sky, attempting to see what the stockman saw. "It looks no different from an hour ago."

Logan smiled as the other man raked the clouds with his eyes and waved his arm towards the mountain. "It's coming in from the west - off the Tasman. It'll be here in a short while. We should be getting back."

Mark shook his head and Hana smirked at her brother's disbelief, biting her lip in amusement at his expense. Logan helped them put the tools away, treading down the soil around the planting with the sole of his cowboy boot. He took the carrycot off the pram and collapsed the frame easily with his strong hands while Hana went to stroke the white mare and feed her long grass from the verge. The mare greeted her with eagerness and it pleased Hana. "Hey girl," she kissed the furry, rounded nose and Sacha sighed a heavy, wet gust of air.

Mark lifted the pram frame back into the boot of the Jeep, feeling inferior next to the capable younger man as Logan effortlessly fitted the carrycot containing his sleeping daughter onto the back seat, securing the seatbelt around it. Mark climbed into the driver's seat and started the engine. "See you back at the bottom," he said with gruffness.

Logan put his hands on his wife's waist and leaned in for a kiss, pushing his hat back on his head. His lips were tender and soft and it left Hana feeling ragged and frustrated. "Tease," she rebuked him. Logan's smile and narrowed eyes made her stomach flip. "You're making Mark jealous," she whispered. "I don't think he likes how perfect you are."

Logan snorted. "Hardly."

"Well, you are to me," Hana breathed into his ear. Logan slapped her bum and pushed her towards the Jeep.

"You can thank me later," he smirked at her retreating back. He smiled and waved as they circled the flattened area and made their way down the steep hill. Reuben's old overgrown driveway, which impeded the volunteer fire brigade's access during the inferno, had been cleared and widened. The burnt out shell of the charred house was later removed by diggers and hauliers. Logan shivered and ran his hand through his dark hair. As Hana looked back, she saw Sacha's head shoot up in answer to Logan's low whistle and set off obediently towards him.

Mark was quiet on the way down the hill, negotiating the difficult terrain with his glasses perched on the end of his nose. Finally, he spoke. "He's very imposing, your husband."

"Yes," Hana said simply.

"Weren't you terrified of him when you first met?" Mark asked, deeply curious, trying to comprehend the dynamic of this unusually matched couple. Hana shook her head.

"He was never like that with me. He was quiet and awkward and seemed nervous. I had no idea within the confines of our school-world, that he was anything like the powerful man he is. I fell in love with the head of the English department, although he's always had this powerful aura around him. Māori call it *mana*. We'd been married for ages before I found out how financially solvent he was, or that he owned this place outright. I'll always see him as the gentle, unassuming man first and foremost, that little boy on the train who watched me so intently while I sobbed into his mother's hanky. But when I need him to be, he's this giant who shelters and takes care of me and Phoe."

"Do you think he's the ideal man?" Mark asked.

Hana looked at her brother, surprised. "Why do you ask that?"

"I guess I need a role model," Mark smiled.

"You can't really be a 'Logan'," Hana mused sagely, "because then you would need a 'Hana.' And fortunately for the rest of mankind, there is only one of me."

Mark laughed and the jovial mood returned, lasting until they reached the stables and thanked Jack for the use of his vehicle.

Mark left after breakfast on Monday, travelling back to Hamilton for his afternoon shift on general surgery. Hana wondered how he coped, never knowing what would greet him when he arrived at work each day but he assured her he loved it and was good at it. He hugged Hana tightly. "I love you, little sister," he whispered. "Let's catch up again soon."

"Yeah, I'd like that," she replied into his shirt, hoping he took her warning about bringing Anka near Logan, to heart.

Mark and Logan shook hands, their relationship soothed and strengthened by the visit and Hana's brother even sought out Alfred, to make his farewells. Phoenix did her cute little wrist wave from her position on her daddy's hip and then Mark was gone, his vehicle straining up the tarmac driveway towards the main road. Logan watched Hana carefully as she waved woodenly until long after her brother was gone, her face worryingly devoid of emotion.

Determined to distract her, he hoisted Phoenix further up his hip and took his wife's arm, leading her away from the car park towards the motel units along a pretty, tree-lined lane. "I spoke to Izzie this morning when you were in the shower," he said, keeping his voice devoid of emotion. "You can call her later if you like. She was nipping out to do the food shop but she'd love to hear from you. She's been ringing your mobile. You should turn it back on, Han."

"What did you tell her?" Hana asked, her voice low and her shoulders stiffening under Logan's palm.

"Nothing," Logan replied. "You need to tell them yourself. It's not my place. But they're going to be really hacked off when they find out that they were the last to know their mother had heart surgery."

Hana ran her hands through her hair, clearly distressed. "I don't know what to say to them," she groaned. "I almost wish they'd found out at the time, I've left it too long now."

Logan pulled her into him, smiling as Phoenix reached over and stroked her mother's cheek and burbled something unintelligible. Hana kissed her hand and the baby squeezed her eyes shut and put her head on one side. "I'm sorry," Logan said with honesty. "It never occurred to me to get in touch with your kids until it was too late. I felt like I was treading water, but I can see how it'll be received now. They'll think I deliberately kept them in the dark."

Hana sighed and tried not to think about the gathering storm. Logan strolled down the lane and Hana kept pace, wondering where they were going. They walked until the motel units were in sight and Logan stepped confidently onto the deck and knocked on the ranch slider of the one furthest away. It was the most spacious in the row, a three bedroomed unit with a small kitchenette, an open plan lounge area and a sofa which converted into an extra bed. Hana remembered it well from her renovation work over the summer. She felt a budding flash of nerves and hung back. "Isn't this Nev's unit?" Hana's voice wavered.

"Yeah, the insurance company pays the bills," Logan said quietly. "I'm just amazed Reuben had insurance. It's not like he bothered with anything else!"

A man in his late teens opened the door and stared at the family on the deck. His handsome face degenerated into a nasty snarl, full lips pulled back from perfect teeth with overt hostility. It didn't take a genealogist to see t he was pure Du Rose, right from the towering height to the olive complexion and dark wavy hair. He possessed the distinctive grey eyes, which right then were black as coals and displayed open annoyance. They all stood looking at each other in a charged gridlock.

"Who is it, Asher?" came a man's voice, and the teenager turned to someone inside.

"It's *him!*"

Nev was at the door in seconds, cuffing the young man around the head and pushing him out of the way as he apologised profusely. He glared at his offspring angrily, their grey eyes locked in battle. "Come in, come in," Nev said with polite embarrassment, his olive skin flushing a rosy pink. Hana noted that in the battle of wills, the young man looked away first.

Nev offered them both a drink, which Logan declined but out of English politeness, Hana felt compelled to ask for something. "Just a glass of water, please," she said, including a smile with her reply. She regretted it instantly as the young man was dispatched. Hana waited, trying to disguise her discomfort as she heard Asher running water in the kitchen. He presented the drink to her without care, slopping it roughly on purpose. Hana prayed he hadn't spat in it by the sink. As she took a tiny sip, she was relieved to discover it tasted of the mountain spring just like it always did.

Logan kept a tight hold on his daughter as they all sat down. Asher remained standing, leaned against the archway through to the kitchenette. Phoenix looked around with curiosity, taking in every detail of her surroundings, pointing at something known only to her up near the ceiling and babbling quietly to herself. Periodically she beamed at Nev, making him look and feel unnerved and awkward. "She's very like the old lady, aye," Nev said wistfully, indicating the baby with his head. Logan nodded once. Hana wondered if he meant Logan's mother or their paternal grandmother, Phoenix Du Rose.

Nev sat back in his chair and opened his hands, palm outwards, silently inviting Logan to make his proposal. Asher in the corner tensed visibly as he anticipated the reason for the visit, which was clearly not a social call.

"You spoke to my business partner about selling your section of the mountain. I'm guessing the property has already been valued by the developers?" Logan asked and Nev nodded. "Depending on how badly they want it, I may not be able to equal or better their offer because they'll inflate it to get you interested, but I am prepared to get some fair valuations and work to those."

Hana's brow creased as she wondered silently why Nev talked to her if he'd already spoken to Logan's business partner. Perhaps he hadn't gotten a suitable reply and come searching for answers. Logan's half-brother let out a huge sigh of relief and nodded with enthusiasm.

"No bloody way!" The young man over by the door held his stance, balling his fists and blurting, "If you can't beat the price the developers have offered, you can go screw yourself!"

Hana's hand shook at his sudden outburst and the water slopped over her wrist and onto the tiled floor. Phoenix jumped and then laughed as though it was a game and her mother mopped at the mess with the edge of her cardigan, feeling embarrassed. Logan's body stiffened and he eyed the young man, newly promoted from distant cousin to nephew, with a steely gaze that seemed to go on forever. Asher looked increasingly uncomfortable as though the look was torture, but he held his ground through some primal sense of ego. "Perhaps," Logan said acidly, without removing his grey eyes from Asher's face, "you should go out to play and let the adults talk business."

Asher's jaw tensed and he rose up on the balls of his feet, like me might lurch towards Logan. Hana grew afraid for the little girl sat defencelessly on her husband's knee and half rose, ready to throw what was left of the water at the young man. The effort of sitting on the edge of her seat made Hana's thighs hurt and the stitches in her chest ached from the tautness being communicated from the rest of her body. Logan's eyes flashed a warning at the young man which he received and understood, but it was Nev who took charge of the unfolding situation. "Just bugger off, Ash," he said to his son and the young man bridled in anger. "I mean it!" his father said and Asher sloped out of the ranch slider, banging it closed behind him. "Sorry," Nev said with feeling, looking directly at Hana. "He doesn't want me to sell. None of my family do." He sighed with a heaviness laced by a sense of failure.

"What will you do, once you've?" Logan asked and there was compassion in his voice as his mind took him back to the agony of his own thoughts of quitting, the memories and burden of it all.

"I honestly don't know," Nev replied and sat forward, putting his head in his hands. Hana felt deep pity for him. Phoenix sucked her thumb noisily and it was the only sound in the room for a few minutes until Logan spoke again.

"I wouldn't blame you for selling to the developers. I'm not selling, no matter what they might think, but my circumstances are less precarious. I own all this outright, apart from that section near the road, but you have the rest of..." Logan paused, unable to mention Reuben's name. "You have *his* side of the family wanting to carve your land up and take a chunk each. What I'm proposing is that you sell to me for a price we both agree is fair, but stay on and run the land as a going concern.

I'd like to stay on as my manager." Nev's head shot up and he looked at Logan in disbelief, his grey eyes widening. Logan continued, "I wouldn't run it the same way as before though, so you'd need to be prepared to accept some changes. I'll want to do it my way, but that's a given. It's a decision you'll have to make anyway; sell to the developers, carve up the money between the family members and go elsewhere or sell to me and stay on. Get Kane and the others off your back with whatever I pay for the land and live in the new house you've built at the bottom of the mountain, as my tenant manager."

Neville looked utterly poleaxed and shock caused his tongue to stick to the roof of his dry mouth, rendering him speechless. His lips moved furiously but nothing came out. Logan stood up, hoisting Phoenix onto his hip while he offered his hand to Hana, to help her up. She looked around frantically for somewhere to put the glass, in the end leaving it on the floor by her chair and hoping Nev's little son, Wiremu, didn't hurt himself on it. Phoenix made a new popping noise with her mouth, sounding like little wet kisses as Hana made her way to the door. "Call me," Logan said as he stood on the deck and closed the ranch slider behind him.

They sauntered down the lane and Hana looked around nervously for the angry young man. "You're a big old softie at heart, aren't you?" she said to her husband, wrapping her right arm around his waist and hooking her thumb into his back jeans pocket.

He smiled down at her with a twinkle in his eye and denied it. "Just a shrewd businessman," he answered.

"Loge?" Hana asked, suddenly curious as the loose stones crunched underfoot. "I didn't know you had a business partner?"

Logan stopped and faced her. His eyes were deadly serious. "It's this woman I met a long time ago. She's gorgeous and we've got this thing going on."

Hana's brow knitted and she felt sad and vulnerable. Logan put his head back and laughed, not wanting to prolong her misery. He leaned in to kiss her and she pushed him away crossly. Logan switched Phoenix onto his other side and ran his fingers up Hana's cheek and into her hair, pulling her in close to him. "Hana, *you're* my business partner, you egg! Nev spoke to *you*, remember?"

Hana leaned back and eyed her husband with suspicion, before deciding he was paying her a huge compliment. A slow smile broke out over her face and she let him kiss her while their baby tugged on the front of Hana's cardigan and repeated the popping sound, keen not to be left out.

The young grey eyed Du Rose watched from behind them on the lane, grinding his teeth and kicking at the loose dirt, oozing hatred and trouble.

Chapter Nine

"Which is the section of land you *don't* own?" Hana asked as Logan plugged her laptop into the charger.

"There's ten hectares down near the main road. Someone else owns it."

"Who?"

Logan eyed his wife nervously. She was trying to distract him. "I don't know. He's just called 'JD' and I lease it on an annual basis. I don't really need it, but it's got a bore hole so it's good in a drought because I can pump water for the stock from it when we're short."

"How come you don't know him?"

"Hana, I don't need to know him. The family's leased that land forever. When Dad nearly destroyed the place, this guy let him have it for nothing for about five years. I keep paying him purely because of that."

"What if it's not a man? What if it's a..."

"Hana!" Logan's retort was sharp. Hana sat in front of the laptop screen, watching her reflection and feeling increasingly nervous. Logan sat out of view, waiting for the programme to register the three-way call about to take place. Two green telephone receivers lit up on screen and Hana shot a frightened look at her husband. He smiled and nodded encouragement at her. Hana clicked on both of the green lights and immediately little screens opened up at the bottom of hers. In one was her beautiful half-Indian daughter, Isobel, peering at the screen. Baby Marcus sat on her knee and her husband, big Marcus' face beamed from behind his wife holding the other twin boy. In the background, Hana could hear Elizabeth singing to herself in a tuneful but dribbly melody. Hana smiled and waved at the laptop, rewarded by the sound of disjointed 'hellos' from the other end of the country.

Hana ached suddenly for the feel of her daughter's arms around her and a small sob caught in her throat as she put her hand up to her mouth, attempting to contain her emotion. Logan leaned over and squeezed her shoulder lovingly, before lying on his side and trying to entertain Phoenix until it was her turn to look into the screen and taste the family gathering. In the other screen was the face of Bodie, Hana's policeman-son. He was also half-Indian, olive skinned and raven haired. On his knee was his son Jas, beaming fit to burst and waving his Action Man, which made a dark green blur across the screen. "Where's Poppa Logan?" Jas asked immediately.

Logan reached his head around so the camera could see him for a second and waved at the little boy. The child worshipped the ground Logan walked on, much to the annoyance of Bodie, who really didn't. Jas beamed even more widely, showing another gap where a tooth was missing. "The fairies left me five bucks, Poppa!" he exclaimed happily, holding up a dollar coin. "I saved this for you. See, half each!"

Logan looked into the screen again and smiled. "Awesome buddy. The cookies are on you then."

Jas jigged around on Bodie's knee with excitement. "Ok, when you coming home? Is it soon?"

"Not long now. A few more days," Logan said and backed away from the camera to give Hana space to talk to her family.

They all made small talk for a while, until the respective children got bored and disappeared from view. Phoenix sat on

Hana's knee for a moment to be admired by her older siblings but fascinated, she kept trying to push the keys and Logan took her away and laid her on the change mat. He undid her nappy and she started singing and playing with her toes, enjoying her bare bottom being out in the open air.

"Is everything alright, Mum?" Izzie asked, always fine-tuned to other people's feelings.

"Is it about Culver's Cottage?" Bodie asked, his face shaping into a frown. "Don't you want to sell it to me anymore?" He rolled his eyes and looked fed up.

Hana deliberately didn't look across at her husband, sensing the tension in the room hike as Logan struggled with his stepson's mercenary attitude towards her. She didn't have to see the irritated look on his face to know it was there.

"I've been texting you all week, asking about the valuations. How come you haven't been replying to me?" Bodie's voice achieved a perfectly pitched whine, despite his twenty seven years on the planet and his job as a police officer.

Hana took a deep breath. "I only plugged my phone in to charge this morning. I haven't turned it on yet. Logan found it with a flat battery in my coat pocket. I...erm...I..." Hana looked across towards her husband, gulping when he wouldn't meet her eyes. Her avoidance tactics frustrated him; like hiding the carrier bag containing her clothing and phone under the bed, afraid to be reminded of her heart attack. Hana ran a fairly effective out-of-sight-out-of-mind policy when it suited her. The coat bore mud and grass stains on the back from her plunge earthwards and Logan put it in the laundry, finding the iPhone in the pocket at the last minute.

Hana opened her mouth to speak, but Bodie interrupted. "Why does Izzie need to be involved in the house sale? It's nothing to do with her." He sounded like a petulant child and Hana winced.

Logan shook his head out of view and contemplated leaving the room before he seized the laptop and said something unfortunate into it. Hana agreed a few weeks previously to consider selling her home in the Hakarimata bush to her son and his fiancé if they could agree on a price. As far as she was concerned there was no great rush as Amy hadn't sold her house yet, but Bodie scented the whiff of victory and wanted to press the issue. "There's another thing, Mum," Bodie began. "Something happened at the school..."

Hana held her hand up to silence her son. She needed to get on with this before her courage failed her. Still, Izzie said nothing, waiting patiently for her mother to reveal the real reason for the call. "I need to tell you both something," Hana said her voice failing her in an agonised catch. She swallowed and looked across at Logan again. Phoenix rolled over onto her stomach on the plastic change mat and laughed at her own cleverness. Logan rested his hand gently on the small of her back to stop her wriggling off the bed and moved next to his wife, his other arm firmly and visibly around her shoulders. Izzie's face leaned forward, growing larger in the little box at the bottom of the screen. She looked concerned and Logan liked her for that, even more than he already did.

"Now she's a credit to your single parenting," Logan whispered. Bodie at least had the decency to finally shut up about his own agenda.

Hana continued, faltering as she tried to remember the sentences she rehearsed earlier. "I was taken ill a few days ago...er..." She turned to Logan, out of view and whispered, "When was it?"

Logan was alarmed to see her reach up to her chest and rub it gently. He pulled the laptop towards him on her knees, angling it so both their faces showed and told the story for her. At the words 'heart attack,' Izzie clapped her hand over her mouth and looked backwards at her husband standing behind her. Bodie actually looked shaken.

"The cardiologist did a valve repair," Logan said. "Your mum has a pacemaker with a defibrillator in it and a stent I believe, although they'll explain more when she goes for her first check up this week. I'll make sure I go with her, so I can tell you more after that." Logan paused and looked around at his daughter, who had peed all over the mat and was patting her hands in it. He grimaced and looked back at the screen, feeling his loyalties divided.

"How bad was it?" Bodie asked and Logan could see that finally, he was concerned.

Hana opened her mouth to play it down, to placate her older children but Logan wasn't prepared to let her do that. He interrupted her before she could tell them it was nothing, pulling the screen further towards him to cut Hana out. "Real bad, as bad as it gets. If her brother hadn't been there, she would've died. The Air Ambulance took us to Auckland and she was in surgery within the hour."

Logan looked across at his wife's pinched face, feeling guilty but not wanting to live behind a veil of lies, especially for Bodie's sake. He didn't deserve it.

Both Hana's children by her first marriage sat silently as Logan finished his sentence. Izzie's hand covered her mouth but Bodie sat rigidly, his face expressionless. Hana kept her eyes facing the bedspread and Logan sensed she was cross with him for his blunt appraisal of her frailty.

Phoenix looked like she was about to lick her hands and Logan pushed the laptop back towards Hana and snatched the baby up, holding her at arm's length out in front of him. He took the little girl into the ensuite and sat her in the sink. She started to squeal with glee, loving it when they bathed her that way. Her father stripped her clothes off over her head, an expert after seven months of experience. Then he ran tepid water into the sink and soaped her thoroughly. "*Paru*," he told her, pulling a face. "Dirty."

Hana sat facing her children, wondering what they could possibly find to chat about now. As the information sank into their brains, both of them asked the same question. "How come you didn't tell us sooner?"

Hana knew they would ask. She would have - if she were them. She coached herself all afternoon, ever since Logan managed to contact her son and daughter earlier and arrange the three-way conversation. Her carefully prepared answer suddenly didn't seem so convincing. There was a pause before Hana spoke and the silence crossed the miles between them as static hiss. "I felt...I feel...embarrassed," Hana said honestly. "I already felt conscious of my age, especially having Phoenix so late and this made me feel ancient. I've struggled to come to terms with it and it's been hard for me and Logan. Nobody else knows either. My father and brother were with us, thank goodness Mark was as it turned out, but I needed some time to get used to it before I told you."

When Hana looked back at the screen again, she saw Izzie swipe her hand across her eyes, her gentle heart distressed at her mother's revelation. More than anything, she wanted to hold her daughter and reassure her. "I'm sorry," Hana whispered and immediately, Izzie sought to make her mother feel better.

"It's fine, Mum. I love you. Please, please let me know what I can do to help? Just name it and we'll do it, won't we?" Izzie's head swivelled round, seeking the approval of her husband. Marcus' face appeared over his wife's shoulder.

"Of course we will. Whatever you need."

Hana felt emotional again, feeling angry with her body for being so uncontrollable. They warned her it might be like this, the trauma of the heart failure coupled with the effects of the general anaesthetic. *'Expect to feel low at points over the next few weeks,'* the cardiologist said.

Bodie was so quiet it was almost eerie. Hana heard Logan washing Phoenix's face in the sink and the 'brrrr' noise she made as he ran his fingers over her lips. She loved that game. He appeared a few seconds later with the baby swaddled up in a towel, her tiny pink feet sticking out the bottom. Logan observed the wet change mat with a sigh and contemplated his next task. Hana held her hands out for her child, putting the laptop carefully on the bed and trying not to knock it as Logan sat the baby on her knee. Her actions were wooden and it was obvious to the watchers how she protected her chest area from the baby's wiggling torso, as she fought the towel.

Logan dumped the wet mat into the shower cubicle and came back to rescue Hana from the flailing child. Izzie and Bodie watched the little girl as she seemed to take off from Hana's lap, not seeing the strong arms of Logan airlifting her out of view. Hana ran her hand over her face and tried to pull her mind back to their conversation. *What were they talking about again?*

"Mum," Izzie said and her voice sounded very small, "I know you rang me a few weeks ago and I'm sorry for not getting back to you. What did you mean about your father and brother, because I'm not understanding?"

Hana exhaled slowly, so as not to be seen on the screen feeling exasperated. It all felt too hard to explain. She looked across at Logan as he sealed his daughter into a clean disposable nappy. Her green eyes were sheltered by tired, drooping lids and her face had lost the day's healthy flush and grown pale. Logan responded to her distress call, laying the baby down on the bed and sitting next to his wife. Slowly and carefully he took the laptop back and spoke into the screen. "It's a long story, but Mark McIntyre is a surgeon from the UK. He operated on your mum's wrist and removed the shard of glass some months ago. Anyway, he's your uncle and he recognised Hana and called her father in England. He was having chemo but came to New Zealand to find her as soon as he could."

"I'm confused." Izzie grappled visibly. "You always said your father was dead. But he isn't?"

"I genuinely thought he was, Izz. I'm so sorry. It's all too hard to explain right now." Hana felt relieved that for once, her son kept quiet about having met Mark instead of enjoying the ready sense of one-up-man-ship.

"I was going to tell you when I rang," Hana placated her daughter. "I'm so sorry I never managed to. In the end, it seemed unlikely they would get as far south as Invercargill but Dad says next time, he definitely wants to meet you."

"He did," Logan interjected. "At the airport, Robert asked me to pass on a message. Next time he comes over, he'll make sure he sees both of you."

Izzie nodded slowly and looked downcast. "It seems I've been kept out of everything." An uncharacteristic sulkiness descended over her at the dissatisfaction with her life in the far south, missing home and the town she grew up in. The harsh winter and feeling of disconnection from her mother began to eat a sizeable hole in Isobel's happiness of late and Marcus sensed a familiar storm would be brewing in their marriage as soon as the call ended.

Bodie was still quiet, feeling guilty for not having got in touch with Izzie when Hana dropped the bombshell about her father and brother. He didn't want to admit he'd already met his uncle, knowing Izzie would feel betrayed. They always told each other everything, forming an alliance behind Hana's back from an early age and sharing a bond outside of their familial relationship. The distance between them made it difficult to maintain their closeness and Bodie didn't know how to put it right. He hung his head and Hana detected shame in his deep brown eyes.

Logan abruptly lurched for his daughter's ankles as she worked her way across towards the edge of the bed. "No ya don't!" he grunted as the laptop wobbled on his legs. He pulled her back into view of the screen camera and persuaded Phoenix to do her cute little wave. "Wave bye-bye," he encouraged as the affable child beamed and flicked her chubby wrist. Hana blew kisses to each of her children and Logan disconnected the call, laying the laptop on the bed while he dealt with the baby.

Sitting Phoenix in the travel cot for a moment while he sorted everything out, Logan turned a concerned face towards his wife. She sat with her head in her hands, looking pale and sad. "That was awful!" she muttered, her voice muffled by her fingers.

"It's done now," he said, squatting in front of her and pulling her hands away from her face with strong, reassuring fingers. "It'll be easier now it's all out in the open."

"I should've done it when you told me to, days ago." Hana sniffed and waited for Logan to pull the I-told-you-so card, feeling more broken when he didn't. He rubbed her fingers in a gentle motion and looked up at her with his beautiful grey eyes. His kindness chastened Hana. "I'm too scared to turn my phone on now!" she wailed, giving into the latent hysterics hiding beneath the ruffled exterior. "I've probably got a million missed calls and texts from Bo about the house and I haven't even given it a second thought this last week. What a mess!" She tried to put her hands back up to her face but Logan wouldn't let hide from him.

"I'll deal with everything so don't worry. Come on, let's go down for some food. I'll dress Phoe and we'll take the pram down in the lift in case she falls asleep. Then we can go to the family room and watch video's on the old TV. Yeah?"

Hana leaned forward and rested her face on Logan's shoulder. "I don't know what I'd do without you," she whispered but it was more than a platitude for a woman once woken by the urgent knocking of apologetic police officers. They destroyed her world in their first sentence, '*I'm sorry to have to inform you, Mrs Johal...*' Hana clung to her husband, winding her fingers into his shirt as she tried to banish the awful sense of foreboding which clung to her like a ghoul.

"You won't have to," Logan soothed. "I'm ordering two pairs of concrete gumboots and I've already picked the bridge."

Chapter Ten

First thing on Tuesday, Logan made the journey to Rangiriri, to the French style restaurant owned by his cousin. Periodically the two men looked at the accounts together, deciding on the direction the eatery should take to remain profitable during the current recession. Alex always greeted his maternal cousin fondly, a childhood friendship stretching with confidence through the years. He was outside before Logan cut the engine, wrenching the Honda's door open and embracing him in a *hongi*. The men pressed noses and kept eye contact, their Māori genealogy calling to each other. Logan clapped Alex on the back and smiled. "You're losing your puppy fat, bro."

"Yeah, bro. Now you're married my wife's lookin' at me more. I gotta look the part." Alex held the door open and indicated Logan should sit at the table nearest the bar.

"This bar was a great move," Logan commented, looking around before he sat. "Extending from the café scene was genius. Your *wahine* certainly knows the hospitality business."

Alex's face clouded over and Logan knitted his brows in concern. "It's fine, it's fine," Alex said, waving away Logan's look of worry. "We work too hard and it's taking a toll on our marriage. The most we see of each other is when we pass with plates in our hands or she's handing me an order sheet. We'll work it out."

Logan shook his head firmly. "It's not *fine*. Family first, bro' otherwise it's all a waste of time. *Whānau* before finery – always. You know that." Logan reached for his cousin's hand and Alex nodded and squeezed his fingers, keeping his eyes facing the tablecloth. "Hey," Logan said gently, "this place works because of you both, but I don't think you need to be tied to it permanently. Let's have a look at the books and see if we can free some money up for another staff member. You could promote someone reliable to under-manager and then take on help." Logan lowered his voice to a lilting tone which couldn't be heard by the bar staff setting up for the lunchtime customers. "What about *tamariki*, Alexandre? You wanted kids. What happened?"

"We got too busy. Maybe it's too late." With shoulders drooping and his forehead lined, Alex Du Rose looked crushed.

Logan shook his head, their temples almost touching as he whispered. "It might not be, bro." His grey eyes channelled hope born of satisfaction with his own changed life and Alex nodded with deliberate slowness.

"Is it good? With your *wahine* Hana and *taitamaiti*, is it as good as you dreamed?"

Logan nodded. "Better, Alex. Being a husband and father, it's what I was born for; I just didn't know it."

The men were interrupted by the new head chef, a large, rambunctious man by the name of Claude. He said his name in a gay-French way which made Logan smirk. Stealing a glance at Alex, he noticed his cousin's jaw set in a practiced smile. "Is he for real?" Logan asked in a low voice as the man minced away, wiggling his hips and promising to bring them a 'special' something to snack on. "What do your customers think of him? He's a bit over the top, isn't he?"

"That guy's great value with the customers. You have to see it to believe."

The chef shimmied back with cat-walk precision and placed before them a silver platter. Logan's eyes widened with horror at the fat brown snails lined up on its surface. He peered again and realised they were made of milk chocolate, with dark chocolate detail to define the shadows on the shell and little white chocolate eyes. "Wow!" he said, staring at the chef with appreciation. "They're scarily life-like!" He pushed at one of the shells, pulling his finger back as the white chocolate eyes stared back at him. "Far out, these are good. Please can I buy some to take away?" Hana hated slugs and snails and it would be amusing to tease her as he popped them into his mouth in front of her. She always said the English hated the French because of the bits of snail shell in their teeth, mocking Logan's French ancestry without reserve.

"I 'ave spent some weeks perrrrrrrfecting zem," the chef simpered, rolling his eyes extravagantly towards heaven. "Mon dieu, zey were impossible!" He made the word 'impossible' sound very French. "It was 'ard to stop zem looking like little turds on ze tray."

Logan was enjoying a swig of his delicious espresso coffee and struggled to keep it in his mouth. Alex had tears in his eyes from keeping the mirth in. Both men eyed the chocolate snails nervously. As the chef swaggered back to the kitchen, Alex looked back at his cousin and business partner and they both snorted with laughter. "Does that guy know we have real French ancestry and French and Māori were the only two languages spoken in our homes until we were old enough to realise English existed?" Logan chortled.

Alex shook his head and shrugged. "He hasn't got a clue!" and they both burst out laughing again.

"Where did you find him?" Logan asked eventually, crunching on a chocolate snail.

"He just walked in here and I gave him a go. This place is getting too big to manage by myself and my off-sider - as you know - left a few weeks ago. It's been hard managing and to be honest, the guy can cook great French food. He comes up with these ideas, like the snails. He calls them *'chocolat escargo'* and no kidding, we sell out of them every service as a novelty dessert item. He does this really cool trail with the cream that looks like fake..." Alex snorted, unable to finish his sentence.

"If that guy's French then I'm an Englishman!" Logan commented. During his time in England he used the summer holidays to travel around Europe alone. He was pleased with how easily he coped in France, the colloquial-handed-down version of the language adequate in his dealings with native French speakers. Angus made him pick up a Year 13 French language class, as a special favour. The principal's 'favours' were usually best fled from, but Logan actually enjoyed exercising a language as natural as Māori for him. "Did he bring references?" Logan asked with suspicion and Alex nodded emphatically, cream squirting from the centre of the snail body. Then he burst out laughing again.

"I rang them. They said he was really a kiwi from Opononi called Clive, but an awesome chef. They were sorry to lose him. I thought he was gay but apparently he's got a wife and a whole tribe of kids with him. The whole gay-thing is part of the act. He's hilarious. I don't think we've laughed in the kitchen that much since...well, forever actually."

"Whatever makes you happy!" Logan remarked, raising his eyebrows at his childhood friend. "Rather you than me."

Two hours later and Alex waved Logan off, his step lighter and his face less lined. "I'll advertise for a new waiter this week and I know exactly who I'll make undermanager," he beamed. His wife emerged from the kitchen door and smiled as Logan pulled out of the car park. "Did he like the extension?" she asked, concern on her face. "He's pulled the plug on all his investments now. It's all in that cursed hotel. How do you know he won't cut ties with you?"

"Because his word is good." Alex turned grey eyes on his wife, noticing Hinga's tired face and the lack of energy in her demeanour. "And he's a good man. There is *aroha nui* between us."

Hinga snorted. "Logan Du Rose is a businessman. He doesn't have deep affection for anyone."

"Well, he does for me!" Alex let his eyes rove down Hinga's body, taking in the portly shape and the flawless texture of her olive skin. "*Wahine*, you're beautiful," he said. "I don't tell you enough."

"I'm thirty eight," she sighed. "And I have a roux to finish for the lunchtime crowd."

Alex smirked, scooping her up in his strong arms. "And I'm forty one and horny as an *ngeru mohowao*," he growled.

"Ooh, a wild cat," Hinga giggled. "That's different." She squealed as Alex carried her into their house behind the restaurant, forgetting about the roux thickening on the stove and not hearing the raucous swearing of the chef as he pulled the pan from the heat and threw the whole thing in the industrial sink.

Logan waved in his rear view mirror and headed west, keen to get home to Hana and Phoenix. His heart ached for his cousin and he felt glad they were able to release some of the profits for extra wait staff. He could see how strained and unhappy the man had become in the last six months. Sometimes it felt wrong to cream off a share of the profits, simply for putting up capital in the first place while other men worked their fingers to the bone to keep it coming. "It can go the other way just as easily," he sighed. "The current economic market sucks." He travelled along the familiar route, making the turns onto smaller and smaller metalled roads as he went deeper into the mountains, enjoying the sense of belonging and whistling a Māori *waiata*.

Logan rounded a bad left hand bend with care. His side of the road was scarred from a deep washout, roped off to stop cars plunging down its yawning maw. The torrential rains earlier in the winter had ripped away part of the steep underpinning of the road, making it treacherous. To Logan's dismay he met a camper van on the wrong side of the white line, cutting the corner without control or regard. Logan fought to keep control of the Honda and not skid off the extremely steep side as the wheels hit the rough edge and slewed across the road and back again. The camper sped by and Logan's vehicle shuddered to a halt, leaving him shaken and sick, inches from the drop on the passenger side. "Bloody tourists!" He exhaled carefully and rolled the Honda forward, moving onto a tiny verge to give himself a moment to recover without being rear-ended by another vehicle. Rubbing a shaking hand over his face, Logan waited for his equilibrium to return, trying not to imagine Hana's stricken face as a policeman informed her she just lost a second husband.

Something drew his attention, a movement from the other side of the road. With horror, Logan saw what the camper van crossed the centre line to avoid – and failed.

The shape of a man rose shakily from the ground, dressed in a camouflage jacket and trousers. He shook a heavy rucksack off his shoulders and onto the ground, bending over for a second while he rested his hands on his knees. Blond hair covered his head and his gear marked him out as army, although the pattern was British forces. Checking behind him, Logan left the Honda and ran across the road, startling the man who immediately took a fighter's stance. "Hey bro." Logan held his hands up, non-threatening but ready to defend himself if necessary. He weighed up his opponent, knowing a fight would be evenly matched in other circumstances, apart from the man was bleeding. "The van hit you?" Logan's voice oozed concern.

The soldier visibly relaxed as he instructed his body to soften and lose its rigidity. He nodded and wiped at a cut on his face, a black eye beginning to swell and bruise, closing the lid. "Need a ride to the emergency room?" Logan asked, "I can take you back to the city."

"Na, thanks. No." He didn't look like he needed an ambulance, shaking his head to indicate he didn't. But he flexed his left arm painfully, alerting Logan to his discomfort.

"The van driver must have realised he hit you." Logan looked along the road. "Maybe he's looking for somewhere to turn around and come back."

The man laughed a hollow sound. "Somehow, I doubt it." He reached down to pick up his rucksack, but his face was blank and Logan couldn't tell if he hurt more than he made out. Something forced the Māori to stand his ground, determined to do something useful and not let the stranger limp on his way uncared for.

"Where are you headed?" Logan asked, aware he was asking more questions than usual.

The man shrugged. "Just to the end of wherever the road goes and then back again." He smiled cynically in a way that didn't reach his eyes. Logan made a decision.

"Look, let me take you back to my place, at least have something to eat and get someone to look you over. Then I'll drive you back here and you can go on your way." Logan wasn't sure why it mattered so much to see this man taken care of, but it did. There was something about the soldier which resonated in his soul, a familiar emotional neglect which Hana's daily presence erased.

The man studied him for a moment and weighed him up, the olive skin and dark hair reminding him of a group who taunted and hassled him a few days back. They were drunk and he defended himself, leaving all but one of them requiring hospital treatment. This man seemed different, able to handle himself; but with no desire to prove it. The soldier looked down at his combat pants which were ripped at the knees after months of wear and washing them in streams. He thought he might smell a little unpleasant too, but couldn't be sure anymore. "I am hungry. And I could use a break from walking." Rubbing his hand across the bushy blond beard which sprang up unchecked and finishing in a movement that encompassed his tight curly hair, the man nodded once.

Logan bent and retrieved the rucksack, crossing the road and putting the bag on the floor behind the back seat. The men got in the car and the soldier settled himself in gingerly, planting his black heavy duty boots on the floor mat before clicking his seatbelt firmly in. Logan turned and offered his right hand without making any sharp moves and introduced himself. His hand was shaken with a firm grip and the introduction returned. "David Allen," the stranger replied with the slightest trace of a smile.

Logan wound his driver's window down so he could hear any approaching vehicles before he pulled out. The blind bend offered him no visual assistance. Hearing nothing, he pulled onto the road and set off. Logan deliberately stayed quiet on the journey through the lower part of the mountains, sensing his passenger's discomfort and unsure whether it was his injuries which troubled him, or something else. There was a look of resignation about the man, which Logan recognised and it tore at loosely healed wounds in his psyche.

Logan Du Rose first saw Hana in London on a Circle Line train. Eighteen and pregnant, she cried throughout the journey and Logan sat opposite with his mother, watching the tears run down Hana's face as embarrassed, she hastily brushed them away. Her red hair cascaded down her shoulders, her tight fitting yellow summer dress exposing the shape of her rounded belly. Logan fell in love, recognising his soul mate even as a fourteen year old and his life acquired an emptiness from that moment on. He left New Zealand as soon as he qualified as a teacher, heading straight to London and riding the tube trains regularly in hope of seeing her. It was like searching for a black and white horse in a herd of paint ponies – utterly impossible.

Logan headed back to New Zealand after a decade, that same look of resignation on his face as he finally gave up on ever finding the girl-on-the-train. He found Hana by sheer luck or maybe even fate, just as he accepted his aloneness. David Allen looked like a man on the run from his dreams and the dark feeling resonated somewhere deep inside Logan, recognising a kindred spirit and wanting to tell him it needn't be terminal. Yet silence dominated as they rode down the long driveway, each lost in his own thoughts.

The view of the hotel came and went as they rounded the mountain following the road. David looked out of the window but made no comment. The Honda swung through the huge iron gates, propped welcomingly open and crunched to a halt in the staff car park. Logan switched off the engine and got out, pulling David's rucksack from behind his seat. He noticed how the soldier rubbed his arm as he closed the car door. The man reached out immediately for his bag and Logan handed it over. Plainly it was all he owned and Logan understood that feeling. "You in pain?" Logan asked, indicating David's arm and the soldier shook his head and lied.

"No, I'm good."

Logan Du Rose spent his twenties living in a grotty bedsit in Brixton and listened to the screams of the 1995 riots. He owned nothing that didn't come with the room, apart from his clothes which were always expensive and imported from Italy. The clothing could be packed away in seconds and was probably the only thing worth protecting. The riots were over the death of a black man in police custody. To the white people, Logan Du Rose was brown skinned and to the black community he was white. He fitted in nowhere but eventually fitted in everywhere. He earned the respect of his students and fellow staff, his demeanour strong, silent and always watchful. Not watching for danger – watching for Hana.

David Allen observed the pristine building, elderly and attractive but well-kept and properly maintained. He saw nothing of the hotel's chequered past, the war, neglect and family feuds. The guest car park buzzed and hummed with excited voices as members of a national Christian organisation arrived for a week-long conference, milling around with their wheeled suitcases. Logan strode towards the huge front doors, giving way as people filed in and out. A male and female receptionist dealt with the queue of people from behind a polished wooden desk but Logan skirted the crowd and turned right down a long passageway. David followed him, confused and wrong-footed, his steps slowing as he second guessed his rash decision to go with the stranger.

Logan opened a door to the right and entered a brightly lit room. A pine dining table took up centre stage, flanked by items of heavy old furniture which stood guard around the walls. Long sash windows let the generous winter sunshine pour in. "Please, sit." Logan indicated the table before going over to an archway to his left. He stuck his head inside an adjacent industrial kitchen and spoke to someone in Māori.

A portly, olive skinned woman bustled into the room carrying a tray of drinks. "*Kia ora!*" she greeted David, nodding and plonking the tray on the table. She unloaded mugs, milk jug and pots of tea and coffee. "Hurry up, Helena!" she called, frowning. A younger woman trotted in bearing a platter of cottage pie in one hand and a bowl of trifle in the other. The wares were set down before David and cutlery provided from the large woman's apron pocket, already wrapped in a serviette. "*Kaikai,*" Leslie said, waving her hand at the food and looking expectantly at the soldier. She put her hands on her hips and screwed up her face as though looking for judgement on the quality of her food.

David stared at the food, suddenly starving. He knew he should portion it out. It wouldn't be good to eat it all in one go. It would make it harder later, when there was nothing and he had lulled his guts into a false sense of security. He regretted there was nothing he could safely pocket. He looked up with wide blue eyes and something in their intensity made Leslie frown. Logan jerked his head towards the old lady, dismissing her with the thunderous expression on his face. David stopped with his cutlery raised, feeling the animosity between them.

Logan poured himself coffee and David indicated the teapot with his index finger, not wanting to speak with his mouth full of the delicious food. His stomach complained violently about the sudden food dump in his oesophagus, used to making a muesli bar last all day. Logan poured tea and pushed the mug towards his guest, pointing at the milk and sugar on the tray before turning away. "Eat what you want," he said, keeping his tone light. "I can get you more. I'll ask the housekeeper to make food for you to take on the road."

He had seen hungry people before, during the lean days of his childhood as Alfred got to grips with his business ineptitude and wrecked the dairying income. It filled him with miserable memories and he stared through the window at the immaculate driveway and the neatly cut hedges, while his brain went back in time to a dreadful rutted track and skinny cows filing past the window. The urgent scrape of cutlery on crockery jarred Logan's nerves with the naked need of the man behind him, knowing that eating required extreme courage because it left the diner vulnerable and open to attack.

Spotting his nephew outside, Logan undid the catch on the sash window and raised the bottom half so he could lean out and shout to him. He called him a rude name and Tama sauntered over, smirking. "Whatever, Uncle!"

"You been with the cuzzies in the township?" Logan asked, referring to Tama's childhood friends. "They're bad boys, Tama. You've been drunk all weekend, haven't you?"

Tama nodded. "I've been with them, but I ain't been drinking. Look at me, bro; I was the sober driver." He jerked his head upwards, looking for Logan's approval.

"For real?" his uncle asked him, genuine surprise in his voice. Tama smiled and nodded. "Well good on ya! There's hope for mankind yet then."

"Where's Ma?" the young man asked, looking hopeful, poking his head through the window. "I wanted to tell her too."

Logan shrugged. "I dunno, I thought she'd be in here. Do me a favour, Tama?" he asked his nephew. "Find her and tell her I'm back. Just check she's all right for me please. She talked to her kids last night and it wasn't easy for her."

Tama nodded enthusiastically and trotted off to find the woman responsible for putting his catastrophic life on a better course. Logan turned back to the room after shutting the window, surprised to find David's plates and cutlery neatly stacked in a pile and the man standing by his chair, gathering up his rucksack. "I wondered if you wanted to look around," Logan asked casually and David wiped his hand over his forehead, smearing the blood from the cut to his temple, right across his face. Logan felt chastened. "Sit down, I'll get someone to look at that. Sorry, I forgot."

Logan went into the kitchen and commandeered Leslie's first aid skills to deal with the man's cuts and bruising. She did her best, washing the head wound and taping it tightly shut with a series of butterfly stitches. David moved his arm gingerly and she insisted he remove his shirt so she could look at it. "Ooh boy!" she exclaimed. "Look at youse muscles!"

David was toned and muscular but painfully thin, his ribs showing through the skin. A set of army dog-tags swung from a metal chain around his neck. There was a spiteful cut on his left elbow from the side panel of the camper van and lots of black bruising beginning already. "It's not broken," Leslie declared, "but it's gonna be painful for a few days." She dealt with the cut, strapping the elbow and arm tightly. She even helped him slip his tee shirt and camouflage jacket over the bandage before patting him on the back and resuming her duties in the kitchen.

"Come for a look round," Logan suggested again. "Then I'll take you wherever you want me to drop you."

David nodded once and looked down at his bag. Logan suggested locking it up in the Honda and he seemed happy with that. Logan strolled him around the property, explaining the heritage of the place and pointing out the different businesses on the site. David seemed interested, especially in the equipment shed. "What was your trade in the army?" Logan asked, surprised when David replied he was in the Royal Air Force. "British?" Logan concluded and the other man nodded.

"Yeah. From the age of seventeen until a few months ago. Gave them the best fifteen years of my life."

As they walked around the shed in companionable silence, David touched the farm equipment and quad bikes with experienced fingers. "So can you mend this crap then?" Logan asked bluntly and the soldier smiled and nodded, continuing to touch the vehicles as though they were old friends. Logan leaned his bum back against the side of a quad. "I could use a good mechanic, even for a couple of weeks." He kept his voice casual, his eyes narrowing as David looked interested.

"I was a fireman," he said quietly, "but I know this stuff, yeah. I've done mechanics courses."

Logan left the conversation alone for a while, leaving the subtle offer to float in the air before coming to rest in the other man's brain like an answer to a prayer. Logan showed him the stables and skirted the hotel, explaining how it was run as a conference centre in part and a hotel for the rest of the time. David seemed impressed in an understated way, struggling with the rare show of human kindness in his lonely life. "Why do you give a damn about me?" David asked, his voice sounding gruff in his confusion as he flicked flaked paint from the wheel arch of a tractor.

Logan shrugged. "Maybe I just have broken crap in my shed." He stuffed his hands in his jeans pockets and sauntered through the door. David followed, kicking his heels and debating with himself.

Rounding the side of the huge building, Logan saw his baby's pram over by the vegetable plot. "Oh, there's my..." His brows knitted and he stopped speaking mid-sentence, causing the other man to stare at him warily. Logan spotted Hana sat on the ground, her back to him and he panicked, unceremoniously abandoning his guest. "Hana?" Logan pulled his hands from his pockets and ran to her.

Hana Du Rose sat cross-legged in the sunshine; her eyes closed and her body motionless. A tray of lettuce perched in front of her on the lumpy earth, many of them leaning haphazardly as they slipped into the space where others had been lifted out. The missing ones sat neatly in a row in front of her, planted equal distances apart. A small black trowel was clutched in her hand, redundant against her left knee. Logan touched her gently on the shoulder, squatting down as she gave a huge shuddering sigh and opened her eyes. "Hana, are you ok?" His voice was sharp with panic.

David stood awkwardly nearby and watched, not sure whether to approach or not, understanding the moment was private. The red-haired woman was of slender build and the sunlight caught her hair, showering it with gold and copper streaks. From the way the Māori looked at her with such compassion, it was obvious she was either his wife or girlfriend. The substantial flash of gold on her ring finger confirmed the alliance, matching the one on the man's. David saw Logan stroke her long hair back from her forehead. "What's wrong?" he asked again.

Her answer caused Logan's brow to knit, consternation filling his face and squaring his shoulders although he tried to hide his sadness. "I'm sorry; if I keep still I can almost remember what it's like to have no pain. It felt good, while it lasted."

Logan Du Rose stroked his wife's hair with tenderness, biting his lip and frowning. Hands which could cause a bull whip to issue the kind of crack which the mountains remembered and echoed back to the valley for seconds on end, were gentle and loving around this woman. David saw the man's body align in a different, more protective stance. It altered everything about him and David looked away, not wanting to recall what it felt like to be so in love.

The woman pitched onto her hands and knees and pushed herself up from the ground, brushing soil off the seat of her jeans. When she turned around, David recognised beauty; a pretty face with neat, perfectly proportioned features and striking green eyes. Registering David's presence she held out her hand in greeting with a forced smile and then looking down at her dirty palm, wiped it frantically on her jeans apologising. "Gosh, how rude. I'm so sorry."

David couldn't help but return her smile, shaking her delicate hand. "It doesn't matter, ma'am."

Logan explained he just met David, not expanding on how or where and the woman didn't ask. She caught the warning flash in her husband's eyes and knew he would tell her later. Hana asked, "Have you eaten?"

"Yes, ma'am." Two offers of food in one day. He hadn't had it that good since before he touched down in his native land over six months ago. David felt comfortable and the feeling alarmed him. '*Never let your guard down!*' the voice of his corporal yelled from inside his head and David Allen hardened himself reluctantly, but out of necessity.

"I need to finish planting these," Hana said, waving her arm at the row of lettuces as Logan tried to lead her towards the pram. "You go and look around with David; I'm fine. I just needed a rest." She smiled at her husband and pushed his muscular arm. "Look, I only have another twelve to plant and then I'll come indoors. Get a pot of tea ready for me." She laughed and pulled a face at him, pretending all was well.

Logan stood his ground for a second and then David saw pram move in his peripheral vision. A little voice issued out of the raised hood. "Dadadadad,' it sang and the tone was happy. Logan's face lit up like a Christmas tree full of fairy lights and he strode over to the pram. There was a click as he flicked aside a set of straps and lifted out a stunning little girl. "Hey, *pēpe!*" he exclaimed with enthusiasm and grey eyes turned towards him, creasing in a beaming smile.

The child was dressed in a tiny white tracksuit with the soccer All White's logo on the side of the leg and the front of the jacket. The hood had turned inside out and hung in a bobble at the back of her dark fluffy head. Her skin was olive but lighter than her daddy's and she had the most haunting eyes. She sized up the newcomer and beamed at him, giving an elegant little wave that was more like a flick of the wrist. Then she pointed at her mother and said, "Mama" as though it was the most important thing David would ever hear.

"David," he found himself replying and she smiled and burbled something unintelligible in return.

"Do you need me to take her?" Hana asked, but she gazed sideways at the lettuces lying limply in the tray.

Logan looked at David. "Are you alright for another hour? I'll run you back to the main road whenever you want."

The man knew what time it was simply by the position of the sun and nodded. He still had time to get sorted out for the night if he could get the Māori to drive him a little further on from where he met him. Logan kept hold of his daughter and pushed the pram one-handed towards the house. He bumped it backwards up the front risers, accepting David's help to lift the wheels clear of the steps. Then he pushed it down the same corridor and dumped it in the dining room they had exited an hour ago.

David's crockery was gone and the table scrubbed. Logan sat his little girl in a high chair near the window and went into the kitchen. David heard conversation and then the tall olive skinned man appeared seconds later carrying a plastic spoon and feeder cup. The little girl made excited noises and waved her arms and legs simultaneously and David enjoyed seeing something so purely innocent and optimistic. It had been a long time since he saw anyone experience genuine glee over anything.

Logan pulled up a chair and helped her with the feeder cup which she tried periodically to yank clean out of his hands. "Is it water?" David asked, showing an interest despite himself.

"Mainly," Logan answered, "with the smallest squeeze of a fresh orange in it. It helps her stomach without rotting her teeth."

David nodded. "That makes sense."

"You got *tamariki* - children?" Logan translated and it was the first personal question he had asked. After his kindness so far, his guest figured he owed him an honest answer.

"Na, me and my...na." David lapsed into sudden silence as Leslie bustled in with a bowl of something which left a haze of steam in her wake. She laid it on the table with a white towel and then kissed the little girl on the forehead. The baby coughed as liquid spurted from the little holes too fast and Logan wiped her mouth with the towel.

"She's a bit young for a feeder cup," Logan said, by way of explanation, "but my wife's been sick lately and Phoe wouldn't take a bottle. This was the only solution at the time. She's a determined little madam and if she doesn't want something, she'd rather starve." He turned his attention fully to his baby, who beamed in response. "You're like your stubborn mama aren't you, Phoenix Du Rose?"

She laughed and seized the spoon with fast-as-lightning-reflexes, taking Logan by surprise and waving it at David, burbling baby talk at him as though sharing a conversation. Leslie watched the father and daughter show, fondness etched in her face. She shot an occasional wary glance at her tall employer and as he caught her eye, trotted back to the kitchen, her rounded bottom wiggling under the ties of her apron. "Mrs Du Rose wanted to plant them lettuces," she protested as she retreated, shaking her head. "I tell her there's no need but she wants to. She says she wants to see something *live*! I tell her it's too early for them, but she want something to do. *Don't blame me she's out there scratching in the dirt!*" Leslie's rear end wobbled heartily as she ran the last few feet to safety. David saw Logan grit his teeth and wondered what the deal was between them. He shrugged, knowing he wouldn't be there long enough to care. It was a shame because he felt a curious kinship with the man who fed squished-up food to his baby with complete concentration.

"Would you be interested in hanging around for a while?" Logan asked bluntly, allowing David to disguise the look of surprise before he turned to face him.

David shrugged as though he couldn't care less, but inside his heart beat with unfamiliar hope. "Maybe," he replied.

"I'm hoping to take over some more land and the equipment that comes with it is shot. I could use a mechanic to get the best of it going again and use the rest for spares. The pay is reasonable and you get your lodging included. There's a bunkhouse I can show you later...if you're interested."

David allowed himself to sigh and think about how good a proper bed and a shower might feel. Still he hesitated, not keen to give himself a break that would only make it harder when forced to hit the road again. Part of his psyche screamed out for normality, camaraderie and decent conversation. Logan stared at him with a fixed look and David sensed a difficult question surfacing. "Is there anyone coming after you?" Logan asked, his grey eyes drilling into David's face as though waiting to read lies there. "I'm not bothered if there is, it just means I do things a bit differently...like not register you for tax, for instance."

David smirked. "Yeah you can register me for tax." He smiled, allowing himself to show emotion openly for the first time in months, admitting to himself how good it felt.

Logan smiled back. "Welcome to the crazy Du Rose firm."

David nodded, his face flushing in pleasure. He watched the little girl scoff her food. "I haven't used my tax number since I was a small boy doing a paper round back in Hamilton."

"I'll sort the forms out for you later," Logan answered, pulling a face at the baby as she pressed food in and out of her mouth.

David pondered on his parents' big move to England, to the lazy city of Norwich tucked away near the east coast. He sighed. *Was it really twenty five years ago?* He remembered his reluctance at leaving his school and friends and shook his head, a whole swathe of his life gone from under him with nothing to show for it.

The child was like a baby bird, opening her mouth for the food, swilling it around and then swallowing, repeating the process as though she would never tire of it. The human instinct for survival no longer amazed a man who had seen people at their very best and worst; often displaying both within the same hour.

The child ate more efficiently and cleanly than David expected. He'd watched grown men eat with less finesse. She gave a huge sigh as the last mouthful went in and slumped back in her chair like a fat man at a free wedding feast. Logan gave her some juice and she sipped more delicately this time, like a fine lady having afternoon tea in a Jane Austen novel.

The Māori housekeeper appeared with a plate of fresh homemade scones and another pot of tea and the soldier tucked in eagerly, eating far more than his share. Logan didn't eat but wandered over to the window, clearly agitated about something outside. The dining room door opened suddenly and Hana came in. Logan's face relaxed as though her presence flicked a switch in him. The male with her was tall and grey eyed like Logan, so similar they could have been father and son. David assessed the newcomer quickly, recognising his voice from Logan's conversation through the window earlier.

"Hey, Uncle Logan," the man said. "I found her."

Logan smiled at his nephew, shaking his head in exasperation. "I found her ages ago, idiot! Get some *kai*." He indicated the food on the table. Little more than a teenager, the male sat down and tucked in, showing a whole buttered scone between his lips.

"Just washing my hands," Hana said and disappeared next door to the kitchen. The men heard water running. She reappeared, running and squealing and making the baby start up in surprise.

"No, Missus Hana!" a thick set man cried loudly, his face scolding and his finger wagging furiously. "Not my sink. You use other one!" He lumbered into the room after her, clutching at her shirt and clinging on. He squealed as Hana flicked her wet hands at him, splattering his face with water. He stuck his long tongue out and licked the droplets from his chin and then he smiled. "You naughty," he said playfully, "you always naughty to me!"

Hana took his face in her wet hands and kissed his forehead and the man looked as though he found heaven. "I love you, Missus," he told her and she smiled, sending him back into the kitchen with a slap on his rounded bottom. It was apparent from the young man's features that he had Down syndrome and David was touched by how natural Hana was with him.

"Stop winding the staff up," Logan said gruffly to her and she responded by sticking her tongue out at him. The baby dissolved into fits of giggles. Logan looked at his wife in amusement as she clapped her hand over her mouth.

"Oh no, she's not still on that one is she? Sorry!"

"Obviously!" her husband said, glaring across at the young man who shoved scones and jam into his mouth as though they were going to be taken away any second. "Thanks to Tama."

"Don't blame me!" Tama said, his mouth chock full of dough. Bits of it spat out and the little girl looked at him with hope in her grey eyes, her body poised to react to some anticipated delight.

When everyone looked away and receded into their own thoughts, the baby watched the young man with abject concentration. Hana poured tea for herself, Logan looked out of the window in a half turned position, his butt leaned against the window ledge and only David concentrated on his surroundings out of habit. The young Māori finished his mouthful, smirked at the baby and then pulled a face. It was terrifyingly warlike, his eyes bugging huge in his face, their whites horribly vivid against his dark irises. Then he stuck his tongue out and flattened it against his chin, tensing his upper body and holding his arms out by his sides as though about to weight lift something heavy from the ground.

Having received what she wanted, the animated baby dissolved into a paroxysm of tinkling laughter, evoking a reluctant smile from David. She laughed until tears appeared in the outer corners of her eyes and Logan spun round to catch Tama in the act. "Quit it!" Logan exclaimed and the young man hid a smirk.

"Tama," Hana said a little more calmly than her husband. "Please don't start that again with her. Last time I went into a school assembly, the boys did the *haka* and she laughed herself sick. All over the Great Hall floor! Then the Year 12's started laughing at her and it was dreadful. I had to leave and Logan was..." Hana eyed her husband and wiped the smirk from her own face.

"I can't help it," Tama giggled, shoving more scone between his lips, "she's so cute when she laughs it's hard not to keep making her."

"It won't be hard if I chop your tongue out!" Logan snapped and David glimpsed the hardness of the man beneath the smooth surface.

Tama shrugged as though not taking him seriously, but as soon as the child caught his eye he smirked and bugged his eyes again, just enough to set her off giggling. Then he adopted an air of complete innocence. Logan's teeth set in a hard line as his jaw bone flexed, showing through the flesh of his cheek. A bad scar looked white against his olive skin just under his right eye and he fixed a hard gaze on his nephew. But it was his wife who interjected. "How do you feel about ridiculing my daughter's heritage for her?" she asked the young man, her tone serious. His face blanched and the scone dangled from his fingers as he looked at her with his mouth slightly open. A suitable retort escaped him and the moment was tense. Then Hana snorted. "Gocha!" she said happily and shoved him as she reached for a buttered scone.

Logan Du Rose smirked and leaned his backside against window sill again after ruffling his daughter's hair. "Don't listen to the bad boy," he said. She smiled up at him and burped.

Hana looked at her in mock disgust. "Come on baby, don't let the side down!" she said and the child grinned, whilst keeping a hopeful eye trained on Tama.

Logan turned back to the room with a fed up look on his face. He sighed and directed his next question at David. "Hey bro, you ok with cops?" David nodded and looked back, his face curious but unworried. "Well, there's one outside," Logan growled, sounding upset. "Tama, could you drive David up to the bunkhouse and get the guys to give him a room? Take the Honda – his stuff's already in it. You'll have to carry it from the second gate; it won't make it the rest of the way. David's staying for a while and fixing up the equipment."

Tama nodded and rose from his chair. He skulled another whole scone and indicated David should follow him with a wave of his outstretched hand. At the door he caught the car keys Logan threw to him.

"What's wrong?" David heard Hana ask as the door closed slowly behind him on its automated closer. Logan's reply dripped with irritation.

"Your son's on the driveway. He's been sitting in the car for the last twenty minutes."

Chapter Eleven

The dining room door opened with a bang and Hana's grandson, Jas tore into the room. Phoenix gave a high-pitched squeal of excitement as she clapped eyes on her five-year-old nephew. She gabbled something in gibberish and tipped forwards and back in her high chair. "Hanny!" yelled the little tousle-haired, part-Indian child, "I saw a real Action Man!" He waved an action figure doll in his right arm and Hana realised he probably saw David on his way out with Tama. "I need to see him," Jas continued, still shouting as though Hana was deaf. "I need to ask him about..." he looked around him, covering his mouth with his hand and whispering. Hana leaned forward to hear, treated to a cheek full of whispery spray. "I wanna ask him 'bout the secret mission. He's been on a con-vert operation with Barbie and I need him to debrief."

"I don't think Barbie's with him, buddy," Logan commented from across the room and Jas whipped around, seeing his favourite person in the whole world standing by the window.

"Poppa Logan!" he shrieked and ran to him, taking off into mid-air as Logan seized him and swung him round. "I've missed you so much, Poppa. I wanted to see you all the time, but daddy's being a git."

"Ooh no swearing, mate," Logan chastised gently. "It's not nice."

"Mummy said it," Jas said, indignation bristling in his voice. He leaned sideways to make sure Logan got the full effect of his explanation. "She had her head down the toilet again this morning and she said, 'I hate that bookin' git.' She did, Poppa, I promise."

"I don't think it was 'bookin' mate, but it's still disrespectful to say swear words about your dad."

Hana smiled at her husband's tact, thinking of all the times Logan must have swallowed his own colourful words about her difficult son. Bodie appeared through the doorway looking nervous and wrong-footed. His eyes flashed with anger at Jas. "Don't ever run off like that again! There were cars and people and all sorts out there and you didn't even look. You need to start doing as you're told!"

Jas looked apologetic for about three seconds. Then he went back to interrogating Logan with questions about David and how he could possibly get to meet the heroic man who dressed in combats. Logan pulled the 'possibly later' card, but Jas wasn't easy to distract. "You need to apologise to your dad, mate. He's right. You can't run through a busy car park without a grown up."

Jas turned sulky, half-lidded eyes on his father. "Sorrrrrry," he said in a sing-song voice which destroyed the effect. Bodie grunted in reply and Logan frowned and relented, sensing a hiking tension in the room.

"Ok, I'll take a quad up to the bunkhouse to see how David's getting on. But you have to promise not to ask questions or hassle him. He's tired and it's not fair on him." Logan thought he was being helpful. He hoped Bodie would deliver whatever was on his chest, secretly hoping it was an apology for his recent behaviour towards his mother. He smiled at Hana as he exited the dining room with the bouncing child, misinterpreting Hana's smile as gratitude. It wasn't. The smile faded as the door clicked shut behind her husband. She sensed Bodie was about to tell her something she didn't want to know, but Logan was already on his way out to the bunkhouse with an excited Jas bouncing on the seat next to him, when Bodie dropped his bombshell.

"Action Man's enjoying himself," Jas announced. Logan glanced down at the doll perched on the hand brake lever, it's legs splayed painfully and a startled look on his face. It was Logan's gift to Jas when he broke his arm in a fall, but as the man took a sideways peek at Jas he noticed the bald and battered head of the old Action Man, poking through his shirt front. Jas leaned forward and patted his chest lovingly and Logan smiled at the child's loyalty. Evidently the disgusting old thing was still in favour. The trait was characteristic of Hana and Logan grinned at the boy and ruffled his hair.

Back in the family dining room, Hana made tea and poured some for her son. Leslie appeared with more scones and a rusk for Phoenix. "Ohhhhh!" the little girl squealed.

As Hana poured milk into Bodie's cup, he broke the silence. "Amy's pregnant. *Again*."

Hana's hand wobbled and milk poured down the side of the cup and onto the table before she was able to regain control. She mopped at the mess with Phoenix's dirty towel, her lips pursed. The baby sighed and peered at the rusk in her hand, trying to decide after all if it was friend or foe. Her rounded tummy looked about to burst.

"I had a fair idea," Hana said with feigned calm. "The day after Jas broke his arm, when you did a disappearing act and I had to babysit, she told me what happened. I guess she must only be a few weeks pregnant at the moment?"

Bodie nodded and slumped back in his chair. His Indian complexion began to lose its uncharacteristic sick look and regain some of the healthy olive glow. "I've been worrying about telling you. I thought you'd have more to say about it though. I've been sitting in the car rehearsing a spiel but Jas got fed up and did a runner, little bugger. Mum, it was all going really well - the no sex before marriage thing but then..."

Hana held her hand up, not wanting to stop her son's unusual candidness but wary of too much detail. "Bodie, you have to work at your own relationship with God. I was pleased when you made the decision not to...you know, but if it was to impress me; it was wasted. And from what Amy told me, it really didn't impress her. You need to do things with the right heart; otherwise you may as well not bother."

"Don't you want me to impress you?" Bo asked, his voice like a small boy's.

"Not really," his mother replied. "You don't have to. I won't be there when you meet your Maker and have to give an account of your life. It'll just be you and Him."

"That's exactly what Father Sinbad said," Bodie answered, looking at his mother in surprise. "Did he talk to you about me?"

Hana shook her head and tears pricked behind her eyes. The old Irish Catholic priest had been part of their lives for over a decade, until a few weeks ago. Hana held his tired old hand as he died and his absence was like a knife to the chest. "I'm not ready to talk about him," Hana said, sounding unintentionally sharp.

"Yeah, I know," Bodie sighed. "I'm still hurt there weren't more people at his funeral. Just me and you and a few rest home staff; yet I know he helped more people than that. Life sucks sometimes." He rubbed at a mark on the table, staring hard at the wood. "He knew everything about me and I know you called in to see him all the time. Don't you ever think how clever he was? Neither of us are Catholic and yet he always managed to get a confession out of us somehow." Bodie smiled but Hana experienced the awful sense of being cut loose again. Father Sinbad was her spiritual barometer and without his patient wisdom she felt utterly lost.

Hana swiped her hand across her eyes and tried to turn the conversation towards something that wouldn't make her tearful. "What are you going to do?" she asked, reaching in her pocket for a tissue.

Bodie's handsome face tightened with concentration as he observed his baby sister. Phoenix pulled the rusk to pieces on her high chair tray and flicked the bits around. Occasionally one went into the slot in her face but most of it looked like the remains of a building site. She caught Bodie's eye and smiled, showing four tiny teeth between her rosebud lips. He smiled back, an involuntary reaction to such a beautiful girl and watched his sister some more before answering. "We were always going to get married. I guess we just need to do it quicker now."

"I guess so," Hana said softly, not helping him out like perhaps he wanted her to.

At the start of the year Logan offered Bodie and his fiancé the opportunity to have their wedding at his hotel as a gift. Bodie took it as a right and when Hana discovered he called Logan 'the spare', she told him to either pay for the wedding himself, or cancel it. He cancelled it, not realising the extent of Logan's financial generosity until faced with a possible invoice. Amy lost her temper and in their reconciliation got pregnant. Hana mentally refused to take responsibility. In the past, she would have seen the catalogue of disasters as beginning with her and tried to fix it. Not anymore. She fixed her face into an impassive mask and let Bodie work through his own problems for once.

"I thought you'd be shocked," her son said, taking another scone.

"I don't think I'm that shockable anymore," Hana replied. "Life's definitely too short for hissy fits over stuff. I'm having a big enough job keeping my own life straight most days."

Bodie wiped his mouth with the back of his hand and Hana caught a flash of the little boy she had adored, hidden away in there somewhere still. It gave her hope. Before Vik's death they were close but her late husband's affair with a colleague wrecked that as the teenage Bodie struggled to keep his father's awful secret. "This might shock you then," Bodie said with far too little warning, licking butter from his thumb. "Alan Dobbs is dead."

It was a stupid thing to say to a woman fresh out of major heart surgery. Hana's cup dropped from her hand and smashed on the wooden floor, the tea spilling through the grooves between the floorboards into the storeroom below. Leslie appeared immediately, hunting the killer of her best china but distracted by the colour of Hana's white face. "Radio Mr Logan!" she called back over her shoulder as she rushed towards the stricken woman.

"What?" A kitchen worker poked her head into the room and retreated quickly.

"No!" Hana struggled for control before they completely over-reacted and called the air ambulance again. She took deep breaths and clutched at the thing in her chest, anticipating the promised electrical impulse. Her whole body tensed in fear, her face a mask of dread. Nothing happened. Bodie was on his feet, his eyes betraying a mixture of guilt and terror.

"What did you do?" Leslie growled at him. Her bristling body said she wanted to tell him to get out, but daren't. Instead she turned her back on him.

"I'm fine - I am really," Hana said, pushing Leslie's hands off her chest. She feared the old woman was about to lay her on the ground and perform CPR and desperately didn't want that. Hana wondered fleetingly if the person performing resuscitation also had to take their teeth out. It made for an incongruous scene of muddled teeth and body parts and she almost laughed.

"It didn't go off!" Hana exclaimed, drawing in a noisy breath and alarming everyone even more. "I was sure it was going to – my heart was doing the Mambo, but it didn't go off." She thought for a moment about the pacemaker in her chest wall and then her face dropped as hysteria pitched her into misery. "Oh no, what if it's a broken one?"

Leslie leaned forward and took Hana's face in her strong brown hands. Hana could smell the coleslaw she made earlier. "It didn't go off, cos it didn't need to," she said lovingly and Hana exhaled a long, slow breath.

"You really think so? Mine's not a broken one?"

"Na, *kōtiro*, never. You sit here and I'll get more tea."

"Don't get Logan," Hana called, her voice sounding strangled as Leslie bustled out of the room, her bottom wobbling under her uniform.

"Too late," came her muffled response.

Now the soap opera was over, Phoenix began to grizzle in her chair. Bodie tried to get her out but couldn't work out the straps. Leslie plonked the teapot on the table and added a fresh cup for Hana, before retrieving the baby and carrying her off. She shot a look of irritation over her shoulder at Bodie as she talked to the baby. "Let's get your face and hands wiped in Leslie's kitchen," she told her.

Bodie looked miserable, his shoulders drooping as he remained standing. "I might as well be on my feet when Logan takes a swing at me," he muttered. He half hoped he would. He deserved it.

"Please can you pour me some tea?" Hana asked and the Bodie obliged, rushing in case Logan flew in the door and took him by surprise. Best not to be playing 'mother' when the Māori decked him. Hana shakily added a couple of sugars, spilling most of it on the table and sighing in exasperation at herself.

"Here she is! All clean!" Leslie brought a squirming Phoenix back in. Hana held her arms out and sat the little girl on her knee. The child made sucking sounds and rubbed her eyes and Hana pushed her shirt up and unclipped her bra. Latching on, the soft baby eyelids closed and the fidgeting ceased. Until her father burst in the door.

Logan pushed the fire door so hard the automatic closer groaned against the explosive force it was made to resist. A horrid clunk issued from inside the mechanism. "What the hell happened?" Logan asked, his voice surprisingly soft as he knelt by his wife. He looked ashen, subdued memories surfacing with awful clarity.

"Where's Jas?" Bodie's tone was sharp. He tensed as he saw the quad bike draw up in front of the hotel spitting gravel behind it and waited for his stepfather to unleash his fury. Logan ignored him. The Māori kissed Hana on her temple and acknowledged the curious grey eyes peeking from underneath her shirt. Little legs kicked momentarily as Phoenix was at first startled by the noise and then reassured by the presence of her capable father. "Where's my son?" Bodie asked again, concerned Logan might have abandoned him in the middle of the bush.

"With Tama!" Logan said through gritted teeth and Hana admired the control in her husband's voice, clearly the product of maturity.

"I'm fine," Hana whispered, enjoying the sense of strength which came with her husband. "It was a bit of a shock that's all."

Logan looked hard at his stepson. "*What* was?"

Bodie took a deep breath and swallowed. "She had two shocks actually. She was so cool about Amy being pregnant, I thought she'd be fine about Alan Dobbs' death."

Logan's jaw dropped and he stood up, his face showing all the incredulity he felt. "Alan's *what?*"

"Erm...dead." Bodie shifted on the spot and bit his lip. "It happened at the start of the school holidays. I did try to phone and let you know."

Logan shook his head. "This is stupid! He can't be dead. What are you talking about?" He turned his anger on Bodie and the young man dropped into his police officer role, recognising a familiar reaction to bad news.

"I'm sorry, but it's true," he replied, keeping his voice low and soft.

Alan Dobbs was the deputy principal at the school Logan worked at. He was Hana's boss for a decade and a half before she left to have Phoenix and she spent most of the time avoiding his booming voice and quick temper. But Logan got on well with him, forming an easy relationship and defending him against criticism. Alan Dobbs was kind to the English teacher when Logan started at the Waikato Presbyterian School for Boys the previous year. "I should call his wife," Logan said, running his hand over his face. "She must be devastated."

"What happened?" Logan asked and sat down on the seat next to Hana with a bump. He reached for her hand and she noticed his fingers shook slightly.

Deciding he was probably safe for the moment, Bodie sat down again, leaving a safe distance between himself and Logan. He reached over and poured himself a cup of tea, but then pushed it across to his stepfather, trying to show compassion for a change. Logan accepted it and drank it black. "It was during the first week of the holidays," Bodie said. "His wife said the alarm company called him in to deal with an alarm sounding in the main building. When he didn't return home she drove down to look for him and found the school locked up but his car still there. She drove to Angus' house and he went back with her and unlocked the school. They found his body at the bottom of the main flight of stairs behind the reception. The medical examiner said his injuries were consistent with a fall...but they're not so sure now."

"What are you saying?" Logan asked and Bodie started to look shifty. Logan's eyes flashed with danger and he shifted in his seat. "What do you mean?"

"I can't tell you too much at the moment; I'm not allowed. But we're looking into it possibly not being an accident."

"Murder?" Logan said with feeling and ran his hand over his face. "No! Poor Alan."

Bodie started to relax a little more. Logan's shock seemed to have overshadowed his concern for Hana, now he could see she was ok. Unfortunately, for a policeman his instincts were certainly letting him down.

"So was that all you came for?" Logan snapped. "Act like the angel of death and spread a little unhappiness in your wake, or was there a particular reason?"

Bodie got to his feet quickly. "I should probably go."

Hana held her hand up, irritated. "No!" she cried. "I've had enough of this. We're going to sort this out once and for all. I can't take any more. I love you both but you can't even be in the same room as each other!"

The room went silent as the two stubborn men refused to speak. Hana slapped the table with the flat of her palm and the sleeping baby jumped. "I feel like I'm qualified to join the United Nations as a peacekeeper; I'm always refereeing between you two and I'm fed up of it." She glared at Bodie, beginning with him. "I know it's been hard for you, accepting someone else in Dad's place, but Logan's a good husband and I love him. He's been kind and generous to you and Jas. Why can't you accept him, for my sake?"

Bodie sat down and leaned back against his chair. He looked uncomfortable, physically and emotionally. "I don't know," he said, his voice laced with a sullen quality. "It's just that Logan's involved with people like the Triads, I guess. It made me look bad when he rang me after Boris was attacked. They took my phone and had it analysed like I was a criminal. I thought I was going to be fired!"

"I said sorry for that!" Logan complained. "And it was me who got locked up in the bloody cells on a jumped up charge, not you. I thought we'd reached an understanding and then..." Logan glanced sideways at the little girl who dozed on her back across Hana's thighs. "It's because of Phoenix, isn't it?" he asked, realisation crossing his face.

Bodie squirmed and looked set to deny it, but with both sets of eyes on him, one green and one grey, he knew he couldn't lie his way out. "No, it's not her fault. She's just a baby. But you're a family unit and I'm on the outside. Mum doesn't need me anymore. I feel like I keep losing ground everywhere – Dad, Mum, Father Sinbad. Now if I'm not careful, I'll lose Amy too. She wants to rip my head off all the time. It's not like I got her pregnant all by myself; she did have a part to play in it."

"You put yourself on the outside," Hana protested without guile. "We want to include you but you act up all the time. Calling Logan 'the spare' was just plain mean. It made me angry. He's helped you out financially and I've lost count of the times you've happily dropped babysitting Jas on him in the last couple of months when it suited you. You're behaving like a brat, Bo and I'm done with it. We're not a resource for you, I'm your mother and you seem to have forgotten that small fact."

"I'm sorry." Bodie looked contrite, a man clinging to a sinking raft. "I wanted things to stay the same, but they didn't. I know it's not your fault."

"You mean you wanted me to stay alone," Hana said softly. "That's not fair."

Bodie kept his eyes facing the table and Hana shook her head, knowing she was wasting her time. Logan squeezed her fingers and warned her to stop and she bowed to his wisdom as he changed the subject.

"So Jas is getting his wish then?" Logan asked and Bodie looked confused. Logan smirked. "He told me a few months ago he wanted you two to hurry up and get married. He wants a little brother so he can start forming his own squadron." Logan tried to keep a straight face at the thought of Jas commanding a group of marauding toddlers and trying to get them to do drill. "He's promoted Izzie's babies to second lieutenants recently, so there's a vacancy."

Bodie rested his arms on the table with a bump, looking miserable. "What if it's a girl?" he asked, as though any prospective daughter might be slighted in his son's pretend army.

"I don't think he's sexist," Logan replied, openly grinning. "Elizabeth's a two star general and Phoenix is already a sergeant, so I think he'll be an equal opportunities employer."

The point was wasted on his stepson. "Isn't a two-star general from the American Army?"

"I think she's been seconded over," Logan replied, no longer able to remain serious. He eyed his stepson, his grey eyes crinkling in mirth. Bodie relaxed and leaned back in his chair.

"Sorry for slagging you off," he said to Logan and the older man nodded, accepting the apology and aware it was all he was likely to get. "Does this mean you're not going to punch me out?" Bodie ventured a smile.

"No," Logan answered, his face serious. "You still upset my wife."

"When's Alan's funeral?" Hana asked, slapping Logan's thigh under the table. There was a prolonged awkward silence and Bodie shifted uncomfortably in his chair.

"Erm...sorry, it was last Friday. I texted and rang you, but you didn't pick up...obviously because of Mum being so sick."

Hana exhaled sadly and covered her face with her hand. "Oh, Logan I'm so sorry. It's just something else my stupid heart attack robbed you of - a chance to wish your friend goodbye." Her head sank lower until her forehead almost touched the table.

"*Me aha koa,*" Logan whispered and kissed her temple. *No matter.*

In Hana's opinion, nobody did death as well as Māori. To be denied the opportunity to pay his respects was a big thing for Logan. On a professional level, there was no doubt Alan Dobbs was irreplaceable. He was Angus' right-hand man in no uncertain terms.

Hana's legs went to sleep under the weight of the baby. She shifted in her chair, relieved some sort of equilibrium had been achieved between the men but desperate to get out of her seat. "Do you think we could put Phoe in the pram for half an hour?" she asked Logan quietly and he nodded and leaned across to peel his daughter off his wife's legs.

He got her over his shoulder and was about to stand up when the door burst open again and Jas and Tama appeared. Tama looked concerned and Jas elated. Tama went straight to Hana and wrapped his arms around her shoulders, burying his face in her neck. "I was so scared, Ma. What happened? Are you ok?" His grey eyes looked red rimmed and Hana stroked his head.

"I'm fine, idiot!" Hana kissed Tama's soft dark hair, seeing Bodie's body stiffen with jealousy.

"I've been promoted to commander in chief by that soldier!" Jas shouted into Bodie's face and clambered up onto his knee. "Dad, Dad, David's a real soldier with medals and stuff. I saw them in his rucksack. He's got a big metal cross on a ribbon and real, live *dog-tags*." The little boy said 'dog-tags' in a whisper as though talking about the Holy Grail. Bodie smiled, until Jas started on the inevitable track. "Can I have dog-tags? Can we get some for me? Please can we?"

A sensation of exhaustion washed over Hana's head and spread down her body, robbing her of the last dregs of energy. The thought of her bed upstairs on the first floor was a definite draw card. She settled for the red sofa in the family room instead, with Phoenix dozing in her pram by the French doors and Jas next to her with his school reading book. The three men hung around for a while and then went for a wander outside, Logan in struggling with being confined indoors.

Jas read in a halting monotone, pushing his finger across the lovely pages about an elephant family, whose mother couldn't seem to get even five minutes peace without a child disturbing her. He looked up at his grandmother and tapped his temple in a deliberate movement. "Guess what?" he said, frowning at Hana's shake of the head. "I bet you know," he informed her boldly, "Mum doesn't think I do but I heard her and Daddy shouting. She's got a soldier in her tummy. It's my new sergeant major called Freddie."

Chapter Twelve

"Eat up, son. We'll go home after dinner," Bodie told Jas as the child faced a sumptuous dinner in the guest dining room. Jas felt like a prince with his grown up chair and his china cup and saucer. Bodie engaged Logan in a conversation about the beef herd which roamed the mountain, feigning interest as his stepfather talked statistics, a twinkle in his grey eyes as he made it deliberately boring.

"Everything ok, Jas?" Hana asked her grandson quietly, noticing the sad set of his lips.

"I miss my kindergarten dreadfully," he replied and her brow creased at the sorrow in his voice."

"Eat your dinner, Jas," Bodie interrupted, drawing breath before attempting to reroute Logan onto politics. Jas sighed and tucked into his food.

"I hate school. Everyone at kindy loved my stories about Poppa Logan and all the wonderful things my family got up to. At big school, nobody cares."

"I suppose it's a different environment so you can't expect it to be the same," Hana soothed. She glanced sideways at her son, his voice jovial but raised as he provoked Logan with a political viewpoint which penalised entrepreneurialism and farmers. She sighed, hoping it didn't end badly.

"Every Monday they do 'show and tell' on the carpet," Jas whispered. "But I haven't been picked for weeks now, not since I listed all Daddy's favourite swear words in alphabetical order. He said all of them when he was trying to fix the shower." Hana bit her lip and swallowed.

"You listed *all* of them?"

Jas smiled with pride in his eyes. "Yep. I thought Mrs Whatsit would be impressed with me, being able to sort out all my letters and phonics so well. But she told me off and now won't pick me. And nobody wants to know about my special army members either." He pouted, mirroring his father's sulky gene. Hana popped a carrot in her mouth, playing a game which stopped Logan worrying about her but avoided indigestion at the same time. Jas watched her chew and continued with his whispered rant. "When the babies are all bigger and can do a proper karate chop, the doubters will be sorry! I just need to stop Elizabeth smiling such a lot. She has to have a mean face to be a war hero. She's way too smiley!" Jas sighed as he thought about school – it gave him a pain in his tummy and Hana watched in concern as he rubbed at a spot near his belly button.

"Tell me about your teacher," she whispered across the table and saw her grandson's pupils dilate. His lips turned downwards. "She hates me," he said in a small voice. "Mummy collected me in the police car to do showings off but it didn't work. She put the sirens on because my girlfriends used to squeal and giggle but now the girls won't talk to me because it woke Jacinder's baby sister up in the pram. So Mrs Whatsit complained to the principal and now Mummy has to leave the police car outside the gates."

"That's a shame." Hana stopped pushing her food around the plate and watched the child's face move through shades of sadness. He popped a pea in his mouth and swilled it around with his tongue.

"Action Man's not allowed at school anymore either. He's banned, since the time his bungee rope got caught on the bully boy's shorts pocket. The bully boy pulled and pulled so hard Action Man came out my hand and slam dunked the boy real good on the floor. He got a panda-eye and Mummy got a phone call."

"What are you talking about champ?" Bodie asked his son, breaking into the conversation.

"Nothing," the little boy replied, pushing his mashed potato piles around his plate. "I love how perfectly round these are, like Waihopai Station's spy domes before the men popped them and got on the news." He pressed his fork into one of them, making it look like a deflated balloon on his plate. Hana watched as he set about hiding his broccoli underneath.

Bodie went back to wasting his time trying to rile Logan. The intelligent Māori played the game, allowing himself to be taken through every controversial topic available, politics, religion, gay marriage. He let Bodie lead, finding out more about what was in the young man's heart than if he argued with him. Hana shook her head slightly as she caught Logan's eye and he grinned at her.

Jas looked up and found Logan looking at him. He bit his lip as his favourite person in the whole wide world smiled and winked at him. Hana saw tears well into the boy's eyes and it caused a lump in her chest as Logan's obvious affection touched something in the child's heart.

"What can we do to help?" Hana asked, keeping her voice low so Bodie couldn't hear. "Do you want me to speak to your teacher? What's her proper name?"

"No!" Jas whined. "I don't know her name. It's foreign and I can't say it. It sounds like Whatsit but it's not and she gets angry when I call her that."

"I'll just keep praying for you then," Hana said softly. "God's bigger than Mrs Whatsit and the bully boy."

"Ok, but don't let Poppa go and see her either. Promise?" Hana nodded and Jas seemed satisfied. "Things are difficult enough at home anyway with Mummy throwing up all the time and Daddy trying to fix the house to sell and breaking more things that he mends." Jas sounded like his mother and Hana fought the smile which budded on her lips, as Amy's exact words were repeated out loud.

A random, unprocessed thought wandered unbidden into the boy's head and as he hid a piece of broccoli cunningly under the mashed potato, he voiced it, a little too loudly. "What's sex?"

Bodie stopped with his fork half-way to his mouth and cringed, his olive colour rising to an embarrassed flush. Hana looked at the little boy with her brow furrowed and Logan let out a snort, which he quickly disguised as a cough. When Jas didn't get an immediate answer, he repeated it a bit louder in case the adults hadn't understood, following the misapprehension that older people were also deaf. "What's sex?"

This time a few of the guests turned towards their table, their curiosity piqued. Bodie's cheeks flamed and he shifted in discomfort, looking hopefully at his mother. As Jas rolled his eyes and opened his mouth wider, aiming to project his voice even more, Hana stepped in, asking in a calm voice, "What sort of sex, darling? Why are you asking?"

Bodie choked on a potato and held his serviette up to his face. Logan bit his lip and observed the scene with amusement. Jas wrinkled his nose and gave an exaggerated sigh which proclaimed his view that all adults were not only hard of hearing, but thick too. "Wer-lij-us-sex," he lisped and the grownups looked at each other, bemused. It wasn't a good idea to ask for a repeat of the words as the volume was already attracting interest from surrounding tables.

Bodie's brown eyes were wide in his face and he shot a frightened look at Hana, who shrugged and pursed her lips. She opened her mouth to diplomatically suggest they talk about it later, when she felt the slight shuddering of the table. Looking down at the jiggling cutlery, she glanced across at her husband in alarm, only to find it wasn't an earthquake but Logan, causing the movement. His elbows rested on the tablecloth next to her, his cutlery collected into one hand. The other was rubbing at his eyes and he looked distressed. "Logan, are you crying?"

Hana peered at him, hearing the huge breaths he took, causing his body to lurch. Bodie had stopped eating and watched as a tear ran down Logan's cheek and plopped onto the table. The Māori groaned a couple of times as though in pain and Hana grabbed his arm. "Logan?"

Jas pressed the potato over the broccoli, feeling annoyed as the green stuff poked through. He patted the growing mess softly with his fork and glanced up as his poppa dabbed his eyes with a napkin. His father and grandmother were both staring at Logan in confusion.

"Oh..." Logan groaned and looked up, his face a mask of pain. He rubbed at the scar from his spleen operation and sniffed. "That boy's killing me." Catching sight of Bodie's perplexed face, he dissolved again.

"What?" Hana asked, growing increasingly annoyed. Logan made several attempts to tell them, but even the thought of whatever it was rendered him incapable. Hana tutted, frustrated.

"What is it then?" Jas piped up, having created a dodgy green and white potato dome which he seemed reasonably pleased with. "You know what?" he mused. "If the Waihopai domes were camouflaged with broccoli bits on them, nobody would have spotted them in the first place."

Logan gave a curious little whimper and struggled to keep the piece of roast pumpkin in his mouth, having only just dared put it there. As Jas opened his little mouth again to repeat the word causing him such trouble, Logan raised his hand and managed to keep it together enough to answer his step-grandson. He swallowed with a valiant effort but his voice still wobbled. "It's a group of people who get together with a common belief. They all think the same thing. You're talking about a religious sect, where people with the same faith group together. But there are political ones and other sorts as well. It's 's-e-c-t' which is the root word for 'section' and other words like it. You have to say the '*c*' and '*t*' sound, mate, otherwise it...comes out as something else."

Logan snorted again as Jas made a humphing sound and waved his fork. A blob of speckled green mash shot backwards and hit the wall next to his father. "Time to go, I think." Bodie placed his cutlery on his plate, humiliation colouring his face up to his hairline. Hana bit her lip, realising her son's need to best her husband was never going to be fulfilled.

"But I wanna stay here with Hanny!" Jas dragged his feet in the car park, being awkward and difficult for Bodie who seemed to have even less patience than usual.

"Na, come on, mate. Do what your old man says." Logan hefted the boy onto his shoulders and walked him over to the Honda, Jas balancing with a giggle as Logan bent and reached into the glove box. The little boy's face lit up, first with amazement and then delight.

"Oh, my goodness! That's wicked!" Jas sat on his booster seat in the front of his father's BMW and balanced the chocolate snail on his palm. "Poppa taught me to say '*escargot*' with a proper French accent. I liked France. They've got the Foreign Legion and everything. I love Poppa Logan. I love the French." He prattled on as Bodie started the car and the young man rolled his eyes, feeling the betrayal of his son in preference for Logan's keenly. "I might join the Legion if school gets any worse," Jas mused, but Bodie made the mistake of ignoring him as he waved to Hana and Logan.

"Poor little guy," Hana said with feeling as she waved back. Logan slipped his arm around her shoulders and kissed the top of Phoenix's fluffy little head as he nodded in agreement.

"It sucks aye? He told me what was wrong on the way up to the bunkhouse. He's not settling at school but he wouldn't let me talk to Bodie about it."

"I offered to go into school, but he almost blew his stack at that suggestion," Hana said, turning to go back into the hotel.

"When they buy Culver's Cottage, won't he transfer to Ngaruawahia or Te Kowhai; somewhere more local?"

Hana shrugged, guilt settling over her pretty freckles. "You mean when they sell theirs and when I *finally* get around to having Culver's Cottage valued."

Logan squeezed her against his strong torso. "Stop punishing yourself, woman. It's not like we've had nothing else going on is it?"

Hana nodded and sighed. "Yeah, you're right, as always. When we discussed him buying the house a few days before the school holidays began, I didn't plan on heart surgery. It did kinda put it out of my mind." Hana looked at the gravel, engrossing herself with the way the light caught the tiny stones, not wanting to hear platitudes. She should have known better than.

"Hey, don't try and hide from me." Logan's voice was low and seductive as he used his index finger to pull Hana's chin upwards. His grey eyes were kind. "I'm a 'fixer' babe, a problem solver, not someone who meets problems with kind but unhelpful niceties. I told him he could show a valuer round while we're away, to get the ball rolling. I'll do the next one when we get back and then I'll ask Angus to recommend another one to keep it fair."

Hana looked confused. "But he left his key behind, that time when he was angry at me."

Logan shook his head. "I sent it back with Jas a few weeks ago; that time I looked after him at work and..."

"And Jas told you his father called you 'the spare'..." Hana trailed off. "I despair of my son sometimes. Of all the idiots I could have married over the years and he reacts to someone as perfect as you."

The look of pain in Logan's face was genuine at the reminder of Bodie's cruel term for him. Hana regretted her tactless mention of something so unkind but saw his eyes regain their light as he registered she just called him 'perfect'.

A dirty Nissan utility vehicle pulled up in front of them with a roar as they reached the hotel steps and Logan smiled at the driver. The friendly *kaumātua* from the *marae* bounced out, jolly as always. "*Kia ora*, Logan." The timbre of his voice seemed to resonate with a sense of safety, causing a gentle rumble in Hana's stomach. He embraced Logan and they pressed noses in a *hongi*, staring into each other's eyes.

"*Aumihi kaumātua*," Logan replied, his eyes warm but his head slightly bowed in deference to the other man's status as an elder.

"Ah, here she is, our *mākoha kuikui*." The portly Māori man repeated his greeting with Hana and she obliged, her brow knitted showing her confusion at the words he used over her. She looked across at Logan and he smiled, offering reassurance.

As the elderly man pressed noses with her mother, Phoenix made a swipe at a large piece of jade dangling within temptation. Unfazed he laughed and kissed her on her tiny cheek, releasing his precious *taonga* from her clenched fist. "You got good taste, little one," he told the baby, lifting her out of Hana's arms. "You will have your own treasures to cherish one day." Phoenix went willingly and settled on his hip, staring at the *ta moko* tattoos on his face as though understanding them. The intricate design identifying the man's cultural identity began on his chin, occupying the area where men often grew goatee beards. It was completed in black ink, swirls and curls weaving their way across his brown skin. They began again on either cheek, similar in design and yet subtly different. It may have looked intimidating on another, but this man was full of life and laughter and his tattoo fitted his personality as though he was born with it.

He was a *marae* elder, recognised for his *mana* and influence and Hana found herself smiling in response to his easy presence. She recalled their first meeting after the fire which killed Logan's birth parents, when he cleansed the area from a spirit of death. Their second meeting was at Reuben and Miriam's funeral or *tangihanga* and it made a nice change not to associate his visit with disaster. Hana smiled as the old man bounced her baby on his hip and persuaded a giggle from her serious lips. "Would you like some tea or something to eat?" Hana asked, her English politeness rousing a smile to Logan's lips.

"No, no. Just a flying visit *kōtiro*," he said, using the term of endearment in his answer. "My *waahine* will have my dinner waiting." His face softened at the mention of his wife and Hana smiled, liking him even more.

In his late eighties and a decade older than Alfred Du Rose, the *kaumātua* was sprightlier. He handed Phoenix back to Hana and beckoned to Logan to follow him round to the back of the truck. "Before I open this door," he said with an air of mystery, "I've been keeping these boxes for many many years, at the request of Phoenix Du Rose." He inclined his head majestically towards the baby, acknowledging her namesake. "She gave it into the safekeeping of my *whānau*, when the Du Roses divided the land. The instruction was to return it at the moment the *whenua* was restored to the family as one complete lot – the same as in the beginning. I have heard the time is now."

Logan's brow knitted in confusion and a flash of irritation lit his grey eyes. "Nobody knows about this." He ran a scarred hand through his dark hair, leaving it tousled and unkempt. "We haven't shaken on it. Neville, my wife and I have discussed it but…"

The *kaumātua* raised his hand and *mana* oozed from him in such an awesome sense of power, Hana felt lightheaded. He was so regal and authoritative even Logan deferred to his greater wisdom. "If youse have spoken, then it will be so," he said, as though it was a certainty. He flicked the rusty catch on the back door of the truck and flung it open.

Hana tried to contain her disappointment as she peered into the space, leaning to see past her curious child's wavy head. All she saw was a half dozen cardboard boxes stacked inside, some looking as though they had been attacked by damp and lost the fight. The cardboard was stained a darker colour at the bottom of many of them and warped. Logan shook his head in confusion. "What is it?"

The old man clapped his hands. "I will return when you have had time to go through the contents and appraise what's there. Phoenix Du Rose was clear with her instructions that the *taonga* were to be returned. To *you*, Logan. And only you," the old man said.

"*Taonga*," Hana breathed reverently, finally understanding. "You mean these are family treasures?"

The *kaumātua* smiled and nodded at her, his eyes twinkling at her obvious awe. The baby pointed an index finger at the boxes and babbled something unintelligible as her daddy stood and surveyed what looked like the remains of a garage sale. "Come, come," said the old man and shoved at Logan's inert body. "I do not want my *hoa waahine* to feed my dinner to the dogs three nights in a row! Let's get these out of here."

He leaned in and shouldered the first box as though it contained nothing but air, shifting it onto the steps with care and respect before reaching in for the next one. Logan galvanised himself and retrieved the boxes nearer the seats, lifting them down to sit by the others. With a hug and a wave, the elderly man was gone, spitting up gravel behind his huge car wheels. Logan stared down at the boxes on the ground and groaned.

"Will there be some sort of handing-over-ceremony?" Hana asked.

Her husband shrugged and shook his head. "Maybe that was it," he said, tiredness leaking into his voice.

"This is really exciting! Family treasures, how wonderful." Hana hugged her daughter, her eyes dancing with purpose. "Don't worry," she said, rubbing Logan's upper arm. "I'll help you go through it. I can't wait to see what it is. I hope it's not just old bits of chipped china your grandmother was fond of though. That'll be disappointing."

"It's not," Logan said, with a little too much certainty. "I think I know what it is and it's nothing but a few boxes full of *māreherehe*."

"What does that mean?" Hana asked, fingering a corner of the nearest cardboard box.

"Trouble!" Logan ran his hands through his hair. "*Roke paroro.*" He left Hana standing by the boxes while he went to fetch some manpower.

"I don't think I want that last bit translated," Hana told her daughter. "I know the last word means storm and the first one is a swear word. I think I can guess what he means."

Phoenix sucked her fingers and burbled nonsense in reply. Logan wasn't long, returning with the new stable hand and one of the stockmen on his heels. Between them they manhandled the boxes into the lift and upstairs to the first floor. By the time Hana climbed the spiral staircase with her baby clutched in her arms, they were hauling the last box down the corridor into her bedroom.

"Hello, Rawhiti," Hana said pleasantly to the young man as he passed. He nodded and returned her greeting, escaping after the stockman into the lift but looking eager to escape conversation. Hana accosted her husband on the threshold of their bedroom.

"I hope Rawhiti didn't get into trouble the other day," she said. "I told him I was allowed to take Sacha. It wasn't his fault."

"I never said anything to him about it," Logan seemed distracted as he stood over the boxes. "I don't know if Jack did."

"I hope not," Hana said with sincerity. "Will you check?"

"No," Logan responded, his tone short. "I don't employ good managers and then quiz them on how they do their job. Nor should you."

Hana plopped down on the bed in their room, feeling chastened. She let Phoenix wriggle out of her arms and crawl on the duvet cover. It was too slippery and silky and she couldn't go anywhere. Hana lay down next to her and watched as she rocked backwards and forwards on her hands and knees, not sure what to do with her hands once she got the motion going. Hana giggled as she rocked forwards, moved one hand and then collapsed onto her face. Unperturbed, Phoenix showed no signs of despondency. "Very shortly, something's going to click and she'll be off," Hana said, watching her daughter with pride. "Then we'll find out what trouble really means."

Phoenix could almost taste success, her face beaming as she chatted to herself in excited baby burble.

Logan quit staring at the outside of the boxes and lay down on the bed next to his wife. "Sorry," he said, "I shouldn't lecture you."

Hana reached over and touched his cheek, feeling the stubble pushing its way through his skin. His colouring was so dark on his pale olive face, his five-o'clock-shadow began right after he finished his morning shave. She pushed her hand around the back of his neck and pulled him down towards her for a kiss. His lips were soft on hers and she loved the feel of his beard growth on her chin.

With a gasp, Logan lurched across her body with his left arm and Hana took a sharp intake of breath from the shock. "Sorry, sorry!" he exclaimed, seeing her reaction. When Hana looked to her right, she saw he gripped her daughter's ankle in his hand and she wriggled and squealed. Logan smiled down into Hana's surprised emerald eyes. "I suddenly saw her out the corner of my eye and she was off and going for it. I could imagine her crawling right off the end of the bed."

Hana looked up at her husband while he leaned across her, wrestling with his daughter who wiggled and protested, keen to give it another go. "S'up?" he asked, staring down at her, confused by the offended look on her face.

"Do you kiss me with your eyes open?" she asked and Logan laughed.

"Not telling," he said, leaning down and biting her neck. The moment was destroyed as Phoenix managed to leave Logan holding her sock and bootie, making her sortie on the little runway that stretched out invitingly before her. "Come back here!" Logan ran round Hana and launched himself at his daughter's legs, just as she reached the other side of the bed at an impressive crawl speed. He caught both her feet and hauled her back to the start.

"That's mean," Hana said, her voice sounding lazy. "It's like putting a snail at the bottom of the wall to start again."

But the child had learned something new and was insatiable. In the end, Logan put her on the floor. Phoenix amused herself by touring the bedroom, picking up things that were formerly inaccessible like shoes and bags and fluff and bits of whatever she could get her hands on. Hana sighed having done this part before and remembering the exhaustion of it.

But Logan hadn't and it was all wonderfully new and exciting to him. He crawled around behind her, giving chase while Phoenix belly laughed and fatigued herself, finally throwing up her lunch on the wooden rimu floorboards. She sat up, a look of distaste on her pretty face, but as she pushed herself up onto her ample nappy-clad bottom, she pitched over backwards and landed with her head safely in Logan's outstretched hand. "You need to get better at that bit," he told the indignant face staring up at him. "First lesson in any use of forward motion, is how to stop!"

Logan took his daughter off to the bathroom for a face wash. He returned carrying her on his hip and she wore only a little vest on top. "The All-Whites have been christened," he announced. "With sick."

"The All-Whites are no longer all white," Hana said poetically. The boxes caught her eye and she sat up. "Do you have to open these as head of the family because they're a *taonga*, or can I?" she asked, curious about the contents.

Logan looked nervous, his eyes darting towards the troublesome containers. "I'm not the head of any family, not Reuben's and definitely not Alfred's. I don't understand why *Kuia* Phoenix left them to me. And actually, I don't know if I want to open them at all!"

Hana heard the irritation in his voice. He registered the confusion on her face relented. "Look, she told me about all this stuff, many times. I just forgot until today, is all. She kept saying she'd put the family treasures safe and one day when I built the new house, I'd be able to get them back."

"So what's the problem?" Hana asked, pulling a face. "She obviously wanted you to have them enough to hide them elsewhere."

"Nev's not signed anything!" Logan said. "He's agreed in principal but that's all. The surveyors will go through the property tomorrow, but there're no guarantees he'll accept. His son is absolutely set against it."

Phoenix cuddled into her father as though cold, pushing her little hands and arms in front of her and resting her cheek on his shoulder. Instinctively he snuggled her in tighter and she shut her eyes.

"So what will you do with it all?" Hana asked, spreading her hands at the huge mess on the bedroom floor. "I don't want to fall over them in the night."

"Hopefully it'll all be finalised soon. Then maybe I'll know what to do with it." Logan turned away from the mess of cardboard and Hana got the feeling the discussion was over.

Logan gave his daughter a bath in the sink and changed her nappy. She was exhausted from all the crawling, but it didn't stop her trying to flip over onto her front while he was doing up the poppers on her sleep suit and making a swift getaway. Logan laid her firmly on her back again and wagged his finger at her. "No, Phoe! I've seen parents chasing their kids around and it ain't happening. My daughter's gonna do as she's told."

Phoenix put her bottom lip out in protest, hearing the authority in his voice. She stared hard at her daddy, watching his deft fingers and the concentration on his face. She studied him carefully, her little brain drinking in information the whole time. By the time the poppers were closed she had moved on mentally and seemed surprised her own bottom lip was still inside out as she tried to smile. He laughed at her and said something in Māori before kissing her on the nose.

"Oh, that reminds me," Hana said, still curled up on the bed. "What did the elder call me before? I didn't know the words."

Logan bit his lip and viewed his wife sideways. His fringe hung in his eyes giving him a sexy, pin-up look and Hana felt desire stir in the pit of her stomach. "Please?" she asked, persisting.

"Ok, he called you the gentle matriarch," he said softly.

"Oh." Hana pulled a face. "That makes me sound really old and infirm." Disappointment stamped across her face in work boots and she felt cross.

"It's a compliment actually," Logan corrected. "You're the mistress of this place and I'm real happy he said out loud something I've known my whole life." He left the baby with Hana and went to clear up the bathroom, leaving her feeling stunned by his words and knowing she'd failed to grasp something important once again.

Feeling the cold, Hana changed into her pyjamas and slipped into bed. She turned the electric blanket on its highest setting, even though sitting on it made the bed into a fire hazard. Logan brushed Phoenix's fluffy hair up into a quiff and then handed her over for a feed. Hana half expected a battle but she fed quickly and easily, falling asleep on the breast and snoring. Hana shuffled down the bed, laying the little girl on her chest and covering her with the duvet. Logan switched the telly on for her and began fiddling around with the boxes, moving them next door into his sister's old room. "Liza hasn't been home for months," he said, almost to himself. "And these are making me nervous sitting here."

"What about if Tama wants to stay in there?" Hana yawned. "Now he's back from playing the sober driver for his out of control mates."

"He's sleeping at the bunkhouse," Logan replied. "It'll be fine."

Inside Liza's room, Logan piled them up neatly in the corner, leaving the worst water damaged one by itself. Then he stood over them, worrying at his thumbnail and remembering his grandmother. "What did you do to me?" he whispered to her essence. "This isn't my problem." Pushing the last box through the bedroom door, he spotted a figure standing in the wide hallway watching. Alfred was transfixed at the sight of the battered box moving slowly across the wooden floorboards. He recognised it of old and his heart went still in his breast.

"What is that?" he hissed, his face aghast as he strode towards Logan. "Where did they come from?"

"Arama delivered them earlier." Logan kept his voice impassive. "*Kuia* Phoenix left them for me."

"No. No!" Alfred's grey eyes bugged and his face flushed. "Reuben took them out of spite, I know he did!"

Logan shook his head. "No, Dad. Arama's father kept them as part of the agreement with her."

Logan's use of the term *Dad*, made Alfred take a step back. "I'm not your father," he said, shaking his head, his eyes filled with pain. He pointed a gnarled finger at the stack of boxes. "Reuben took them. We fought the same day I went to see him to tell him to stay away from you. He bloodied my nose and weakened my *mana* and then he bedded my wife again and again just to prove it!" Spit issued from Alfred's lips and Logan took a step back, horror making his eyes dark.

"This is not my fight," he whispered. "It never was."

Alfred shook his head and raised his voice. "Reuben was his usual arrogant self. He refused to stop giving you the guitar lessons she took you to. '*He's my son,*' he shouted at me. I told him, '*You never had any rights to him, not when you bedded my wife and definitely not now. He calls me father, not you.*' He cried like a baby!" Hysteria seemed to embrace the old man, straightening out his bent spine and bringing insanity into his grey eyes. "He cried like a baby. '*They're just guitar lessons,*' he said. '*I haven't told him who I am. I'm begging you. Please don't take this from me.*' He told me he didn't have the *taonga* but I knew he was lying, just like he always lied." Alfred balled up his fists in fury, dribble coating his chin in a white film. "Him and that *kairau!*"

Logan's eyes flared at the use of the derogatory term and he swallowed. His voice was low and menacing. "Don't call my mother that!"

Alfred waved his arm at Logan. "It's what she was!"

Logan stared at the old man, hardly recognising him as the loving father of forty one years. The question was out before he could stop himself. "Why didn't you let him teach me?"

"Because you were mine!" Alfred snarled, drawing his lips back from his gums like a wild animal.

"But not now?" Logan's eyes bored into the old man's, grey on grey. "Now there's no challenge involved, you don't want me anymore?"

Alfred looked sick, his breath coming in short huffs. His eyes cast about the offensive boxes with a wild quality and he refused to meet Logan's gaze. "Get them out of here!" he snapped, rubbing his hand across his mouth.

"No!" Logan's voice held authority and his eyes were hard like pools of ice. "This is my property, my land and my house." He took a step forward, his body stiff and unyielding. "The only thing that no longer belongs here, is you!"

Alfred's lips parted in surprise and his eyes lost their fire. His body softened and realising his error, he took a step towards Logan. "Get out!" the younger man hissed. "Get out of my face and out of my life."

The awful forty-one year old mystery unravelled more of its bile for Logan and he stayed in Liza's room, reaching for an inner calm that wouldn't come. Despite her seven month absence from the hotel, Liza's expensive perfume still lingered in the air. Logan conjured up an image of his sister in her judge's robes. She was formidable and feared in legal circles, the kind of judge barristers cringed before, but Logan was one of the few people who knew the other side of her. He had seen the tearful, vulnerable woman abused by a psychotic husband, needing her brother to dig her out the awful, spiralling mess. Logan sighed. For forty-one years she was his big sister, cruelly relegated to half-sister by a painful revelation. Logan balled his fists, knowing she had always known. He pressed his toe against one of the boxes, hearing glass moving around inside and sounding broken. "Yeah," Logan whispered to the empty room. "As broken as me, Michael and Liza. Thanks for the reminder."

Back in the bedroom, Logan found his wife fast asleep on her back and the baby snoring on her chest. He peeled the child off and laid her gently in the travel cot, covering her up with blankets. Hana looked pink and overheated and becoming worried, he laid a cool hand on her head. She was burning up and he panicked until he noticed the red light peeking out from under the valence. "Bloody hell, Hana!" he tutted and turned the electric blanket off. "Hasn't this family had enough of fire?"

His wife sighed in her sleep and turned onto her side. Logan stripped off to his boxers and got into the red hot bed, kicking the blankets off and pressing the light switch above his head. The room plunged into darkness apart from the television's flickering light, until Logan cancelled that too. He fell asleep, lulled by the rhythmic steady breathing of his wife and the gentle snores of his daughter.

Logan woke with a start, his heart pounding as he struggled out of sleep, aware something was wrong. He put his feet on the floorboards and was instantly awake, a skill honed from years of dangerous living. The noise which woke him came again and he moved quickly across the room, tracing its source until he found it.

"What's all this crap?" Liza rounded on him as she tripped over another of the boxes abandoned in her bedroom. She looked fraught and upset, more rattled than usual. Logan leaned against the door frame and rubbed his hand over his face. His state of undress seemed to irritate her even more and she glanced at his shorts and waved her hand towards him. "Put some damn clothes on, Loge! I don't need to look at your bloody, mangled body!"

Logan's eyes widened and his mouth opened, thought nothing came out. It was a cruel thing to say. Already self-conscious of his scars, her verbal attack was unexpected and hurt filled his grey eyes. He took his foot off the doorframe where it rested, stood up straight and left.

He went back to his girls and shut the door quietly. He didn't hear the whispered '*sorry*' as his sister realised her mistake and he deliberately ignored her quiet knock on his door a few minutes later.

Much to his surprise, Logan dropped off to sleep again, snuggling up to Hana as the bed grew colder. Hana grunted and turned into his body, taking the pressure off her surgery wounds and pressing her face into his downy skin. When Logan woke in the morning she was cuddled tightly into his side with her head in his chest. Love seemed to surround him like a protective shield and he lifted up her nightshirt with gentle, roving fingers and sought to ground himself in what really mattered.

Chapter Thirteen

"Mmnn don't move. I'm comfy." Hana resisted Logan's attempts to disentangle his arms from around her. He tried to pull away but she snuggled in closer, following him across the bed and clinging on harder. Her tangled, messy hair spread out across the pillows behind her like a red carpet and Logan smiled and kissed the top of her head. She wouldn't let him escape, wrapping her legs around his and forcing him to stay with her.

"What's wrong, babe?" he asked.

"You feel so cuddly and nice," came her muffled reply. "I want you to stay here."

Logan shifted on his side and started to kiss his wife's tender lips but tensed, his body becoming rigid as he felt her hand move over the rugged scar under his right armpit. Hana opened her eyes and looked up at him perplexed. "What did I do?" she asked, concern in her voice. "You did that before. Does it hurt?"

Logan shook his head; the mood ruined. "Do I look...mangled, to you?" he asked. His voice was husky and low, as though he was getting sick.

Hana looked shocked. "Who put those awful words in your head? No, Logan, I've never thought that!"

From the doubt in Logan's grey eyes, she knew words were pointless. So she showed him just how mangled she thought he was, kissing every inch of his long scar and leaving him in no doubt about her view on the matter. But when Hana groaned, Logan put his hand over her mouth, his face panicked. "No, we have to be quiet," he hissed.

"Phoe's snoring," Hana giggled, nipping the soft skin on Logan's collar bone.

"Yeah but Liza's here," Logan muttered into Hana's and she heard what sounded like distaste in his voice. She kept quiet, sensing the spiteful vibes coming through the wall behind the headboard.

"Oh. Great." Hana sighed. Even the mention of the judge's name brought back memories of the night Hana travelled with her up to the site of the fire. Logan's sister was deliberately cruel, impatient with Hana's lumbering, pregnant body, abandoning her at the top of the slope to fend for herself. Liza returned to Auckland the day after her mother's *tangihanga* and Hana hadn't seen her since.

Arriving back at the hotel after Logan's stressful and emotional goodbye to the various *whānau* members who travelled from far and wide to pay their respects to Reuben and Miriam, Hana found a cute little outfit for her new-born baby. It lay on the kitchen table with a scribbled note. *'To Logan. For the baby. Liza.'*

Hana knew from the start Liza didn't like her. The woman made no secret of it, treating Hana with disdain and openly scorning her blossoming middle-aged pregnancy. "She hates me." Hana cringed and pushed her face harder into her husband's downy chest. He held her closer, picking up on her anxiety. For once he didn't try to infer she was imagining it or suggest she read too much into Liza's behaviour.

"She hates everybody." Logan ran his hand gently down the length of Hana's long red hair, enjoying the familiar kinks and curves, careful not to snag the knots with his fingers and earn a reprimand. "I should get up," he said softly, kissing the top of her head. She groaned, not wanting to lose the heat of Logan's body or face the fact she should get up too.

As if on cue, Phoenix started singing her morning song from the cot in the corner. It consisted of running the words '*mama*' and '*dada*' together in a nonsensical mixed up sentence. She grunted as she stripped her socks off again and Logan extracted himself from his wife's tight grip and pulled his shorts on, before traversing the bedroom and retrieving his daughter. "Pooh, stinky!" Hana heard him exclaim as he headed to the ensuite with the baby held at arm's length.

Hana vacated the bed and scooted after him, running hot water into the shower cubicle and jumping in quickly to avoid getting any colder. Logan cleaned up the baby on the bathroom floor. "Can she come in with you, Hana?" he asked in desperation. "She stinks."

"Fine," Hana agreed, "but don't disappear because I'm not sure how long I can hold her. Hana sat on the cubicle floor and played under the hot water, trying to soap the child with shower gel and then not drop her as she became slippery. Phoenix loved the hot water and squealed with excitement, beaming and waggling her arms and legs like a turtle. Hana grew tired trying to hold onto her and the operation wounds felt tight against their waterproof dressings. "Loge, she's too wiggly," Hana giggled. "She's like a fat bar of soap."

The little girl whinged when Logan came back to claim her and left Hana to shower in peace for a few minutes. When she was dressed, they swapped over, her giving the baby a feed while he showered and dressed.

A frantic knocking on the door began as Logan sat on the bed, pulling his socks on. His brow knitted and zipped his jeans up, making the person wait as he pulled his checked shirt on over a tee shirt. Hana watched his precise movements with concern. "Stop being daft, Loge. It's only Leslie or one of the staff and I'm sure they've seen it all before." She giggled at the glance Logan shot in her direction. "Leslie's seen it more than once, *all* of it. She told me. Apparently it's the stuff of Du Rose legends."

She bit her lip as Logan gave the faintest of smirks and relaxed into the pillows. But her heart sank when the door opened and Liza's sour face peered through the gap.

"What?" Logan's tone was more rude than abrupt and Hana stared in confusion. Phoenix twisted her head to see who was at the door, curiosity making her nosey. Hana covered up and sat the baby on her knee to wind but Phoenix kept trying to turn towards the raised voices in the doorway. "Bugger off, Liza!"

Logan turned and walked back into the bedroom with Liza hot on his heels. But for the automatic closer over the door, he would have let it go in her face. "I want that crap out of my room!" she said with force, putting her hands on her hips. Logan ignored her, going into the bathroom to clean his teeth. "Oh, you're so juvenile!" she snapped at the sound of Logan scrubbing his teeth and spitting into the sink.

Liza spotted Hana sprawled on the bed and sneered. "Still clinging on then?" she said with venom and Hana gritted her teeth and ignored her. Liza's eyes strayed to the baby on her knee and she did a startled double-take at the tiny mirror image of her brother. Hana patted her daughter's back gently and Phoenix stared at her aunt with open curiosity, their grey eyes locked in a battle of searching one another out. To Hana's surprise, Liza looked away first.

Logan reappeared from the ensuite, looking fed up to see Liza still standing there. Obviously the judge expected people to follow her orders with immediacy. "Get lost!" Logan said aggressively and she bridled with anger.

"That's no way to talk to..." Her words trailed away and she looked at the floor.

"My what, Liza? Sister? Half-sister? Lying, deceitful piece of..."

"Logan!" Hana's rebuke stopped him and he turned to see her holding her hands over Phoenix's ears, although her efforts were proving ineffective.

Liza swallowed. "I want you to get that crap out of my room, I..." she began but her words were cut off by Logan's shout.

"I don't bloody care what you want! This is *our* business and you can't just turn up when you like. I've told Michael and I'm telling you, ring before you come in future and we will see if we can *fit you in*."

Phoenix's bottom lip shot out at her father's sharp tone and her little face crumpled. A hitch began in her throat and Hana cuddled her into her chest, wrapping her cardigan around her child's body so only her eyes peeked out. Logan saw and if anything, it made him angrier at Liza. They faced each other, flashing grey eyes filled with unspoken accusation and years of deceit. It had taken its toll on both of them.

"This is my family home," Liza yelled and Logan shook his head, his face oozing a pain Hana recognised.

"Not anymore!" he bit. "Mum's gone and Alfred couldn't give a damn about this place. None of you cared when it was falling round their ears so don't come whining now. We own it - so get over it!"

"Who's we?" Liza said snidely, glancing over at Hana. "Oh, right, you and *her*. I get it. So much for family loyalty! What about your proper *whānau*?"

Liza's voice rose to a screech and hysteria hovered near the surface. She was more out of control than Hana had ever seen her. It was so uncharacteristic of the hard woman, Hana felt the urge to make her husband stop. Something was wrong.

"*What proper whānau?* Since when have you shown *me* any loyalty?" Logan hissed, so close to Liza her fringe moved with his breath. "You knew Alfred wasn't my father but you never said anything. And you and your little best mate, Caroline; did she know too? Every time she screwed me over, you must have had coffee and a giggle at my expense. *Funny was it?*"

As Liza looked at the floor her action confirmed Logan's statement and his face flushed with fury. "Oh, she did! So everyone knew except me? What a bonding experience for you all. Don't you ever consider me *whānau* again! You're nothing to me!"

Logan was into his stride. Age old resentments spewed from his mouth and a tell-tale vein pulsed dangerously in his neck. The awful scene reminded Hana of another family and another time; her father and brother saying words to her which could never be unsaid. Her hands trembled as she gathered the distressed child to her breast and slipped off the bed. She saw all the warning signs the argument was getting out of hand and wanted to be as far away as possible. Hana felt angry at Liza's complete disregard of her and the rude invasion of her safe place, but she was also upset with Logan and wasn't sure yet why that was. Perhaps it was because the stuff he screamed into Liza's face came from the heart and betrayed wounds he hadn't felt able to talk to his wife about.

Hana used the spiral staircase to get to the ground floor and sought solace in the family dining room next to the huge industrial kitchen. Phoenix had calmed by the time they pushed the heavy door open and her tears were like dobs of glitter on her pretty cheeks. Hana stuck her head through the archway and Leslie spotted her, bustling over and fussing the baby girl as though she was her own flesh and blood. "*Kia ora, mokopuna*," she addressed the child. The baby rubbed her nose and hid her face under Hana's cardigan. Leslie asked Phoenix in a baby voice what was wrong.

"Liza's here," Hana informed her, pursing her lips and looking shaken.

"Oh." Leslie's response said it all. "Is her ladyship coming down for breakfast?"

Hana shrugged. "Only if she and Logan don't kill each other."

To her surprise, Leslie let out a huge laugh. "So, your *tane's* finally seen through the glitz to the *kerakera* underneath?" The other women in the kitchen looked at Hana and nodded to her in sympathy.

"I don't know what that is," Hana said, the unfamiliar word passing her by.

"Filth!" Leslie spat.

Hana shook her head, refusing to be drawn into slander with the women, sensing by some strange instinct that Liza was in pain of a kind requiring more than a doctor.

Phoenix tucked into a plate of porridge, which Hana felt sure had far too much sugar in, but the baby's tears dried up as she became stuffed full to bursting. During a slack moment, Leslie trotted through with a beaker full of boiled water, laced with the tiniest scent of chamomile tea. Phoenix drank with eagerness. "It helps with digestion," Leslie assured Hana. "It's a very old recipe. All our *tamariki* had it."

Hana sniffed it and thought it smelled like silage, trying not to look overtly disgusted. Leslie stood over her while she ate some dry toast. "Youse not lookin' after yourself right, *kōtiro*. Youse not givin' your poor body a chance to heal!" She waited for Hana to finish before bustling back into the kitchen and Hana seized the opportunity to escape.

The pram was still in the dining room and as Phoenix began to show signs of wanting a nap, Hana laid her in it. She pushed her down to the mud room to retrieve the boots she had left there the day before. It was damp outside, but she thought her child might appreciate some fresh air. The thought of returning to the bedroom filled with angry adults made her squirm.

The walls of the mud room were lined with shelves containing boots and shoes, odd bits of outdoor clothing and a rack mounted a foot from the ceiling where hats were stored. Hana's Jillaroo hat should have been there and she raked the shelves with her eyes looking for it. It was brown leather with a flat top and a decent brim. A plaited leather tie ran around the brim and she loved that Logan gave it to her after Miriam's death; the birthday present from him which his mother never wore.

"Move!" Liza's spiteful command made Hana jump and she leapt out of the way as the woman barged past. Her long fingers were in the process of planting Hana's hat on her neatly trimmed boy-cut hair. Hana stared open-mouthed, disgusted at the fear which stopped her challenging for it. "Go on, get out!"

Lisa ordered and Hana gritted her teeth. *Just let it go,* she told herself charitably. *It's only a hat. My hat. My favourite hat*

"Why are you still here?" Liza bit and it was so unexpected, Hana had no ready reply.

"Here as in; *here in this room*, or here as in; *still married to Logan and at his hotel*?" Hana's voice sounded more courageous than she felt.

Liza's lips curled back to reveal perfect, white teeth. "You must be elated, a little free loader like you. You've married the rich guy, produced the offspring and now you can sit back and collect. Nice work!"

Hana felt stunned, her lips parting and her eyes widening in horror. It seemed pointless telling her that Vik had left her amply provided for and she actually owned two houses of her own. "What did I ever do to *you?*" she asked, her voice sounding small.

Liza attempted to pull a pair of black leather chaps over her jodhpur boots and jeans, struggling with the zip. An irrational sense of satisfaction crossed Hana's addled mind as she saw the long fingers trembling. "You've turned my brother against me, that's what you've done! You and your English rose act! Now your filthy, mixed race little brat will make a mockery of everything this family stands for!"

Hana glanced at her innocent, sleeping baby and swallowed. Maternal fury as strong as a lioness' lit the touch paper in her heart and she found her voice. "How dare you!" Hana pushed her daughter's pram safely out of the way and took a step towards the vitriolic woman hopping around on one leg, still yanking on the zipper of the chaps. She leaned in close to Liza's face, bending to ensure she drove her message home. "If you ever speak about my child like that again, I'll slap you into next week without a second thought! Hana's voice dripped bile and Liza's jaw dropped. "People like you make me sick!" Hana finished, glaring at the hat on Liza's head. "And when you've finished with *my* hat, kindly put it back where you got it from."

Hana felt Logan's presence before she saw him, her heart plummeting into her stomach. She breathed through pursed lips to avoid panting in fear and avoided his eyes as she stuffed her feet into her boots and seized the pram handle. She cringed as she heard his next words. "Just go," he said to Liza as she looked up in surprise, the colour draining from her face. Hana heard Logan's teeth gritted together in temper as he made his awful decree. "Get out and don't *ever* come back!"

Hana felt the draught as he turned on his heel and left. She heard the click of his cowboy boots on the tiles, taking him away to another part of the house. Her pram blocked the doorway as Liza put her hand up to her face and the unmistakeable sound of crying filled the small space.

The compassionate side of Hana felt instantly sorry for Liza. But it was like watching a wild animal cornered and snarling – she felt sorry for it, but didn't particularly want to get bitten. Hana rocked the pram gently from side to side as Liza rested her forehead against the external door and sobbed noisily. Phoenix stayed asleep, removing any decent excuse for Hana to avoid the judge's obvious grief.

With a sound like an exasperated 'tut', more at herself than Liza, Hana left the pram in the doorway and ventured towards her. Gently she put her hands on the woman's heaving shoulders, expecting at any second to be slapped. To her absolute surprise, Liza turned and wrapped her arms around Hana's neck and sobbed into into her cardigan. Hana patted her on the back, soothing her as she would one of her children. A river of tears emanated from the judge, soaking into Hana's clothing until she was soaked.

Hana spied a roll of industrial cleaning cloth on the windowsill and reached out for it. Liza disturbed and took a step backwards, wiping her face on her sleeve. She was flushed with crying but Hana sensed embarrassment adding to the mix. "Here you are." Hana tore off a length of the heavy-duty roll the men used to clean their boots and tack and offered it to Liza. She took it with muffled thanks and produced an enormous blow into it. Then she snagged another piece and blew her nose again. Hana stood back, abruptly aware once again of her role as 'interloper' into this complex, tortured family. Liza wiped the harsh tissue across her nose and balled it up to throw into the huge trash can in the corner and sensing the rising tension in the room, Hana seized the handle of her pram and left.

At first, she sought Logan, looking for him in the stable yard and then the equipment shed. Finding him in neither place, Hana acknowledged a definite sense of relief which became quickly accompanied by guilt. "It's not like he'll tell me how he feels anyway," she muttered, absolving herself of responsibility. Hana pushed her daughter around the property, admiring the gardens and sitting on the bench by Miriam's favourite rose garden for a while, delaying the inevitable moment of return to the house. Eventually the cool wind and spitting rain sent her scurrying for cover, hoping for an afternoon without more fireworks.

Taking the lift up to their bedroom, Hana planted the pram in the corner of the room, next to a slightly open window. Hurling herself onto the big bed face down, she gave in to an incredible wave of boredom. Having finished the only novel she brought with her and in the absence of Logan to seduce, there was nothing to do. Rolling onto her back, Hana debated the wisdom of moving up to her new house on top of the mountain, even if the generator wasn't there. "I'll be so bored," she informed the empty room. "Logan won't be able to leave the hotel and the farm alone, not if we're that close to it and what will I do stuck in a house on the edge of a cliff? I might not see anyone for days!"

It was a miserably isolating thought and Hana became grumpy as it took hold. She decided it would be intolerable. Her hand ran over the place where the pace maker lay under her skin. The doctor was right when he said she would get used to it. It hadn't gone off yet, so perhaps her poor old heart was holding its own. But the question remained unanswered; what did God save her *for*?

THE DU ROSE PROPHECY 191

Hana Du Rose was not unrealistic. She aware that wise men went to their graves still wrangling over the meaning of life and she didn't consider herself wise. She morbidly wondered what was in store for her and what her true purpose might be. "I'd like to see Phoenix married or at least following a career that consumes her passion," Hana prayed. "Don't let me die like my mother did, right in the middle of everything. If this is my second chance, at least let me give it a go?" she pleaded.

Rolling onto her side, Hana sighed. "I'm not doing anything right though, am I?" she said out loud. Even with Logan, she still consistently put her foot in it. He hadn't loved the strutting, posturing go-getter, Caroline, but nor did he want the simpering bimbo type who hung on his every word. *What did he want and how could she be sure she was it?* Liza's presence made her feel insecure and out of her depth.

Hana's mind wandered to Alan Dobbs and the news of his death. A frightening man, she managed to make avoiding him into an art form. Liza's spite reminded her of Alan Dobbs and Hana shuddered at the memory of her argument with him, years before. "See, you can stand up to people," she reminded herself. Hana allowed her brain to toy with the recollection, venturing into futile territory, especially now he was dead.

'*How dare you?*' Dobbs screamed at a much younger Hana. '*Staffing decisions are nothing to do with bloody admin nobodies! Mind your own damn business, or find yourself another job!*' Hana shivered at the memory of the purple, apoplectic face and bulging eyes, his wig wobbling tremulously on his head.

'*I thought he was going to hit me!*' she complained to Vik later, her voice echoing down the years. '*All this drama over a stupid mistake!*'

The staircase behind reception was Alan Dobbs' customary vantage point, from where he observed the behaviour of staff and students. Hana wondered why he would stand there during the holidays. It seemed ludicrous; why would he watch an empty school? If the administrative director had died on school premises during the break, it would have seemed more logical.

Everyone knew Donald Watson practically lived there, turning up for work at some ridiculously early hour and leaving long after the day became evening. Bodie said something about the alarm sounding, but even that was odd, because Donald always attended those calls from his house on the street behind the school.

Realising boredom made her pick holes in things best left alone, Hana pottered around making herself a drink. A quiet knock on the bedroom door revealed Liza standing on the threshold. Hana stood back to let her inside but waited in front of her, expecting the woman to say her spiteful words and leave. "I came to say sorry," Liza said and Hana struggled to keep the shock from her face. "You were kind to me earlier and I didn't deserve it." Liza's eyes were still bloodshot and her face was puffy and swollen.

Hana nodded and offered a smile of encouragement. "I'm making tea, would you like some?"

Liza nodded and wandered further into the room. While Hana made drinks, Liza stood by the pram and stared down at the sleeping baby. "She's very beautiful," she commented in a whisper. "It's like she's all the best bits of us, put together in one person."

"*Us?*" Hana asked, confused.

Liza took the mug of tea, sipping it slowly. "*Us*. The Du Roses. Both parts of the family. I can see my mother and Uncle Reuben in her. She has Loge's hands and eyes and I can even see you in her too."

Hana smiled at the last comment in disbelief. The child was dark haired and olive skinned, whereas Hana was red-haired and as porcelain skinned as a person could be and still be alive. She looked down into the pram, her heart swelling with love at the oblivious infant, laid with her little arms raised above her head as though she didn't have a care in the world. Hana's brow knitted and her face held doubt as she watched the tiny chest rising and falling.

"She does," Liza persisted. "She has that same sense of peace you have. You know who you are. It's more powerful than you could ever imagine. It sort of shines...out of your face."

In view of her internal agonies only seconds before, Hana shook her head in denial. "Oh, I don't think..."

But Liza cut her off sharply. "I'm not saying you have all the answers, Hana. You have this surety somehow. I envy you."

Hana chose to say nothing, staring at the carpet between her socks. She felt no surety in her life at all most of the time; apart from her faith. God loved her; she knew that without a shadow of doubt. She wondered if that was what Liza meant, but instantly dismissed it. Liza couldn't possibly know what Hana did or didn't believe because they'd never had a conversation about anything. Liza avoided her like the plague, ever since their first introduction the night Logan announced to his family he had married Hana. She shivered involuntarily at the frightening memory and Liza watched her with interest, like a lion waiting for its lunch to stop walking around and sit down.

Offering her sister-in-law the armchair by the ranch slider, Hana sat down on the bed and brought her legs up underneath her. Having Liza on her territory was a new experience and she decided not to care if the other woman thought her rude for laying on the bed. A feeling of exhaustion pricked at the back of her brain and Hana attempted to fend it off with rest.

"Are you ok?" Liza asked and Hana nodded.

"I had a heart operation a week or so ago and I still get tired."

Liza looked surprised and her jaw dropped. "Oh." The single word held guilt and contrition. "Then my appearance can't have helped much. Sorry." She looked wrong footed and with the hardness of her soul suddenly gone, her face became pretty. It was incredible how like Miriam she looked. A piece of Logan's complicated emotional puzzle clicked into place as Hana saw his yearning for his mother mirrored in his sister like a physical ache. But having Liza appear unexpectedly, a carbon copy of Miriam, would be enough to send him over the edge. Hana sipped her tea and contemplated it all.

"I meant what I said, about envying you," Liza said, the words seeming to stick in her throat. "You have it all. You've got Logan and a lovely baby. Anyone can see how much my brother worships you. It must be great, feeling so...safe."

"Safe?" Hana repeated. "I wouldn't think of it as safe."

"Of course it's safe!" Liza scoffed. "You have this secure family unit. Nobody can take that away from you." She sipped her tea and sulked, her prettiness disappearing underneath a dark shroud of misery and veiled anger. Hana drew in a deep breath and let it out again slowly.

"Nothing in life is safe, Liza; or certain. God gives and takes away. There're no guarantees. I loved my first husband very much and he went to work and never came home. The lorry driver who killed him will live with that for the rest of his life, but I'm sure he didn't set out on his journey with the intention of taking a life. I spent most of my pregnancy in hiding from men who hunted me without care for my safety as long as they retrieved what they wanted; I gave birth to my daughter in the bush, miles away from civilisation and a couple of weeks ago I had a heart attack and was dead for a few minutes. Believe me; it can all be gone in seconds!"

There was no comfort for Liza in anything Hana said. There were no guarantees in life. "You have to make the minutes you have count for something," she said, speaking as much to herself as to Liza. Hana sipped her tea slowly, beating herself up. She wasn't making anything count. She watched the other woman out of the corner of her eye.

Liza was used to getting her own way. In chambers she had people to do her bidding, summoning powerful barristers at will and watching them crumble in the face of one of her stony silences. Hana kept her composure, even though inside she collapsed like a rugged outcrop attacked one time too many by the weather. Judge Liza Du Rose was terrifying. Liza looked at her – those grey Du Rose eyes piercing Hana's soul as she whispered, "What can I do? How can I get Logan to forgive me?"

"I don't know," Hana answered, her face sad. "Try talking to him instead of shouting."

"It's my fault," Liza interrupted, her voice cracking, "Not his. I'm sorry; I've caused such a mess. He said I should have told him about Reuben being his father and he's right. Of all of us, I should have been loyal to him and not them. I owed him. But I didn't know how to do it. How do you tell someone something like that?"

Hana nodded in sympathy. "I don't know, Liza." Hana bit her lip, not wanting to admit she found out the truth too before Reuben died, but never found the words to enlighten Logan.

"Do you think Logan was serious before, when he told me to leave?" Liza's voice sounded small but Hana wondered fleetingly if she was being played by Liza, looking for Hana's allegiance. Liza never shared as much as airspace willingly with Hana before now, let alone an apology. Hana chose to give her the benefit of the doubt.

Getting off the bed, Hana walked past Liza to the ranch slider and went out onto the balcony, seeking fresh air and space to think. On the driveway at the front of the hotel, she watched a couple arrive in an expensive car. The man started getting suitcases out of the boot and the woman waited while he lumbered them over to her. They made an unhappy couple. The woman left the man to lump the cases by himself, setting off towards the hotel reception. Hana heard him grumbling and complaining to himself as they came level with the balcony. They didn't look up or even notice Hana. Her red hair flew out behind her in the wind and her socks soaked up the rainwater from the smooth tiled floor, doused in the passing shower.

"Stop moaning, Jerry!" the woman exclaimed, frustrated as she whirled around to face him. "A couple of days away; that was all I asked for."

"Yeah!" the man retorted angrily, "but you had to pick these particular days!"

The woman stood still and put her head down. Hana realised from the set of her shoulders she was crying and felt guilty for her voyeurism. She stepped back from the rail and her foot landed in a puddle, the water rendering her socks sodden. Groaning, she lifted her foot and peered at the mess, noticing Liza standing just inside the doorway. Her eyes stared past Hana, towards the couple below. A shout made Hana whip round. "Fine!" the woman shrieked, not caring what the other people in the large car park thought. "Fine. I've had enough. Take me home and then you can get out. Pack your stuff and leave!" She marched back towards their vehicle, a determined air about her as she stepped across the gravel in stilettos. The man stood for a moment, his hands still on the handles of the suitcases and his relationship hanging in the balance. Neither Hana nor Liza witnessed the conclusion of the row as the couple climbed into the vehicle, leaving the cases outside.

"Another one bites the dust," Liza said sadly. "And if there're kids, they'll probably end up in the family court."

"You sound like my son, Bodie," Hana said, holding her wet foot off the floor. "He gets cynical with his job."

Liza nodded. "I haven't given you much of a chance, have I? I'm sorry for that."

Hana smiled back at her sister-in-law at the same moment as a little squeak issued from inside. It was accompanied by the sound of rattling as Phoenix whacked the animals on the mobile over the pram to tell her mother she was awake. The women went back inside and Liza shut the ranch slider behind her.

"Hey, girlie!" Hana unclipped Phoenix from the pram and lifted her out, still wearing her little pink harness. Her hair stuck up, dark against her flushed cheeks. The little girl rubbed the back of her hand repeatedly across her button nose and put her face on Hana's shoulder. Then she noticed Liza and stared at her hard, her eyes flicking from the stranger to her mother and back again. "Aunty Liza," Hana said to her and the child frowned, looking exactly like her father.

Emerging from the bathroom after a swift nappy change, she found Liza by the ranch slider. "They haven't left yet," she said, turning towards Hana. "So maybe it's just a spat."

Hana nodded. She sat her baby down on a towel which she laid on the floor, offering her a rusk at the same time as lifting off the reins and pushing a bib over her head. Phoenix took it slowly, sizing it up as though not sure if it was acceptable or not.

Liza smiled. "Her father was picky as hell. Sometimes money was so tight on the farm there were boil-ups filled with meat fat and Logan would purse up his lips and refuse. Then the rest of us would fight over his portion like a pack of wolves." The memories didn't fill Liza with any comfort and as always, she switched them quickly off. "How old were you, when you fell pregnant?" she asked Hana instead. Hana looked up in surprise.

"I was forty-four. I thought I was past all that, but obviously not." She looked embarrassed and turned her attention to peeling off her wet socks.

"I was pregnant once," Liza said sadly. "A little girl. I lost her at five months. Michel was devastated. I don't think either of us got over it. It was the beginning of the end really." Hana tried to keep the surprise from her face. "Logan doesn't know," Liza added, looking worried. "Nobody does...anymore. Mum knew but now she's gone."

Hana shook her head. "I shan't say anything; it's your business." She threw her socks at the laundry basket, and watched them land next to it on the rimu boards. "For what it's worth though, I'm sorry. I think out of everything I've ever had to deal with, grief's the worst. You never know when it will take its next bite of your soul, just that it will."

The women looked at each other, green eyes to grey and reached an understanding. Liza looked almost normal. She had lost the hardness and no longer displayed the familiar prickly aura. Phoenix sang to her rusk and Liza watched her with interest, the edges of her face softening.

The click of the bedroom door drew their attention. Logan stood on the other side of the bed, his face unreadable and his hands squarely on his hips. He looked both gorgeous and formidable and both women tensed involuntarily as though caught out in some misdeed.

Chapter Fourteen

"Don't stand like that," Liza snapped. "You remind me of an effeminate boyfriend I had in law school."

To Hana's surprise, Logan put his hands down by his sides before remembering he was still angry with his commanding sister. "Whatever!" he growled. Hana realised there was more in play than she understood. She sighed and Logan looked down at her from his great height. "Have you been overdoing it?" The patronising edge in the question irked her. She gritted her teeth and didn't reply.

Phoenix finished grinding her new teeth on the side of the biscuit and decided she wasn't impressed with it, squeezing the crumbly mess between the palms of her hands and making whispery noises. Hana wiped her face and hands quickly before she could object, swiping the biscuit away with it. Phoenix patted her palms on her splayed knees and Hana hauled herself up to her feet, openly rejecting Logan's offered hand and dumping the dirty wipes and biscuit into the bin. She snatched her daughter up and pushed her feet into a pair of slippers without bending down, leaving the room wordlessly.

Outside she spoke to Phoenix, who started to whimper, "Let's go and get some peace in the family room and Mummy can give you a little breast feed."

They took the spiral staircase at the end of their floor and Hana settled herself in the bright little private room at the back of the house near the stables. The sitting room was one of the few which hadn't been decorated for years, left alone in its rustic comfort. The red leather sofas were squashy and safe and the ancient television gave a poor reception. "When your Grandmother Miriam was alive, she and Poppa Alfred spent their evenings in this room," Hana told her daughter. She remembered how the fire roared savagely within the confines of its grate and Alfred wound balls of knitting wool for his wife. Only latterly Hana could see it for what it was - a picture of fake, domestic bliss, carved out to fool the world.

Miriam had been the lynch-pin for the family, the cornerstone holding them all together. In her absence, they were in-fighting and drifting on a rising tide of disaster. It was ironic how Logan's brother and sister returned home within weeks of each other, seeking something they both knew they wouldn't find. With their mother gone as housekeeper and Alfred disconnected from everything, there was nothing here for them. It was Logan's business and nothing more. Hana's brow creased as she thought of Alfred. She hadn't seen him for days and he no longer bothered to come and see the baby, hiding out in Jack's bunkhouse like a hermit.

It was irritating the way Logan's siblings turned up, expecting to be waited on hand and foot, but Hana saw the craving in their eyes. She knew Logan hadn't come to terms with his mother's suicide, but wondered if any of them were coping. Hana sighed and spoke to her daughter. "I don't have the energy to get involved," she said.

Logan repeated to Liza almost word for word, what he threw at Michael a few weeks before. *'You weren't interested!'* Hana always assumed he bought the failing farm section by section, paying off the suffocating debts from the other side of the world.

She hadn't known he asked his siblings for help. There were lots of reasons why they might have turned him down but Logan drew his own conclusions in the light of the revelation that Reuben and not Alfred was his father. She realised with amazing clarity that part of her husband's recent angst was fear that Michael and Liza rejected his business rescue plan because they weren't full siblings. In which case they rejected *him*, not his proposal. It made perfect sense.

The old Hana would have rushed upstairs, spewed out her conclusions and demanded they all have a group hug. The new Hana knew better. Constant clashes with Logan over 'family issues' about which he claimed, she knew nothing, had long since dented her confidence in any counselling skills she may have possessed. "No baby," she whispered to her suckling daughter, "Mummy's learning to play the long game."

Phoenix stopped feeding and beamed at her mother, reaching out with her hand for Hana to kiss it. Then she babbled something helpful along with a deep sigh and buried her face back into Hana's breast. Hana lay her head back against the old sofa and closed her eyes, enjoying the peace of the room and the rhythm of her baby's feeding. It was soporific and Hana felt herself drifting off to sleep and finding resistance futile.

She jumped as someone came into the room and she heard the chink of crockery. "Sorry, love," Leslie said gently as she sat on the sofa next to her. "I went upstairs looking for you. I wanted to know if I could have your little girl this afternoon for a few hours, but your husband's up there with *her ladyship*. You could cut the atmosphere with a knife, so I figured youse might be hiding down here."

Hana laughed but it was a sad sound. "Am I that predictable?"

"Only to us that know and love you," Leslie answered and put her arm around the younger woman. Hana leaned in and kissed Leslie's brown cheek and thanked her. Then she sat the dozing baby up on her knee and patted her back.

"You've not long woken up, missy. How can you just nod right back off like that?"

Phoenix yawned and rubbed her eyes, letting out a wet burp and grinning at Leslie.

"Maybe she's like her daddy," Leslie said, chucking the baby under the chin with her finger.

Phoenix giggled, but Hana shook her head. "No, Logan sleeps terribly at the moment. He's often up in the night wandering around. Especially here."

Leslie tried to lighten the mood but realised her mistake too late. "Not like Alfred then. He lays on his back and snores like a piggy!"

Hana's eyes twinkled as Leslie covered her hand with her mouth in embarrassment. "Naughty Aunty Leslie," Hana said to the baby. "Doing rudies with Grandpa Alfie; who'd have thought it?" Leslie looked mortified, her body tense as she observed the empty fireplace with unusual intensity. "Actually where is Alfred?" Hana asked. "I know he's staying away from Logan, but he's been reasonably attentive to Phoe since I got home from the hospital. I haven't seen him for a few days."

Leslie stood up and walked over to the French doors, peering outside at the drizzling rain and grey muted landscape. She didn't answer immediately and Hana felt besieged by everyone else's problems. She sensed Leslie was about to confide in her and tried not to visibly wince. Settling her baby onto the other breast, she reached for the mug of tea on the tray and waited. When it came, Hana was relieved to find there was little in it she didn't already know, apart from maybe the finer details.

"I knew about Miriam and Reuben; I've always known. I passed messages for years and watched Logan grow up. When Miriam was depressed and beating herself up, I took news of the boy to his father; silly little things to make him smile. I always liked Reuben as a friend. He was only ever interested in Miriam. Everyone thought they would marry and then they fell out and not a soul knew why. Reuben left for a while and when he came back, he was wed; to Miriam's sister. The old lady was mad as hell with him but she took it out on Alfred more. Rumour was he'd shown too much of an interest in Miriam and as the older brother, Reuben would have to step aside. Sure enough, Miriam took up with Alfred and nobody will ever know the truth but them. They all lived together here and the babies were born in this *whare*, Kane and then Liza, Nev and Barry. Life settled and it was fine for a while. Reuben's wife loved kids. She was always picking up strays from around the wider *whānau* and the house was full of little ones running around, making a noise."

Leslie sighed and ran her hand over her face. Hana was struck by how her seventy-odd years pressed her down in that moment. "Something happened – and Reuben's wife went away for a while. Everything was ok when she came back and we were told she went to care for a sick relative. She was gone for the best part of a year. Then one day that blondie turned up, Caroline Marsh. Nobody was sure where she came from. She was a delicate little tot but a cuckoo if ever there was one; real hard to manage. She was a few years younger than Liza but those two were trouble together, like sisters. Reuben's wife died the year Michael was born and Reuben got real sad. He and Miriam struck out again together not long after that. I don't think they meant to; it was just one of those things.

"I came to work one morning in the cowshed and the word was that Alfred had gone; took off in the night. He went up north to work with an uncle who ran a beef farm and didn't come back for months. The old lady followed him up there and tried to talk to him. She never said why he went and Miriam was dead quiet about it, but I guessed about her and Reuben and figured Alfred did too. By the time he came back, Miriam must have already been pregnant with Logan. Ain't no way that child was born two months early, not the long legs on him. Besides, you only had to look at him to see that he was pure Reuben Du Rose.

"It blew up bad one day. Alfred came in to find Reuben holding Logan and lost it. He took a swing at his brother even though he was cuddling the *piripoho* and Reuben laid him out flat. But the old lady wouldn't tolerate it no more. She sent Reuben and his lot packing. She divided the land and fenced them out. She gave her son the money to build that house and then washed her hands of him. They lived in tents while it was built and him with all those small kiddies across the winter. She was a hard woman and punished them all for Reuben's wrong. That was her *utu* and those *tamariki* never forgave her. It was wicked but she wouldn't let nobody from this side help him out. It broke his heart being banished from his own son and he never got over it." Leslie's voice ceased and Hana let the word *utu* roll around her mouth without speaking it out loud. It was a form of plundering aimed at righting a wrong after battle, but what Phoenix Du Rose took was more than just possessions.

Leslie sighed. "It wouldn't have worked, not Reuben and Alfred under the same roof trying to raise the boy. The older boys knew about Logan and word always gets out with kids. They hated that poor *tamaiti* and he had no idea why."

Leslie pressed her forehead against the cool glass and let out a long breath. "I should never have taken up with Alfred when I moved upstairs. It was an accident, two lonely old people finding a bit of happiness. I know the other staff hated it and I forgot my place, especially with you and Mr Logan. I dealt with things all wrong. I felt such guilt over all the times I covered for Miriam while she met with her lover and I saw what it did to Alfred, how he used to watch her with his heart all cut up inside. He didn't deserve it and I shouldn't have helped them. When I realised Logan knew, I thought he would tell Alfred. I'm too old for all the drama so I decided to do the right thing. I went to see him at the bunkhouse and told him myself. He was devastated."

Hana lay a towel across her shoulder and put the baby over it. She was almost long enough to balance her toes on Hana's thigh and felt heavy. She put both of her little arms around her mother's neck and snuggled in. Hana kissed the side of her face and pulled her in closer. Leslie was silent and Hana watched her. "What do you want?" she asked eventually.

The old woman looked at her strangely, as though not understanding the question. "I don't know. Why does it matter what I want?"

"It always matters," Hana replied. "Because if *you* don't know, how can you expect other people to?"

Leslie looked stunned and Hana felt sad for her, remembering tales of the abusive gambling husband who robbed her blind their whole married life and then dropped dead, leaving her to pay off his loan sharks. If Logan hadn't intervened, Leslie would still be in that derelict house without any furniture, watching them take her wages week after week for the rest of her life. "Do you want to be with Alfred?" Hana asked and Leslie blanched before nodding, her cheeks flushed with embarrassment. "Then tell him," Hana said. "See if he can forgive you and then carry on enjoying each other's company."

Leslie's eyes almost popped out of her face with shock and she gaped like a fish. "That's the thing," she stammered. "He asked me to marry him and I knew I had to tell the truth. But part of me knew there'd be a big scandal. He's meant to wait a year, until after the unveiling otherwise the *whānau* will believe he never loved her."

Hana shrugged, regretting getting involved. "It's your life, Leslie, not theirs. You need to talk to Alfred, but you won't know anything until you try. I've spent far too much of my life avoiding stuff and running away from issues which blow up out of nowhere. What I'm learning with the Du Roses, is to either put up or shut up. I'm sitting in here now because I've come across something to '*shut up*' about, but I'm picking my battles. There's a '*put up*' coming, believe me."

Hana thanked Leslie for the tea, standing up with Phoenix still draped over her shoulder. Giving a little sigh, Phoenix stuffed her hands between her body and Hana's and turned her face to the other side, closing her eyes and dozing. Hana decided the little girl was auditioning for family sloth. "Good luck," she said kindly and left the room, hoping she hadn't set the older woman up for one heck of a fall. "I think I've given enough advice today," Hana whispered to her daughter. "It's wearing me out!"

The Du Roses didn't do 'talking' or 'feelings.' Hana discovered that major problem soon in her marriage, although Logan had softened since the baby. He had become far more adept at explaining the things that bothered him, yielding significantly less run-ins and misunderstandings. He was also better at listening, but it had taken a number of brave moments while Hana blocked his escape route and forced him to explain himself, in order to get this far. Standing in front of an angry, frustrated Logan Du Rose who had all the signs of detonation in his eyes, was no mean feat. What she said to Leslie was true, she was learning to pick her battles. This last generation grew up in a world of secrets and lies and there was no wonder they were scarred by it. Then again, Hana's sedate upbringing hadn't been as perfect as she believed. She shook her head and climbed the spiral staircase.

Liza was no longer in their room and Hana couldn't see any blood on the floorboards. Logan lay on their bed re-reading 'Lord of the Flies', ready to teach it to the Year 11's next term and the corner of the room was piled high with the boxes from next door. Hana eyed them with amusement. She resisted the urge to make any snide comments about the title of the book in Logan's hand, in which the character names could easily be substituted for those of Du Rose family members. Logan closed the book as Hana turned the heat pump on again, memorising the page so that he didn't have to splay its cover. "Sorry about before," he said, holding out his arm towards her and shifting over. "I was being an arse. I shouldn't take it out on you."

"No, you shouldn't!" she replied. Hana plonked herself down on the bed and hearing her father's voice, Phoenix reached out with both arms towards him, almost tipping herself out of Hana's grip. He took her and settled her on his chest. "Liza hung around for a bit. We thought you might come up for a group hug." There was a smirk in his voice and Hana turned away to hide her smile. She looked back and wrinkled her nose and shrugged. Logan looked hard at her. "Don't you care anymore?"

"It's not that." Her voice betrayed her tiredness. "I've got too many scorch marks on my backside already. And anyone who tries to get between you lot is always the one who ends up burned. I think you need to sort it all out yourselves. It's probably the only way I'll to survive being in this family."

Logan lay back against the pillows, patting his daughter gently on the back. He looked as though his striking grey eyes were closed but Hana perceived the swish of his long black lashes as he observed her covertly from the side. "Well, you're no fun anymore," he said. "I enjoyed that smack in the face you gave Kane a while back. And I know Michael appreciated the matching pair of black eyes a couple of weeks ago. You're getting a worse reputation than me."

Hana sighed and put her head on his shoulder. "I didn't think you saw me whack Michael with that plate. You had your face in the tea towel, bleeding. He actually took a swing at you, even though you couldn't defend yourself. Violence isn't the answer anyway. I thumped Kane and then look what happened to that naughty hand."

Hana looked down at the angry scar on her wrist. Life was peculiar sometimes with its twists and turns. "Then I defended you against Michael and had a heart attack a matter of hours afterwards. Being in this family is lethal."

Phoenix grinned at her mother from her prime spot on Logan's chest and Hana smiled back. "Nope, I think God's trying to tell me something."

Logan laughed, "What like? Stop hitting *whānau* members, or stop defending your husband?"

"Both," Hana replied. "He says you're big enough and ugly enough to stand up for yourself."

"Na," Logan said with a low chuckle, "now I know you're lying. Cause I'm not ugly."

Hana drew in a loud breath and slapped him on the thigh, calling him vain and openly laughing at him. The rain hammering against the front of the hotel made her jump. "This weather is crazy!" she exclaimed. "I thought I'd go up to the memorial gardens and see how they're coming along but the rain made it pointless. I don't know how your stockmen cope with it.

"They're all back," Logan said with a yawn. "They'll do inside jobs with tack or machinery or go back to the bunkhouse. But it works both ways because the jobs still need doing."

"Do they have to catch up tomorrow?" Hana asked and Logan nodded.

"Yep, or the weekend. They don't care. It's just the way this industry is and they're mostly glad of a well-paid job they love. If they didn't like it, they'd move on, wouldn't they?"

Hana nodded, figuring it helped that Logan spent many long hours fencing in the rain and wind and calving or foaling in the middle of the night with his men. His work ethic was faultless and it left no room for anyone not wanting to do the same.

Feeling chilled to the bone, Hana ran a mid-morning bath. Phoenix heard the water running onto the bubbles and began an entertaining striptease, pulling at her cardigan buttons and when that failed, pulling it over her head and getting stuck. Hana piled her hair onto her head in a scrunchy and sank into the deep bubbles. It felt like heaven; until Logan appeared in the doorway with a naked Phoenix and plonked her on Hana's stomach. "Oh don't, Loge!" Hana protested as Logan stripped off and climbed in as well, making the water slop over the edges. "What happened to my five minutes peace?" She laughed as he grimaced, trying to get comfortable at the plug end.

Phoenix came alive, shrieking, squealing and slapping the water in a frenzy of excitement. She was wriggly and slippery and hard to hold onto. Logan spent ages showing her how to make funnels from his mouth with the bathwater. She laughed like a drain, even when he got her in the face by accident. "I'd stop doing that soon, if I were you," Hana suggested. "We should probably get her out before she pees."

Logan pulled a face and wiped his wet hand across the back of his mouth, adding, "Or worse."

Hana laughed but before she could speak, he held his hand up. "Please don't remind me. It was horrible."

Logan stepped out of the bath and reached for a towel, looking bashful as Hana ogled him without shame. "Not in front of the children!" he chastised.

Phoenix kicked up a fuss when he lifted her out and Hana heard him telling her they were going to get lunch in a minute, which seemed to stop her high pitched squeal. Hana used the soap and let out the cold water before running hot back in. "Aren't you coming down?" Logan asked, appearing in the doorway with the baby, both of them dressed.

"I'm not hungry," Hana admitted. "I feel so tired today. You go down and I'll stay here for a bit."

Logan looked unsure, not wanting to leave her alone in the bath. Hana rejected his offer of bringing something up from the kitchen, suddenly craving time alone with her thoughts. Reluctantly he left her there and went to feed his grumpy daughter.

He returned an hour later and he was alone. Hana lay on the bed in a towel, warming herself under the heat pump which was on sauna level. "Leslie asked for Phoe," he said, climbing onto the bed and slipping his arm around his wife's shoulders.

"I think she's going to see Alfred," Hana commented. "Did she drive or walk? It's awful out there."

"She drove. I gave her the Honda keys because it already had the car seat in it." Hana nodded and sighed. "What's the matter?" Logan asked and Hana shook her head.

"I honestly don't know. Maybe I'm stir crazy with the weather and being so tired all the time. I seem to have a lot of worries going round and round my brain and don't know how to sort them out. Sorry. I'm not good company am I?"

Logan smiled and pulled the scrunchy out of her hair, feeling it drop easily from the silky red tresses. He kissed her neck and Hana squirmed and giggled. "I've got very definite ideas about how a rainy, childless afternoon should be spent," he breathed, running his hand along her thigh and as he tugged Hana's towel loose, began to show her.

Hana's fingers trailed down his strong chest, feeling the defined muscle through his skin. She pushed him onto his back and smoothed her palm along the scar tissue on his torso, seeking the mess of ridged flesh down his side. Hana kissed Logan's pectorals in turn and let her lips slide over his nipple, hearing him inhale. "I love your body," she whispered, her breath snuffing over his soft skin. "I never want to hear you say it's mangled again. Do you understand?" She sank her teeth into the bud of his nipple and he let out a groan and flipped her on her back with force.

Hana squealed as her towel disappeared over the side of the bed and Logan's lips pressed against hers, his tongue questing for entry. He paused, his eyes the colour of stone. "*Tutakina ake,*" he whispered and covered her mouth again with his.

Chapter Fifteen

Leslie stayed at Jack's place with Alfred and Phoenix for most of the afternoon. When she finally returned, she discovered Hana and Logan sitting on the floor of their bedroom, going through the boxes and containers from the *marae*. Phoenix was bright eyed and alert and sat on the rug next to Logan, watching him closely and attempting to grab every object emerging from the boxes.

Leslie sat on the bed and chewed her lip, angst present in her crinkled face. "Agh, youse shouldn't be doing that!" she said, worrying at the fingers in her ample lap. "Them's *tapu*. I can feel how sacred they are from here."

"The *kaumātua* seemed to think it was fine for us to go through everything," Hana reassured her, piling the framed photographs up to one side as Logan handed them over. "Who are all these people?" she asked and Logan shrugged.

"Alfie might know," Leslie ventured and Logan's body tensed in irritation at the nickname the housekeeper used.

"Well, sod off and ask *Alfie* then!" he hissed under his breath.

Hana heard and fumbled the frame in her hands, clanking it roughly against the others. "Sorry," she said, staring at her husband. Logan kept his face pushed into the box and wouldn't look at her. Turning to Leslie, Hana raised her eyebrows in question and Leslie smiled and gave her the thumbs up. Hana jerked her head towards Logan, asking with her eyes if she could tell Logan. Her face fell with guilt as she saw Leslie's complexion pale and found Logan looking straight at her, annoyance in his eyes.

"Would you like me to leave the room?" he asked crossly and Hana shot a look at Leslie. She blanched and Hana shoulders drooped. This wasn't the way things were meant to happen and now she had ruined it.

"Don't be silly!" Hana chided him. "We can talk about sore boobies and periods and nipple creams perfectly well with you here."

Logan looked at her sideways and narrowed his eyes. He knew he was being bluffed but his eyes channelled warning to his wife. He would get it out of her later. "I've had enough of this now," he said, placing large piece of jade back into the box nearest him with extreme care. Phoenix made a capable swipe at it and almost ended up with it on her head.

"What is that?" Hana asked, stroking the smooth surface as it lay on top of another stack of framed photographs and pictures.

"It's greenstone or *pounamu*," Logan answered, pushing himself to his feet and catching up the baby, who squealed with delight. "It's a *mere*, a weapon, like a club. Depending on how old it is, it can have great *mana*, which increases as it's handed down. We need to find out more about all of this stuff. Maybe the *kaumātua* will know."

"Are the cops any nearer to discovering what happened to that poor man who fell down the stairs at your work?" Leslie asked, making herself sound interested in the stranger's death and trying desperately to take the conversation away from herself and the *tapu* objects on the bare floor. She shifted with discomfort as Hana hefted a leather bound book back into a box. "Ooh, careful missus," she groaned as a frame clattered against another. "I'm scared you don't understood how Māori ways work." She wrung her hands as though in pain and eyed the opened box with fear in her brown eyes. There was something powerful coming off the objects which made her feel unsettled and nervous. They were so precious, more precious than Hana understood.

"I don't know," Logan said with a sigh, his voice sounding sad. "Initially it looked like an accident but Bodie seems to think they've revised that and are looking at it differently. He wasn't real clear about why. I guess we'll find out in a few days." He threw his daughter up in the air and fearless, she squealed and wiggled her legs, wanting it again.

Leslie smiled. "I saw your dad," she said, tentatively venturing into quicksand. Logan bit his lower lip and said nothing. "He'd probably like to see you, if you're up that way."

Hana saw all the signs of tension appear in her husband's body and reached out to touch his bare foot with her hand in warning. Looking up at him, she saw his jaw as a hard line through his cheeks and he ground his teeth. "*Tutakina ake, rūruhi,*" he snapped, his voice acerbic. He kissed his daughter's forehead. Come on poo-bum," he said to Phoenix, carting her off towards the bathroom.

Leslie swallowed and let her breath release. Hana's face bore confusion and she cocked her head. "What does that mean?" she asked, making a mess of the words Logan used earlier. She assumed they were words of agreement but the different context made her wonder now.

"It means I'm in the poo!" Leslie hissed.

Hana tried to say it again, remembering Logan's urgent kisses as the words whooshed from between his lips. Leslie rolled her eyes. "*Tutakina ake?*"

"Yeah! It means, ok, doesn't it?"

Leslie shook her head and glanced towards the ensuite bathroom where Logan's black presence seemed to ooze through the partially open doorway. "Na! Ok, means, ok. *Tutakina ake* means shut up!"

Hana's eyes bugged in horror and her jaw dropped open. Thinking she'd exacted a promise from her husband, she allowed his hands to rove over her warm body and take his pleasure. "He told me to *shut up?*" Her cheeks flushed with humiliation and anger.

Logan's unwitting face appeared in the doorway with a naked baby in his arms and Hana heard water sloshing into the sink. Phoenix kept looking behind her and waggling her legs with excitement. Still sore about the mention of Alfred, Logan let fly his poisoned arrow. "Alfred only stopped being my dad because he wanted to. There's nothing in a name or genetics. He knows where I am. I'll be here waiting when he finally decides to get over himself and talk like a man!"

Hana looked down at the picture in her hands and sighed as Logan went to turn the tap off. The frame was worn and tatty, the glass cracked. A Du Rose ancestor stared up at her regally from a sepia brown photograph, his frilly collar and cuffs looking European and expensive. She couldn't see the colour of his eyes because of the sepia, but she sensed they were the same striking grey as her husband's. "I can't believe he told me to shut up," she muttered.

"What did you think he said?" Leslie asked, curious as she stood up to leave.

Hana's instant blush gave her away and Leslie pursed her lips and raised her hand. "I don't think I need that image, if it's all good with you. Thanks for lending me the baby, she was a good distraction for us both."

"No, thanks for taking her," Hana answered, pushing herself to her feet and laying the frame with the others. "It gave us a chance to..." She bit her lip and looked cross.

"A chance to *tutakina ake?*" Leslie's full brown lips spread into a grin. "I need to remember that name for it."

Hana pushed her arm and gave her a hug. "It'll be ok, don't worry. Logan feels like Alfred's rejected him and it's easy to see why. They'll have to sort it out between them, but they will, I feel sure of it. They both need each other."

Leslie nodded and turned to leave, smirking as Logan's angry shout issued from the ensuite, covering the noise of Phoenix's happy singing. "I can hear you whispering about me!" He sounded snarky.

Leslie giggled and patted Hana on the shoulder, offering an encouraging jerk of her head. Hana tossed her red hair over her shoulder. "Logan?" she said, letting her annoyance leach into her tone. "Just *tutakina ake.*" She heard his low chuckle cross the distance between them and scowled.

Logan took Phoenix downstairs for dinner, demanding Hana came too. "You haven't eaten properly all day!" he said, sounding worried. "We're a family, so get your ass downstairs and act like part of one!"

Chastened, Hana pulled her slippers on and hung her head. Logan's strong fingers pulled her chin up to face him and she saw the fear in his eyes. "You need to tell the doctor tomorrow, in case something's not right." His face looked pinched and drawn.

"Fine!" she snapped. "Now *tutakina ake!*"

Logan smirked and he slapped her backside. "No, you shut up!" he smirked. "I'll have to watch myself from now on," he conceded.

They opted not to go to the formal restaurant, but hung out in the family one next to the kitchen. A roaring fire made the room cosy and surrounded them with a sense of wellbeing. Phoenix's sat in her high chair and messed around with her own cutlery, without Hana feeling self-conscious about the presence of a joyful but noisy baby among the paying guests. Phoenix beamed whilst trying to chew a pea between her new front teeth. It kept slipping in and out and entertained her for ages until she dropped it in her jumper somewhere and spent the next five minutes looking for it.

Logan polished off a hearty looking homemade steak and cheese pie with roasted veggies, while Hana pushed a pile of macaroni cheese around her plate as though sweeping the stable yard. When Logan went through to get dessert, she managed to palm some of it off on the baby, whose eyes were huge and round with delight at the tubes of pasta and dripping cheese sauce. "Saw that!" Logan said, sounding annoyed as he returned unnoticed. In his hands were two bowls of Leslie's special dish; cream and yoghurt whisked up with marshmallows with other sweets and lollies buried inside it.

"I'm just not hungry," Hana said, angry he had made her jump and feeling guilty. "Now look what you did!" Phoenix's next mouthful subsequently missed and splattered her tray and she used her tiny fingers to pick it up, piece by piece.

"Oh, sorry," he looked concerned, his grey eyes dulling to the colour of grit. Unsettled, Logan put his spoon into the dessert and whirled it around a long while. "I've been thinking about Alan," he said eventually, his voice laden with sadness. "Do you think someone from school could have pushed him?"

Hana snorted. "At the risk of sounding cruel, there are generations of boys and staff who would probably have liked to!"

Logan fixed his intense gaze on Hana and she felt the sadness radiating out of him. "Sorry, that was unkind. I don't know, Loge. Leave it to the cops."

"Ooh!" Phoenix squawked and her parents turned to look. The baby put her head on one side and sneezed and the errant pea shot out of her nose and landed in Logan's desert.

"Ugh!" He pulled a face and laid his spoon down. "We should probably take more notice of where she's actually putting her dinner."

"Could we take some of that stuff back upstairs with us?" Hana asked, pointing at the sickly sweet mixture in his dish. Phoenix leaned across towards Hana while her back was turned, digging into her mother's bowl with her special little spoon. Pleasure radiated out of her and the tiny dextrous hands pushed it in fast without wasting a drop.

"Why?" Logan asked.

"I'd like to do some research. I've got a bit of an idea and I want to see if it's feasible."

Logan didn't answer straight away but his eyes lit up and he shot a look at his daughter. "Will it be noisy?" he asked with a smirk. He glanced at his bowl, deliberately filtering out the green pea in his mind's eye.

Hana bit her lip. "Oh, no, I didn't mean...never mind. I just meant I don't want to stay down here so can you finish dessert in our room? I want to go upstairs and look in the boxes a bit more." She pushed the point a little further. "I know it's *tapu* and really precious. I could see Leslie wasn't happy with me touching it, but I want to take some of it back to Hamilton with us."

"It's not *tapu*," Logan said, licking his lips, disappointment souring his expression as his evening of cream filled debauchery slipped away. "*I* wouldn't have touched it if it was."

Hana looked confused, feeling the cultural divide yawn open between them with her lack of understanding. Logan sensed her withdrawal. "What's wrong?"

Hana sat back in her chair and sighed. "I'll always be an outsider. I never know what you're saying when you speak Māori or French. I don't know *ok* from *shut up* and I don't understand how *tapu* works." Hana felt the alienated from his world as though she had married into it by default and could be ejected at any point. Instead, she turned her attention to the baby, engrossing herself in something she could understand.

Logan turned sideways, pushing his bowl away and reaching for her hand, holding tightly onto it and not letting her pull away. "These things are *taonga* - family treasures passed down the generations. They accumulate *mana* as they pass through the family. Some of the items could have been declared *tapu* at some point, especially if they were associated with birth, death or burial and we can't possibly know that now. Things which were useful can also have increased *mana* and importance. The *mere pounamu* would've gained a lot. But the *kaumātua* blessed it before he handed it over, Hana. He wouldn't deliberately put us in danger. It's his job to know all that stuff."

"What sort of danger are you talking about?" Hana asked, honing in on the one-liner.

"Oh I don't know," Logan replied, making his answer sound casual and instantly regretting his slip of the tongue. "Mythological stuff I guess. *Tikanga ā-iwi* - customs of my people." He translated the native word for her and Hana sensed him making an effort to explain.

Still she looked at him, studying his strong, striking features. He was lying to her. She raised her eyebrow in question and saw Logan squirm. "It's just stories, ok!" he bit crossly. "My grandfather allegedly took something that didn't belong to him – I don't know what it was, so don't ask me. But he died not long afterwards because whatever it was, it was *tapu*. And look how it's gone from then on in. We're a great family aren't we? *Not!*"

"Are you saying, you think the family is cursed?" Hana asked and Logan bridled.

"No! Don't be ridiculous!" He denied far too emphatically, clearing up the dishes and carrying them next door. When he didn't return, she realised he had slipped through the kitchen door without her noticing and felt annoyance bud in her heart.

Leslie popped her head through the archway, bearing a plate of dinner for herself. "I just gotta eat this quick," she announced. "There's a party of twenty due soon." She glanced at Hana's thunderous face. "What's up with youse?"

Hana sighed and pushed more dessert into Phoenix's rounded cheeks, hearing the small groan of satiation. "I asked Logan if he thought the family was cursed and he flipped out and left."

Leslie looked nervous and lowered her voice, glancing back through the archway where the women raced around with platters of food. "We don't talk about *that!*" she hissed.

"So it's true?" Hana sat forward in her chair. "If you don't tell me, I'll have to ask him again and there'll be blood on the walls! Probably mine."

Leslie gave a moan and looked at her plate of food as though it had turned to ash. "Don't ask Mr Du Rose again," she advised. "I'll tell you what I know. Phoenix Du Rose...*the original one*," she added as the baby looked at her and smiled, "married a complete waste of oxygen. He was a gambler and a drunk. She didn't have much choice because the marriage was arranged by her father. He was *rangatira,* a tribal chief and wanted to reunite the two disagreeing halves of his wife's family. After the marriage, Phoenix's husband thought he would rule the roost, but Henri Du Rose bit off more than he could swallow and his wife was a strong woman. She had *mana* and he didn't, so nobody listened to him and he grew bitter. Phoenix's father was sore about the union after and made no secret of the fact.

"When the *rangatira* died, objects were buried with him, *tapu* things meant to go in the ground with him. Something went missing during the *tangihanga*. Nobody knew where it was and it caused a big upset at the *urupa* when it was discovered missing just before the body was interred. Nobody would admit to being stupid enough to touch a sacred object and anger the god, *Atua*. The thing never turned up again but Henri Du Rose was accused by Phoenix's sister. Phoenix just stood there with her face like concrete, staring at the grave while they lay her father in the earth. I was a child but I remember my father talking about it. Alfred was not much older than me, but Reuben was a tiny wee thing, bein' carried on his mama's hip."

"So, what was stolen?" Hana asked, watching her daughter's head droop forward as she dozed.

"Nobody remembers anymore." Leslie stabbed at a tube of pasta and shook her head. "But Henri was dead before six months passed and everyone knew why. My parents took me to his *tangihanga* and it was bad day. It was like the whole township was stunned by the weight of it. Phoenix Du Rose carried Reuben on her hip the whole time, his big grey eyes taking it all in. Alfred says he doesn't remember but he does. There were whispers Henri brought a curse on the family and for a while, local men avoided the mountain. Phoenix ran the farm herself with her boys and she turned it right around. She was a hard woman and she made herself the biggest employer in the area. She got workers from Auckland and Hamilton at first

- fair wiped the grin off township faces when they came begging for work in the hard times."

Hana waited while Leslie chewed and swallowed, her mind running through images of a grey eyed woman barking orders at burly men. People said Logan was like her with his no-nonsense approach and the way he engendered loyalty and respect. He had *mana*.

"When he was a tiny boy, Reuben got real sick. He started bleeding and it wouldn't stop. People said he had a bleeding curse and it would kill him. It never did. He learned to live with it, although many times he looked like a bull mowed him over; black and blue with cuts always oozing. It never stopped him doing anything, even though sometimes he looked half dead. He had such *mana*, did Mr Reuben; he was pure Phoenix and so handsome. He was cleverer than anyone in this area; I wish you could have met him..." Leslie remembered herself and tailed off, staring across at the snoring child with cream round her rosebud lips. "He would have loved his little *mokopuna*," she said with a catch in her voice, "just like he loved her daddy more than life itself."

"I did meet Reuben," Hana said, her voice little more than a whisper. "A few days before he died, he appeared in Logan's room. He spoke to me and touched my stomach. I knew straight away who he was – the banished uncle. I felt this incredible draw towards him and sensed he was Logan's father; my husband is a carbon copy of him. Phoenix moved in my belly like she was doing a flip. I think she knew too."

Leslie put her cutlery down on her plate, her jaw slack and her eyes lighting in amazement. "He passed his *mana* on to her, through you!" she whispered and put her hand over her mouth. "He bequeathed the essence of himself and his mother." She pointed a shaking hand at the little girl, whose almond shaped grey eyes flickered under her closed lids. Leslie's awe caused Hana to panic.

"No," she said, shaking her head in denial. "He said he just wanted to meet me. It was during all that mess over the land so he was probably looking for Logan. I don't believe this family's cursed or that he passed his *mana* onto Phoe. It's superstitious rubbish!" Hana stood and pulled Phoenix from the high chair, almost forgetting in her haste to undo the buckles holding her in.

"It's what we believe!" Leslie said, the offence clouding her face. Hana realised her error, rejecting something simply because she didn't understand. Her faith demanded that anything not issuing from God was dangerous opposition and her senses told her to dismiss it and run. Superstition and talk of curses whilst possibly in existence, were definitely not the hand of her God. It confused and frightened her and she recognised Logan's fumbled attempt to spare her such conflicts, by opting to end the discussion.

Leslie stood up as Hana hoisted the baby over her shoulder and instinctively, Hana knew she was doing the 'ignorant European' thing. Her position in the family was tenuous at best and her behaviour was ill-bred and insular. With a gargantuan effort, Hana turned to Leslie and forced herself to meet the indignant brown eyes. "I'm not sure how I feel about the whole 'curse' thing," she conceded. "But my father prayed over most of this property when he visited and blessed it. That's what he does, he 'prayer walks.' The bible tells me no curse can withstand the prayers of the righteous and I refuse to cohabit with the remnants of evil. Maybe there was a curse here, but it's not here now. The heart attack should have killed me, I know that and my mother died of the same thing. But only a few hours before, my father anointed me with oil and prayed against my fears of this place. I know God kept me that day, despite my body's betrayal." The fingers of Hana's right left hand strayed to the wound under her shirt and she met Leslie's eyes. "I don't know why God kept me alive, but I know he did."

Leslie nodded and her face had an essence of victory in the soft expression. "We both believe in the supernatural, Hana. Just different versions of it."

Hana bit the inside of her bottom lip and left the room, leaning back against the closed door. She understood the darkness and sense of doom hanging over Logan, with sudden clarity. If Reuben's blood disease were perceived as punishment for Henri Du Rose's guilt, Logan's would be also, even though haemophilia was passed through mothers. Hana shook her head at the weight of the burden her husband carried, growing up under the shadow of death. His older brother's death from the disease in his teens had sealed Logan's fate and Hana felt tears prick behind her eyes. "I shouldn't have opened the boxes," she whispered into her child's downy hair. "I bet he thinks the stolen item will be in there; if it ever existed." Hana felt anger at herself burn in her breast. She had trampled on the *whānau's* beliefs without care and would reap the consequences.

Feeling ashamed of herself, Hana walked the maze of hallways to the family room at the back of the building, her steps slow and heavy. As Phoenix napped, Hana lay her on the squashy red leather sofa near the window, plumping cushions around her so she didn't roll off. As isolation surrounded her, Hana curled up on the rug, pulling her legs under her and glancing over her shoulder at the dozing child as she dialled the number on her phone.

Bodie Johal answered on the first ring, surprising his mother with his curt answer. "Sorry," she said, her heart sinking. "Am I disturbing you?"

"Hey Mum, no, not at all," he said, exasperation in his voice. "Amy's bathing Jas. He took that bloody Action Man in with him – the new one Logan sent him and it's got the same problem as the last one now. Every time he tips it upright; it pees out of every joint and hole. Can't you hear him crying?"

"What - *Action Man?* Crying?" Hana asked blankly and Bodie tutted with impatience.

"No! Jas," he laughed.

Hana concentrated on the background noises and heard Jas' hysterical voice in the distance. His little voice wailed something about the 'emergency room' and Amy's raised voice told him, "*No!*"

Hana bit her lip and stifled a snort, wanting to ask her son why he allowed history to repeat itself but tactfully refraining.

"S'up Mum?" Bodie asked, sounding keen to avoid going back to help Amy.

"Nothing," she lied, "I wondered how you all were."

"Same as the last time you saw me," he chortled. "Overworked, underpaid and messing up everything I touch."

"Don't say that," Hana soothed, dropping into mummy-mode. "You're doing great."

"Yeah, about that, Mum. Izzie ripped my head off after that Skype call we had. She said I acted selfish and I figure she was right. It's what I drove up to tell you, amongst other things. I never got the chance to apologise, so for what it's worth, I'm sorry."

Hana felt warmth towards her son returning and Bodie regaled her with a few minutes of aimless chat. The conversation turned to the school and Hana admitted she felt reluctant to go back. "Even the thought of the tiny staff unit depresses me," she confessed. "I used to love the school and now it's like a prison."

"Yeah, I can imagine," Bodie sympathised. He paused and then delivered his newest snippet of police information. "Hey, Alan Dobbs was definitely murdered," he said, swearing as he heard Hana's sharp intake of breath. "Sorry, I did it again, didn't I? Are you ok?"

"I'm just a bit shocked. I mean, you mentioned it might be but I don't think I expected it to be anything more than an unfortunate accident. That's awful. And I guess it means there's a killer running around the school too."

"It does. Don't repeat this to anyone, Mum, but it was way more than just a fall downstairs. The call Dobbs got asking him to go and turn off the alarms, didn't come from the alarm company. It came from a throwaway sim card which isn't traceable. The phone provider says it was a 'pay as you go' sim and they can't track it. They say it's been destroyed. The original call bounced off an aerial near the school grounds though so someone made the call and intended to lure him there. The security camera pictures are rubbish and only show grey lines and shadowy people, which is typical of a budget system!"

"Poor Logan," Hana said softly. "He'll be devastated."

"Seriously? He actually liked the guy?" Bodie snorted. "Only person on earth who did then!"

"Oh, he well got on with Alan Dobbs. Apparently they went hunting and fishing together when Logan first arrived in Hamilton. Logan thought he was awesome. I'm sure he's been to the house for dinner with Dobbs' wife too and he was always defending him. It's just the rest of us who were terrified of his temper." She shuddered at the memory of Alan's purple face yelling at her.

"That's interesting," Bodie mused. "I might pop over and have a chat to him when you get back. Maybe he knows something about the man nobody else would. All I can find are people who're glad he's dead, apart from his poor wife. She seems broken."

"That's sad," Hana said. "Being widowed sucks! I might bake something and take it to her."

"When are you back then? I'll take a background statement from Logan."

"He won't tell you anything," Hana said, regretting the sentence the moment it was out of her mouth. Bodie's silence spoke for itself and Hana sighed. "I meant he's good at keeping confidences. If Dobbs shared something with Logan which he didn't want anyone else to know, Logan won't tell you."

"If it potentially solves a murder, he won't have any choice!" Bodie bristled and Hana foresaw even more trouble in her little family. She felt a tug on her hair and looking around, found Phoenix wide awake and looking at her. The little girl kicked her legs and put her thumb in her mouth again, looking up at the ceiling.

"Mum," Bodie said, sensing Hana distraction. "Someone sent Dobbs hate mail. Can you think who that might be?"

Hana stifled a snort. "It could have been anyone, Bo. I fell out with him over a tennis trophy which accidentally had the wrong name on it and he hardly spoke to me with any degree of civility a decade later! Dobbs was completely unreasonable in every facet of his working life. The man was terrifying when he was angry, even when it was over *nothing*. Maybe I should be a suspect too," she added facetiously. "Only I would have done it years ago and spared a few more other people their nervous ticks and breakdowns."

"Mum!" Bodie admonished her. "What happened to forgiveness? That was hundreds of years ago! Way to hold a grudge; I'm telling Marcus you're being a bad Christian."

"Do it!" Hana said, reaching back and stroking her baby's arm. "And it was about ten years ago actually, not hundreds. It happened just before your dad died."

Bodie snorted. "Still a long time to hold onto it, Mum."

"He never gave me any reason to *stop* holding onto it," Hana retorted huffily. "You're right though, I should have forgiven him and it's too late now, so that's on me. But you went to the school for five years; you must remember how hard he was on everyone. You can't have forgotten the detentions he gave you and Marcus for the stunt you pulled with that whoopee cushion! You were picking up litter for the best part of a year, weren't you?"

Distracted, Bodie laughed. "Oh yeah! I forgot about that. How he didn't notice the cushion, I'll never understand. Oh that's right, Marcus hid it under the tasselled cushion on the throne in the Great Hall. When Angus stepped back off the podium all dressed up in his robes and sat down, it went off like a diarrhoea explosion." Hana heard him snorting and degenerating into schoolboy humour as he recalled the moment. "The microphone was still on because Dobbs was about to start ranting about litter and Angus sat down and let out this ripper of a fart. It was stunning – the whole assembly hall was dead silent apart from the sound of Marcus crying with laughter. Oh crap! Oh my goodness..."

Every time Bodie got control, he remembered some other part of the memory and spluttered again. Hana pulled faces at her daughter and shook her head. "I don't remember any humour attached to that particularly humiliating visit to his office."

"Thanks for reminding me of that," Bodie said, his voice wavering with mirth. "I needed a laugh. I wonder if Marcus remembers. I might ask him. We were in such trouble; we sat in Dobbs' office knowing we were about to get it so bad and all Marcus could say was, "Sorry I blew it up too much.""

"You were a pair of idiots!" Hana remarked. "If you're going to pull a stunt like that, you don't write your name on the evidence in black marker pen!"

That set Bodie off again, remembering his horror as Angus lifted the offending whoopee cushion up between finger and thumb in front of fifty staff and six hundred stunned boys and read the name carefully written around its bright red edges. "Marcus Hauser".

"Why did he write his name on it?" Hana asked and she heard Bodie snort and blow his nose.

"His mother made him name everything!"

Hana laughed into the telephone connection, almost 100km apart but enjoying a shared memory from a decade ago. Phoenix watched her mother with amusement, her little mouth smiling on either side of her thumb.

Hana was caught out by the door opening and Logan strode in. She was in the process of wiping her eyes with her hand and Logan's brow knitted in concern. "What's going on?" His presence filled the room with dark foreboding, sucking the laughter from Hana's lungs and dampening her lightened atmosphere.

"I should go," Hana said and rang off quickly as Logan studied her, his muscular body dominating the room.

"What is it?" he asked.

Hana suffered a dreadful dilemma, having to explain how his friend had definitely been murdered, whilst stifling snorts and giggles. Logan looked at her with an odd expression and it made the situation worse. The more pressure Hana felt under to stop laughing and behave with respect, the more her brain wandered to the image of Angus, sitting regally on a farty cushion. The look of surprise on his face was priceless, forcing another inappropriate snigger from Hana.

"And how is this amusing?" Logan bit and Hana pursed her lips. "A man died, Hana! It's hardly funny!"

"No, it's not," Hana conceded. "But you wouldn't understand what was, so I shan't even bother trying, especially seeing as you're so determined to suck the life out of everything lately!" She snatched up her baby and stalked from the room. Too late, she remembered Bodie asking her not to tell anyone and it made her wince. But Logan wasn't anybody. Surely Bo would understand that she would tell *him*.

Something nagged at the back of Hana's brain all evening. Her recollections of the trophy incident dislodged some other little detail in her mind and she scratched around for it. "What was the name of the boy?" she mused. "Who won the silly trophy in the first place?" She saw his adolescent face swim across her inner vision but his name wouldn't come, drifting out of reach like a trail of shifting fog. It wasn't until she crawled into bed exhausted that it unexpectedly crashed into her memory, like a coin making the satisfying clunk in a vending machine and releasing the chocolate bar. *Lachie Dobbs*. That was it. No, that wasn't right. *Lachie* something else, surely. The vending machine only released half the chocolate bar, but Hana slipped into slumber, confident the rest was imminent.

The hospital appointment the next day went well. Hana was healing well and the doctor was pleased, transferring her future appointments to the Waikato Hospital, as promised. Logan took her up the Sky Tower for lunch in the revolving restaurant and Phoenix spent the whole time pointing out of the window confused. "Dah!" she exclaimed, fixing on a landmark but as the view changed, she pulled a bemused face and held her hands out palm up, as though saying, "What the heck's going on?"

"You're so entertaining, baby." Hana smiled and stroked her soft cheek. "Eat your bread."

"Hey, I'm sorry about yesterday," Logan said, running his hand through his hair and waiting until Hana gave him eye contact. "I don't mean to suck the life out of everything."

"Will you tell me what's wrong?" Hana asked, handing Phoenix another piece of bread roll.

"I wish I knew," Logan replied, watching the changing view through the glass. The reflection of the winter son reflected on his grey irises and his face screwed up in pain. "It's everything and nothing. I miss my Mum. I didn't realise how angry I was with Liza until I heard it come spewing out of my mouth. She said my body was mangled and I've got that thought in the back of my mind and I keep seeing you collapsing on the grass every time I close my eyes." Logan wiped the back of his hand across his mouth. "Everything feels like this huge weight on my head. I think it'll be good going back to work and teaching the boys. It'll give me some structure and a direction while I try and sort my head out."

Hana smiled and kept her misgivings hidden. The thought of the tiny unit made the bile rise into her throat but she saw Logan's need and tried to bury her concerns. *It'll be fine*, she told herself.

Logan began moving around the property over the next few days, getting ready to leave and leaving copious instructions with his managers. He went up to the new house with Flick, returning revitalised and filled with excitement. "Flick's done an amazing job," he told Hana. "He's awesome at project management. I kinda hopes he stays on when the house is finished because I've got heaps of projects I can trust him with."

Hana smiled with grace and nodded in all the right places, knowing in her heart she wanted neither the house on the mountain, nor the staff unit in town. As the valuers trooped through her home in the Hakarimata hills she tried not to feel as though life was robbing her once again, nodding at their suggested values and stepping back so Logan took charge.

Liza stayed for a few more days. She actually smiled a little and even held Phoenix, unnerved by the way the child sought out her eyes and stared, as though penetrating her damaged soul. They parted on reasonable terms but Logan refused physical contact with her, fostering the wounds in his heart as he nodded a curt dismissal. Tama stayed with Jack and Alfred in their chalet behind the bunkhouse but asked to return to Hamilton with Hana and Logan. "I wanna see Lucy for a few days before I go to fire brigade training," he said with a twinkle in his eyes. "Can I bunk on your floor for a few days?"

"Please, yes!" Hana exclaimed. "I know I'll be ok but if you're with me for Logan's first few night duties, it'll make me feel happier."

Tama smiled and kissed Hana's forehead. "It's my role in life to make women happy," he joked, ruining the moment. She slapped his arm and he ducked out of range but Hana's heart felt lighter.

She sorted their gear into suitcases in the bedroom and piled it up near the door ready to leave. It felt as though they arrived a few days ago, despite the world of experiences they passed through in the last two weeks. The bulging cardboard boxes lurked forebodingly in the corner of the room and whenever she turned around, Hana felt as though they watched her. "Ridiculous!" she said out loud to herself, giving a fake little laugh as Phoenix snored the morning away in her travel cot, oblivious. "Curses," Hana scoffed, nudging one of the bottom boxes with her toe in demonstration of her disdain. The sharp edge seemed rigid and unbending and Hana rubbed her sore digit. Leslie's words hung over her like a challenge and Hana stared at the boxes, unable to resist the lure of the history sequestered within. With hindsight, she would have done better to leave well alone.

On the pretence of finding the object which clanked deep in the box as she kicked it, Hana poked around in the one already opened, noticing a few interesting pieces of jewellery tumbling from an open wooden box. Logan told her to pick one box to take back to Hamilton, so Hana grunted as she pulled her hand out. "I'll take this one," she said, hefting it towards the bedroom door. It was heavier than she expected and as it came away from the haphazard pile, the box behind began to fall. Balanced one on top of the other, except for this open one, the cardboard sides of the box underneath bent at a horrid angle and Hana jumped out of the way as the top one crashed to the floor.

The chunky wooden frames of photographs spewed onto the rug and Hana bent to right the box and pick them up with a careful touch. Their historical value screamed out at her and she felt fearful for their exceedingly delicate state. As Hana reached for the uppermost one, it completed its fall, taking the rest with it like dominoes. Hana froze, closing her eyes in dismay until the last frame finished its clattering.

The sudden silence was as jarring as the crashes and Hana was almost afraid to look. The glass on one of the pictures looked cracked and she groaned in misery. "Why me?" she wailed. "Oh, no!" She panicked, peering into the bottom of the cardboard, her eyes seeking the precious *pounamu mere* and praying it was still in one piece. It was. "Thank goodness for that," she breathed, stroking her shaking fingers across its hard surface. The foolishness of her panic made her shake her head. "Duh! It's a weapon, you idiot. They'd hardly hit someone over the head with something breakable, would they?" Hana crouched on her knees while her heart rate settled, smelling the musty air from the box, accompanied by the scent of old cardboard. Her eyes caught the edge of a brown box and Hana reached in to give it a careful tug. The *mere* slid to one side as she seized the smallest edge of the wood and brought it into the daylight.

Immediately she recognised the colour and fine lines which identified the wood as swamp kauri. It was beautifully carved, an intricate, delicate pattern almost an exact copy of the tattoo on Logan's shoulder graced the ancient surface. Hana traced the fine lines and swirls of the *koru* with her forefinger and understood. It was the Du Rose *whakapapa,* the distinctive family lineage of twisting unions and births. She was gripped by a sense of fascination and turned the box in her hands, looking for an opening. No catch presented itself although a seam around its entire circumference betrayed its ability to be opened. Hana turned it this way and that, determined not to be beaten by the object. After a good ten minutes of searching, she discovered a tiny hole in the underside, half way along one of the lengthier edges. It was so miniscule she had missed it countless times.

Hana hunted around the bedroom for something to shove into the hole, finding a thin sewing needle. She jammed it into the hole and after a few attempts heard a satisfying click. The box came apart in two halves, fortunately on the bed, as Hana almost dropped it in surprise. She beamed like a child with a coveted toy. "Well, how about that?" It wasn't a box at all, but a book filled with pages of neat, crabbed handwriting in formerly black ink, now faded and light brown in places.

It was bound at the centre near the hinges, but Hana couldn't see how without pulling the two wooden pieces apart and it creaked and groaned enough already. Water had gotten into the wooden housing and much of the thin, wood pulp paper was stained and degraded. The words were English, but it was poor, as though the writer had no formal education and little understanding of the language form. But it was readable still, in those places where time and liquid had not stripped out the writer's secrets. Hana held her breath as she struggled to decipher the words on the first written page. A tiny coiled silver fern was tucked in between the first pages and left its imprint on the surface of the paper. Its edges were crinkled and dried and Hana tried not to disturb it as she carefully turned the page.

She was stunned by the name of the writer. *Phoenix Te Whai*. Surely there couldn't have been another Phoenix in the family. The tiny crabbed date on the next page revealed it was July 1944. "Oh, my goodness. I'm holding the diary of Phoenix Du Rose!" Hana felt at once like a naughty child who finds a chocolate stash in a parent's wardrobe. She knew she should hand it over to Logan and be honest about her discovery, but some irrational, subconscious reasoning told her not to. She wanted to keep it secret, read it and drink in its revelations in peace, savouring the moment without the complications the Du Roses would bring.

But the power of the secret was in its concealment and the owner of the family curse went quietly into Hana's suitcase, tucked underneath her freshly laundered clothing. In the same way Eve handled the forbidden apple and discovered the curse to be not in the taste of the fruit, but what it brought about, Hana Du Rose was to discover likewise.

Logan returned from his tour of the farm happy. "David's awesome," he announced. "He never mentioned he was a good rider and he's already fixed the big truck."

Hana accompanied Logan as he dragged his girls around for one last look. David Allen nodded at Hana and she smiled back. Logan shook the outstretched hand and looked relaxed, confident with leaving. "David's mended the old quad," he said to Hana, turning away before she could react.

"Nice," she said, faking a smile and glaring at the dreaded machine. "He needn't have bothered," she muttered under her breath. The quad seemed to grin at her from between its headlamps and Hana shivered. It reminded her of so many bad memories, falling into the foot well when Michael lost his temper driving downhill last summer and she glared at the metal bodywork, holding it responsible for her premature labour. She hated it on sight, remembering the way it stubbornly refused to start on the dark mountain, leaving her stranded and forced to deliver her baby on the sacred site at the top of the world. Staring at the paintwork brought back the scent of fire to her nostrils and Hana shivered at the vehicle which carried her up to watch Miriam's death.

Logan congratulated David on the quad's unusually contented purr, but when he turned away again, Hana gave the machine a swift kick and wished it nothing but ill. "I hate you!" she hissed at its inert form. Not satisfied with the kick, she bent the wing mirror over at a jaunty angle, surprising herself with her vehemence. Logan noticed but said nothing, knitting his brows and pondering the sub-surface of his pretty wife's look of determination.

"It's good to have you here, mate," Logan told the soldier as they parted ways and David Allen grinned and nodded his head. His blond curls wobbled in the breeze, growing out into a fuzzy white halo.

"I like it with the Du Roses," he answered with a cryptic smile. "I'm fed and housed and left to go about my business with nobody screaming orders or dictating what I should do. I'll work hard for you and I won't need telling twice."

Logan nodded and recognised a man who needed to keep busy to stop his mind running overtime. The mindless tinkering with engines was a welcome distraction from whatever drove him out of the army and half way across the world to escape. "See ya, then," Logan said as the little family turned away.

David watched them leave with a hankering in his heart for what the tall man had. It wasn't the money or the land he would trade for, but the beautiful redhead and the cute child, the sense of family and belonging. He leaned against the corrugated wall and drew in a sigh. Days before, Jack threw him up onto a huge bay Kaimanawa with a grunt and a smirk, waiting for him to fall flat on his face as the horse pawed the ground and wheeled. David steadied his seat and eyeballed the old man. "Too bad!" he mouthed, making sure the deaf stable manager understood. Jack shrugged and turned away, his joke no longer funny.

"Top paddock," Toby yelled at him, opening the gate at the end. "And don't fall off because I'm not stopping!"

Deep into the mountains they rode, to fetch a group of mares due to be sired. David didn't know how to round up or use the loud bull whip, but the other man was instructive and blunt, using him to close gates and bring up the kicking, protesting stragglers with the formidable bulk of his mount.

David laughed out loud into the wind as his horse galloped dangerously downhill, following the herd as though it was the huge gelding who would be covering them. The soldier choked on his own spit as the rushing air gagged him with it. It was exhilarating and he felt the sense of death and pointlessness drop from his shoulders. He whooped into the air, hearing his words stolen from his lips and thrown behind him in the downward run.

There were no bureaucrats pushing toy soldiers around a plastic map in a board room somewhere, decked out in their medals and finery as they tried to decide if this green, plastic soldier should be the one to die today in someone else's futile war. He was no longer cannon fodder for a politician's whims, but a man on a horse going at breakneck speed down a mountainside, fetching a group of mares for a randy old stallion to shag. David felt every movement of the muscular powerhouse beneath him and the horse plugged into his psyche, using his sense of release to gallop harder, faster and further. David Allen's numb heart touched life and broke free, reminding him that for once, he was exactly where he chose to be. The colour streamed back into his cheeks and his life in a powerful rush of unstoppable emotion.

Chapter Sixteen

The boarders were due back on Sunday ready for the new school term and as hostel manager, Logan's presence was required on site. The little family made the trip back to Hamilton with heavy hearts the day before. Even Phoenix was grotty and whinged for most of the journey. Hana screwed her face up. "I don't know what's wrong with her, Loge. The car normally puts her to sleep." She leaned forward and stroked the puckered face next to her, crooning whispered words of comfort.

Logan watched his wife in the rear view mirror as he pressed the code into the keypad at the back gate. His girls were his priority and if Hana even started looking uncomfortable at the staff unit, he fully intended to get her out of there, even if it meant jacking in his job.

Logan pulled over to the side of the small road and went back to open the gate for Tama, who followed behind in his ute. The younger man rolled down his driver's window and nodded to his uncle as he passed, turning into the lane between the staff houses. Logan climbed back into the car and smiled back at Hana. "It's weird with nobody here, isn't it? Pity the boys have to come back."

"If they didn't, it wouldn't be a school, idiot!" Hana shook her head and watched through the window, concentrating on dispelling the misery blossoming in her heart at the sight of the end staff unit coming into view. "I'm glad Tama's here," she said softly. "I forgot he had his own key."

The front door was wide open as Logan parked behind Tama's vehicle, squeezing into the small space allocated to the two bedroom home. Tama stood on the front steps, talking on his mobile phone. He turned away as Logan put the handbrake on and seemed to be arguing with someone. "Oh well, here we are baby. Back to the shoebox." With a huge sigh, Hana climbed out and walked around to the boot. Just being on site made exhaustion wrap itself around her throat. "Can we just get unloaded please guys, before Phoe starts grizzling again?" she called, looking each of the men in turn. Tama ignored her.

"Yup, coming." Logan pressed the button inside the cab to activate the back door and Hana hauled the nearest suitcase towards her.

"No, no!" Tama called with an urgent tone in his voice.

"Hana! Don't be stupid!" Logan arrived next to her, his eyes flashing in irritation. "How is lifting a heavy suitcase gonna help your...thing?" He waved his hand towards her collar bone and Hana bridled.

"I'm not an invalid!" she snapped.

"Yes you are!" Logan smirked. "So behave."

Tama slammed the front door of the unit with a bang and ran down the steps, holding out his hand in front of him. Logan picked up on his angst and put a restraining hand on Hana's arm. "Oh not you as well!" she groaned, glaring at Tama's hurried approach. "I won't break!"

"No, it's not that!" Tama's grey eyes were wide as he sent out a silent appeal to Logan.

"What's going on?" Logan's grip on Hana's arm increased.

Tama bit his bottom lip nervously and looked from one to the other. "Don't freak out!" he urged. "I've called the cops. The front door was already open. Someone's forced it. It's a real mess inside."

Logan made to sidestep Hana but for once, it was Tama who had the cool head and stopped him, barring his way with his body. "I've got a bad feeling about this Loge, I think we all need to stay out until the cops get here."

Logan pushed at the young man's chest, but Tama held his ground, indicating Hana, who sat down on the rear bumper looking pale. Logan stared at him narrowing grey eyes the colour of grit and nodded once. '*Please?*' Tama mouthed.

"Ok." Logan strode over to Hana and wrapped his arms around her. "It's nothing, babe. I'll sort it all out."

Tama relaxed, but it was obvious his aim was to keep Logan out of the unit. Every time his uncle moved, Tama jumped and stationed himself on the tiny front steps.

"The cops will be hours if they come at all," Hana sighed from inside Logan's shirt, the muffling of her voice not hiding her distress. "Burglaries aren't a priority."

Phoenix grizzled in her car seat, wondering where everyone had gone. Tama lifted her out, keeping one eye on the door in case Logan decided to try and get in while he was distracted. Phoenix put a tiny arm around her cousin's neck and snuggled into his shoulder with her bottom lip sticking out, picking up on the seriousness of her trusted adults.

"Walk along and see if the other units are ok," Logan said quietly to Tama, but the young man shook his head and refused.

"I'm staying right here. You just want to look inside and I know it's a really bad idea."

Logan narrowed his eyes, not understanding Tama's determination to keep him out. "This is ridiculous!" he grumbled. "It's freezing out here!"

"Look, just ring Odering...or Bodie, yeah, ring Bodie. Either of them will tell you the same," Tama urged. He pulled out his mobile phone again and looked at the screen, punching keys before lifting it up to his ear. Phoenix made a swipe for it and tipped her face to watch Tama, as though he was a zoo exhibit. "Lucy," Tama said as soon as the call connected to his policewoman girlfriend, "Hey yeah babe, I'm back in Tron. Thing is, our unit's been broken into and trashed. I've dialled 111 but they said to wait. Is anyone coming?" He listened carefully to the disjointed voice issuing from the handset, nodding a couple of times. Phoenix copied him, bouncing her head forwards and back and smiling at her cleverness. Tama disconnected and put the phone back in the front pocket of his tight jeans. "She said definitely stay out," he informed Logan and Hana. "They're actually on their way right now and you can't go in. You'll mess stuff up."

"I didn't think cops came for burglaries anymore," Hana repeated disconsolately. "I know someone who called after a burglary and they gave her a crime number and told her to ring her insurance company. The cops never even attended and two days later she got a letter saying they'd investigated and couldn't solve it." Hana pushed Logan away from her and stood up. "How can they say they've investigated if they never even showed up?" She took a decisive step towards Tama as he blocked the steps. "They're not coming. We might as well go in and try to tidy up. How bad is it?"

"No!" Tama said again, backing up the steps towards the doorway.

"Tama! Move!" Hana snapped. "I'm tired, I'm fed up, I'm in the last place on earth I actually want to be and I need to sit down!"

"Sit there!" Tama said, pointing back at the rear bumper Logan's brows rose in alarm. Something was wrong.

"Dit der!" Phoenix chuntered cutely, pointing her whole arm twice at the bumper of the car and repeating what Tama said.

"Tama? What's really wrong?" Logan cocked his head and took a step forwards. The sound of sirens rent the air as a number of emergency vehicles spun up to the rear gate, lights flashing like a daytime disco. They couldn't get in.

"Tama gate the gate, please?" Logan asked. "The entry button's on your right."

Tama shook his head. "No, Uncle Logan. I won't."

"What the hell's wrong with you?" Logan bridled as his temper came to the fore. The sirens shrilled loudly in the quiet street and Tama stayed on the steps, his legs splayed and the baby caught up in his muscular arms.

Logan gritted his teeth and made no move to go. The sirens didn't cease but the gridlock continued as the men faced each other angrily.

"Oh for goodness sake!" With a huge sigh of exasperation, Hana set off down the road towards the gates, making the turn at the end and walking briskly towards the awful noise.

"What are you playing at?" Logan asked roughly, striding up the steps and getting into Tama's personal space. "You better tell me what's happening right now!"

Tama gulped and bugged his eyes, biting his lip and looking shifty. "Well," he began nervously, "it's just that..."

The first police car roared around the corner and screeched to a sliding stop alongside the Honda, blocking the narrow lane. Two young cops piled out and ran to the front of the unit. "Who called us?" one said, bristling with busy importance.

"Er, me," Tama answered, glancing sideways at Logan.

"Excuse me, sir," the policeman said, indicating with his hand they should get away from the front of the building.

"It's only a bloody burglary!" Logan said, astounded. "You lot a bit bored today or avoiding some paperwork."

"Come aside, sir," the other cop said, moving Logan bodily by the arm. The Māori stared down at the fingers on his forearm and narrowed his eyes. The young policeman smiled and moved his hand, using his body instead to herd Logan. Tama followed Logan, responding to a jerk from the first cop's head.

"Key?" the man asked and Tama dug around in his back pocket and produced his, handing it over. The policeman poked it into the lock and opened the door.

"This is a bit overkill!" Logan exclaimed as another two police cars squealed to a stop behind the first. He glanced at Tama.

"Hey bud, your girlfriend's here. All we need is Hana's son and we'll have the full set."

Lucy shot out of the third car. Without even looking inside the unit, a male police officer opened the boot and began unpacking crime scene equipment. Lucy went up the steps up to the front door and poked her head through the opening, saying something to the officer inside. Turning towards Logan, she asked him, "None of you went in here, did you?"

"No..." Logan sounded bored. "We just got here. It's only a burglary – probably kids or junkies. They might have done the other units as well. All the staff went elsewhere for the holidays. We're first back."

"I know," Lucy commented. "I was here after they found the body of the teacher."

Logan conceded the point with a nod. A quick tour of the site a week ago would have revealed all the staff units were empty. Nobody in their right mind stayed at work in the holidays. "How soon can we get in there and clear up?" Logan asked Lucy's back. She peered through the front door, seeming reluctant to enter. "It's just Hana's been real sick and could probably use a lie down."

Lucy turned and looked at Logan, trying to weigh up if he was serious or not. Tama shot a look of panic at his uniformed girlfriend realisation dawned in her face. "You haven't been in, have you?"

"No!" Logan snapped. "This jerk wouldn't let me! Can we please go in now?" Lucy stepped back and turned to face him. "You won't be in here tonight, Mr Du Rose. You need to find somewhere else to go."

"I don't have time for all this crap!" Logan huffed in exasperation, seeing Hana come back around the corner. Her face was deathly pale and her body language oozed exhaustion. "Look at the state of her," he said to Tama in an undertone. "We've only been back five minutes and she already looks like she should be hospitalised."

"It's gonna be ok, Logan," Tama promised, his eyes wide.

Logan shook his head in concern, knowing how quickly Hana's tiredness could descend and leave her wretched and unable to cope. Sunday would be a busy day for him with the boys returning and he needed her to be strong enough to look after the baby on her own. As he watched, Hana looked over her right shoulder and veered to the side of the lane. She stopped to allow a big vehicle to negotiate the corner between the front of St Bart's and the first of the staff units. An ambulance lumbered slowly into view, two uniformed paramedics in the front seats. They emerged from their vehicle and slammed the heavy doors behind them. "Where's the body?" one of them asked Lucy.

Chapter Seventeen

"Get her away from here." Tama spoke with authority and nodded towards Hana as she sauntered down the small road, winding her way through the emergency vehicles and hurriedly disgorging personnel. Logan looked at him, wondering when on earth the teenager morphed into this powerful figure, so full of *mana* and presence he felt compelled to obey him.

Logan took his daughter from Tama's arms, smiling at her as she tipped forwards into her daddy's muscular embrace. He dug around in his jeans pocket and handed his nephew the Honda keys. "Take care of everything for me?" The scar next to Logan's eye crinkled as he looked at his nephew with hidden cues. "You'll let me know?" Turning, he redirected Hana towards the soccer field and the front doors of the boarding house. She followed his pointed finger with her eyes and pouted crossly.

"I'll tell them where you've gone," Tama said in a low voice, snatching the baby's bag from the boot and slipping the handle over his uncle's hand. Logan nodded.

Phoenix grizzled all the way across the field to St Bart's. Hana wasn't far behind in the complaint stakes. "This is ridiculous.

I don't even *want* to be in this stupid place anyway and now I can't even get a sit down and a cup of tea!"

Logan was quiet. In fact, Logan Du Rose was *too* quiet and Hana modified her tone and took the irritating whiney screech out of her voice, in case he was becoming fed up with her. He unlocked St Bart's front doors and let them swing shut with a hollow clang. Hana followed her husband through the eerily silent building, up to the staff restroom on the first floor. "Wow!" she exclaimed. "This looks so different from before!" The area was spotless, cleaned the first weekend of the holidays after a full upgrade. Brand new kitchen units stood in place of the tired old ones, sporting gentle beige surfaces and smart metal handles. The cooker, fridge and microwave were new, top of the range stainless steel and to Hana's relief, the horrid old carpet was completely gone, replaced by beech-effect laminate. "They got rid of your blood," she commented, scuffing at the new surface with the toe of her shoe. "I hated seeing that there."

Gone were the disgusting, saggy sofas left over from the 1970's and Hana wondered if the awful beds and mattresses from the staff bedrooms had finally found their way to the dump. "Incredible!" she raved, but then her brow knitted. "I thought the boarding house was struggling."

Logan pulled a face and shook his head. "Not anymore. We solved that mystery and it picked up straight away."

"Well, I have to admit, I hadn't realised the impact my business savvy husband could have on a place."

"Yep, we're full now," Logan said without pride, undoing the buttons on his daughter's little jacket. It was a difficult task one handed, not helped by her wanting to look down and see the action of his fingers, putting her head in the way and dribbling on his hand. "It's turning over a decent profit again but needs a tidy up before enrolments for next year start. It was one of the comments at Open Day - that it's a bit tired looking."

The words shabby chic rose uninvited into Hana's brain and she instantly dismissed the chic.

"Flick the water heater on," Logan said over his shoulder at Hana, as she stood aimlessly in front of the sparkling metal sink. She turned the power switch on behind her, hearing the water begin filling up inside.

"It'll take ages to reach boiling point. The cops will be done by then and we can go back to the unit and get something to eat and drink," she grumbled.

"Er...I think they'll be a while." Logan raised his eyebrows at Phoenix and she giggled.

"Fine!" Hana sulked and clattered around with mugs, coffee and tea bags, tutting when the brand new fridge was empty. "We'll have to drink it black," she mused to Logan as he poked his head through the doors of the bedrooms and nodded his approval. "Loge?" Hana said, her voice holding a note of enquiry as she opened and shut the new microwave. It even smelled new. Logan stood still in response, holding Phoenix with a worried look on his face.

Hana was about to ask him if he picked the fittings for the restroom, but something in his face alerted her. "Look, I don't care about the burglary," she reassured him. "I mean, it's horrid and everything but it's not like that's our proper home and we took all the important things with us, didn't we? I suppose if they've wrecked and vandalised, that'll be awful but I've realised there's more important things." Her right hand strayed to the site of the pace maker and Hana's face stilled in thought.

Logan bit his lip and nodded. Phoenix stroked his chin with her fingers and giggled at the feel of his stubble against her soft skin. "I should probably feed her, shouldn't I? We don't have anything solid to give her." Hana held her arms out for her daughter, who instantly made a grizzly, hitching sound in her throat as soon as she saw her mother settle herself in the folds of a plush sofa.

Logan handed Phoenix over a little too quickly in his desire to go back to the unit. "I'll run back and see how they're getting on. I'll be back before the heater finishes boiling and I'll make us both a drink. There'll be some milk somewhere. Will you be ok?" He flicked on the new television in the corner, finding with irritation it hadn't been tuned in properly. "Can you give this a go? It shouldn't be too complicated." With an apologetic smile, he handed his wife the remote control for the television and satellite box. They were still in their respective wrappers and Logan knew full well she probably wouldn't manage it, but she would at least be distracted. He ran down the stairs and out the front doors, pelting across to the staff units, the sound of his cowboy boots changing as he went from the tiled corridor floors to the concrete outside.

In the restroom, his oblivious wife fumbled with the wrapper and struggled to avoid the octopus-reach of her infant. "Phoe!" she chided her daughter, who was suddenly more interested in the rustling plastic than feeding. "This is a waste of time," Hana grumbled. "He knew I wouldn't be able to do it."

Growing impatient, Hana lay the remotes on the sofa with a clatter and closed her eyes. She lay her head back and settled, attempting to block out the fuzzy screen on the other side of the room. Phoenix finally got the hint and resumed what she was supposed to be doing.

Hana woke up half an hour later, coming up through the layers of sleep as though being pulled through a hedge backwards. It wasn't pleasant, but at least it was no longer quite so shocking. She was getting used to it, the exhausted sleep she seemed to pitch into without warning and wake from like a douse of freezing water was tipped over her face. Instinctively Hana's fingers sought the pacemaker, feeling its hard edges under her skin. *Still there. Still silent.* The water heater in the kitchen made hopeful sounds like it might be boiling and Hana looked down at her sleeping daughter in contemplation.

Hana shifted under the weight of the child, switching her to the other breast and tickling her tiny feet to wake her up. Phoenix pulled a grumpy face but latched on, finding every time she dozed off, her mother played with her toes to disturb her or called her name. Eventually the child was full, her head lolling back on her neck and a line of milk dribbling down the side of her face. When Hana tried to rouse her then, the little lips moved automatically in the olive face, but only for a second and then ceased.

Satisfied, Hana laid her on the sofa, making sure she couldn't roll off. She made herself a cup of black tea, pushing the bag around in the mug. "So much for believing you'd be quick, Logan Du Rose," she breathed, loneliness creeping up the back of her neck and infusing her with a sense of abandonment. The day was grey and overcast, although not raining yet with any serious intention. Hana ran her finger down the window and peered at the ground level, wishing she could see what was happening at her house instead of the dark view of the gully. New Zealand winters seemed endless without Christmas to break them up. Hana looked down at her clothing, jeans with ankle boots, a pretty blouse and a cardigan. "I guess at the equivalent month in England, I'd have been sporting a big overcoat and probably a hat and gloves. Maybe it's just perspective," she comforted herself.

The canopy of native trees along the tributary made a pretty backdrop, but it was still suburbia. Hana missed the expansive views from the hotel and the sense of space and openness. "What are we doing here?" she asked herself out loud. Bored, she nosed around the staff bedrooms, approving of the new desks, wardrobes and single beds, but it took only minutes, leaving her just as trapped and stir crazy.

Bodie found her kneeling on the floor in front of the television, struggling to tune it in and failing miserably. Hana smiled at her son and held the remotes out to him. "Tune these for me will you please, babe? I keep seeing channels float past but by the time I press the button to name them, they've gone again in a haze of fuzz. Logan knew I wouldn't be able to do it; he was just keeping me out of the way. I know his game!"

Bodie strode over, his police uniform giving him a smart, capable air as he took the electronics from his mother. "It can't be that hard." He zapped the telly remote once, producing a plain black screen and then pressed a button on the other one.

Instantly the television burst into life with a crystal clear picture. Hana pulled a face and looked back up at her son in disgust. He laughed. "At least you managed to put the batteries into the remotes."

Hana humphed and didn't have the heart to tell him the batteries were already in. Bodie squatted down next to his tiny half-sister and Hana watched him for a moment, feeling tenderness towards him but knowing if she disturbed him, the moment would be over.

Instead, she went back to the kitchen cupboards and tried not to clatter around as she made him coffee. "No milk, sorry," she said with a tired smile as she handed it over. "Is there much clearing up to be done over there? I could use a lie down. I sat on the wrong side of the car and the seat belt has rubbed on this." Hana pulled her blouse aside to show the reddening of the skin over the pacemaker. Bodie bit his lip and tried to keep the cauldron of mixed emotions out of his face. He gently took her hand, pulling it away from her collar bone and righting her blouse with abject care. Then he dropped his bombshell.

"You can't go back there tonight, Mum. It's a crime scene now. Logan's taking you all up to Culver's Cottage. He'll be along in a minute."

Hana tutted. "This is crazy! How bad can it be? There was hardly anything there." She beamed at the thought of going to her house in the Hakarimata Hills and distracted, asked, "Oh, how did the valuations go? I'm ready to look at the figures as soon as you are and agree a fair price."

Bodie bit the inside of his lip and tried not to get frustrated. "They went fine, mum. I've got some figures for you. We can sort that out soon..."

"How's the marketing going for Amy's place?" she interrupted. "Did you decide whether to go to auction or not?"

Bodie nodded, trying not to get diverted from his task, but finding it hard. "Mum, it feels like there's too many obstacles working against us at the moment, with finances and selling Amy's lemon of a property in Claudelands. I seem to spend every spare moment decorating it or mending something terminal."

"Oh," Hana said, instantly curbing her enthusiasm.

"We've got the first 'open home' tomorrow," Bodie said. "And we go to auction in a month's time. I don't think it will sell though..."

"Think positive!" Hana chided him. "It's a gorgeous house and you've done heaps to improve it recently. It'll be snapped up by someone who wants to restore it or..."

"Mum!" Bodie interjected. "Please listen to me for a minute! In fact, look...sit down here." Bodie steered his mother towards a neatly arranged circle of comfy seats at the far end of the restroom.

"I bet these don't stay in a neat circle for very long," Hana smiled. But the expression slid from her face as Bodie pushed her down into one of the seats and hunkered down, resting his forearms on her knees. She glanced across nervously at Phoenix as she saw a little leg raise up into the air and then sink back down, realising she probably should have changed her nappy before expecting her to sleep. Hana smiled at her son with maternal encouragement, hoping he hurried up with whatever it was he wanted to say.

"A guy's lying on the floor of your unit with his head bashed in, Mum. Tama saw him as he got up the steps and called us. The forensic guys have arrived and will be a while. We can't move him until they've done all their stuff. So that's why you're going up to the other house, initially for tonight, but probably for a few days at least."

Hana's porcelain face lost all colour and her right hand strayed involuntarily to her collarbone, comforted by the presence of the tiny box under her skin. Her heart beat slightly faster than normal, but no dreadful kick was administered to her heart. She withdrew her hand and put it over her son's, smiling down into his concerned face like a lunatic. "I think it's ok," she said with a sigh. "I've had a few shocks now and it hasn't gone off! I need to stop *being-afraid-of-being-afraid* and I'll be fine."

Bodie took a deep breath in, letting it slowly out through his nose like he did when Jas was being a pain. He stood up and looked down on his mother as quick footsteps heralded the arrival of his stepfather.

"Ok?" Logan asked him, as they passed in the centre of the room, one coming in and the other escaping. Bodie shook his head and Logan's eyes widened in his face. "What? Why?"

Bodie jerked his head in the direction of his mother and issued through gritted teeth from under his breath, "*Lost. The. Plot!*" Bodie kept walking briskly towards the stairs; his rubber-soled black work shoes making an odd squelching sound on the laminate flooring. Logan looked nervously at his wife. She sat in an armchair with her hands clasped neatly in her lap, but she looked composed and strong which wasn't what he expected to find. He felt a flash of irritation that Bodie got to her first, but Detective Inspector Odering detained him, wanting details of exactly when they'd pulled up outside the unit.

Logan had plaited Hana's hair at the back of her head for the journey to Hamilton and the front of it escaped, drifting around her face and neck in a sexy haze of red and gold. Logan's eyes softened and his stance relaxed. He touched her lightly on the shoulder. "You all good to go, gorgeous? Odering wants to speak to you, but not today. He said we could go."

Hana sighed and stood up with a look of determination on her face. "Fine," she said softly, "but I'm never going back to that unit."

Logan ran his hands across his face and sighed heavily. "I thought you might say that."

Chapter Eighteen

"Who died?"

"No idea."

"Bodie said we were going up to Culver's Cottage!" Hana complained as Logan swung onto Amy's driveway. Tama cruised in behind them and between the two vehicles, there was no room for anyone else to park.

"Well, Bodie doesn't make the decisions about this family, I do. So stop making problems and get in there."

"You're not telling me anything! Why won't you tell me who died?"

"Because I don't know, Hana. And we're staying here for tonight."

"But..." Hana began again and then wisely looked at her husband's angry face. She would get her own way but might have to wait. She stepped out of the car as Tama opened the door for her, muttering under her breath, "Fine, I'll just wait until you're not looking then," in a bolshie-teenage-sing-song-voice.

Tama smirked over her head at Logan and the other man narrowed his eyes and shook his head, under no illusions whatsoever about what he was up against.

"Oh, nobody's home," Hana said with mock dismay, knocking and then quickly turning away. "What a pity."

Logan produced a key from his jeans pocket and Hana looked thwarted. Tama retrieved the car seat with the sleeping baby from the Honda and stifled a snort at Hana's antics. It was hard not to laugh at her when she was cross. "Hey," he leaned in close to her ear as he passed. "Don't stamp your foot, not unless you want to see Logan blow a gasket!"

Hana glared through narrowed eyes and stuck her tongue out. Tama grinned. In no other area of his life did anyone dare to disobey Logan Du Rose openly, quite so vehemently and with such class.

The house was spotlessly clean but cold and Hana moved around it in misery. An idea occurred to her and caused her face to light up in victory. "We can't stay here!" she exclaimed, putting her hands on her hips. "They've got an 'open home' tomorrow. We'll make the place look untidy. It's not fair on them."

"Hana!" Logan said forcefully to his wife. "Stop this! A guy is dead in our lounge! We have bigger problems."

Hana put her hands over her ears and hummed a tune to herself, not wanting to listen. Awake in her car seat, Phoenix laughed at her mother with glee. She tried to copy but ended up with her little hands on her cheeks instead. She moved her head from side to side and squawked, "Bleh, bleh, bleh," and looked uncannily Hana. Tama stifled a laugh as Logan gave him a warning look. "Avoidance won't work this time, babe," he muttered.

Tama went back outside to fetch the luggage as Hana decided to kick off. He heard her raised voice even with his head in the boot and smiled, shaking his head as there it was - *the stamp*. He decided it was probably safer to hang around outside for a while.

"I want to go home!" Hana demanded, but her protestations fell on deaf ears.

"What, like by yourself, Hana? Miles away from anywhere while I'm busy at work? What happens if you collapse or get sick? Who's going to be there for you? Who's going to be there for my daughter?"

"Tama!" she responded, daring to raise her voice, her eyes flashing and her hair making its final escape from the plait and tumbling around her shoulders.

"That's not fair," Logan retorted. "He's got stuff to do, people to see and he leaves early on Monday. You can't pin him down just because you want to be somewhere else!"

"I'm sorry I'm such a burden for you all!" Self-pity oozed from Hana and angry tears shone in her eyes. "Maybe you should have left me at the damn hotel!"

"I wish I had!" Logan retorted, immediately regretting it. His shoulders slumped and he shook his head, frustration in the set of his jaw.

Phoenix opened her mouth and started to cry, a wide open wail of fear and confusion. With shaking hands, Hana undid the restraint buckles and lifted her daughter out, cuddling her tightly and ignoring her husband. Logan stood by the doorway running his hands through his hair and looking awkward, his cowboy boots shifting on the tiles as he fidgeted.

"Hana..." he started to say, spreading his arms out wide in front of him in a placatory fashion. But she was already through the door into Amy's lounge, shutting it with the heel of her shoe.

Tama poked his head through the kitchen door. "I thought it was probably safe to come back," he smirked. Logan stared through the window into the overgrown front lawn, his face downcast.

"She's right," his sighed to his nephew. "It's not fair on Amy. They desperately want to sell this place and here we are, moving in and messing it up."

"It'll be fine," Tama replied. "We can live out of suitcases and pack up and leave before the 'open home' times. The three of us can put it straight easily enough." He laughed and tried to lighten the mood, "Nobody's as anal about clearing up after themselves as you..." *Not funny*, he realised too late as Logan glared at him. Now was not a good time to mock his uncle's compulsiveness. He beat a hasty retreat with Logan's credit card, visiting the supermarket on Mill Street for some essential food items.

Logan left it a while before braving the onslaught and striding into the lounge with purpose as though nothing was wrong. He put a confidence into his step and stuffed his hands deep into his jeans pockets, completing the air of nonchalance with a low whistle he used to calm the horses.

Hana played with his daughter on the tiny fold-out change mat, smiling at the baby as she rolled around on her back, catching hold of her feet and singing softly to herself. "Let's find you a clean nappy," Hana said in a baby voice, delving around in the bag next to her. The nappy lay on the floor, folded into a neat sealed rhombus. Hana ignored her husband, but her body was tense and rigid as though someone had fixed a metal bar from her head to her knees.

Logan leaned against the mantelpiece in front of the empty grate and observed his wife with an intense stare. He knew she hated it. Hana slammed the bag down onto the floor and got up, smiling at her baby. "Be a good girl while I nip to the car for a clean nappy."

Phoenix sighed and slotted her big toe between her lips, indulging in some alternative thumb sucking. Hana walked past Logan, so close he felt the air move around him. She knew he couldn't follow her and leave the child alone on the floor. Logan looked down at the perfectly formed creature on the mat, her creamy olive skin and cute fluffiness making her seem angelic. She swapped the toe for a thumb and stared around her with interest, her grey eyes missing nothing.

Hana returned with the car keys and a nappy, unfolding it ready to slip onto the baby's clean bottom as she walked wordlessly past her husband. "Hana stop! I can't stand this!" He seized the tops of her arms, halting her sassy saunter past him, his eyes widening in surprise when she made it into a wrestling match she surely couldn't win. Hana found herself tipping over backwards as she forgot to move her feet and Logan took her weight, banging his elbows into the door behind her. She squeaked as their feet tangled and she heard the sound of her husband's watch clank against the wood in his struggle to keep them upright. Logan's face was close to hers and she was also trapped. "*Get off me!*" she hissed.

Logan's grey irises shone, pale and smoky, his pupils standing out black and huge in contrast. His grip on her upper arms was painful and Hana's irritation soared. "Get off or I'll kick you!" she threatened, glancing down at his vulnerable shins.

Logan's voice was soft. "But then you'll bruise me so badly, you'll feel guilty for weeks while it heals."

Hana's eyes flashed in anger at the truth, Logan's haemophilia owning the ability to extend both their punishments indefinitely. She was dismayed to see the smirk play across her husband's lips as he read her mind. Temper flashed through her breast like a hot poker, invigorating her and offering renewed strength through righteous indignation. But it still wasn't enough to best Logan. He kept a firm hold on her upper arms so she couldn't hit him and settled his lips on hers, feeling the breath go out of her.

Hana Du Rose detested her body for always responding to his, letting her down even when she tried so hard to resist. With a flash of smug satisfaction, she kissed Logan back, letting his tongue enter her mouth and feeling his tenuous hold on self-control waver as he let go of her arms and pushed his hands under her shirt. Hana bit his bottom lip and heard the hiss of desire as the tempo increased and Logan's breath came in short pants. The baby squeaked on the mat and laughed at something unseen as her father got very much into his stride, until her mother called time on it. "I don't think so," Hana whispered. "You wished you left me at the hotel and that's not nice, is it?" Her eyes were teasing as she pulled away with a last, teasing kiss.

Logan groaned and his eyes pleaded as Jas burst in through the lounge door, whacking it against Logan's cowboy boot with surprising force. Logan fixed a ruffled, uncomfortable face on his wife and wasn't his usual jovial self with the child who demanded to be picked up. "Hooray!" Jas yelled, making Phoenix jump. "Now we're all together like a fambly! One big, happy fambly!"

Hana smiled to herself serenely as she fixed the nappy onto the baby, enjoying the small sense of revenge. Logan looked across the room at her with longing, the passion still cooling in his eyes. She felt at the same time, cruel and victorious – not a wholesome combination.

Amy threw herself down on the sofa, looking tired. "Jas, for goodness sake! Just leave Poppa alone for a minute, please? Let him breathe!"

"Long shift?" Hana asked, deliberately not looking at Logan's pained expression, knowing it wasn't Jas that was bothering him.

Amy nodded without enthusiasm. "I was in the charge room. We've had a busy day. Bodie said you guys were staying here until they finished with your place." As Hana looked up, Amy raised her hand and instantly allayed her fears, "It's absolutely fine. You can stay as long as you need." She hauled herself off the sofa and went out into the hallway. Hana heard her open the airing cupboard door and fossick around inside.

"Leave the bed," Logan called out to her, dangling Jas upside down with one arm wrapped around the boy's waist. "Hana will help me do it later." He looked pointedly at his wife. "Won't you, Hana?"

"In your dreams," she muttered under her breath, enjoying the rare upper hand.

"You're only punishing yourself," he sniped in a low voice and Hana laughed out loud. Actually, she thought she might have a lot of fun at his expense over the next few days. She could get her own back on him for assuming unilateral control of her life and redress the balance a little. Hana sniggered to herself with the thought of driving him insane but the dark look he gave her crossed the room and brought her to her senses. Logan Du Rose had a streak of danger in his soul that was not to be trifled with.

Besides which, Hana knew she was rubbish at holding out on him, especially with sex.

Tama returned from the shop with some staple food items, including some cheats for Phoenix in the shape of baby food jars. She scoffed one of them within minutes, wrinkling her nose at the mush described as beef casserole.

"Sorry, baby," Hana whispered softly as she pushed the stuff between her lips. "You've been a bit spoiled with Leslie's homemade dinners."

Logan and Jas whipped up jacket potatoes with a variety of fillings and Phoenix topped off by tucking into the mash and melted cheese from Hana's plate. Logan was a lot more liberal in the kitchen with Jas than his mother and as the little boy plonked his plate down on the kitchen table and climbed into his chair, Amy spotted the marmite blobs on the top of his potato and rushed off to the toilet to vomit.

When poor Amy finally emerged from the only bathroom, it was to find the rest of the household desperate to go in for differing reasons. Except Tama, who went outside and peed in the bushes. Unfortunately, Jas spotted him through the lounge windows and tore off outside happily to copy. It took great persuasion on Logan's part to dissuade him. "Jas, you can't!" Logan argued.

"But Tama did, I saw him." Jas looked at the young man with a mix of accusation and admiration and Tama smirked.

"Yeah, well nobody took the trouble to house train him." Logan glared sideways at his nephew and then back at the small boy. "It's no ok to pee in bushes, unless your miles away from a toilet."

"I am miles away from a toilet!" Jas argued. "Someone's in ours and school is miles and miles away."

The sound of a distant flush ended the debate and Jas conceded.

"I just want to go to Culver's Cottage!" Hana hissed at her husband. "I want my own space and my own things. I knew it would be like this!"

Logan ran his hands through his hair and ignored her.

Amy went to bed as soon as Jas was bathed and in his room, leaving the Du Roses to sort themselves out. Logan and Hana shared the other double bedroom with Phoenix in an old travel cot from the attic and Tama took up residence on the sofa. "Sorry," Hana apologised to the young man, "this is your last weekend in Hamilton and it's turning into such a disaster."

He soothed her, telling her it was fine and heading to town to meet Lucy. "I'll try and find out some information on the body in the lounge," he promised.

"He'll forget," Logan said grumpily as he lay on the double bed in their room, watching Hana get undressed. "He'll be too busy trying to get into her knickers."

"No he won't!" Hana chastised him in a loud whisper, aware of the thinness of the walls. "Lucy's a Christian so they won't be doing any of that!"

Logan humphed and stretched, muttering something vaguely expletive under his breath. Hana turned around to stop the giggle escaping. She stopped fluffing around in the suitcase and hopped into bed, frantically rubbing at her cold limbs. "This house is freezing!" she hissed. "How do they stand it?"

Logan grunted and Hana rubbed at a splinter in her thumb. Her fingers had brushed over the ridged wooden surface of the diary as she pushed her hand into the suitcase. Phoenix Du Rose Senior pulled at Hana's interest with powerful, clawing hands, inciting a hunger that seemed insatiable.

With her mind elsewhere, Hana snatched the sheets over herself and Logan pounced, pulling her on top of him. He kissed her hard on the mouth and suppressed the little squeak of shock that issued from her. "So where were we?" Logan breathed as he ran his fingers over the soft skin underneath his wife's nightdress and settled them in the space above her hip bone.

"No way," Hana struggled. "These walls are like paper!" She felt Logan's smirk in the darkness as he pushed his face into her hair and placed careful, erotic kisses on her bare neck.

"Then you'll have to be quieter, won't you," he whispered, sensuously peeling her underwear down one-handed.

Hana sighed, already beaten. She exacted her revenge for his earlier dominance in part, but ended up driving herself just as mad as her husband and gave in far quicker than she meant to.

Nobody heard Tama come back because he didn't. Lucy blew him out, working late with Odering and Bodie over at the school. Disappointed, Tama hit the Hamilton nightlife with his old school friend, Gareth, crashing on his university room floor around four in the morning.

Chapter Nineteen

Phoenix was into her crawling in a big way, proving hard to contain as her expertise increased. At Amy's place, the rugged floorboards with random nail heads poking out and the presence of Jas, who crawled around behind her, drove Hana to distraction. By mid-morning on Saturday, she was ready to quit and walk out altogether.

Tama showed up around ten thirty and collapsed width ways across Hana's double bed, where he stayed until after lunch, maintaining he wasn't hung over – just extremely tired.

"You flamin' liar!" she raged at him. "You're boozed up!"

But it was pointless. Tama lay like a dead man, his head sagging off one side of the bed and his feet lolling off the other. Jas used him as a trampoline for a while but got quickly bored when there was no response. Logan shot off to school on foot for an emergency meeting with Angus, joined by a small but available contingent of the board of trustees able to make it at short notice. Item one on the agenda was likely to be - the presence of the body in the staff accommodation.

By lunchtime, the fated 'open home' loomed and help had not arrived. Amy was on shift and Bodie, evidently still tied up at the school site with the dead body. It left Hana completely alone with two small children and a house which got messier by the minute. Hana's endless tasks involved cleaning, putting away valuables, stowing the Du Rose's possessions in the boot of the Honda and trying to make the place presentable enough for potential buyers to traipse through the house. The two excitable children drove her almost mental with their antics and Jas got the baby so wound up, Phoenix didn't sleep at all, offering her mother no relief.

Hana finished loading the last suitcase into the Honda – a mission with the roving children – feeling a tightness in the wound on her collar bone. She touched it gingerly just as the baby squealed so hard with excitement in the hallway, she projectile puked milk and sandwich all over the hall rug. Hana rushed up the stairs just as Jas stood up, looking guilty.

"Oops!" he said. "I was only playing doggies with her on our hands and knees. I thought she liked me chasing her."

"I've had enough now!" Hana snapped. "I just asked you to behave for a little while." She snatched the baby up and changed her, faced then with shampooing the sick stain from the rug. In desperation, she hid the elderly carpet in the garage at the back of the property.

The buoyant, male real estate agent let himself into the kitchen just before one o'clock, full of enthusiasm and bonne homie. "All set are we?" he asked with a patronising air and Hana gritted her teeth as he inspected the house. She listened to his expensive shoes click around the floorboards as he readied himself to show perfect strangers around Amy's house, in the hope they were serious buyers and not just nosy voyeurs. He popped his white-blond head around the kitchen door. "Er...there appears to be a body in the second bedroom," he said, hopping from foot to foot nervously. "I think it might put people off."

"Oh no!" Hana wailed. "Tama!" She raised her eyes to heaven in misery as Phoenix pulled her earring and Jas snorted. "Oh, don't worry. Just sell him as a fixture."

The agent stood outside the Honda with a grizzling Phoenix under one arm and a giggling, spinning Jas gripped in the other. Hana found Tama uncooperative, stumbling bare foot down the hallway and falling down the side steps. With difficulty, she peeled him off the driveway and shoved him in the front of the car and the little children in the back. The agent pointed at something behind her. "You might want to move that out of the way first."

Hana groaned as she discovered Tama's ute still parked behind her. In a temper she snatched the keys from its comatose owner and cranked the elderly gearstick into reverse without care, shooting the ute out onto the street backwards and abandoning it there at a jaunty angle. "Bloody men, I'm sick of the lot of them!" she cursed as the agent shot inside the house and slammed the front door.

The stitches in Hana's chest pulled, tight and painful as she struggled to cope with this latest drama. It seemed so unfair. Every fibre of her being screamed out for her safe place in the Hakarimata Bush, but she knew Logan would be furious if she took off there; besides which, Jas and Tama would still be with her and their juvenile behaviour was one of the problems.

"You probably shouldn't leave my truck there," Tama slurred. "It's not really the look that they're going for; that kind of shabby chic."

"Well, what do you want me to do?" Hana shrieked, alarming him with the hysteria in her voice. "I've done my best. If you don't like it - you move it!" She hurled the keys at him, feeling guilty when they hit him straight in the groin with her appalling underarm. Tama slumped in the passenger seat with a groan and went back to sleep, clutching his crotch.

Hana drove across to the boys' school, determined to seek out her errant husband and son. "Who the hell do they think they are?" she raged. "Leaving me to do everything all by myself. I've just had heart surgery! They knew that."

"Who the hell?" Jas piped up, loving the sentence a little too much and repeating it like a parrot. "Who the hell? Who the hell?"

The back gate to the school site stood wide open but the narrow street to the staff unit was cordoned off by police tape. Hana parked the Honda on the grassy edge of the soccer pitch, realising as she turned in her seat that all her passengers were fast asleep. "Typical!" Exasperated, she stomped off towards her unit.

"Hey, Mum, how you doing?" Bodie called as she got to the police tape. He stared at something intently on the ground before writing on a clipboard. The tape fluttered white and flimsy in the breeze with 'Police-Incident' printed from one end to the other in a navy blue font. "You ok?" her son asked, looking at her frazzled demeanour as she ducked under the tape and got it caught in her hair tie.

"Not really!" Hana snapped, flushing with rising humiliation as she fought with the tape. She yanked her hair tie out and her amber locks tumbled down her back. At that exact moment Logan emerged from a side door of the boarding house looking like he didn't have a care in the world. He sauntered across the lane with his hands deep in his pockets, treating Hana to a wink and one of his lazy smiles.

She felt the angry red mist descend over her eyeballs and heard the vitriol pour from her mouth, as though she were a bystander. Logan stopped dead in the middle of the lane, his eyes widening in shock as she launched. "So, this is how it is then?" she screeched. "You make me stay somewhere I don't want to be, prevent me going home and then abandon me with two small banshees and one big drunken idiot. I get left to clear up for the 'open home' all by myself at a house that isn't even mine and then have to find somewhere to take them all for two hours. Thanks for nothing! I'm not supposed to be lifting and yet that's all I've done all morning. I'm sick of being dictated to! I've managed perfectly well for the last nine years and I refuse to be dumped on *anymore!*"

Hana reached flipping point, not helped by the extra uniformed spectators who poked their heads from various doors and windows around the property. She jabbed a pointed finger first at Bodie and then at her husband. "*You* can go and get your son out of the back of my car and *you* can get your lump of a nephew out of the front! And *both* of you can stick your orders up your..."

Detective Inspector Odering's amused face appeared on the front steps of Hana's unit, quickly followed by the rest of his lanky, smartly suited body. He made no attempt to control his enjoyment at the floor show. Hana's impromptu diatribe ceased and she bit her lip as embarrassment flushed her porcelain complexion. The detective shoved his hands in his trouser pockets and leaned against the doorframe, eager to hear more.

Bodie's eyes lowered in guilt and he muttered a hasty, "Sorry."

But as ever, Logan's face was unreadable. He raised a dark eyebrow in challenge and Hana gulped, backing away from him and sensing his distaste for her childish scene. She caught Odering's eye and played for an audience of one. "Oh, don't worry," she called in a casual sing-song voice and jerked her head towards the grinning detective. "Take as long as you like. I'm never coming back!" Then she turned on her heel and stomped off to her car.

Neither of the men followed her with any intention of retrieving their respective charges. Arriving at the vehicle, it seemed a mean to tip the sleeping Jas and Tama out onto the wet grass and leave them there, much as she wanted to. Instead, Hana gunned the engine and did a full circle. She successfully stripped off a huge arc of precious-first-eleven-soccer-pitch-grass on her heavy tyres and almost wiped out a red Lexus saloon. It pulled out from behind the boarding house, jamming on the brakes and making a dreadful skidding sound as Hana sped by.

The ghostly, familiar face of a woman peered through the windscreen as the car screeched to a halt, her hand half raised in greeting. Ignoring her, Hana headed through the back gate, still consumed by her fury at the selfish men in her life. *How dare they tell her what to do? How dare they leave her to do it all by herself? Who did they think they were?* "One minute I'm too fragile to leave alone and the next, I'm capable of vacuuming, cleaning bathrooms and managing rowdy children. *And* loading heavy bags and people into the car!" she fumed.

Her other companions snored and dribbled and her rant was entirely wasted. It was only as Hana reached the main road west out of Hamilton, she realised why the other driver looked so familiar and a heavy ladle of guilt poured over her heart. "Oh, no!" she groaned. "I almost crashed into Alan Dobbs' wife, Dora."

The children woke as the vehicle reached the coastal town of Raglan. Hana had no idea why she ended up there, but the hour long drive had allowed her to cool off. As she parked up in a small street next to the harbour, she remembered with horror that the doctor hadn't cleared her for driving yet. *Which meant she was uninsured and driving illegally.*

It wasn't the parking of the car which woke its occupants, although it was a pretty shocking display of parallel parking, but the sound of Hana's unrestrained crying. Her tears were full of injustice at the men who regulated and dictated to her and then left her to deal with the consequences alone. Tama reached an unsteady hand towards her. "What's wrong, Ma? What happened?"

Hana's reply was unintelligible, hampered by the wad of tissues in front of her face. Tama attempted to comfort her, but ended up sitting in the passenger seat with Jas crying on one knee and Phoenix on the other. Only Hana knew why she sobbed like an inconsolable child and the others sat and watched with sour faces. Jas put his arm around the baby, who wiped her nose on his sleeve and they all looked accusingly at Hana "What?" she sniffed crossly. "How is it all my fault?"

"Hey, come on, let's all go somewhere for a drink and something to eat. Then we'll all feel a bit more...human." Tama seemed decently apologetic for once and took control of the situation. He led them all to a hotel facing the sea and seated them in a booth by a large, picturesque window. He fetched soft drinks and ordered copious amounts of food, paying at the bar.

"Thanks," Hana sniffed. "That's really generous of you. It can't be cheap."

Tama grimaced and held up Logan's credit card. "I still had this from last night when I nipped out to get some groceries." He held up his pint of cola. "Cheers Uncle Logan."

Jas sat with tears still dappling his cheeks while Hana fed her baby, trying to be surreptitious in the corner. Her eyes were swollen and red and Tama looked genuinely sorry as he wrinkled his nose and contemplated her misery. "Sorry, Ma. I didn't mean to be such a dick," he offered.

"I'm not supposed to drive," Hana whispered across the table, her voice hitching after the painful sobs and her eyes welling up with tears again. "I'm still sick. Logan just left me to it. He knew when the 'open home' was and he still didn't come back. The kids were crawling around driving me mad and I had to clean everywhere again. Oh no!" Hana clapped her hand over her mouth. "I don't think I got the chunks of sick off the wall and the bed was all rumpled where you got off it."

"I know what you can do," Jas said, poking his index finger up his nose. "You can ring Poppa Logan and shout really loud down the phone *'I'm going to knock your bookin' head off!'* That always makes Mummy feel heaps better."

People in the hotel restaurant looked their way as Jas did a talented impression of his mother without volume control engaged. Hana's chest hitched again and she grabbed involuntarily at the pacemaker. Jas crawled onto Tama's knee and as the young man reached out and put his hand over Hana's, Jas added his tiny paw to the pile. "Sokay, Hanny," he said, his face earnest. "Gimme your phone and I'll shout it."

As if on cue, Hana's phone rang out into the quiet restaurant, bleeping from inside the change bag under the table. "Leave it!" she said with force, forbidding Tama or Jas reaching for it.

Especially Jas. "It'll be Logan or Bodie grovelling and I don't want to hear it."

"Naughty Poppa and naughty Daddy," Jas whispered, pushing out his bottom lip and looking grumpy. Hana closed her eyes and felt guilty. Her phone rang again and then when it stopped; Tama's began trilling in his jeans pocket. "Turn them *all* off," Jas insisted. "Then the baddies can't get us."

To Hana's surprise, Tama did as he was told for once.

Without meaning to, the little gang of runaways entered into Jas' imaginary world of covert operations and undercover spy tactics and the child showed his metal as a budding combat operative. He stared around the restaurant making mental notes of who was there, creating an alternate reality in his mind. "That man in the corner with a newspaper is a terrorist," he announced and horrified, Tama took a look at the innocent customer and put his hand over Jas' mouth. "He is!" Jas asserted, biting Tama's finger. "His glasses are strange."

"Oh, my goodness!" Hana hissed. "We don't need this right now."

"I need to pee, quickly," Jas complained. "It's gonna come out on your legs in a minute, Tama."

Hana groaned. Tama held his hand up and shuffled sideways off the bench, taking Jas with him. "I'll go," he sighed, rolling his eyes as Jas made him walk around the room so he could get a better look at the man.

A briefcase at the man's feet held all the possibilities of an incendiary device and Jas wondered if he would get to use his bomb disposal skills. He tried to execute a perfect drop and roll on the way past but Tama, thinking he had stumbled, hauled him up and led him back to the table. Jas sunk further into his alternate reality. "This kid's weird!" Tama complained to Hana back at the table.

She narrowed her eyes and shook her head. "Don't say things like that in front of him," she chastised. Tama smirked.

"Yeah but you didn't disagree, did ya?"

When his fish and chips arrived, Jas managed to drag himself successfully back into the real world for the duration of his chewing. Hana ate a few hot chips, helped out by her daughter who sucked them to death and then squashed them on the plate. The baby's eating habits made Jas feel sick and he gagged a few times. "That's disgusting!" he breathed and stared at the little girl with a screwed up face. If he thought too hard about what she was doing, or watched the long strings of saliva that dangled between her tiny fingers and the golden fried potatoes, it made tears come into his eyes and his food launch dangerously up his gullet. "Baby Phoenix," he said without looking at her, "I'm promoting you to the military police division. Then you can eat by yourself with the prisoners. It can be a sort of torture for them."

"Dah," Phoenix replied obligingly as she squished a chip through the gap between her front teeth.

Jas distracted himself by covertly scrutinising the man in the corner. He was definitely up to something, looking at his watch and appearing shifty. Jas made sure he memorised everything about his fellow customer; his hair, face, clothing and shoes. The little boy even registered the make of his spectacles, which had a tiny 'DG' in the corner of the frames. *Dolce and Gabbana* – Jas knew that. He was so interested in the man that twice, he almost toppled off Tama's knee. Phoenix enjoyed the look on the little boy's face as he pitched precariously forwards and laughed like a drain at him.

Tama was fed up though and eventually plonked him back down on his own seat. "Mate! Pack it in!" He turned to Hana. "What are we going to do now?" he dared to ask, regretting it when her eyes automatically filled with tears. She shrugged, not having thought past parking the car, which was difficult enough. "Want to get a hotel for the night?" Tama suggested and Hana shook her head miserably, not knowing the answer.

"Logan would kill me and then you. Actually, I think he'd kill you first."

The man in the corner table squeezed himself through a gap between the chairs and left. Hana was astounded to see Jas bob his head down into his hoodie and mutter something into the cloth tassels dangling down from the neck. *"Suspect is on the move. Repeat, suspect is on the move."*

Hana sighed with an air of hopelessness as Tama smirked at the child. "I can't decide if he has an overactive imagination or genuinely requires a psychiatrist," she whispered.

Jas watched with beady eyes, concentrating as the man went into a jewellery shop across the street. It wasn't a flashy chain store affair but a local tradesman who made individual one-off pieces, largely influenced by the seaside location. The Māori craftsman specialised in expensive *pounamu* or jade work. As he went across the street, Jas watched intrigued as the man pulled his hoodie up over his stubbly blond hair and a baseball cap further down over his face as a shield. The watcher's interest was almost obsessive, knowing deep in his core that something was about to happen. As the man shot quickly out of the jewellers not five minutes later, Jas leapt to his feet screaming, "*10:31-crime in progress!*" and bolted across the hotel restaurant floor, almost legging up a waitress carrying two bowls of chowder.

Tama looked at Hana in alarm, but she pointed to the baby on her knee and he swore. The young man stumbled from the booth and pelted after Jas, leaving Hana panicking in her seat.

"Jas!" Tama grabbed the little boy's arm as he managed to get out of the hotel door, whipping him around with an angry look on his face.

"No, no! Tama, get him!" Jas yelled. "He's a terrorist!"

At the word terrorist, the whole street went into a panic and emptied as tourists shot into shop doorways and hid. The man from the hotel wrenched open the door of a bright red Ford Sierra across the street, hurling himself into the passenger seat as it screeched to a halt alongside him. He only just got his legs into the vehicle as it took off at speed.

"What are you doing, kid?" Tama yelled at the boy in his grip.

"Shut up! Shut up!" Jas squealed, bouncing on the balls of his feet and closing his eyes, memorising the registration plate of the vehicle. He repeated it over and over, not wanting Tama's chastisement to wipe it from his quick brain. He slapped his hands over his ears and refused to take them off until the cops arrived.

Chapter Twenty

"I know where she went," Bodie sighed with exasperation, turning up the volume on his police radio. With small steps he approached his angry stepfather, trying to listen. Logan grunted and carried on dragging the two seater sofa across the wooden floor by himself, screeching the legs as though the thing was in pain. "Wait up!" Bodie snapped, "I needed to listen to that message."

He knew the tall man was rattled and upset. It seemed like rough justice that he had spent all morning organising somewhere else for his little family to live and when he finally secured the old principal's house on the edge of the grounds, he was yelled at by Hana. "Let's get this sorted out, then I'll deal with *her*," Logan replied gruffly.

Bodie shrugged and lifted the other end of the sofa, carrying it into the lounge of the old house. "The renovations in here are nice, aren't they?" he commented, looking around him in appreciation. "I think you might be staying in it alone though." He cringed when Logan fixed him with a forceful stare.

The older man gritted his teeth and pulled the coffee table straighter with white-knuckled fingers. "You shouldn't have left her to sort out that 'open home' with your kid in tow. It wasn't fair. You have no comprehension how sick she's been; she nearly died - in fact, she did die. You need to wake up, kid."

Bodie bit his lip and turned away, finding Logan's gaze hard to return. Logan sighed. "Where are they?"

Bodie hurled his backside into one of the two sofas and his olive face broke into a grin. "Well..." he began.

The jeweller had run from the shop sporting a cut to the side of his face. His hysterical assistant emerged after him, pouring herself out onto the street in a frenzy of tears which attracted the attention of nearby shop owners. Someone called the local police and they arrived from their station just up the street. The uniformed men were dismissive of Tama and Jas, joined eventually by Hana and the baby. But the little boy was insistent and his information comprehensive. "Write it down," he wailed, adding frustrated tears to the mix. "Quick, write it down before it falls out of my head!"

With no other comprehensive witnesses, they finally took him seriously, accepted his description of the man and his clothing, the registration number of the getaway vehicle and the item about his *Dolce and Gabbana* glasses. They apprehended the robbers on the mountain road between Raglan and Kawhia with surprising ease. The policemen on the scene made a tremendous fuss of Jas, calling him a have-a-go-hero.

"I'm a havaho-hero," he repeated over and over. "You have to buy me stuff now. Havaho-heroes need lots of stuff."

"Yer dad'll get youse a cape and I'm sure you can wear yer undies on the outside of your trousers," Tama joked but Jas wasn't amused.

"You can be satisfied with an ice cream," Hana agreed. "I think your daddy can provide the obligatory stuff." She eyed Tama sideways and he nodded in agreement.

They walked on the beach and shivered through an ice cream, despite the miserable westerly breeze blowing off the Tasman Sea. Then Tama drove the little family back to Hamilton, with Hana safely in the passenger seat and both children fast asleep in the back. Black, iron-rich sand, so familiar on the west coast, littered the floor of the vehicle. "Where do you wanna go?' Tama asked Hana, reaching for her right hand with his left and clasping her fingers in an attempt at solidarity.

"I still don't know," she sighed, gazing at the ridged mountains as they whipped past.

"Why don't you turn your phone on?" Tama suggested.

Hana found four missed call symbols floating around on the screen and a text from Logan. *'Go to the old gatehouse on the edge of the grounds nearest to the Maui Street entrance,'* it said.

"Unbelievable!" Hana started, cranking herself into a fury again. "He didn't even say sorry!" She huffed and puffed in her seat. "Well, I'm not doing what he says!" she postured.

"Yeah, well I'm the one behind the steering wheel fortunately," Tama replied. "So let's just do as we're asked."

"Your loyalties are so skewed!" Hana bit. "Now I wish I hadn't read it to you. I should have guessed you'd take his side. I want to go to Culver's Cottage!"

A traffic police car sat outside the front of The Gatehouse. The name plate on the porch had once been ornate brass but the attack of the elements had reduced it to a verdigris mess of green indents. The driveway was short and the proximity of the house to the front school gates made it undesirable as a residence for anyone who valued their privacy. Tama put the Honda wonkily on the grass verge. "Wow, you're staying in the palace," he commented and blew out a long breath. "Lucky. I always wondered what it would be like to spend a night here."

"Well, you can sleep with Logan then, can't you?" Hana replied rudely.

The house was a beautiful structure and there was talk of the school selling it a few years ago, expecting it would raise a fortune. But nobody wanted a listed building which could only be accessed from inside the school grounds, so the property was withdrawn. One builder had wanted to remove the house entire, but the local council refused permission. The beautiful heritage building became an albatross.

The original garrison school met in the house for the first twenty years of its life and successive principals lived in the huge attic room above the classrooms. As the school grew and St Bart's boarding house was added after the war, the house became the principal's residence until the late nineteen nineties. Angus and his wife, Iris, broke the trend, buying their villa in Gordonton in pursuit of privacy and the house lost its status as a home. In later years it served as an overspill classroom; a unit for children needing extra tuition; a storage facility; a dumping ground for surplus textbooks and lastly, a refugee centre for a displaced family.

Hana looked up at the tired red roof and the ornate verandas stretching around much of the lower and upper storeys. Repainted the previous year by a particularly elderly painter wearing white overalls, he was so doddery the staff expressed concerns about his safety as he tottered around on the scaffolding and laboured up the rickety ladders. A year later his work reflected his skill and the white boards sparkled next to the old fashioned beams, which were a muted green.

"I'll wait here with the kids," Tama offered, while Hana negotiated the finer details of her tempestuous marriage. She shot him a nervous look of thanks, accepting his hug of encouragement and his kiss on the top of her head, grateful for his support.

"Fine, I'll meet with him. But if I don't like what I hear, I'm going up to Culver's Cottage and he can go...he can..." She caught the end of Tama's smirk and felt irritated. *Did nobody ever take her seriously?*

Hana made her way slowly up the front steps, dragging her feet like a naughty child fetching the slipper for a whack. It reminded her of her childhood. The hallway in the vicarage used to stretch out in front of her and it seemed like a mile to the spot under the stairs where her father kept his slippers. She would do 'fairy steps' all the way back, knowing he would justifiably whack her backside hard with it over some misdemeanour. It was pitiful how Logan managed to make her feel like that still, the adult in her rebelling as she lifted her hand to the latch on the front door.

Bodie yanked the door open and startled her. He was still dressed in police uniform, his radio chattering on his breast. He halted when he saw her and his cheeks flushed with guilt. "Hey, sorry about before, Mum. I shouldn't have left Jas with you like that, not with the 'open home' going on. It was a bit of a muck up."

Hana nodded and gave him a faint smile. The parent in her knew she should forgive with more generosity, but the rampant child inside wanted to scream and kick and protest about the injustice of it all.

"I'll get Jas," he concluded as they stood facing each other in an awkward stalemate. The young man found it hard to deal with this new version of his mother, who didn't put up with his abuse of her good nature without fuss. Perhaps it was the heart attack, he realised with a stab of guilt. "Erm...it went good, the 'open home.' One of the viewers is interested in making an offer."

Hana's smile was wooden. "Good. I'm glad for you."

"About Culver's Cottage..." Bodie began, taking one step down.

Hana raised her hand between them. "Not now, Bodie! I don't want to talk about it standing out here."

"Oh, ok. I'll just get the boy then."

Hana took a deep breath and pushed the front door open, stepping across the threshold and hearing her pulse beat in her head. She touched the ridged pacemaker and realised she was holding her breath. The ceilings seemed miles away and the walls and skirting boards were neutral and clean. A room to the right was packed full of text books floor to ceiling, but the other rooms looked clear. Hana trod slowly down the hallway, hearing the noise of someone shifting things around. Furniture scraped against the polished wooden floors. A huge chandelier hung overhead making the walls sparkle and glint with the reflection from its myriad candle bulbs. It was a phenomenal house with so much history in its walls. It was as though the collective whispers of a century and a half of principals and generations of Hamilton's finest wafted over her being.

Logan was in the enormous downstairs classroom. He looked up as his wife peeked in the doorway and stopped hefting the two seater sofa closer towards the wood burner. She didn't notice him as she looked around the room. The furniture from the unit had somehow been transported across the fields and installed in the house. The room was massive and the few items from the unit hung around the centre in a lonely circle. Hana felt the familiar flip-flop in her chest as she sensed her husband's presence and sought him out with her eyes, finding him stood with his hands on the back of the sofa watching her. A flash of anger reared its head and she beat it down as best she could, recognising its irrational origins. "What did you want to see me about?" The question sounded ridiculous but Hana managed to keep her voice level.

Logan watched her for a while, imagining his fingers stroking the soft skin on her cheeks and the feel of her curves under his palms. When he felt ready, he approached her at a casual pace, his eyes never leaving hers. Hana felt her teeth grit involuntarily and her body stiffen. She hadn't decided yet whether to slap him or ignore him. Logan stepped the last few metres boldly up to her; his gaze frighteningly intense.

Reaching out his left hand, he stroked her face, tracing an invisible line around her eyebrow and down under her jaw line. Then he did that thing she loved, pushing his hand around the back of her neck and underneath her hair, gently caressing the back of her head. Hana sighed and closed her eyes, silently rebuking herself for always being such a pushover. She hoped he would kiss her, sorely disappointed when he didn't.

Hana opened her eyes, her green ones locking onto his smoke grey irises. Logan was so close the electricity arced between them, causing almost physical pain. Hana hated him for how much she wanted him to kiss her, touch her, anything. It made anger rise up again - that he could control her as easily as the mares and big stallions on his property, bending their will to his like a magic trick. She balled up her fists and contemplated knocking the satisfaction she saw glimmering in his face, right out of his stupid head.

As she lifted her fist, it was met by the open palm of his hand and quicker than she thought possible, he dipped his body and collected her over his left shoulder. It rendered her angry fists and feet useless in his grasp. "*Frickin' Māori!*" she ranted into his shirt, deliberately trying to enrage him with her racist expression. He laughed and slapped her on a backside that was temptingly close to his face.

"You have no idea how hot you are when you're mad," he snorted. "I wish I could have you to myself for half an hour."

"You'd only need two minutes at most," she sneered, attempting to squash his unbounded ego and Logan laughed and slapped her backside again.

"I wanted to say four hours, but I figured half an hour was modest."

Hana wished she took more notice of Jas when he spent an entire Sunday afternoon trying to explain how to fart-on-demand. That would have wiped the smug look off her infuriating husband's physog. Hana couldn't see the smirk, but sensed it was there.

She saw the wooden stairs passing underneath her from her upside down view; the sides of the treads painted a glossy cream. An ornate banister rail passed quickly by and she heard the heels of Logan's cowboy boots thrumming on the floorboards. He negotiated carefully through a doorframe with the original pale wooden door and then bodily downwards, settling Hana's bottom on a soft surface. She slithered past his neck and saw the duvet cover from the staff unit beneath her. "Welcome to your new bedroom," he whispered, his tone seductive and his breath light on her face.

Hana's anger flared and as her hand came up to slap him, he seized both her arms and pushed her backwards on the bed. Hana tried to bring her knees up against him but Logan was on top of her before she could do anything to stop him, his face inches away from hers. He looked at her lips and then again at her eyes, as though judging his safety. She was pinned to the bed and there was nothing to stop him kissing her, but still he didn't.

Relaxing his grip, Logan reached out a hand and tenderly pushed a lock of stray hair away from Hana's forehead. Her eyes flashed and sparked and it seemed to make him sober a little. "I'm sorry about before. It was crap."

Hana waited for the excuses, disappointed when they didn't come. She would certainly have qualified her apology with a pitiful justification and some heart-rending reason she had ended up in the wrong. *Nothing*. Logan's 'sorry' was exactly that. Hana realised how disarming it was and how infuriating. No debate – *sorry*. In a peculiar way, it made her madder. *She should forgive him. She would forgive him*. "Pig!" she said with vehemence and he laughed and pressed his firm lips over her angry open ones. Hana felt the breath and fight leave her as Logan's tongue began its familiar dance with hers. His hand crept underneath her tee shirt, working its way upwards towards her bra and promised oblivion. "No!" she said, her voice coming in a gasp.

Logan's eyes snapped open and Hana pushed him away. "Tama's outside. I'm not doing this." With reluctance, she pushed her husband's chest to get him off. Frightened by the catch in her throat, he slithered onto the duvet next to her; concern etched in his face. "I'm fine," Hana admonished him, "but the kids are outside waiting for me."

"Ah, the driver and the getaway car. So you weren't planning on staying?" He narrowed his eyes and she felt chastened by his glare. "Angus gave us this place for as long as we need it," he said with warning in his voice. "And I'm not staying here by myself like a loser, so get your ass outside and get my daughter."

Hana thought about disobeying him for the sake of it, but wisely dropped the idea. The house was beautiful and she couldn't wait to explore, feeling the eager anticipation of spending the night here bubbling up inside her. She thought she gave nothing away, disappointed when Logan got up and offered his hand to help her, a look of satisfaction on his face. As she released his hand and passed him, he reached out and ran his finger down the side of her face with seductive precision. "We'll finish this later." His grey eyes flashed as they burrowed into her soul and the scar under his right eye looked white against his olive skin. He kept her paralysed there with the intensity of his look and Hana felt her fire slipping away.

On the way downstairs, Hana manufactured all kinds of rebellious thoughts, formulating all manner of smart retorts or dismissive answers to demonstrate he hadn't won. But he had. It was futile. If Logan gave her 'that look' later, she would give in, she knew it. And she hated him for it. And herself.

Tama sat sideways in the passenger seat, playing a protracted game of 'hidey boo' with Phoenix, who slumped in the back showing all the signs of being bored and fed up. She was positively vitriolic and glared at Hana as her father lifted her out of the car seat. Evidently playtime with cousin Tama was second best to whatever she had missed out on inside. *Little do you know*, Hana thought to herself with a smirk, which Tama saw and correctly interpreted.

'Skank,' he mouthed to her and she looked first surprised and then outraged. "That must have been a very quick quickie," he whispered as they both reached for the baby's bag.

"I'm shocked!" Hana retorted and pushed his rock hard body.

"Bet you were!" Tama snorted and Hana retreated, losing another Du Rose fight.

They trooped around the house, initially exploring together and then separating. It was enormous, far bigger than Culver's Cottage which was big by most people's standards. There were three floors, unusual in the current fear of earthquake damage which made such properties a risk, especially after the crisis in Christchurch which sent architects and councils back to the drawing board. The top floor nestled in the apex of the huge roof and made up one giant room with an integral bathroom and kitchenette. The central floor possessed huge bedrooms, originally decent sized classrooms. At some point, an ensuite was added to each in addition to the enormous bathroom near the stairs.

The bathroom, as big as the average family lounge, was converted from the original toilet cubicles. It had a full sized, claw foot bath, a shower cubicle and a toilet, in addition to a double set of wash basins. Its opulence was stunning for a principal's residence. The stairs from the attic were wide, ornate and majestic, leading down to an open landing below. A beautiful stained glass window graced the split level hallway, glinting in the watery late afternoon sunshine. Downstairs at ground level, the hallway was enormous by the front door with intricate designs in the tiled floor. The stairs swept diagonally across it, splendid enough for a bride to swish down the wooden treads on her wedding day. A narrower corridor ran from front to back with the front door at one end and the back door at the other. Another four huge classrooms came off left and right, one now including the huge kitchen, which had wall to wall cupboards and decent appliances.

"I remember it being renovated," Tama said as Hana walked down the open staircase with him. "I was in Year 11 and helped to make some of the kitchen cupboards in woodwork."

"Really?" she replied. "The bathroom looks quite turn of the century."

"Ah yeah, that is," he admitted. "We just did the kitchen."

Wow!" Hana exclaimed with genuine interest. "That's so cool. I love how they're natural wood. It fits the place really well." She rubbed the young man's arm with encouragement and he pushed his shoulders back with pride.

"Yeah we had to study period methods and make the cupboards exactly in the style of the house. It was surprisingly difficult and very manual."

Hana dragged him off to the kitchen to see if he could identify his craftsmanship and Logan heard her exclaiming with enthusiasm alongside the sound of a cupboard door opening and closing. He looked down at his daughter and raised one eyebrow at her. He smirked when she almost managed to do it back, cuddling her into him and kissing her soft forehead. "You'd better not be as fiery as your mother," he warned her. "I can't cope with the both of ya."

Tama fetched the bags from the Honda and the box of *taonga*, which sat in the hallway by the front door. Then Logan heated up a jar of baby food for Phoenix, while Hana breastfed her on the sofa. Hana seemed happier and Logan was relieved. He sent Tama out in the Honda for hot chips, surprised when the boy refused his cash. "He's still got your credit card," Hana said quietly as Logan watched his nephew reverse the car off the grass outside. "Thanks for lunch, by the way. You paid for it." Logan pulled a face and sat down next to her, massaging Phoenix's little feet with his big hand. "Sorry, I was a bitch before," Hana sighed and Logan shook his head and slipped his arm around her. Phoenix popped her head out of Hana's tee shirt and looked at her daddy with her brows knitted. He reached over with his other hand and resumed the impromptu foot massage.

"We kinda deserved it," he mused, "and it was good actually. The cops must have felt sorry for me because they helped us carry loads of this stuff over. Odering even wheeled a couple of suitcases and bought all the bedding in his car. I think they're all a bit scared of you."

Hana looked sideways at him but couldn't tell if he was joking or not. She didn't think she was that formidable. "Who was the poor man that was murdered?" Hana asked and Logan shifted in his seat in sudden discomfort.

"I've been dreading that particular question," he admitted. "I think you knew him. He was a guy named Lachlan Reynolds. Hana, they found tennis gear in his car and he fitted the description of the mystery guy you played tennis with a few weeks back. Remember?"

"The man only I saw," she sighed, her breath exiting as a loud whoosh. "A million times I wished someone else had seen him and could vindicate me and you'd all know I didn't make him up. Now it's come true but he's dead." Hana kept her hand raised to her mouth and her eyes closed, defying her body to be sick and let her down again. It had done enough of that lately.

"You ok?" Logan asked and Hana exhaled with more control, relieved nothing untoward had happened in her chest.

"Maybe the police got it wrong," she stated with false hope lifting her tone. "I mean, they can't be sure yet, can they?"

"They're certain," Logan answered, watching his wife as her posture deflated like a popped balloon. "He looked exactly like you said, right down to the tennis racquet cover with 'Lachlan' written on it and the ball machine in the boot of his car. He had a key to the tennis courts and to that shed. What they don't know is why the hell he was in our living room with his head bashed in. He bled out a bit onto the flooring, but Angus will get it replaced and…ah, Hana, sorry babe, sorry."

It was far too much information for Hana and Logan gritted his teeth, furious at himself as the first sob broke. "All I can think about is the smiling, handsome young blond man who hero-worshipped me for past glories which nobody else remembered. He made me feel like a superstar and he seemed so innocent." Hana cried into Logan's shirt over her baby's prone body. The young tennis enthusiast had sparred against Hana with deadly accuracy and incredible humility, at a time in her life when she felt most lost. He remembered her from her doubles tennis days with her late husband and tried to persuade her to come out of retirement. Hana stumbled across his practice session by accident and played with him twice in secret. It gave her control in her powerless world. "To think of him dying that way, his life snuffed out like an unwanted candle is just too hateful," she sobbed. Hana handed her daughter roughly to Logan and just made it to the first-floor bathroom, where she threw up in the toilet, christening the house in unforeseen ways.

Hana couldn't eat the chips Tama brought home but laid a little too heartily into the bottle of red wine he had scored on the way. "Steady with that," Logan warned. "You'll get Phoe drunk at her night feed."

Hana glared at him and Logan bit his lips and rolled his eyes at Tama. "Which room do you want?" he asked the young man as they sat eating at the dining table, which was shoved in the centre of the kitchen.

"Can I have the attic?" Tama asked, looking excited. Logan looked across at Hana and nodded when she didn't reply.

"Yeah, that's fine. Move your stuff in."

"I don't have any," Tama said, his mouth full of chips as he pushed even more between his lips. "I slept on the floor at the unit, remember?"

Logan nodded and watched his wife mindlessly pushing baby food into Phoenix's little mouth, obviously struggling not to retch again. Toothpaste and red wine didn't seem like such a good combination. Her brain rebelled as she tried not to think about poor Lachlan Reynolds. Not even when a droplet of red wine on the surface of the pine table made her mind wander to the issue of his spilled blood on the laminate flooring of the staff unit. "You said his head was bashed in?" Hana asked, her voice sounding loud and jarring in the peace.

Logan fixed his eyes on hers and didn't speak until she felt the connection. "Hana, stop it."

She turned away, flustered and pushed another spoon into the baby's mouth, tutting as the little girl shot it straight back out again. "What will you sleep on?" Hana asked, distracting herself from her morbid thoughts.

"Floor. I've got a sleeping bag."

"Don't be an egg!" Logan waved away Tama's insistence. "Na, drive the Honda up to the shopping centre at the top of town before it closes at nine o'clock. "Get one of those flat pack beds – it should go in the car if you put the seats down. Just get what you need, sheets, duvet, stuff like that."

Logan gave Tama a price limit that made his eyes bug in his face. "Gosh, thanks Uncle Logan!"

"Yeah, well maybe you should give me back my credit card afterwards."

Tama looked a little guilty but only for a second. "Damn!" he smirked. Moments later he was gone, pulling out of the school gate on his exciting errand.

Phoenix fell asleep in her dinner and Logan took her upstairs. He wasn't gone long, changing her nappy and putting her in her cot. It looked so incongruous, the gigantic bedroom with only a cot and set of drawers on one wall. Logan arrived back downstairs to find his wife loading the dirty plates into the dishwasher. There were a couple of mouldy cups in it, possibly the discarded product of a sneaky staff visit. She took them out and threw them in the bin. "Hey gorgeous." Logan came up behind her and lifted her long hair, kissing her neck with butterfly movements. Hana groaned and leaned her head back into him. "Come on," he whispered, "let's finish what we started."

"But Tama doesn't have a key," Hana protested, quickly stopped by Logan's lips on hers. She moaned and allowed his fingers access to the catch on her bra, giggling as her swollen breasts tumbled against her tee shirt. Logan's lips were soft on her neck.

"He'll be there until closing time," he whispered. He's got my credit card and sixty-four shops to look round. He'll be like a kindy kid at 'choosing time' – he'll be hours. Come to bed with me." Logan nipped her bottom lip and struggled with the button at the front of her jeans. "Otherwise I'll make you do it here."

"It wouldn't be the first kitchen romp," she snorted, silenced by Logan's fingers and lips.

Logan was eager to restore their relationship to its previous secure footing and stripped off quickly in the dark bedroom, sliding between the covers with a groan at the freezing sheets. "Get over here!" he demanded.

"Be patient!" she chastised him with a smile, closing the floor to ceiling drapes and savouring the expensive weight of the material beneath her fingers. The curtains were a dark grey fabric, matching the growing darkness outside. As Hana swished them shut, she caught sight of Dora Dobbs' car again.

It was over on the other side of the playing fields near to the boarding house. A long way off, the colour was indistinguishable in the dark but instinct told Hana it was the same vehicle she almost crashed into earlier in her temper. She paused for a moment looking at its profile side on, the headlights off but exhaust fumes blowing visibly into the cold air from the running engine. The person inside sat rigidly still, her white face producing a ghoulish effect in the dusk. "I wonder what she's doing," Hana muttered. "Maybe she misses her husband so much she wants to sit there. It's like she's waiting."

Hana squealed as Logan's strong arms gripped her behind the legs, swinging her up into the air in his muscular arms. "Bloody hell, woman!" he complained. "You've punished me enough. Now get in that bed and let me show you how sorry I am." Logan's lips were warm and his fingers rough as he divested Hana of her remaining clothing. He sighed and appreciated her laden breasts and by the time he pulled her over onto his naked body, she was responsive and desperate for him.

Hana had been asleep for an hour by the time Tama arrived home, excited with his wares. He and Logan carried the furniture inside, trying to disturb the girls in the echoing hallway. They assembled the queen sized bed and the chest of drawers with lots of whispered swearing and bickering. Then Logan sat downstairs with Tama watching television, waiting for the cuts on two of his fingers to stop bleeding after the spanner slipped and he sliced them on a bolt. "Sorry about the cuts," Tama said, yawning into his can of beer.

"Yeah," Logan replied, his voice sounding grumpy. "Your laughter conveyed that."

"I wasn't laughing because you hurt yourself! It was the use of all those incredible swear words, all whispered so you didn't wake your scary wife."

"I'm not scared of her!" Logan bridled and Tama shrugged.

The young man fixed his grey eyes on his uncle's face and imparted one of his rare pieces of wisdom. "No, you're not scared *of* her, but you are scared of losing her. You shouldn't be; she adores you. Just don't balls it up and you'll be fine."

"Why, thank you counsellor," Logan responded, a snarky quality to his tone. Tama smiled as he watched his uncle's brain working.

"You don't know what I mean, do you? You don't understand what her limits are."

"Sod off, Tama." Logan peered at the weeping cuts and wrapped them back up in the tea towel.

"I'll tell you anyway." Tama ducked out of range of the fist Logan swung in a haphazard arc.

"I don't need you to analyse my marriage, thanks!"

"Yeah ya do. There's three reasons she'll leave you. If you cheat on her, if you lie to her and if you don't value her."

"Whatever!" Logan's face held warning and Tama shrugged and ceased trying to help. Logan's grey eyes watched the action unfolding on the screen but his mind was elsewhere, considering the mistakes of another man in another time, who subjected Hana to all three.

In the end, they both fell asleep on the sofa and didn't get to try out the new rooms. Tama had his mouth open snoring and his long legs over the arm and Logan had his hand wrapped up in the tea towel and a crick in his neck.

Chapter Twenty-One

Logan crawled into bed at five o'clock the next morning, freezing cold and aching from his unnatural sleep position. The cuts on his fingers had stopped bleeding, but he encased them in plasters to prevent blood going on the sheets in case they were only fooling him. He waited until his body temperature had increased enough to snuggle up to the back of his wife, feeling her warm silky softness under his hands.

For a moment, he thought he heard his baby disturb next door, but the loud click coming through their open doorway indicated she had lost her thumb for a moment. Logan smelled the shampoo in Hana's hair and felt a slight grittiness between his fingers from the beach as he stroked the long tresses stretching over his pillow. Her skin was so warm and peachy and he felt a familiar desperation for her, pushing his hand gently up her nightdress and resting it on her warm thigh. He debated it for a while, eventually falling asleep still wondering if he dared disturb her.

Another hour later and he awoke to her thrashing about in the bed next to him. The sheet between their bodies and the duvet had become a tangled mess and she had worked up to the night terror without him realising. Her forehead was wet and her hair matted with sweat. Daylight approached and Logan knew by Hana's frenzied, staring eyes, she was immersed in a nightmare. "It's ok, babe," he whispered. "I'm sorry, I should have known." He held her tightly, soothing her, kissing her damp forehead and making her feel safe, pinning her thrashing arms and reassuring her all was well. "Hana, you're safe. I'm here."

The dead man in their lounge was easily enough to set her off and Logan was relieved it happened with him sleeping next to her. Often in her terror, she ran. In a strange house, she may have fallen down the stairs. Logan chastised himself for his neglect and allowed it to create a heaviness in his chest.

Hana's first night terror poleaxed her brand new husband. Responding to a memory of her late husband, Vik, Logan was devastated to hear her calling another man's name as she argued in her sleep. Since the kidnapping and injury to her wrist, Hana often work screaming as the memories she bound in the daylight, worked themselves out at night. Sometimes she woke, holding her left wrist so hard her fingers were white and the scar would be aggravated for days afterwards. It could take him hours to sooth her and reassure her that her artery wasn't pumping blood in every direction. Logan stroked Hana's damp hair and counted it a blessing that Phoenix slept so deeply, wondering how he would cope with both of them distressed. Hana's screams once woke Amanda in the unit next door and Logan needed to do some serious explaining the next day, not that he cared overly much what Amanda thought.

But it was the first nightmare since the heart surgery and Logan felt fear descend over his soul. He spoke gentle words of sanity into her troubled sleep as he pressed her body into his so nothing could trespass between them. Eventually, her struggle ceased as she identified his voice and the constancy of his words, filtering through the fences and barriers of her mind as recognition and safety. As the violent hitching in her chest was all that remained, she drifted back into slumber. Logan felt her heart rioting in her slender body, reverberating through his broad chest wall and terrifying him. In time, it slowed, matching the beats of his which were strong and steady.

Hana snuggled hard into him, pushing her face into his chest so her nose turned up like a little pixie, leaving a red line across it. As her breathing steadied and grew heavy and sleep induced, Hana spoke. Her voice was little more than a whisper as she said the most curious words. "Lachie Dobbs' trophy...it wasn't my fault."

There were a number of other mutterings and Logan tried to rouse her and get her to talk but it was no use. Hana buried her face in his downy chest hair and sleep came and snatched the tortured woman away, taking with her the important piece of information her husband suddenly felt certain she knew.

The next morning it was pointless. Hana had no recollection of the nightmare. Logan didn't repeat it for her, not wanting a repeat performance which would leave him exhausted for class on Monday. So he filed it away in his quick brain and left it to marinade.

Logan and Tama drove a tired and unusually quiet Hana up to her church, calling by Amy's to pick up the ute on the way back to town. They found Bodie having a late breakfast with his son and fiancé, being regaled yet again by Jas' tale of extreme heroism in the face of dastardly criminals. The story had become completely unrecognisable, especially with the presence of a Barbie doll, a Ken doll and four Action Men, all acting out the scene on the breakfast table. "No Dad!" the child protested as Bodie reached for the jam. "Put the jewellery shop back on its spot!"

Tama eyed the food longingly and Amy took pity on him, handing him a piece of toast. "Sorry, but the butter dish is the getaway car," she apologised as the young man bit into it dry. Logan declined her kind offer altogether.

"Right then, I'll be ready in a minute." Jas climbed down from the table and clattered down the hallway. "There's another 'open home' and I'm coming with you. Hanny's gonna look after me but I hope she doesn't keep crying like yesterday. That was just silly." His voice petered off as he clumped around in the distance, getting ready.

Bodie looked at Logan who struggled to hide his irritation. He shook his head, angered at the couple's presumption they could dump their son on his wife without notice or permission. "Not today," he said in an acid tone, looking them both in the eye simultaneously. "Hana's not up to it. Yesterday was too much for her and she had a rotten night. She's gone to church and then I'm taking her for lunch."

"We've got another 'open home' today," Bodie began, trying to guilt his stepfather into it. "It's hard to find places to go with a hyperactive boy."

"Yeah," Logan added with a disarming smile. "It must be. But Hana managed yesterday at short notice. You'll have to be inventive." Logan felt sorry for Jas, who looked put out when his poppa hugged and kissed him and told him they would go for afternoon tea one day that week.

"With Hanny and Phoe and Tama?" Jas insisted and Tama shook his head.

"Not me, buddy. I'll be in fire service training after today."

"Whoa! Calm the farm! Really? Like a proper fireman with muscles and everything?" Jas had found a new hero to worship and it was difficult to get out of the house after that.

Logan was aware he had caused difficulty but didn't care. "You know, Bodie Johal blows hot and cold as it pleases him," he complained to Tama in the car. "Everything's about payback and owing favours to him."

"Ha, are you sure he's not a Du Rose?" Tama quipped and Logan glared at him.

"Not even funny!"

"If anything, it's Bodie who owes you, isn't it? Didn't you lend him a grand last week for that auction?"

"Yeah, but don't tell Hana. Little git promised to pay me back when he got paid but he hasn't. I try so hard with that kid and yet the more I know of him, the less I like him."

"Are you sure he needed it for the real estate agent's fee? How do you know he's not got a bad habit?"

Logan shrugged. "I don't. But the 'Auction' board went up on the property the day after I lent him the cash."

"Yeah, but if they couldn't even afford that, how are they gonna raise the money to buy Culver's Cottage from Hana? You don't reckon her son's about to try and take Hana for a ride, do ya?"

Logan let out a low growl. "Maybe. But I think he might find her unexpectedly shrewder than previously. And I've got my eye on him!"

The Māori men ran some errands in town as Tama stocked up on the things on his kit list for the fire brigade. Logan grew irritated as he prevaricated over simple items. "Just choose the bloody socks, already! Who cares what they look like; they go in your damn shoes!"

"Yeah, but they gotta be the right ones!" Tama protested. "Hey, how're you gonna to stop Bodie's lot turning up at your place for the afternoon and making themselves at home?" He saw the momentary flash of anger ride across his uncle's face.

"I honestly don't know," Logan sighed. "Wonderful as Jas is, he's too much for Hana lately and his parents seem either unwilling or unable to rein his behaviour in."

"You thinking of your brother, Barry?" Tama asked, putting black socks into his trolley. "Poppa Rueben said he began that way, all cute and endearing but manipulative and forceful."

Logan blanched as he contemplated how that story ended. The face of the spiteful teen passed across his memory like a ghost of misery. Logan heard the sound of his own ragged breath as they chased him through the bush and the noise and feel of the machete as it rent his skin apart. Logan involuntarily touched the space on his side with his opposite hand and gave a noticeable shiver. He shook his head, thinking of Jas' cheeky smile. "He'll never become that sadistic or cruel. Besides, if I see him heading that way, I'll step in to prevent him taking that particular route, just like Alfred should have done with Barry and didn't."

Tama nodded and left the painful subject alone.

Back at the house, the men shifted some of the furniture around, trying to stop the place looking so empty. Logan lit a fire in the wood burner in the lounge to get some heat going. "I'm gonna take a walk over to the main building," he told his nephew. "There's something I need to check."

Tama watched his uncle as he strode across the playing field, a determined set to his posture and his face thoughtful. He went back to his packing and watched the clock, knowing Hana would text when church finished.

Logan stood in the front reception area, peering through the glass of the trophy cabinet when Angus came silently across him. Logan's hand shielded his eyes from the reflection of the glass, trying to read the inscriptions on the cups and shields inside when the principal made him jump. "Boarding house all ready, Mr Du Rose?" Angus boomed, his Scots accent sounding rather too jovial for the start of a new term.

Logan nodded, feeling irritated and knowing the older man did it on purpose, catching him out and making him feel like a fourteen-year-old student at the grammar school again. Angus enjoyed Logan's discomfort, his eyes crinkling in a smile of victory, always acting the adult in their twenty-eight year relationship. "What are we looking at?" Angus asked, pressing his nose up against the glass of the cabinet.

"I'm not sure," Logan replied, "I think I'll know when I see it. And yes, your boarding house is ready."

Intrigued, Angus stroked the various pieces of bling with his eyes and relived the memories associated with the success of each cup. Except one. He stared intently at a spot between a soccer shield and a large ornate brass cup, on a wooden base. "That's odd," he said, sounding confused. "I hadn't noticed that before."

Logan waited for him to explain, growing frustrated when the principal stared in silence. "It's gone," Angus finally said.

"The championship trophy from 2003 is missing." He touched the door of the cabinet in obvious confusion, expecting to find it securely locked. But at his touch, the catch moved easily, the mechanism undone and the glass door slid back. Angus looked at Logan, his eyes wide. "Is that why you were looking? Because you noticed it missing?"

Logan shook his head, perplexed. "No, Hana had one of those night terrors last night – after we told her about the tennis player being killed. She always maintained he had the name 'Lachlan' on the tennis racquet cover, but last night she said 'Lachie Dobbs' and something about a trophy. I guess I should have looked for a tennis trophy because she said he was a good player, but when you arrived, I was looking for his name on any trophy. But there's no trophy, tennis or otherwise with that name on it." Logan sighed and stepped away from the glass, giving his shoulders a little shake. "I probably shouldn't get involved. I think I'm wasting my time somehow. It all just seemed a bit too coincidental in the early hours, the surname being the same as Alan's." Logan ran his hand over his face, feeling tired.

"I'm sorry about Alan's death; I know he was your friend," Angus said gently and Logan looked at him, his brows knitting.

"I thought he was your friend too?"

Angus looked away. "He was once upon a time." His voice sounded heavy and sad, the timbre of his Scots accent uncharacteristically dull.

"How long did you know each other?" Logan asked, sensing some hidden undertone but unable to grab it.

Angus gave a deep sigh. "I met Alan and Dora many years ago. We all taught together at the North Shore Grammar School up in Auckland. I'm surprised you don't remember. You were there."

Logan's jaw dropped. "I remember you. I don't remember either of *them*. It must have been before my time."

"No," Angus shook his head. "They both left after your first year and went...elsewhere. But they definitely both taught that year. You may not have come across them in your classes and

Alan was very different then, both as a man and a teacher. He was calmer and less controlling. And he didn't wear that blasted stupid wig."

"So what happened?" Logan asked. "Why did they leave and what changed him?"

Angus blanched and his guard dropped for a second, putting Logan's senses on alert. "I'd rather not say. But he's been a good deputy and I've been glad of him on many occasions, despite his fastidiousness. Professionally, he was faultless. Which brings me to a new subject. I'm in need of a replacement for our Mr Dobbs and I think you're the man for the position."

The conversation did not go as the principal had planned. Anyone else would have jumped at the opportunity offered, grovelled and scraped and at least been flattered. Not Logan Du Rose. "Thanks but no thanks," he replied in a casual, infuriatingly offhand way, leaving Angus feeling perplexed and angry.

"Why?" The principal's voice went up a number of octaves and Logan took a step back, unused to hysteria in Angus. "Bloody hell, Du Rose! You've foxed this old man since the age of fourteen, when you walked into my maths class and I first clapped eyes on your scraggly, grey-eyed Māori face. Why do you never perform to type, not even just once?" Angus fumed, his eyes flashing in his pale face. The sun caught his hair and made him look as though the wispy remains were on fire. "At least think about it before you throw it back in my face, you arrogant little *rangatira!* I'll get a contract drawn up and call a meeting which you *will* attend!"

Logan snorted at the contradiction. The idea of a powerful chief being an arrogant little anything was incongruous. "Yeah, I'll think about it," Logan agreed, "but it won't change anything. Thanks for the opportunity but it's not where I want to be." He waved a hand in Angus' direction as he left through the front doors, sinking his hands into his front pockets and setting off in the direction of the boarding house.

Angus stood for a long time in front of the old cabinet, contemplating the issue of 'foolish men', which sadly included himself. "*Lachie Dobbs,*" he mused, running his hand through his thinning amber hair, thinking how strange it was that the boy's name should come up again after all those years of silence. "*Now that is an unfortunate coincidence,*" he mused.

The principal looked again at the space in the cabinet, noting the dust mark around where the offending trophy should have been. Then he rolled the glass doors closed again, unlocked his well-proportioned office and went inside, closing the door behind him.

Tama stayed at The Gatehouse getting his gear organised and packed up, ready for his trip north the following day. He was excited to begin his new life, but at the same time felt a deep sadness at what he was leaving behind. The faces of Hana and Lucy drifted in and out of his mind as he acknowledged how much he would miss them both. Lucy popped round to see him, tired from two weeks of constant murder enquiries but determined to make her boyfriend's last afternoon in Hamilton cheerful and positive. They made a scratch lunch in the kitchen and then went for a walk around the grounds, holding hands and chatting with an easy companionship.

St Bart's received the first of the returning boarders and buzzed with parents, boys and suitcases. Logan stayed for a while, troubleshooting and chatting to a number of mothers, eager to make the tall, handsome man's acquaintance. One of them was like a wasp around his head and wouldn't go away. "Oh, Mr Du Rose, would you say my Charlie's settling well? He doesn't really talk much at home so I can't tell. His father left a few years ago so it's been hard work bringing up a teenager on my own." She widened her heavily decorated eyes and gave Logan an uncomfortable once over, touching his forearm with an obvious sexual undertone. He pulled his arm away and glanced across at the woman's son, who talked without breathing and high-fived anyone who came near him.

"Charlie looks pleased to be back," Logan said, keeping his voice droll. "But my wife would have mentioned it if she noticed. She spends a lot of time over here with our baby. The boys love her."

The mother put her hand down by her side and the interest in her eyes was replaced by defeat. The adoration in Logan's eyes when he talked about his family could not be ignored. When the woman opened her mouth to speak again, Logan pointed towards the office down the corridor. "If you've got any questions, feel free to see my colleague. He'll sort you out."

The woman glanced through the open doorway, her face wrinkling in distaste at the sight of Peter North picking his nose with a ballpoint pen. While she was still processing the vision, Logan beat a hasty retreat.

In the upstairs staff area, Logan responded to the trill of his phone, wrenching it out of his pocket. A text from Hana flashed on the screen. *'Gone to Pastor Allen's house for a cup of tea. Will wait for you there. No rush. xxx.'*

"You be ok here? I need to go and fetch Hana," Logan said, sticking his head through the office door. Peter North nodded and smiled, his mouth moving in a chewing movement. Logan grimaced. "Touch my stationary drawer and I'll kill you," he threatened. "It will be a creative death, involving the stapler and your nuts, so don't think I'm joking."

"I haven't touched your stuff!" Pete argued. "What's your problem?"

"Charlie Patton's mum saw you picking your nose with a pen," Logan said. "You're gross!"

"Oh, not *her!*" Pete wailed. "I fancy her. Why didn't you warn me?"

"Because it never occurred to me, that's why! If I catch you doinking any of the mothers I'll fire you myself!"

"Ok, I won't, I won't!" Pete promised, swivelling on his chair like a child.

Logan watched a prefect holding the huge double doors open for a tiny Year 9 whose suitcase was bigger than him. The young man nodded politely at the equally small woman following the child, accompanied by a surprisingly large and burly husband and walked back towards the common room. A thought came to Logan and he turned back to Pete. "Hey, did we have a boy called Lachlan come here in the last ten years?"

"To St Bart's?" Pete asked, pulling a face.

"Not necessarily. Just in the school. It's not that common a name is it? Would you remember?"

Pete leaned back on his chair so far it looked dangerous. He scratched his wispy hair with the end of the ball-point pen and dislodged a veritable snowstorm of dandruff. Logan tried to ignore it, even though the sight of it made him want to break the vacuum out. He tapped the toe of his cowboy boot on the floor impatiently. "Yeah, nah, yeah, reckon," Pete concluded. Logan gritted his teeth and understood how frustrating it was for Hana when he used the familiar kiwi expression himself to say absolutely nothing. He snuffed in anger and Pete realised he was heading into trouble. "Yeah," he said finally, eyeing his friend sideways. "We had a Lachlan about the same time as Hana's boy. They probably went through school together. Lachie, we called him. Tennis player, I seem to remember." Pete scratched his head with a knobbly finger and released more flaky skin.

"What was his last name?" Logan pressed.

"Dunno," Pete answered but he made the mistake of widening his eyes just a fraction. The men had been friends a lot of years and Logan knew the signs of guilty-Pete. He closed the door behind him with a click.

"You bloody do!" he exclaimed. The mirrored glass hid his actions from the surrounding corridors and Pete panicked as Logan came up behind him.

"Ok, well yes I do. But I'm not telling, so get stuffed!"

"Fine!" Logan replied. "I'll check the archives department tomorrow."

"Oh, you won't find what you're looking for there." *Scratch, scratch* went the fingers and the skin continued to flutter down. Desperately trying to ignore the flakes of skin on the seat material, Logan seized the chair and pulled it backwards. It was a typist's chair, a comfy seat supported by a single shaft on four plastic casters. With very little effort, Logan tipped it back onto the two rear wheels. The whole thing creaked dangerously and Pete struggled to sit up, finding gravity against him. His legs flailed around in the air comically, making the creaks and groans of the heavy duty plastic worse. "Let me down!" he hissed and Logan smirked with an evil glint in his eye. They were transported back in time just shy of twenty-eight years, to another time and place, two schoolboys torturing and pranking each other in the name of friendship.

"Oh, I'm going to let you down for sure," Logan chuckled, enjoying Pete's squeaks of fear as he tipped the weight of the chair almost horizontal.

"Angus is coming!" Pete faked, rewarded by the chair groaning as it dropped yet further. Logan held it at the optimum point, where at any moment the casters might lose their grip on the carpet and spin away underneath him, dropping the sports teacher on the back of his head. A quick look through the mirrored windows revealed the lie. Angus wasn't coming at all.

"Going down..." Logan whispered, wrinkling his nose as another hailstorm of dandruff peppered his boots. He let the chair shudder in his hands to make his point.

"Ok, ok, don't drop me!" Pete begged. "Henrietta's due back in Hamilton this week and I can't have serious injuries. It'll stop us doing our aerobics videos. But if you want to give me a few cuts and bruises, it might be good for some sympathy."

Logan bit his lip to stop him laughing at the thought of skinny Pete and bouncy Henrietta swathed in spandex, leaping around to an exercise video. Was the staff unit lounge even big enough for that kind of activity? Would the pilings hold, or the whole thing fall off its foundations? A snort escaped his nose and Pete panicked. "Please Loge, I'll tell you. But if you tell anyone there will be big trouble. You can't even mention that kid's name around here without it causing Dobbs to go loco...oh." Pete remembered at the last minute Dobbs was unlikely to go loco ever again.

Logan sat the chair upright, fortunately just as a parent knocked on the door. The tall Māori opened it with a smile which made the yummy mummy's insides flip flop hopelessly. Logan handed her an exam timetable for the end of the year, even though she could have got it off the website. Then with a final paralysing smile, Logan shut the door and turned back to his prey. "Don't make me ask you again, tufty," Logan said to Pete, his eyes dark and threatening.

"Then don't call me that," Pete complained, running his fingers carefully up the two quiffs either side of his ears. Goodness knows why the man parted his hair at the back. Logan grew impatient, desperate to get up to his wife and daughter. He gritted his teeth and jabbed his head forward in warning. Pete caved. "Lachlan Reynolds was our tennis champion. He won that big trophy in the cabinet in reception, the big silver one with the gold bits on it and the marble base. Anyway, there was this massive upset after it went to be engraved. The tennis club organised it, not the school, but when the trophy arrived, it had a different name on it. The name was *Lachie Dobbs*. It seemed like a silly mistake and the trophy went back for re-engraving. But it caused the biggest stink in the top corridor and Alan Dobbs called me in and gave me a verbal warning.

"He wouldn't listen. I tried to tell him the boy put his own name on the entry form; I only drove the group to the games in the minibus. I was so mad I went to Angus and he told me to 'let it go.' I was really upset with that verbal warning on my record. What made it worse was they put the wrong name in the newspaper as well. Kid must have had a field day giving a false name. I figured it was a joke, but it caused a heap of bad trouble. Wasn't nobody laughing either."

Logan rubbed his hand over his face, contemplating his next question. "Was he a boarder? And don't lie to me or I'll text Henrietta now and tell her you fancy Mrs Patton."

"If you do that, I'll kill myself," Pete threatened.

A genteel grin spread across Logan's face and he reached for his phone. "Now that's an opportunity too good to miss."

"Logan, stop, I'll tell you," Pete whined. "I think he must have been a border because I drove him to the tennis club with Hana. Otherwise his parents would've taken him." He took a risk and popped out of the chair like a jack-in-the-box. "You can check the records here. We must have a list somewhere. Why do you want to know all this anyway?"

"Because he was the dead body found in my lounge," Logan said and Pete's eyes bugged like a frog's.

"No way! After all these years? Why your place?"

"I'm not sure. Would he have known Hana at school?" Logan asked as he turned to leave. "You said you took the boys in the minibus with her. Why her?"

Pete nodded with enthusiasm. "Heck yeah, her and Vik, her...husband, they were an awesome doubles team. They used to win heaps down at the tennis club. Vik went straight from work but Hana came with me and her son in the bus. It was every Wednesday, I think, yeah every Wednesday." Pete bit his lip and waited for a reaction from his friend, knowing how much Logan hated mention of Hana's previous husband.

To his surprise, Logan looked at peace with the conversation. "Hana said she practiced with Lachie Reynolds last term, only nobody else saw him. Why wouldn't she have known it was him?"

"Ahhh, so there actually *was* a tennis player?" Pete adopted a look of superiority. "I thought she was going a bit cuckoo." He put both hands either side of his head and mimicked the action of pulling a cloth through his ears as though there was nothing in between. Logan's eyes narrowed and he concentrated on his breathing to prevent himself putting Peter North through the mirrored glass head first. If anyone had an empty head, Logan knew he was looking at them.

"Erm, Hana might not have recognised him if he was all grown up, but she hasn't changed at all in the past ten years, so he'd know her easy. Man, she used to look hot in that tennis dress. I bet if she put it on now..."

Logan moved menacingly towards him and Pete's jaw snapped shut, figuring he should be quiet. With difficulty, Logan turned and left the room, leaving the door wide open. His heels clicked sharply down the hallway and Pete wafted at the air space behind his backside, releasing the 'fart of fear' he had been desperately sitting on.

On the way up to the pastor's house in Rototuna, Logan used the time to dial Bodie, sliding his phone in the cradle on the dashboard and keeping it on speakerphone. Bodie was snippy with him at first, clearly struggling with his son in a fast food restaurant somewhere while Amy was at work. "Don't take it out on me!" Logan snapped. "He's your kid so get over it!"

Bodie's attitude changed as Logan imparted his new information about the trophy and the upset surrounding it and the call ended with his stepson feeling grateful. Odering would be impressed with his new sidekick. Bodie rubbed his hands together and made the phone call, enjoying telling his superior that the dead man was an Old Boy of the school *and* had also been in the same year as him.

A sudden thought made Logan dial the boarding house as he pulled onto Thomas Road. Pete picked up, impressively on the third ring. Logan wondered if he was waiting on a call from his lady love. "Pete," Logan intoned, hearing a deep sigh coming across the airwaves. "Did Hana know about the trophy – about it being engraved wrong?"

There was silence as Pete's skewed brain ticked audibly. Then he answered, "Yeah. Yeah, she did. She thought it sucked that I got a verbal warning for it. Hana was the one who got the club to re-engrave it. But it was a waste of time because the kid never got the trophy. There was meant to be a big assembly and presentation, but it never happened. The thing just went in the cupboard and got dusted every now and then. Hana was real mad about my warning. She went to see Dobbs about it and he shouted at her. She never talked to him again. I didn't forget it because she was the only one on my side."

Logan thanked Pete and rang off. "How bizarre," he said out loud. He always liked Alan Dobbs but realised Hana never had. They never discussed why but she showed clear disinterest when Logan talked about the man in friendly terms. The possibility that Lachlan Reynolds either was or simply wanted to be, Alan Dobbs' son was becoming a distinct possibility. It was the only logical connection between the two men and oddly, their respective deaths. The missing trophy was simply an added complication, or a clue.

Chapter Twenty-Two

Logan picked Hana and Phoenix up from the pastor's house and took them for a late lunch in their favourite café on Victoria Street. "It's nice being back in town," Hana admitted and Logan snorted and knitted his brows at her.

"Is this the woman who never wanted to come back to the school site and hates Hamilton?" he jibed, seeing the sulk descend over his wife's pretty face.

"Actually," she flounced, her red hair bouncing on her shoulders, "I'm relieved I don't have to make our lives work in the staff unit, which is no bigger than a shoebox. I love The Gatehouse. I hope we'll be allowed to stay there permanently." Her face clouded and she stopped talking, staring off at an indeterminate point across the road and Logan watched her. He touched her fingers gently with his, feeling the softness of her elegant digits under his scarred flesh.

"What're you thinking about?"

Hana jumped and withdrew her hand, seeing the hurt look that crossed her husband's beautiful face. She put her hand back on the table and intertwined her fingers through his. Their skin colour was so different, his a rich bronze and hers the white of alabaster. "I keep thinking about the tennis player.

I talked to Pastor Allen about him. I was cross with you that night I stormed outside and wandered around. I thought you and Amanda were starting an affair and I couldn't deal with it. I just came across him practicing. He was an excellent player. He invited me to spar and I thoroughly enjoyed it. He remembered me as a doubles champion and it made me feel good about myself at a time when I felt useless. Playing tennis was something else I lost when Vik died so suddenly."

Logan nodded with encouragement and his fingers kept their steady stroking motion on her skin, taming the fidgeting fingers with his patience and love. "I was scared Odering and Bodie would think you killed him." Hana bit her lip. There, she had said it.

"Why?" Logan shook his head in confusion. "We were at the hotel...and the hospital. You couldn't have given me a better alibi if you tried." He smiled, but the humour was wasted on his wife.

"You all thought I was crazy." Hana sighed at the memory of her humiliation in front of the two policemen and her husband, when she told them where she had been. Lachlan had seemed like some bizarre figment of her imagination and Hana knew Logan doubted her story of his existence. It made her both infuriated and desperately sad, that she so easily fitted into the category of 'crazy-lady.' Now the poor man was dead, *properly* gone as though he really never existed. Apart from the bloody puddle on the floor of the staff unit, it was as though he was a ghost, sent to disturb and unsettle her in this new and complicated life she had chosen.

"What did Allen say?" Logan asked, gritting his teeth against the hurt he felt when Hana confided in someone other than him. He quashed the feeling quickly. "Did talking to him help?"

Hana nodded. Pastor Allen had listened patiently to her ravings, smiling kindly when she faltered. Lachlan Reynolds, as she now knew him to be, was sunny and optimistic. He was one of those 'glass half full' sorts of people. With the racquet in her hand Hana faced the net and the man's beaming smile, no longer a forty-six-year-old widow on her second marriage. She had morphed into an amazing tennis player ten years younger, full of life and hope for the future, not tired, confused and completely lacking in direction. "I can't believe someone so vital was just snuffed out like that. It's like Father Sinbad. It doesn't seem possible somehow, that someone so amazing could disappear so easily without anyone noticing." Hana withdrew her fingers from Logan's and ran them fitfully across her face, spreading lipstick over her cheek. "How could he lie on our lounge floor for so long without anyone noticing?" It made Hana's stomach churn, thinking about it.

"I sniffed the furniture," she admitted, guilt colouring her cheeks and Logan bit his lip to suppress the laughter bubbling up inside him at the incongruous image. "Does that make me a shallow person - because it's the first thing I thought of? It doesn't smell of dead-person." She looked hard at her husband. "But it could have, couldn't it? Am I am bad person because I inspected it all?"

"No," he replied, leaning forward with a serviette and dabbing the line of lipstick from her cheek. "You're just human and I worried about it too. So if you're bad then I'm wicked." Logan concentrated hard on his task; his eyebrows knitted and his gaze intense. He babied Hana like Phoenix sometimes. He balled up the tissue and wedged it inside a dirty cup and then fixed Hana with a tender smile. She felt her heart plummet into her toes. "I checked it all out before I brought it across. And I sprayed it all with deodoriser before you got back from Raglan. It's fine."

Hana sighed with relief and smiled, her eyes sad. "I sprayed it too, with that aerosol from under the kitchen sink. It makes me feel better you checked too."

Logan smiled at his wife, his eyes laughing. "You sprayed it with bug spray then!"

"No, I'm sure it was air freshener." Hana bit her lip and Logan saw her fretting.

"The only aerosol under the sink was bug spray, but hey, we won't get bugs so there's an upside." The flare of love translated from amusement into passion in his eyes. He felt desperate to take Hana home and hold her tightly in his arms. "Do you want to get food and coffee to go?" he asked.

Hana transferred her hand from the table to his thigh, feeling his powerful muscles through the cloth of his trousers. She walked her fingers gently up his leg, watching him bite the inside of his lip and persuading her imagination to focus on life and not death. "Could do," she held his grey gaze in her emerald eyes, knowing a couple of hours in bed with him could banish every negative thought, even if it was only temporary.

"These yours?" The waitress thumped the two plates down between them, ignoring the under-the-table seduction happening right under her nose. Hana's salad looked colourful and Logan's pie was topped with a sprinkling of parsley.

"Missed your chance," Hana smirked at her husband and he sighed heavily.

"We could just leave it and walk out. I've paid," he goaded her, his eyes laden with desire. "I'd make it worth your while."

"I said I wasn't hungry," Hana retorted. "You're the one who said I had to eat."

"Yeah," Logan sighed again, trying to control the raging testosterone that Hana's touch on his body whirled into a maelstrom. "Eat it quickly then."

Phoenix whimpered in the car seat and Logan hoisted her over his shoulder. She snuggled down and drifted off to sleep again. He at one-handed, scoffing the pie with enthusiasm and Hana smirked, knowing where his true hunger lay. "I hate you being on nights," she said, pushing the salad around her plate, knowing in a few hours he would be across the field and inaccessible.

"I know," he reached out and clasped her hand in his strong fingers and stroked it gently. "But it's only once a week now we're up to full strength staff-wise. It shouldn't ever be as bad as it was a couple of months ago." Keeping hold of her fingers, he asked her the question burning his curiosity, "Han, did you know that the dead guy was an Old Boy of the school?"

She put her cutlery down neatly on her plate, angling the metal with precision and care. Lunch was over for her. Hana looked at her baby, lying so innocently across her father's shoulder and wondered how on earth she was going to keep this tiny person safe from the world. It was a horrid, wicked place. She nodded, her heart and head seeming to weigh her down. "I didn't know who he was when we played that couple of nights, although he clearly knew me. I never got to ask how – we just played and went our separate ways. I almost wish I'd talked more to him now. As soon as you told me his name, I remembered that damn trophy. Pete got into so much trouble over it and it wasn't even his fault. Dobbs was bloody unreasonable. I liked Mrs Dobbs heaps. I sat next to her at a couple of staff events but not him. He was a dreadful, bigoted little man."

"So what do you think the issue was, with the trophy?" Logan asked.

Hana thought for a moment and then confirmed his suspicions. "I thought at the time the boy was his son and for some reason Dobbs wanted to keep it quiet. You'd need to go back through the old records to see if there were any parents by the name of 'Reynolds,' I guess. He was a St Bart's boy as I remember, because Pete used to transport him to the tennis club in the school van with a group of other boys. I went along for the ride and Vik met us there and coached after work." Hana looked off into the distance, watching the traffic stop at the lights outside. "I'm kicking myself I didn't remember him, but I seem to think as a teenager he had sandy red hair and this guy was very blond. It's possible he dyed it, but it certainly put me off the scent. He was also muscular and toned, but as a little boy he was this spindly wee thing with these long spaghetti legs. I don't remember liking him as a teenager, I recall him being very devious, but as an adult he was lovely. I wonder if Bo remembers him – they must have been around the same age."

Logan nodded. "Yeah, he does now."

"How long was he lying in our unit for?" Hana asked. Her voice was quiet and sad, masking a sense that she didn't want to know the answer. Logan squeezed her hand again.

"He'd been there maybe a day or so according to Bodie. There's definitely a connection between him and Dobbs but the other thing, which I discovered this morning, is the trophy's missing."

Hana gaped. "What *the* trophy? With the wrong name on it?"

Logan nodded and then looked confused. "Wrong? Pete said that you got it changed at the club."

Hana shook her head. "I tried but they refused. They showed me his entry form. He put his name down as *Lachie Dobbs* and they paid for the trophies to be engraved. The club chairman said it wasn't their fault and refused. There's a big version of the trophy which stays in the cabinet at the tennis club and has all the previous winners on it, but they also gave out individual miniatures for the winners to keep. That's the one the school has. They go into the school cabinet and boys have the option of taking them when they leave. Mostly they take them away, but that one's sat there for the last ten years or so. I wondered if the boy left it on purpose to annoy Dobbs. That man was always maniacally particular about the trophy cabinet."

Logan sighed and patted his baby's soft back through the little fleece she wore.

"Loge," Hana said suddenly and he refocused on her, turning his grey eyes on her face like a spotlight. "When I told you and the cops about playing with a mystery tennis player a few weeks ago, did you believe he was real? Or did you think I was losing the plot?"

Logan Du Rose could spot a loaded question when it was pointed at him. It was one of those where he was 'damned if he did and damned if he didn't' so he thought carefully about his answer. "You had no reason to lie to me," he said after a decent pause. He remembered the night he went after her and found her crying outside the darkened tennis courts. She was wearing her sneakers and tracksuit bottoms. The cops were looking for the groundsman's killer and Hana blurted a story about playing tennis with some guy nobody else had ever seen or mentioned. It looked bogus. The man hadn't come that night for his regular practice and never would again. It certainly seemed like a dreadful waste of a life.

Hana watched her husband for a moment. His mother's Bi-polar disease made him study the women he loved with something like intense fanaticism. She wondered that night if he thought her a lunatic too, going through some mental high before plunging deep into the pit of despair, where Miriam regularly went. He hadn't treated her that way and Hana realised she would have to be satisfied with his answer. Her sanity had been proven but at the expense of a life.

"Please can I have the car on Tuesday?" she asked, changing the subject in the hope Logan didn't notice she had pushed her full plate to the side of the table. She half wished Jas was with them. He was great at disguising his least favourite foods under other things. She once watched him hide a whole carrot under his cutlery.

The feel of Logan's touch on her hand made her look up. His face was questioning and Hana looked blank. Giving up, he repeated himself and it wasn't a question she had missed, but a statement. "You shouldn't be driving yet."

Hana pouted and looked grumpy. Logan stopped her as she was about to launch into a monologue about how he left her to drive to Raglan with a car load of children, only the day before. "Do you need it all day?" he asked with absolutely no inflection in his tone.

"No, just a few hours," she replied, remaining deliberately obtuse. Hana wasn't sure she had the courage to go there yet and didn't want her strong-willed husband running interference. She secured the Honda for a few hours, knowing she would have to be up and off early in order to achieve what she wanted, before Logan figured out what she was up to.

Phoenix stayed asleep while Logan undressed Hana in the makeshift bedroom. Sometimes the elderly house seemed to ring with the ghostly sound of children long since turned to men and she shivered. Logan pulled his wife underneath the covers, securing her trembling, naked body to his. He realised as his lips settled tenderly over hers and his passion spiked, it wasn't the cold that made her body shake, but the anticipation of his caress.

Chapter Twenty-Three

Logan went off to work mid-afternoon, leaving Hana alone in the huge old house with Phoenix. She rattled around it feeling lost until she remembered the diary upstairs still in her case.

Hana knew enough to know she shouldn't put her bare hands on the delicate pages and managed to sort out a pair of new cotton gloves which came with some hand cream. She slipped them on and turned the pages with care, trying not to do any further damage. The writing was childlike and lapsed into unfamiliar dialect. It was highly unlikely Māori women were given schooling in the early 1900s, apart from that informally gleaned but Hana sensed the woman through her writing, despite the poor English grammar and the glaring spelling mistakes. "What are you trying to say to me, Phoenix Du Rose?" Hana mused, stroking the tattered pages and ruing the water damage which made some impossible to unstick.

The first of the diary pages began with Logan's grandmother as a young woman. She was twenty-two and stated her lineage in the first few lines in a laboured *mihi i*n Te Reo Māori. Hana's smattering of the language limped her through the woman's documented heritage. The Frenchman, who drove off the English invaders was her grandfather who married his eldest daughter to a prominent Māori leader - the *rangatira* from the *Ngati Maniapoto* tribes everyone spoke of. Phoenix *Te Whai*-Du Rose was a product of that marriage, also the eldest daughter. There were obvious links to the *Ngapuhi* tribe also recounted, but Hana's knowledge of the Māori language failed her. Phoenix listed her *waka* as the Tainui, which sailed her ancestors from Hawaiki to Kawhia and her river as the Waikato. The mountain or *maunga*, which Phoenix belonged to was called Mātakitaki and she had been birthed at the summit. A hand-drawn sketch depicted the old kauri tree at the top of Logan's mountain. "I never knew that," Hana said to her baby as the little girl wriggled around on the change mat, sucking her toes and gurgling with happiness. "Mātakitaki - the mountain has a name. You were born there too. Daddy buried your afterbirth under the tree." Hana shuddered involuntarily at the unsavoury thought. It seemed such an un-western thing to do at the time, but Logan performed the rite without a second thought, offering a whispered *karakia* as thanks for his daughter's safe arrival and prayer for their safety down the treacherous mountain.

The Second World War wiped out the sons of the family and a rift between successive daughters meant that Frenchman's estate passed to Phoenix as the oldest granddaughter. The *rangatira* was of the Te Whai lineage and although he lived on the land with his half-French wife, never lay claim to it even by marriage. After a chunk of rigid pages Hana couldn't open without damaging them, the diary began in earnest on the day of Phoenix Te Whai's wedding.

'I do not want this. Matua insists. He say the world changes. The war has brought hunger for whenua in its wake. I will need the Du Rose name to write on paper, not just to run through my veins so I can keep it. He knows I do this only to obey.'

Phoenix hadn't wanted to marry Henri Du Rose. Leslie told Hana as much, but to see it written down in the woman's own heavily slanted hand brought a sadness to her chest. Phoenix did it in return for the French name which would safeguard her land. The diary rambled on for a few pages about how she would do her best to honour her *matua* - father, but it seemed Henri was damaged somehow in the war and wasn't the person the *rangatira* though he was anymore. The fact was sobering and dispelled the ready judgements Hana inadvertently formed against her daughter's paternal great-grandfather, who was styled by others as a gambler and a drunk. The war destroyed many lives, not only those of the dead but the men left to crawl through life ruined.

Water made the next pages unreadable and Hana sighed in frustration. The wood pulp paper had turned brown as the liquid seeped through, rendering the words illegible; black blood on the pages. The next decipherable words showed an improvement in both the handwriting and use of language and catalogued an event eight years later. It was August 1952 and Phoenix Du Rose's father was dead. She detailed the *tangihanga* and named the visitors who came to pay their respects to her father as he lay in state at the homestead. The names formed an endless list of forgotten lives. Phoenix recalled with bitterness, the inappropriately drunken behaviour of Henri and some of his friends during the three-day event. *'He was kakī mārō!'* The exclamation mark had been written with such force, it punctuated the next two pages.

Hana knew the words meant pig-headed and stubborn in Māori, because she heard Leslie whisper them under her breath when Logan irritated her. One of the other kitchen girls told Hana what the word meant, whispering behind her hand. If Henri Du Rose was stubborn, he had handed that little gem down the generations, at least as far as Hana's husband and daughter.

'Aunty try to tell me the homestead is now of her son, Henri. My māmā would be screaming in Hawaiki about now, ready to come from the underworld to slap her heahea face. She is disloyal sister and always was. Matua give me papers. It is mine. Only mine.'

"*Heahea* means stupid, doesn't it?" Hana asked her daughter and Phoenix laughed, her mouth making a delicate half-moon in her dribbly face.

More damage. This time the paper completely disintegrated, leaving huge holes in the page as though blasted away. The crumbled pieces were littered throughout the remaining book like decayed autumn leaves. Hana persevered, losing herself in the memories of a woman she never knew, the nuances of the Du Roses slowly becoming clearer.

'Aunty wants a betrothal between my boys and her girls. Antoinette and Miriam, her mokopuna. Disloyalty cannot be rewarded. My māmā could not forgive how her sister try to get Matua to take her as second wife. Nor can I. The rangatira would not. He have only my māmā. Te aroha. He love only her.'

Hana closed the wooden cover and bit her lip. She sensed conflict swirling through the pages, making her party to things she shouldn't know. "I'll take it to Daddy," Hana told the gurgling baby." But she knew she wouldn't.

Logan idolised his grandmother and Hana lay the book on the bed while she played with her daughter. The wooden cover called to her, desperate to involve her in its intrigue. Hana sighed. "Daddy wouldn't be pleased to know his mother and her sister were maneuvered into marriage with Alfred and Reuben from childhood and his grandmother was against it," she told her daughter, shaking the rattle and speaking in an engaging baby voice. "No he wouldn't."

Māori often took more than one partner in the early days before the English made bigamy a crime. That fact wasn't astounding. But a woman eagerly seeking the affections of her sister's mate was an uncomfortable revelation and it was clear Phoenix's aunt continued to be a problem with the next generation also. "It's generational sin," Hana whispered to her daughter. "That's what's wrong with this family." She'd seen enough of life to recognise its dreadful track marks and it raised its ugly head in Miriam's behaviour with the brothers, Reuben and Alfred. Of course she copied the example of her elders, especially her grandmother, the spurned Te Whai sister.

As baby Phoenix fed, Hana balanced the book in one careful hand but its next revelation left her clutching her chest and fighting for composure.

'Matua wanted māmā's aurei with him. It was to go to the urupa. During tangi, I see Aunty trying to take from his dead breast. I make sure she cannot do what she wants. It belongs to my whānau. Not hers!'

Another exclamation mark was scored into the page as though the writer's fury was fresh on the delicate leaves. Hana sat, riveted to her seat. Phoenix spoke of the cursed 'thing' removed from the body during the *tangi*. Its proximity to the *rangatira* and association with his burial made it *tapu*, sacred. Was it possible the Te Whai sister stole it and not Henri Du Rose? It put a whole new perspective on things. The *urupa* was the burial ground, but Hana had no idea what an *aurei* was. "How can I find out?" she asked her suckling baby. The little legs kicked but she showed no interest.

Desperate to continue reading, the sound of Tama's ute pulling onto the driveway caused Hana to jump with guilt. She laid her dozing child on the bed and rushed to hide the diary in the built-in wardrobe in the main bedroom, burying it beneath a stack of pullovers she already stored away. Tama came upstairs to find Hana, following the lights glaring out of the bedroom. "You look loved-up," Hana teased and he smirked happily, throwing himself down on the bed next to the baby. She squealed with excitement at the rude start and gritted her jaw, looking like a maniac.

"I met Lucy's parents last night," Tama said, playing with the baby's fingers. "I think they liked me."

"Naw, that's awesome babe. You've passed some unwritten relationship test."

"Yeah, it's a whole new experience for me," he mused, "actually dating a girl properly instead of satiating myself with some stranger against the bins outside a nightclub."

"Eugh!" Hana pulled a face and chased the comment from her mind. *Or bedding a friend's mother.* It was spiteful and she culled the thought as quickly as it settled. "I thought you were leaving today," she said, attempting to change the subject.

"Na, yeah, na," he replied, playing hidey with the baby. Hana gritted her teeth at the kiwi-ism. "Sorry." Tama looked up and saw her squirm. "That means I wasn't, then I was, then I wasn't."

"Oh great, I'm glad that's so clear!" Hana shoved Logan's shirts haphazardly on hangers and put them in the wardrobe.

"You know he'll want to iron all those again now, don't you?"

"Well, he's very welcome to," Hana replied.

Phoenix reached for Tama's cheeks with dribbly fingers, laughing at the roughness of his stubble. "You're gorgeous," he told her, blowing a raspberry on her cheek. He glanced at Hana. "The course starts on Wednesday and I meant to go up today but tomorrow's fine. I've allowed myself enough time to get settled."

Hana nodded and stopped with the next shirt half on the hanger. "I'll miss you," she said with sincerity.

Later, Tama sat with Hana for a while in the huge classroom they tried to disguise as a lounge, feeling the weight of her sadness. "S'up, Ma," he asked. "Is it the dead guy in the lounge?" To his surprise, Hana shook her head.

"I meant what I said. I'll miss you." She struggled to stifle a sob. "I don't know why, but your leaving feels far worse than any of my other children. It's probably because I worry more about you."

"Thank you," he whispered, feeling gratified. He hugged her and teared up over her shoulder, secure in the knowledge she couldn't see his weakness. He loved this woman more than anyone else on earth, even Logan, who had backed him since forever. The young man's downward spiral of self-destruction was single-handedly halted, by the intervention of someone whose closest friendship he destroyed. "Remember how we hated each other?" he mused. "You couldn't stand being in the same room as me."

He felt Hana nod against his shoulder. "Yes. I hit you with my handbag. I'm so sorry about that."

"And you threw me out of the house when Logan said I could stay." His voice contained none of his juvenile pique.

"You kinda deserved it," Hana sniffed.

"Yeah, I did. I owe you so much, Ma," he whispered into her hair. "Everything I do from now on is because of you. You gave me a chance when you didn't have to and you saw who I could be, not who I was. I'll always love you."

Danger and adversity pushed them firmly together countless times since their early clashes and it was as though all the sticking power of the hatred created a different glue. They were cemented closely together and it caused jealousy issues with Bodie recently – and undoubtedly would again.

Hana slept badly, the fact Tama was leaving in the morning weighing on her heart. It didn't help she kept reliving memories of Lachlan Reynolds, which merged in her sleep with an image of a small sandy-haired boy coveting a large silver trophy in a tennis club cabinet. *Lachie Dobbs*.

As daylight broke through the curtains of the huge bedroom, Hana was disturbed by the sound of snuffling somewhere by the side of the bed. She lay for a few moments, pretending she imagined it, but the noise came again. As quietly as possible, Hana shifted over to Logan's side of the mattress and peeked over the edge.

Tama lay on his back on the rug. He must have come in during the night and he had his mouth wide open, snoring. On his chest was a small baby girl, lying on her front and snuffling into his muscles. She seemed to be trying to blow raspberries and a long line of dribble ran down Tama's side onto the rug below.

"Yukky!" Hana whispered at her daughter and Phoenix craned her neck round to see her mother. As she caught sight of the fuzzy silhouette above her, the baby grinned and turned her face away, splatting her cheek into the puddle of dribble and cooing to herself. She flapped her legs and tried to get up onto her knees and crawl away. Tama had wrapped a blanket around the both of them and Phoenix became unhappy about being cocooned inside. As she waggled her legs and grew frustrated, Tama disturbed. His eyes were ringed by dark shadows of tiredness and his hair was on end. "What a sight!" Hana mocked.

Tama smirked. "Says the woman with hair like a long, fuzzy, red halo and her flannelette granny nightdress making her look like a pensioner." He lifted his torso off the rug, showing off using only his stomach muscles even with the weight of the child on his chest. Phoenix held her arms up for Hana, demanding a breast feed, reminded now of the presence of the comforting appendages.

"Oh baby," Hana grumbled as she reached for her wiggling daughter, "aren't you even going to let me go to the toilet first?"

Tama shuffled off to the kitchen downstairs to boil the kettle and make tea for the nursing mother. He returned some time later with a mug each and sat on the bed in his boxer shorts, pulling faces and distracting Phoenix. Both of them knew the big goodbye was coming, but neither wanted to progress it. "Tama," Hana started and he stopped her quickly, sliding his arm around her shoulders.

"Don't say anything, Ma. We did this already, when I left for college after the summer, remember?"

Hana nodded and let out a tiny chuckle. "I remember. But you're not allowed to quit the fire brigade, ok? You've got to keep doing it until you're so old you have to wrap the fire hose around your wheelchair!"

"I won't quit, I promise. You and Logan have been amazing over everything. I love you both so much."

"You wouldn't let me get mushy and now you've gone and done it!" Hana sniffed, wiping at the falling tears with the corner of her sleeve. Tama laughed and tickled her, making Phoenix squeal with excitement as Hana jiggled around to get away from him.

"What's an *aurei*?" Hana asked as he cleared the empty mugs away. Tama scratched his head and looked at her strangely. He repeated the word but added the correct punctuation, making Hana feel a stab of irritation.

"It's a...kind of pin, I guess. Like what you'd put in a cloak or shawl to keep it together. It's an old word. I haven't heard it for years. Often they were made of bone and decorated with greenstone or *paua*. Why?"

Having broached the subject, Hana had no ready reason for her enquiry. She fudged it, muttering something vague about the *taonga* in the boxes. Tama's eyes grew wide. "You don't want to be touching that stuff," he said sagely. "You know the stories aye? It's bad news. I don't know how you can have it in the house. It gives me the sh..." He thought hard about the swearword and managed to prevent its full escape.

Hana craved understanding, realising as she pushed for answers the thing she most desired was acceptance into the Du Rose *whānau*. In some small way she subconsciously reasoned that knowledge might gain her entry where marriage had failed. "Do you know what was stolen?" she asked. "From the *rangatira's* coffin?"

To her great disappointment Tama shook his head. "Na, just something precious to the *whānau*. They say Henri Du Rose took it off the body and tried to sell it. He was dead within a year."

"That doesn't mean it's in those boxes though," Hana argued, not believing her own words. Tama shrugged.

"Probably not. It'll be long gone by now. Nobody knows what it was anymore either, so it could be anywhere or nowhere. Leave it to Uncle Logan to deal with, Ma. Don't be messing in that stuff."

The young man left early after loading the box of *taonga* back into the Honda for Hana. Possibly he hoped she was heeding his warning. "I'm gonna try and hit Auckland between the work and school traffic to avoid getting snarled up in either of the staggered rush hours," he said. Tama enfolded Hana in a bear hug and felt the fragility of her body in his arms. "Take care, Ma," he said, a catch in his voice.

Hana waved him off through the front gates in his old ute, proud of Phoenix, who did a perfect little wave at her cousin's departing tail lights. With a guff of dodgy looking exhaust fumes and a hard rev he was gone, out into the traffic on Maui Street and into the rest of his life. "We're gonna miss him, aren't we Phoe?" Hana said with a sniff. She walked slowly back into The Gatehouse, feeling unbearably sad. Her daughter sat high on her hip as Hana tried to ready her mind for the next task. Thoughts of the lovely tennis player attempted to crowd into her brain and she pushed them away, throwing herself into busyness.

Half a kilometre away, Tama drove in through the back gates of the school site and made his way round to the boarding house. He managed to catch his uncle before Logan headed off to tutor group. "Thought I'd better say goodbye to the old git," Tama smirked. "Just don't cry on me, I've got an image to uphold."

"Yeah, you have!" Logan laughed. "But it isn't the one you think it is."

They chatted for a short while before Logan accompanied Tama to his vehicle. "Hey, I transferred some money into your account," the older man said as he shook his nephew's hand in a firm grip. Tama's hand became still within the handshake.

"Why?" he asked, surprised.

"You might need some stuff when you get up to Auckland. I don't reckon you'll be paid for a couple of weeks, so it's to tide you over."

Tama let go of Logan's hand and wrapped him up in a masculine embrace instead. He fought overwhelming emotions of gratitude and the Du Rose men didn't do tears in their hard, unyielding world. Logan held onto the teenager for far longer than he would have managed a year ago, Hana's influence softening and blurring his hard lines. He kissed the side of

Tama's shaved face and ruffled his hair, ignoring the stares of the boarders as they headed over to the main building. Both men were well over six feet tall and made an incongruous scene, blocking the pavement to the front door of St Bart's. The moment became awkward and Tama turned to leave.

Logan stopped him. "Hey, before you go, what's she up to?" he asked, jerking his head in the direction of The Gatehouse across the field.

"I dunno," Tama responded, shaking his head but looking concerned. "I couldn't get it out of her. She cried out in her sleep and was real disturbed. I heard her about four o'clock and went down, but she didn't wake up. Phoe did though. I cuddled her on the floor by the bed."

"Hana?" Logan asked roughly, struggling with the image of his randy nephew cuddling his wife on the floor.

"No, the baby!" Tama spluttered. "I laid on the floor with the baby."

"Oh." Logan had the decency to look contrite. "She's up to something. I hoped you might be able to find out what it was before you left." His dark brows knitted in worry.

Tama slapped him on the back. "Ma will be fine. She's got more about her than any other woman I know. Whatever it is, it'll be something good, a surprise to take her mind off what's happened. It's been a rough few weeks. Don't worry about her. She knows what she almost lost and there ain't nothing gonna make her sacrifice that. Not now."

Tama couldn't have been more wrong. The huge ochre-red gate to the *marae* was open wide, but there was nobody in sight. A big notice pinned to the wall indicated it was a sacred Māori site and entry was prohibited without invitation. Hana stood on the pavement and shifted awkwardly from foot to foot. The website said the event which dominated the weekend before and the Monday clean-up was over and Hana gathered her courage to enter the gates. "Oh, what am I doing?" she whimpered to the baby on her hip. This is madness." Traffic moved quickly past on River Road and she was aware she looked like a random Peeping Tom or worse, a nosy tourist looking for entertainment.

"*Kia ora*. Can I help you?" The thickly accented voice came from behind and Hana jumped like a scalded cat. Feeling embarrassed, she turned to face the small Māori lady, discovering a tiny wee thing; her brown face wizened and crinkled. A *moko* tattoo decorated her chin and although it looked momentarily incongruous to the white Englishwoman, the markings added to the elderly lady, defining her in some ethereal way.

"My husband's *Ngapuhi*," Hana began, realising the ridiculousness of statement as it tumbled from her lips. Why on earth would a woman from the Waikato tribes allow her access to a Tainui *marae*, the seat of the Māori King no less, when she just told her Logan was from the fierce *Ngapuhi* Northland clan? She took a deep breath and started again, "He's also..." Hana gulped and the lady raised an eyebrow. The latter tribe took care of Māori driven south by the English and they remained forever welcome on *Turangawaewae Marae*. She tried to continue, her voice halting. "The thing is, I need advice about some *whānau taonga* which recently came to my husband. I have an idea about how to care for them, but I want to make sure I'm doing the right thing."

"Ask your *tahu*," the woman replied with a smile, referring to Logan. Hana noticed she had a beautiful smile, undiminished by missing teeth at the front.

Hana cringed and it compounded her awkwardness. "He doesn't want to deal with it. It reminds him of...of things he'd rather forget for now. I want to sort it all out but...I honestly don't know what I'm doing." Hana's frustration leaked through and her exasperation put itself on show. "I thought someone here might be able to give me some advice."

"Come," the woman said with another smile, perhaps taking pity on the *Pākehā*. before her. The tiny girl in Hana's arms was appealing and sweet, catching and holding the woman's attention as the tiny fingers gripped a soft toy horse. The woman stared at Hana and then appeared transfixed by Phoenix's grey eyes. A softness engulfed her crinkled face and her eyes brightened. "Yes," she said. "I see now."

Hana followed the lady as she limped through the *marae* gate. The roof was slanted over it, ending in an apex at the top. Intricate carvings and painted designs covered the underside and Phoenix looked up at the lines and patterns denoting something important. The green and turquoise colours of *paua* shell were dotted around, glinting in the light from their position hammered into the wood. Hana emerged into a huge concrete courtyard.

On two sides were seating areas where guests and tribal members would sit facing one another during a *hui* or *powhiri*. Hana had been to a few of each at Logan's *marae* on the outskirts of the township. They were long affairs where representatives from both sides conducted eloquent speeches in their native tongue. She had heard her husband's *mihi* numerous times and it never ceased to fascinate her. It detailed his heritage; who his family was; which waka or canoe his family came to New Zealand on; which mountain he was born in sight of; which river flowed through his birthplace. All these things were essential components in establishing who he was as a man, linking him to the earth with unbreakable threads.

The colour scheme of every surface as always, was the traditional rusty red, black and white, each stroke of the paintbrush signifying some other coded message to the generations. It made Hana tired, thinking about the intricacies and the heritage associated with the place. "Come, come." Her elderly guide led Hana towards the river path but turned off abruptly into a building on the right. She halted on the porch and kicked off her shoes, waiting while Hana did the same. The younger woman hopped from foot to foot, wrestling with her boots whilst clinging to the baby, eventually laying them down next to several other pairs of shoes littered around the walls of the covered area.

Phoenix, clipped neatly onto Hana's reached down with her tiny hands and tugged at her little cloth shoe. "Oh, I don't think yours count," Hana said, looking for help at the old lady. Hana wondered whether the custom extended to miniature people who couldn't walk but the little girl seemed determined to disrobe her feet. "Ok, then. Fine." Hana jiggled around a bit more, yanking off the shoes and stuffing them into the long neck of her boots. One of the baby's socks came off in Hana's hand and Phoenix wiggled her tiny toes in the cold winter air. Hana fought down words like *disaster* and *nightmare* to describe the visit thus far.

Inside the building the floor was wooden and looked original. Photographs lined the walls of the *wharenui,* a hall used to house sleeping guests. The roof met in an apex at the top, supported by huge red beams. Carvings decorated them, male and female with the characteristic three fingers and thumb and wide mouth with the protruding tongue.

Mattresses were placed around the room, still in the process of being stacked away. "We celebrated the king's birthday," the elderly woman said with a smile. "*Whānau* slept here."

Hana nodded and smiled, her green eyes raking the room with interest and fixing on a vibrant male carving above the mattresses on the left. It looked particularly ferocious but Hana's eyes widened at the sight of the phallic object pointing rigidly from the wood. It was massive. Hana bit her lip with a smirk and looked away, feeling amused at the boastful fertility symbol some unsuspecting visitor had gazed up at all night. The old lady followed Hana's line of sight and snorted. She jerked her head towards Hana's olive skinned child and her face creased into a grin. "You know, don't you?" she chuckled and Hana felt her cheeks flame.

The old lady laughed, not bothering to cover her mirth. Hana cringed, hoping nobody else asked what was so funny. She scurried quickly after the old woman as she shuffled away, fanning her hot cheeks with her spare hand and trying to dispel images of her well hung husband from her mind. At the other end of the long room, a man emerged from a cupboard backwards, wielding another mattress. His hair, once black was in the process of changing through greys to white in honour of the march of time. His wide brown face and squashed looking nose sheltered eyes which were coal black and vigorously alive. "Hey Aunty," he acknowledged the woman. "We're nearly done here."

"This *taitamāhine* would like some help," the old lady said and then to Hana's surprise, she winked at him and limped back towards the door. The man looked after her oddly before switching his gaze to Hana.

"Oh, thank you," Hana tried to say as she passed, but the woman waved the words away with a trembling hand and a smile. She shuffled along in luminous orange socks and too-large tracksuit bottoms with a curious look on her face.

"I won't be a minute." The man placed the mattress in a gap between two others, his solid frame making the action seem effortless. Then he turned his attention to the redhead, as though he had all the time in the world. The ready smile became transformed half way across his face as he noticed Phoenix in Hana's arms. The baby stared at him, her grey eyes unblinking as she demonstrated the freaky maturity she often seemed to have. "Ah." The man's brows knitted and for a moment he looked wrong-footed, until Phoenix did a curious little dip forward in Hana's arms and bowed her head. The man faltered for a moment and then, with a strange sense of resignation, he leaned towards Hana's baby and pressed noses with her in a *hongi*.

"*Morena Rangatira,*" he whispered. Hana fought the urge to yank her baby away, even though Phoenix started it first.

"Apologies, Mrs Du Rose," he said, turning to Hana with a smile which was hastily plastered to his face. "Your *kōtiro* has much *mana*. I recognise the line of Rueben Du Rose."

It wasn't a question, but a statement which left Hana flustered. The elderly Māori instantly identified her child's genealogy with accuracy and it left her speechless. In her confusion, Hana failed to realise her mouth was open and she gaped unattractively until Phoenix poked her finger between her mother's lips and grinned. It was a reprimand and Hana felt simultaneously humiliated and irritated.

"Tipene," the man said, holding his hand out for a European handshake and trying to put her at ease. Hana accepted the large brown fingers with trepidation, already feeling out of her depth and wishing she hadn't come.

"Hana Du Rose," she replied, knowing that her naming was academic.

"So, how can I help you?" Tipene asked, but it was clear Phoenix transfixed him, diverting his attention as her gaze locked on his face. He stared between the females with a look of bemusement.

"It all seems a bit stupid now, to be honest," Hana fumbled. She felt overwhelmed by the cultural gulf between Logan, Phoenix and herself. She had the irrational desire to throw the artifacts into the Waikato River and pretend they never existed. The pressing sense of urgency to deal with it all had driven her out into the miserable rain, urged her up to the *marae* and then abandoned her. Hana sighed. "Logan's grandmother gave the family *taonga* to the local *kaumātua* for safe keeping before she died, about thirty-six years ago. My husband has recently attempted to reunite the family property and effectively unify the family and Mr Hika brought them back to Logan. Apparently that was old Mrs Du Rose's wish."

"Phoenix did that?" Tipene asked and Hana became instantly suspicious. She had credited the man with a spooky paranormal skill, when really he knew the family – and by implication – her.

The tiny Phoenix Du Rose looked at him hard, as though expecting him to speak to her because he mentioned her name. Tipene smiled at the baby and his lips cracked wide with the action, changing his face into that of a jolly man with a ready sense of fun. He nodded in understanding. "Ah, you gave your *kōtiro* her name."

The baby smiled with ethereal radiance and Hana felt even more left out.

"Come," Tipene said, indicating the door. "Let's walk."

They retrieved their shoes from the porch and Hana was halfway across the courtyard before she worked out what the uncomfortable bulge was in her left boot – Phoenix's cloth shoes. They bunched up at the toe, causing her to limp. They went into a *ruma-kai* – a large dining room and Tipene seated Hana at a long wooden table with low bench seats. He was gone for a while but emerged from the kitchen with two steaming mugs of coffee and some sugar sachets which he laid in front of her. Phoenix sat on her mother's knee, clutching her toy horse and looking around her with an interested air.

"I must confess to an unfair advantage." Tipene confessed as he climbed onto the bench next to her. "I came to the *tangihanga* for Reuben Du Rose. I saw you but didn't link you with Logan at the time, although there was *kōhimuhimu* - gossip as you can imagine. I know the Du Rose family, or rather – I knew the older generation. I understood Logan Du Rose married but only saw him to offer my condolences that day. He seemed so shocked I doubt he'll remember." Tipene sighed and ran a coarse hand over his face, making a scratching sound against his beard. Hana listened to the rain pattering on the tin roof and watched the grey light kiss the inside of the dining room with ineffectual lips.

"Reuben was my good friend for many years," Tipene began. "He boarded with an aunt of mine here in Ngaruawahia during term time and we both attended Hamilton High School. He occasionally attended *tangis* here at the *marae*, but I hadn't seen much of him in the last twenty years or so. We wrote to each other regularly though. Not on the computer like you young people, but with pen and paper and stamps." Tipene laughed at his own outdated persona and Phoenix jumped, disturbing in her light nap against Hana's chest. Tipene watched her settle with a tight smile. "Perhaps your husband would like the letters Reuben wrote to me? They belong to him now."

Hana visibly cringed. "Logan only found out Reuben was his father the day after he died in the fire." She added, "It was dreadful."

Tipene shrugged and screwed up his face, showing a crease in his nose from a break. "It wasn't a decision Reuben agreed with, but he respected it. The letters contain many references to his son. Perhaps one day, Logan will find it in his heart to read them."

"I don't know," Hana sighed, aware of the hopelessness of her task. "He's had his world upended. He's not who he believed he was and it's been hard for him."

"Of course," Tipene said. "Our *mana* validates us and he feels his is skewed. It hasn't changed because it always came from Phoenix and Reuben Du Rose, its essence living through him. But Logan didn't know that and it's as though he's been plugged into the wrong power point his whole life. He'll right himself but it will take time, *taumano,* long time."

The elderly man led Hana around the *marae*. He pointed out the powerful *waka*, beautiful canoes which came out once a year for the annual regatta. The legacy and heritage of the tribe decorated them in powerful and stunning patterns and shapes. There were five huge ones and one quite small. Tipene made her laugh. "Each year we look for small men to put in it. It doesn't matter if they can row or not, as long as their combined weight doesn't sink it!"

He showed her the outpouring of the spring down near the banks of the Waikato River where the first Māori king bathed decades ago. "It's a place of great spirituality," he told her, "and a good place to sit and think. The water is said to have healing properties from the *mana* of the king."

Together they strolled in the watery sunshine, enjoying the peace and seclusion of the place and grateful of a break in the rain.

"I am truly glad you want to preserve the *taonga*," Tipene said to Hana with a sigh, as they looked at the heavy black doors of *Mahinarangi*. "Nothing is more important." He indicated the doors with his outstretched hand. "This was originally intended to be a hospital for the 1918 flu epidemic, so we could nurse our own kin. But the Ministry of Health refused to certify it, forcing our people into white hospitals where they were second class citizens and suffered great neglect. The building now houses all the gifts to the tribe and treasures collected over the last century earlier. It's all that remains of our heritage."

Hana studied the carving on the doors, depicting legendary tribal members and detailing the history of the land. She stroked the complicated patterns with a forefinger.

"Sorry I can't show you," Tipene said with regret. "Only the king can decide when it's open for viewing. If you'd like to come another time, I will request it."

"Thank you," Hana replied. "I'd like that very much. It would give me an idea of how to display the *taonga* to its best effect without breaking *tikanga* and *kawa*."

"Ah, customs and tradition," Tipene agreed and his eyes widened as he smiled.

"I know I have to protect it for my daughter," Hana sighed, her voice stained with humility. Her fingers lingered on Phoenix's sleeping back, tracing a gentle circle. "I just don't feel properly equipped."

Tipene shook his head, disagreeing vehemently. "On the contrary. Your fascination equips you and your love of Māori, added to your willingness to try. Logan is a fortunate *makau*. This generation doesn't care. We oldies used to listen to our elders in the long meetings on the *marae* as children, learn the stories of our heritage and sing the *waiata* they taught us. One day the world will wonder what our carvings mean and there will be nobody to tell them. Māori lore and customs are being filtered until they are no more and the special people of our songs forgotten. *Marae's* will become overgrown and dusty as my generation passes on. When the spirit of the last custodian leaps from Cape Reinga into the sea and makes their way home to Hawaiki, it will be finished."

He sounded mournful and Hana touched his arm lightly, offering comfort. The irony wasn't lost on her, an Englishwoman with a boot full of Māori treasures. "Not the Du Rose's," she said, injecting confidence into her voice. "I intend to find out about every single item and if I can get my husband to agree to my idea, perhaps we can preserve it all for my daughter's line."

Tipene smiled and his eyes crinkled. He squeezed Hana's shoulder in a firm but surprisingly gentle grip and felt hope burgeoning in his tired heart. The elderly man accompanied Hana off the *marae* and out to her car. "Please may I take your phone number, so I can contact you about the letters?" he asked.

"Yes, of course." Hana snorted as Tipene produced an expensive phone from his pocket, technology jarring with his philosophy. "I thought you didn't use computers like us young people," she joked.

"Ah, I do and happily, but Reuben, not so. He was a man of tradition and his life moved slowly. The world stopped for him the moment he stepped from his son's understanding and never restarted." Tipene looked up at Phoenix, lying in her car seat with a thumb plugged between her twitching lips. "But he was so proud of Logan. You'll see that from the letters. We all need to be loved, Hana; Logan's heart will find healing once he sees how much he was adored."

Hana gave Tipene her number, watching in amusement as the gnarled fingers moved quickly across the smart-phone keypad entering her details. It was an incongruous sight, the arthritic joints flashing speedily across the touch screen.

Tipene examined the contents of the box in Hana's boot. "Yes, yes!" he nodded. "Your idea is a good one. You're *whānau* and within your rights to handle what's here. I know the *kaumātua* of Logan's marae. He will have restored it all to a state of *noa*. The *tapu* will not affect you."

Tipene gave her the name of someone who could deal with the broken picture frames and offered sound advice on archive-keeping. Then he wished her well with a firm handshake and a wave.

"How did you know?" Hana asked his retreating back, needing an answer to the thing which bothered her. The old man turned and looked at her, his eyes filled with mischief. "How did you know Phoenix belonged to the Du Roses?" Hana repeated.

Tipene's weathered face broke into a smile and his eyes looked to a faraway, time-trodden place. Dragging himself back to the present, he gave a regal nod and wagged a forefinger at the baby's sleeping face. "The grey eyes," he said. "Her father is far too serious for his own good, but Reuben...he was not. She has the same twinkle as her *tipuna tāne*. You'll have to watch her later." Tipene gave a low chuckle. "Yes, Reuben Du Rose was a right little bugger!"

He moved back through the gate onto the *marae* and Hana watched as he unhooked the huge wooden structures and closed them against the world. Inside, life carried on almost as it had for hundreds of years, untainted by the western influence outside which relentlessly sought sameness and destroyed anything of difference. Untainted for now; but the wasteland was coming.

Chapter Twenty-Four

The name and address Tipene gave Hana caused her great consternation as she pulled up outside. She checked the GPS on her mobile phone, convinced she took a wrong turn or misread one of the directions it gave her. Hana was expecting a shop front or at least a business address for a picture framer, but the Honda pulled up outside an extremely derelict looking state house, with weeds springing from the gutter as though neglect was in residence. A gate hung off its hinges out front, the paint long since flaked and gone in the harsh climate, leaving the illusion of its having once worn a coat of white.

Hana looked down at her sleeping daughter and decided not to risk getting out of the vehicle. "I think your father will yell into next week," she whispered. "Getting out would be pretty stupid." The area looked poor and unloved, indicative of those low socioeconomic areas of New Zealand which tourists didn't see in the proffered '100% Pure' image. If Phoenix hadn't been with her Hana might have chanced it, but a definite atmosphere of hostility shrouded the area and net curtains twitched along the street.

Hana looked at her baby's peaceful face and made her decision, based on Logan's disdain if she deliberately took his daughter into foolish circumstances as much as her own instinctive fear. Turning back to the ignition, Hana gulped in a sharp breath as a man's face stared down at her. His brown skin was decorated across his chin in a traditional *moko* and his hazel eyes were shrouded by long black eyelashes. He looked in his mid-forties, with a body thick-set and powerful enough to have tossed railway sleepers for a living. His hair was shaved close to his dark head and he stood next to the driver's door, legs slightly splayed and arms folded. Hana whimpered in intimidation.

Then unexpectedly, he smiled. His eyes crinkled and his face split in a cheeky grin and he looked completely different. Yanking the car door open, he offered Hana his giant paw. "Welcome, Mrs Du Rose." Hana shook his hand, her own engulfed in it. Her face struggled to maintain a neutral appearance despite her rapidly beating heart and sweating palms. "I'm Jayden," he said, stepping back so Hana could slide from the Honda. "Tipene said you needed Father's help."

Hana nodded as her brain tried to figure out her next move. "My baby's asleep," she faltered, "would your father be able to come and look at the *taonga* out here?"

Tipene frowned and shook his head. "No ma'am, sorry, he can't. You take the child and I'll carry the gear in for you."

Hana felt powerless. That was how she ended up carrying Phoenix into the house over her shoulder, while the huge Māori lumped along behind, hefting the box of treasures on his broad shoulder. Inside, the house was clean but sparse. The floor was uncarpeted and the furniture old and neatly arranged, as though someone took great care over its placement. A tartan blanket lay over the back of a brown corduroy sofa, folded tightly into a perfect rectangle. A fire roared in a grate beneath a 1970's tiled mantelpiece, tired but still functional. The room was open plan, a sitting area and dining room taking up the majority of the space. The dining table was a round wooden one, with curious three legged chairs pushed tidily underneath it. Hana worried Jayden might require her to straddle one of the peculiar chairs.

The man lifted the box onto the dining table with exaggerated care. "Sit, please." His arm pointed to one of the corduroy chairs before he disappeared through a doorway into a tiny hall. Hana shifted her heavy child further over her shoulder and sat waiting, biting her lip in anxiety. *Logan's going to kill me.*

The room she sat in was homely and loved. Framed photographs lined the walls and mantelpiece, depicting smiling family members, adults and children. A small table next to the fireplace contained a photograph of an elderly lady beaming into the camera lens. Balanced precariously next to it was a tiny wreath of silk flowers, bent into shape to enfold the left-hand corner of the frame. A number of sympathy cards were propped around it, making Hana feel guilty she had imposed on a grieving *whānau*. Noise came from the other end of the house, filtering down the narrow hallway as the dull throb of male voices. Hana continued to wait.

She wasn't prepared for the wheelchair. The sound of the wheels passing over the floorboards made a peculiar noise and the man in it, banged his knuckles on the door frame as he hauled himself through. Hana got to her feet, contrition pinching her heart for having suggested he come outside and she hovered by her chair, unsure what to say. The man was in his late-sixties, dark haired and swarthy, very much like Tipene. He wore a white tee-shirt, exposing strong muscular biceps and a tattoo reaching from shoulder to elbow on his right arm. But his body ended above the knees, exposed stumps pointing forward and blunted. Wheeling himself over to her, the man paused and looked up at her, his face breaking into a broad, handsome smile, undimmed by age or misfortune. He held out his hand. "Will Hohaia," he said politely, a deep voice resonating within the small room. "Tipene's my brother. He rang and said you would come. Welcome. *Kia ora.*"

After shaking her hand, he indicated Hana should sit again. Jayden reappeared and reached for the tartan blanket, putting it gently over Will's scarred legs. It was a gentle, tender action, revealing much about his nature. Hana smiled in response.

"Jayden," Will said kindly, "take Mrs Du Rose's little *rangatira* will you? Just so we can look at the *taonga*."

The young man reached for Phoenix and Hana was forced to either appear churlish or let her sleeping child go into a stranger's arms. With a moment's nervous hesitation, she allowed Jayden to take her burden. To her relief, he walked over to the brown sofa and sat down, cuddling the baby into his breast and switching on the television.

"Come, let's see what problems the wily old woman has left you with." Will indicated with his head towards the dining table. Before Hana got there, the old man reached blindly into the battered box, pulling out the objects nearest the top. He sat in his wheelchair while Hana handed other things to him and they became engrossed in the items.

"So you know the Du Roses also, Mr Hohaia?"

"Call me Will and yes I knew Reuben Du Rose," he chuckled. "He and Tip were inseparable. There were only ten months between us and we were a real band of brothers when he lived with Aunty Celia. They kept contact all these years too, until...well, I didn't get to his *tangi*. I was having my other leg amputated."

Hana knitted her brows and looked sorry, but Will waved her sympathy away with a practiced movement. "Nah, diabetes. It had the other leg away a few years ago and this was always on the cards. We were all damaged goods, us three boys. I had diabetes and Reub had haemophilia. Tip had polio when we were kids and has a fat leg." He did a guttural laugh which ended in a cough. "Reub was always the one for the ladies and he had a wicked sense of humour." Will's whiskered face creased at his memories and he paused for a moment handling an old photograph. "Ah dear. Seems only yesterday," he sighed.

Hana handled the familiar polished *mere* in her hand, smoothing her fingers over its hard surface. "Why did Reuben go to school in Hamilton?" she ventured. "The other township kids went to Auckland, from what Alfred Du Rose told me."

Will put his head back and laughed, the sound huge in the small room. "He was expelled from there!" he chortled. "Law unto himself, that boy was. They couldn't contain him. So his mother sent him to live in Ngaruawahia with our *Whaea* Celia and she fair sorted him out. Man, she whooped his arse from there to Hamilton and back again, just like his ma knew she would. It made him sullen and rebellious for a while, but eventually he saw the sense of it and ended up grateful to her."

"I wonder what he did to get expelled," Hana mused, almost to herself.

Will guffawed. "Probably some money making scheme that made him rich and everyone else poor. He had the best business head of anyone I ever met. He would have given Bill Gates a run for his money that's for sure. He could sell fridges to Eskimos that boy. He bought an old motor scooter off our *pāpā* for a couple of dollars, pushed it home up State Highway 1 to Aunty's house because it didn't go. In his spare time he fixed it up real nice, changed the reggo plates, spray painted it and sold it back to our *pāpā* for ten times what he paid for it. Our *pāpā* never realised it was the same bike. When he was dying years later, Reuben swung by to pay his respects. He had half an hour with the old man and I think he told him. The old man died with a smile on his face after saying a whole string of swear words which all ended in '*Reuben Bloody Du Rose*,' but he died happy. He liked a good joke did our *pāpā*."

"That's where Loge gets it from then,' Hana remarked. "He's got a really good head for finance. Yet Alfred doesn't. It's fascinating really because Logan had no knowledge of Reuben his whole life, but he has so many striking similarities."

"That was a real bad business - all that stuff between those bro's. Reub always liked that girl, Miriam. It was a mess. They were both impetuous and look where it got them. Stupid teenage mind games. Neither of them could have guessed how it would end, now could they?"

"What did they fall out over?" Hana asked. "I've got the bones of the story, but that's about all."

Will shook his head. "I sure don't know. Maybe Tip does, but he won't tell another man's secrets, so no point asking. I think there was an interfering mother in there somewhere, usually is. Now then, are we looking at these *taonga* or not?"

Chastened, Hana went through the contents of the box until it was all neatly laid on the table. There were six small picture frames bearing black and white images of people and five larger ones. Some of them were broken, either the frames warped and snapped or the glass hanging off them in shattered curtains. Will peered at them, stroking a finger over some of the faces and nodding. "You know them?" Hana asked, her voice hopeful and he nodded. "Would you be able to fix these and possibly write something about who they are and what they did? It'll be important to be able to display them with the correct history."

Will smiled. "I can fix the pictures in the workshop out back. It's my hobby really. Jayden can help with some writing for you. He's got one of them computer things."

Hana nodded with pleasure at the man next to her. Together they handled the rest of the contents of the box, the jade pieces and some wooden plaques with engraved pictures of tribal leaders. Age had dulled and chipped them and Will assured her he could bring them back to life. Jayden wandered over to look at the stash with Phoenix was wide awake in his arms. She was unconcerned, rubbing the palms of her hands over his stubbled face like she did to Logan and Tama and giggling to herself. She looked at the objects on the table and pointed a tiny finger at them. "Da?"

"Yes little *mokopuna*," Will said, sounding wistful, "this all belongs to you."

The little girl studied him for a moment with frightening perception before her face degenerated back into its baby self. Will shivered and it made Hana uncomfortable. Phoenix was just a child, a baby. There was nothing spiritual about her, other than the innocence Jesus attributed to all children. It made Hana feel threatened as the two cultures clanged together once again, electrifying the atmosphere and leaving her worn out.

"Photograph all the artifacts of your phone," Jayden insisted. "Then you know what my *pāpā* has."

"Please can you do it?" she asked, handing over the expensive phone. "I suffer from camera shake on this. We won't recognise anything if it's left up to me."

"Now, lots of things you need to think about," Will said, turning his chair to meet Hana. "Everything needs to be properly digitally photographed and a record kept somewhere safe, once it's all restored."

"Oh, then I fell at the first hurdle." Hana's face dropped in sadness. "I had no idea it would involve all that."

"I'll take care of it." Will patted her hand, his face downcast, the brown eyes dulled by sadness. "It's not like I've anything else in my life."

Jayden shot Hana a look of alarm as he photographed a broken picture frame and Phoenix stopped stroking her mother's cheek and stared at the old man. She burbled something in baby talk and Hana made her decision. "There're another six boxes back at the hotel, and I'm told there are heaps more in the attic."

Will's eyes seemed to brighten with interest and his weathered face cracked in a smile. "Really?"

Hana nodded. "Yes. There's heaps apparently but these were the ones Phoenix hid." She turned to Jayden. "Can you put your number in my phone when you're finished with the photographs and I'll stay in touch with you? I will need an estimate of cost though, because I'm paying for it myself."

The dark man smiled at her and nodded, keying numbers into her phone. As she left, Hana turned to Will, the crumpled body in the wheelchair seeming to have regained some of its dignity. "I hope you're in for the long haul. It might keep you busy for the next twenty years."

Will gave her the benefit of his beatific smile and looked pleased with the idea. "I don't got twenty years, *kōtiro*, so we best get on with it."

Phoenix gave a regal little wrist wave as her mother carried her back down the steps to the car. "How does he know how to look after all this?" Hana asked Jayden as he walked her to the Honda.

"He used to be the custodian for Tainui," Jayden replied. "He took care of all the gifts in *Mahairangi* and all the artifacts. The Waikato tribes were fearsome and showed no mercy in the old days. They avenged wrongs through *utu*, plundering those who did them wrong in order to put the situation right and restore their *mana* or honour. There are many precious objects in that building and my father used to take care of them all, cataloguing them long hand. He could tell you everything in there up to about four years ago. When he lost his first leg, he carried on for a while with a prosthetic but he's had other health problems since and had to retire. The tribe has been kind to him, but he struggles to make ends meet. He's lost a lot of his confidence and *mana* since the other amputation. This will give him purpose. He'll enjoy himself."

Jayden leaned forward towards Phoenix and the little girl bobbed her head, accidentally nutting him on the nose instead of performing a decent *hongi*. To make matters worse she laughed. "Practice required little one," Jayden said graciously rubbing his nose. To Hana, he said, "My sister works at the photographic shop in town. When Father has finished with the pieces, I'll take them to her for digital copying. She'll put them on a disk for you to keep safe. They've survived this far - we owe it to their custodians to honour their struggle. Phoenix Du Rose must have had good reason for hiding them at the *marae*."

Hana nodded in agreement. "I just wish I knew what it was."

She strapped Phoenix into her seat and travelled back to the school site, where she fed her daughter mushed up casserole and gave her a breast feed. They crawled around downstairs for a while, playing chase until Hana's knees were sore and then both of them curled up on the double bed in the upstairs classroom and dozed off to sleep.

Chapter Twenty-Five

Logan Du Rose stood in the doorway and watched his girls sleep. Phoenix sucked her thumb so loudly, it sounded as though it might come off. Hana was wrapped around her daughter, her long red hair hanging over the baby like a blanket. Both were pink-cheeked and flushed from their combined body heat, despite the cold winter afternoon. He leaned against the doorframe with all the time in the world for this particular activity, watching his soul mate and his child sleep. '*Never take this for granted, tamatāne. Never grow tired of enjoying them.*' Reuben's voice pricked Logan's heart now he recognised it, imparting wisdom from the grave where it couldn't while alive.

Logan smiled at his sleeping girls. Twenty-six years was far too long to wait for his turn at bliss, but to have this kind of surety he would willingly do the lonely years again. He ran his hand over his face and up through his hair noticing the satisfying glint of his wedding ring in the dramatic sunset his girls were missing through the west facing bay window. They would never know how often he stood this way, drinking in the contentment washing over him. Their presence centred him and made life worth living.

Logan kicked off his boots and walked around the bed, settling himself behind his wife, so as not to wake her. He nuzzled into the back of her hair and smelled the sweet scent of her shampoo, unable to resist laying his arm over her body and drawing himself in closer. Hana disturbed and sighed, but stayed asleep. Logan knew his wife was up to something, but didn't get the feeling it was anything dreadful. He settled down to play the long game with her as though she was a stubborn mare up at the farm he needed to break in. Slowly but surely he would tame her, bend her to his will without subduing the passionate fire he loved so much in her. "I love you, *hoa wahine*," he whispered to his wife.

Phoenix woke first, laying peacefully, her eyes staring around the huge empty room. She felt arms snuggling her and smelled the familiar perfumed scent of mummy and as she lay silently sucking on her thumb, she smelled daddy too. His scent of hay and sunshine comforted her. A familiar sensation snaked around her tiny stomach like a brace and the little girl wiggled her legs and made snuffling noises, alerting her parents if she didn't get nourishment soon, she might die. When her mother instinctively cuddled her in harder it was no good, she turned up the decibel level to be understood.

"Bad night?" Hana asked Logan as he lay next to her dozing while she gave Phoenix a feed.

"Not really," he replied. "I can't sleep there properly. I'd rather be wherever you girls are."

Hana ruffled his hair softly with her free hand, letting her fingers stray to the scar under his right eye. It felt ridged and rough to the touch, but she loved it. It was part of her husband. "Gorgeous man,' she whispered. She gave Phoenix to her father for winding, not that his version was particularly effective. He lay on his back with her sitting on his taut stomach, jiggling around and laughing. Hana could just imagine the clean-up operation if the bubble of air came up without warning. "How come you're home so early?" she asked, standing up to stretch her legs and looking out of the window.

"I had a free period and then they called a Chapel service last thing, so that screwed my Year 11 Classics class."

"Hmmnn," Hana replied, her attention elsewhere, focusing on the woman walking past the front of The Gatehouse.

The school bell rang loudly in the main building, creating a distant trill across the field. It was followed by an outpouring of male bodies which streamed across all available surfaces like fleeing ants. The woman outside was almost white blonde, her hair scraped back into a tight bun at the nape of her neck. She was stick thin and her body had a wooden quality to it as she strode across Hana's view. She walked a fluffy white and ginger Cavalier King Charles Spaniel, which stopped to pee on the verge between the driveway and the playing fields. Hana watched, her nose wrinkled in annoyance as the woman looked directly up at the window and raised her eyebrow in greeting. There was something unsaid there, something important and Hana didn't realise she held her breath until she sensed her chest becoming inexplicably tight.

Leaning into the bay window to see further, Hana noticed the woman walk around the corner, past the end of the section heading for Maui Street. *Dora Dobbs*. "I just need to go downstairs," she blurted, turning to run as an uncomfortable mantle settled on her shoulders. *Dora Dobbs was trying to get her attention*.

"Oh, crap!" Logan shouted and Hana turned to see her baby wide eyed, in the first stages of tears. The air bubble in the baby's gullet had worked its way up to the top and she projectile vomited right down her father's expensive work shirt. In the ten minutes it took to clean up Logan and Phoenix in the shower and then strip the bedding, Hana knew she had missed a valuable opportunity.

As father and daughter splashed and shrieked under the hot water, Hana changed the duvet cover and pillow cases, running the dirty ones down to the laundry room at the back of the house. She peered through the laundry window which faced the main road. It was a dull, overcast day and the headlights from passing traffic glared off the glass, obscuring other things. "I know I'm not imagining this," Hana mused. She made up her mind to track Dora down and have a conversation. She couldn't rid herself of the overwhelming feeling the other woman was deliberately trying to get her attention.

Chapter Twenty-Six

Hana couldn't sleep. She lay on her back and sighed as Logan breathed next to her in a regular, even rhythm. It was a beautiful noise to her former widow's ears. A romp with her gorgeous husband had left her breathless but still wide awake. Hana nudged Logan's strong thigh with her bent knee and wondered if he would be interested in tiring her out some more. He was an attentive and energetic lover and usually wore her out thoroughly, but tonight, sleep eluded her. "Logan," she whispered, trailing her index finger up his hairy thigh into the hem of his shorts. Logan grunted and turned his back on her.

Hana counted the yellow spots on the ceiling, adding up the glittering reflections from the street lights around the driveway which sneaked between the curtains. The face of the tennis player wafted across her mind's eye, handsome and blond, stunning blue eyes and a muscular physique. He was an awesome player - *had been* an awesome player.

Lachlan Reynolds, Lachlan Reynolds. Hana ran the name over and over through her brain, but only produced the skinny, red-haired child. Something about the name and the boy tugged at her memory but wouldn't come loose. If Vik were around, he could tell her what it was. He coached the tennis team for a couple of years, even after Bodie lost interest. Something jarred in her memory but still, Hana couldn't nail it.

Tired of driving herself mad, she got up and slipped a fleece over her nightdress. With a pair of woolly slippers on her feet which a lady from church knitted her, she padded downstairs in the dark, using the moonlight through the stained glass windows on the landing to guide her. The coloured patterns on the floor were eerie and the stairs creaked as they launched themselves into the lobby, but Hana made it to the kitchen of the strange house without disaster.

Shutting the door before turning on the light, Hana placed the wooden shell of the diary on the table. As she reached into the wardrobe for her fleece it was there under her fingers, calling to her with a tantalising invitation, asking her to plunge herself back into the depths of its memory. Hana hunted in a drawer for a needle and used the long metal inserted into the hole to lever open the hidden clasp. Then she made tea and settled down to read, like a closet chocaholic with her next fix.

The cotton gloves were stuffed inside the diary and Hana groaned as only one came out, realising she must have dropped the other one in the bedroom or on the stairs. Using only the hand with the glove, Hana continued her expedition back in time, drinking in the writing as a personal conversation with Logan's grandmother. Feisty and independent, Phoenix Du Rose was impossible to dislike. She wrote truthfully about her life, her fears and worries. Hana felt a deep empathy with her daughter's namesake, yet the burden of her secrecy burned in her heart. The more she learned, the more she worried about her husband's ability to forgive her deliberate concealment of the diary. There were things in it he really should know, but others Hana would rather he didn't.

By the early hours, Hana knew for sure that Phoenix Du Rose and not Henri removed the *tapu* pin from her father's burial cloak. It was done in panic, to prevent her mother's sister, Rangi, from taking it instead. There was mention of a dispute between Rangi's family and Phoenix's father, which was serious enough for him to send her and her family away. Hana turned the pages but found no information about the cause. The attendance of Rangi's family at the funeral distressed Phoenix.

'I knew they would come like birds of prey, circling around the dead. They came to pay their respects she said, whining like an old steam engine. While they were here, they capitalised on the sympathy of my unwise whānau and got drunk and fat at their expense until their whatuaro hung over their trousers.'

Hana bit her lip and rubbed her tired eyes. "That's belly fat," she said out loud. "Logan's said that to someone. Tama? Phoenix? Someone, anyway."

Hana read up to an entry dated 10th February 1952. She got up and reboiled the kettle, feeling the pull of the diary even from across the room. Already addicted, she slipped the glove back onto her right hand even though it was a left-handed glove and noticed something. Phoenix's handwriting slanted to the left. Logan was left-handed and his daughter favoured that side when sucking her thumb or grabbing for objects. It made Hana feel an even stronger kinship with the matriarch. Loneliness seeped from every page and Hana recognised and felt its keen bite.

'The boys are well now, although Reuben continues with the bleeding at times. I manage to hide it - I do not want Rangi's whānau circling. Alfred is a quiet boy but Reub is hard to manage. He wants to do everything Alfie does and rivals his older brother without care for his own harm.'

Hana wondered how Phoenix coped with her haemophiliac son, living miles away from medical help. The tattered pages contained recipes for herbal remedies, parts of them missing or water damaged. Phoenix found natural ways of dealing with Reuben's condition and Hana shuddered at the fear a bleed engendered in her, when she had ambulances and hospitals available. "It must have been horrific," she breathed. "How did you cope, Phoenix?" Often Logan bled without relenting and ended up in hospital on a drip and Hana shook her head, imagining a bowl of mashed kawakawa leaves as a ready substitute. An entry on 28th February 1952 revealed a dramatic change in Phoenix's ability to manage Reuben's disease.

'Reuben's condition is not showing improvement. The Pākehā doctor has done what he can. The boy insists he can ride and muster and he is always in trouble at school. I don't know what to do with him. I fear for him permanently. The blood disease is the curse of the women. Will there be no end to it? Almost all the men are gone because of it. Matua predicted this.'

But as Hana read on, a few pages later revealed a pitiful entry. The writing was heavily slanted and untidy, as though the writer struggled to keep it together. Hana knew that feeling well.

'The hapu think Henri died because of the tapu. I feel so guilty. Henri has been a stubborn man, but we learned to love each other. He knew I took the aurei, but he understood. Life has been cruel to us. What the curse has not stolen, the war took. It was only a matter of time. The shrapnel in Henri's head from the injury was always moving. He knew it. His sight had become worse of late. I miss my husband. Nothing seems to take the pain away. Not even the laughter of my boys.'

Hana blew her nose into a piece of kitchen roll. Phoenix's grief rolled over her like a wave, agonisingly familiar. In Hana's mind, it became all about her. She was back in that world of loss with her dead husband and two teenage children. The misery felt like an old friend, tempting and attractive. Hana wanted to pick it up and wrap it around herself again, knowing if she accepted its embrace she would find it impossible to break free. So she resisted, drinking her cold tea and skipping pages, avoiding the worst of the sadness for now. The diary continued as Phoenix grew busier with the farm and the entries became more spread out.

'Reuben is a terror. They have refused to have him at school. The payments were so much to keep him there, but they have sent notice he is not to return. Alfred is to continue to stay with Matua's whānau in the city and attend, but Reuben must come away. The teachers beat him so badly this time I feared he would not

recover. His body was black from it. The kaumātua has been here permanently since they sent him back on the cart. He has used all the old knowledge to help my son. Reuben is not sorry. They beat him for using the language of our forefathers to another boy and so he refused to stop. I know not whether to be angry with my child or proud of him.'

Hana's hand strayed to her mouth in horror. She had heard tales of Māori children beaten for speaking their language, but never encountered anyone willing to talk about it. It was horrific, barbaric. The words for it were endless. A glance at the clock showed it was after three in the morning. Hana gently closed the pages, intending to go to bed finally. But the book fell open and a loose tattered page fluttered out, bearing a curious statement. There was no date.

'*The women are the curse of this family. But the men will be its ruin.*'

Perplexed, Hana reached towards the page but her hand didn't quite get there. She felt the presence of Logan in the room, even before she saw him. Not only was he a master at breaking into locked doors, but somewhere along the way he acquired the ability to move his six foot, four inch frame in complete silence. Hana gaped, caught out in her deception. Logan pointed towards the table and raised one eyebrow. Hana bit her lip. "It's your grandma's diary, Loge. I was reading it. It's incredible; I've learned so much about your family. None of what you've been told is true. She..."

"You had no right!" Logan's voice rapped out into the silence, halting Hana's babble. She felt stunned.

"You *gave* me the right! You said I could deal with it, take care of it. That's why we brought the box back, so..." she stopped, knowing by the look on his face her words were a waste. Her acceptance into his *whānau* was nothing but a smokescreen.

Hana's ungloved hand strayed to the cover of the book, attempting to draw strength from the woman who poured her heart into it. But the feeling of shared confidence was gone, stripped away from Hana the moment Logan opened his mouth. She withdrew her hand, grief wrapping itself round her soul. The cultural and emotional divide between them yawned wider and deeper, an insurmountable chasm she was powerless to breach. Hana mentally withdrew and after a year and a half of wrangling with her marriage; she gave up. Her shoulders slumped and the fight went out of her. With shaking fingers she pushed the wooden cover towards Logan and let go, resignation filling her eyes.

Logan struggled to maintain his composure. Rage leaked out of him like water from a laden sponge, seeping and dripping from every part of his being. His grey eyes glittered with a hard-edged-danger and Hana held her breath. His muscular body was taut and rigid, compressing his anger within and Hana looked away from the display of power, filled with terror and longing, a heady mix of competing emotions. *"You. Are. Not. The. Person. I. Thought. You. Were,"* he snarled, each word coming through halted and blunt.

The words were laced with cruelty and cut Hana like a sabre, renting her flesh from her bones and causing equally as much pain. The old Hana would have thrown the book at him and run away to lick her wounds, lashed out with some smart remark that aimed its own low blow, but that Hana was gone. This Hana clasped her hands gently over the offending diary and closing her eyes, hung her head. She reached inside herself to the 'pit of despair,' the place where fear and rejection hung out. They could be relied upon to feed her ready grasp with barbed comments, defensive actions and bile. But Hana found nothing there.

Fear and rejection had been de-installed and replaced with nothing. There were no spiteful words to hand and nothing to hurl back at her husband, who just told her he didn't love her. He loved an image of her which wasn't really Hana. He just admitted it and the fragile vase of their marriage cracked against the blow.

Logan watched with knitted brow, his fists balled in frustration while he waited for Hana's inevitable detonation.

When nothing came, he looked lost with no idea how to handle this silent version of his wife. He knew what he meant to say, but once it was airborne, it emerged as something else and they both knew what that was.

Hana looked up at him and her eyes were steady, focussed and calm. Her palms rested gently on the cursed book as though drawing strength from its presence. "I can never be the person you thought I was, Logan," she said and smiled at him with something like apology. "Because that person doesn't exist. You didn't know me when you decided I was worth pursuing as your soul mate. I was just a terrified, lonely, disgraced girl on a train who you could 'fix' and then fixate on. It was just a snapshot of who I really am, a single unit of time in forty-five years of a life well lived. I'm tired of bowing to an illusion, trying to be someone you've spent more than two decades manufacturing in your head. I'm *me*, Logan, nothing more, nothing less and I'm reasonably happy with who that is. I'll never be accepted by your *whānau*, because no matter how hard I try, you want to keep me on the outside. I'm tired. I'm over it. And I'm *done* here."

Hana got carefully to her feet, but when she walked towards her husband, she glided like a swan with more superhuman grace and dignity than she could have humanly mustered. Calm and serenity exuded from her like a covering. Her green eyes sparkled and shone with inner beauty as she gazed into Logan's stunned grey ones for a long moment. It was uncomfortable. Then she held the wooden casing out towards him, pushing it gently into his chest when he resisted, leaving him no choice. "Read it, Logan," Hana ordered. "I'm glad I did. I now know all the things that are great and awful about the Du Roses. There's a lot of wisdom in your grandmother's words and you'll find it releasing. It might help you work out who *you* are. Good luck, Logan."

The smile Hana bestowed on her husband was both kind and sane. It held compassion and no trace of the expected hysteria. With a final tiny smile, Hana turned and walked away from him, drifting down the long corridor without hurry and up the majestic wooden staircase with the same degree of dignity and poise. Logan stayed rooted to the spot, clutching the wooden box in his hands. Its surface felt gnarled and ridged under his fingers and he glanced down at his white knuckles. The markings of his lineage winked back at him in the wood, enhanced by the fluorescent light overhead, mocking him in some understated way. He wanted to throw the *taonga*, to smash it to the ground in anger, but for only the third time in his life, his body refused to do his bidding.

The angry sweat dried cold on his torso and his shirt stuck to him and made him chill. His lithe, athletic frame with its one fatal flaw seemed incapable of taking orders from his brain, ignoring the urgent signals to flee by remaining glued to the floorboards. Logan's jaw worked furiously, grinding his teeth until his head hurt. A voice inside his consciousness yelled at him, *Stupid, stupid, stupid man!* And he knew he had inadvertently made Hana believe he didn't love her. It wasn't what he meant; but it was his inference.

As the blood flowed back into his feet, Logan drew a long deep breath and knew this couldn't be easily fixed. He had some thinking to do, but needed to get away from the house to do it. The first time his body refused his bidding, he was fourteen and his mother clouted him hard around the head. They should have got off the train at the last stop but Logan delayed, getting slowly out of his seat and dragging his feet down the carriage towards the automatic doors. The dirty underground furniture had looked dull and lifeless in comparison to the glowing, vital, pregnant girl in the yellow dress opposite. In his memory she remained on fire, her auburn hair complimenting the dress and her reddened, tear streaked cheeks.

Miriam needed to get off sooner, to get to the hospital and visit her terminally ill brother. Logan's dallying caused them to stay on the underground too long and they were forced to double back. They were too late and the dying uncle was gone. Logan's body froze up that day too, refusing to take another step away from the redhead, transfixed by the sense of knowing she belonged to him.

It was a turning point in his life, the clever boy who until then wasted his talents suddenly had a goal, an aim in life - to find *her*. His failure was almost his undoing, until there she was, grappling around on the floor for her dropped belongings on the wrong side of the world. Logan experienced the same rigidity in his soul and did nothing. He was late for the first day of his new job, stuck in the car park waiting for his body to listen to his screaming brain.

Logan stood in the kitchen of the old schoolhouse and ordered his body to move. "Just move, Logan, damn you!" he hissed, to no avail. The memory of Hana gliding across the room towards him, clutching the *taonga* to her chest, was burned onto his inner eyelid like a brand. "What have I done?" he breathed. She was every bit as beautiful as on that first day, dignity and composure etched into her very being. Logan cursed his body for locking up and refusing to move, responding to a presence which left him breathless. She got too close to the core of him and he froze her out.

Hana got into bed and snuggled down. There was a tightness in her chest from keeping the tears confined but when she reached for the sadness and permitted its escape, it didn't come. A numb, emptiness took over her soul and left her struggling. She prayed, not knowing even as the whispered words tumbled from her mouth, what it was she was asking. To her amazement, sleep collected her quickly and the tears remained unshed.

Downstairs, Logan acknowledged an overwhelming need to scream out loud, but the sound would contain far too much of himself and he couldn't allow it. He retreated to the office at the boarding house where he spent the night in a stunned contemplation of his beloved grandmother's words.

Hana woke feeling surprisingly refreshed the next morning. The numbness had devoured her heart, allowing her room to breathe. It was a reliable defence mechanism. As soon as she was dressed, she rang Peter North's mobile, confused by how puffed he sounded as he answered the phone. "What are you doing?" Hana asked, alarmed by the degree of heavy breathing.

"I'm running!"

Hana peered through the glass of the upstairs bay window at the sports field. "Really?"

"Yeah, I'm gettin' fit. Haven't you noticed?" His voice held an edge of pique and Hana raised her eyebrow at her daughter. Phoenix sucked her thumb and pointed a delicate finger at the tiny figure lumping around the athletics track near St Bart's. The figure stopped and bent in half from the waist and Hana continued.

"Well, after you've finished 'running' could we have a chat? I'll walk over to you in the next few minutes."

"Well don't be long," came the panting voice, "I'm only doing a short one."

"How short is short?" Hana enquired.

"Five minutes and I've already done three."

Shaking her head, Hana rang off, stuffed Phoenix into her pram and after locking up the house, strode over the fields to meet her old colleague. By the time she made it across the lumpy grass, Pete lay flat on his back staring up at the sky. His face was a dreadful shade of tomato-red and his chest heaved in unhealthy gasps. Phoenix took one look at him and lay back in her pram with her thumb and squeezed her eyes tight shut. Hana straightened the bobble hat and blanket and gave Pete time to recover his dignity. "I thought you'd be in tutor group," she commented, wincing as Pete hawked up phlegm and spat dramatically on the grass. He shook his head with enthusiasm.

"Angus took them off me. He said it'd do the student teacher good to manage on his own. Said I'd be doing him a big favour."

Hana rolled her eyes. It was common knowledge Pete was currently taking 'a long walk off an increasingly short pier.' Logan had vouched for him becoming deputy manager of the boarding house, promising no doubt to keep a really tight rein on him; otherwise, it was a dead cert Angus would have biffed him out of the school for good. Angus didn't usually dodge issues, so Hana wondered if the student teacher story was made up by Pete to hide his incompetence. She waved her hand at him and tried not to focus on thoughts of her husband. "Please can you get me the private phone number for Alan Dobbs?"

Pete alarmed her by jumping to his feet. He laid a hand firmly on Hana's shoulders and got way to close for a sweaty man, reeking like he hadn't showered since Henrietta left, over ten days ago. "What?" Hana pleaded, trying to dodge his ministrations without waking the baby.

Pete gripped both her shoulders in his pudgy hands and breathed pickle breath over her face. He leaned in so close Hana could see the hairs nestling up his nose and then he uttered his words of wisdom. "I'm sorry to have to tell you this, Hana. But Alan Dobbs is dead."

Hana couldn't help herself. She shoved the little man hard and he stumbled back over the pram wheel, landing on his backside with a thud. She looked down at him sitting on the ground in the frosty grass and felt a stab of guilt. But before she could make the fatal mistake of showing any weakness, Pete grappled around his backside and looked up at her in annoyance. "You've wet my pants! Now I'll come back to yours for a shower!"

It was so like Peter North, it infuriated Hana. Within a three hundred metre radius of his lardy backside were four available showers for him to use; one in the male toilets in the main building, one in the school gym, one in the staff area of St Bart's and Pete's very own shower, in his staff unit, in view of his seated position. "And you'll have to cook me a full English breakfast while you tumble dry my pants," he added.

Hana felt exhaustion wash over her. "I'm sick of men!" she snapped. "You're all dicks!" She stomped off, pushing the pram ahead of her and racking her brains for another way of getting the deceased man's phone number, so she could contact Dora.

As the bell rang for first period, Pete saw Logan's confident stride heading over to St Bart's. He decided to add an extra minute's run onto his exercise regime, in order to confess he'd broken the news about Dobbs' death to Hana and she hadn't taken it well.

Hana pushed her pram up the disabled ramp and into the reception area of the school. She hoped to get up to the student centre without going through the pain of writing a visitors' badge but was out of luck. Despite being due to retire, it hadn't daunted the receptionist's dogmatic enforcement of the rules. She bobbed her grey head as Hana protested the ridiculousness of writing out a name badge for herself. "This is silly," Hana grumbled, pen in hand. "Not only am I a former employee, but I still live on site. If people don't know who I am after sixteen years, it's a bit sad!" Feeling facetious, she wrote herself a name tag and slapped it on her jacket.

"Nice one, miss," a boy chuckled as he held the door open for her. He jerked his head towards her name tag and Hana smiled. Emblazoned on her front was the name 'Minnie Mouse' and on the carbon downstairs was the reason for her visit; 'looking for Mickey.'

Walking up the stairs having left her pram in the kind bursar's office and carrying her baby, Hana ripped the sticky label off her jumper. In case of a fire it was hardly likely the fire brigade would pull the building apart looking for 'Minnie Mouse.' At the top of the stairs, Hana paused and looked over the bannister to the parquet floor below. The broad staircase was an original feature of the old building. Two sets of steps approached a wide landing, running diagonally towards each other, symmetrical and identical like a pair of open arms. The boys were meant to go up and down one side, leaving the other free for staff, but often both sides were a free for all in the rush between lessons. The wood was a dark chocolate brown, shining from over a hundred years of polish and wear. It still felt as solid as the day it was installed, despite the daily heavy foot traffic of stomping, growing boys.

Hana peered over the balustrade at the administrative corridor below, stretching out either side of the stairs. Her best friend, Anka once used an office at the end of the left-hand corridor and Hana missed her after the affair with Tama ended her career. Anka's office had been a site of much giggling and hilarity. Now a quiet, studious lady worked there and that end of the corridor was silent, but for click of a keyboard and the periodic squeak of a chair.

Kissing Phoenix's downy head, Hana shuddered as she thought of Dobbs falling down the stairs. She had no idea which of the two flights saw his unintentional descent, but it would have been a painful end. "It's so awful," she mused. "I know I didn't like him, but I wouldn't wish that on anyone." Hana stood on the landing and peered at the floor, entertaining the ghoulish pondering. Her body gave an involuntary shiver. It was a dreadful way to die, crashing over the worn treads, feeling bones breaking and not knowing if the next crash would be his last.

"I hope you're going to give me a receipt for these things!" came an angry shouted voice behind her. It shocked Hana and she let out a small squeal. The school archivist, a gentle, elderly man in his late sixties appeared from the direction of the staff room, in hot pursuit of a uniformed police officer. He was pink-cheeked and agitated, scurrying after the burly cop. "These items belong to the school!" the white haired archivist stated in a loud voice. "You shouldn't be removing them without the principal's express, written permission!"

The cop ignored his plaintive cries, taking the steps two at a time downwards, disregarding the fact a man had died on account of them already. He carried in his arms a long photograph depicting the whole school, including students and staff from some bygone era. Hana knew even from a distance where her face would be in the photo. Dobbs glared out at her from the seated front row of the picture, causing Hana to recoil as she felt his printed eyes boring into her. Then his face was gone, along with what looked like a number of year books and a computer disk.

"Damn rude man!" the archivist grumbled to nobody in particular and Hana looked in his direction. He was flustered and sweating, his precious artifacts now long gone. "I'm responsible for those," he said to her pleadingly and Hana smiled in apology. She felt the same about the diary, as though it belonged to her. Again she felt the lack of it, resenting her husband's ability to take it away. She suspected he probably hadn't even read it.

"Were they taking pictures of Dobbs?" Hana asked the man.

He shrugged in a verbose, exaggerated movement. "Him and Lachlan Reynolds," he grumbled, "and someone else, but I'm not supposed to say." The archivist pursed his lips and went carefully down the staircase to the left.

With a sigh, Hana turned to face the archway leading to the upstairs rooms. The senior common room was in front of her, accessed through wide double doors while the staffroom was through another set of doors to the left. The student centre, Hana's old workplace for fifteen years, lay through the common room with the guidance counsellors' suite adjacent to it. It was the one place she could potentially get the phone number for Alan Dobbs' wife without too many questions. Failing that, it would have to be the phone book, but something told her the cautious man would have been unlisted.

Taking a deep breath and turning away from the crime scene of a few weeks ago, Hana marched with confidence through the double doors and into the common room. Over sixty faces turned towards her from their study, two whole classes of boys reading quietly. Hana knew some of the faces and they smiled. Nodding to the study teacher, she hoisted her baby over her shoulder further and knocked on the student centre door.

Heather, Angus' new love interest opened it with a smile. "Hello, love," she said with a smile. "Come to take your old job back?"

"No thanks," Hana answered, knowing that part of her life was long gone. Hana rarely visited her old workplace anymore. Her world moved on in unrecognisable proportions, yet a thin trace of grief could still be unexpectedly felt and an inexplicable sense of longing for her old, simple life. Her battle with Logan in the early hours left her feeling raw and jaded.

As Hana stepped into the room, the familiar chaos surrounded her like a comfortable shroud. Heather jerked her head towards a familiar piece of A3 paper on the brown carpet, depicting the layout of the school and the classrooms being used by presenters for the upcoming expo. "Be very glad you're not involved this year," Heather whispered. "All I'm hearing is how amazing Hana was at everything and how rubbish I am."

Hana winced and stared at the paper. It denoted the marks she put on it in years gone by, showing where wall sockets offered power for projectors or laptops. Next to it on the carpet were numerous squares of paper with names of organisations hastily scribbled on each. "Oh, yeah, I remember this bit. It was known as the pitch frenzy, when locations were allocated and then moved over and over. No, you're right; I definitely don't miss this part of the job."

Heather rolled her eyes and lowered her voice. "It's like working for a banshee on crack."

Hana snorted and a face peered from the corner office. "Oh my gosh, Hana!" Sheila Jennings tore from her office and wrapped elegant arms around Hana and the baby. Miraculously, Phoenix stayed asleep.

Rory, the Year 13 dean and Sheila's son-in-law stood up from his seat behind the door and greeted Hana with fondness. He looked as though he had a whole pile of marking in the centre of his desk, but reached out for Hana's baby anyway. "Holding a child is a good excuse for not working," he chortled, cuddling Phoenix into his chest. The group exchanged pleasantries and Rory wandered off into the common room with the baby, heading for the staffroom. Hana stared after him, torn between trusting an old friend with her child and wanting to run after him and rip the baby out of his arms.

"He'll be fine," Sheila said gently, seeing the conflict on Hana's face. "He has got three of his own."

"I know," Hana said, "it's just that..."

"You haven't really got over all that business at the start of the year, have you?" Sheila asked knowingly. "I can't say I blame you. It's been a horrific year for you and Logan." She pulled at Hana's arm and barked at Heather, "You can hold the fort for a while if I go and catch up with your predecessor, can't you?"

Hana cringed, feeling the rub in the comment. But Heather merely smiled and winked at her. Sheila blew out of the student centre dragging Hana after her and together they tracked Rory to the coffee. "We've got a machine now," Sheila said with excitement, tucking her arm genially through Hana's. The machine was a forbidding looking vending unit and the charge a dollar. Sheila put in one coin each.

"A latte, please," Hana said, watching Rory chat to colleagues at the social studies table. Phoenix was still fast asleep and her mother made a mental note to stop being so fussy and paranoid. Each morning, Hana said a prayer for Bodie and Izzie, in her absence placing their well-being into God's capable hands. It occurred to her it might be a good idea to include the baby. Perhaps then, she wouldn't be so inclined to do it all in her own strength.

Despite desperately wanting to show off the 'improvements' to her working world, Sheila couldn't get the coffee machine to produce a latte. She pressed the button four times and nothing happened. Resorting to brute force and ignorance she kicked it hard and got four cups for her dollar. The cups then made quite a tower, which when filled, wouldn't go past the spout without tipping and pouring the liquid into the drip tray.

Undaunted, Sheila set about retrieving Hana's drink. She left her standing by the machine while she ran back to the office to fetch a pair of scissors.

"Where's she gone now?" Rory asked, wafting past with Phoenix.

"To get scissors."

Rory tutted and pushed a little button above the chute. The front part of the machine flipped open enough for Hana to grab her latte, ensconced in its four cups. "She hasn't improved with age, has she?" Rory smirked and Hana giggled.

When Sheila returned brandishing scissors, she was relieved to find Hana already sipping her too-hot-drink. Admitting defeat, she settled for a cup of tea. They chatted about their respective lives in a belated catch up. "My divorce came through last week," Sheila said, not sounding too sad. "Twenty-six wasted years."

"Never totally wasted," Hana chided.

"No, I've got the kids I suppose. And it's working really well living in the granny flat at Rory and Maria's place. I'm on hand for babysitting and it's nice and private if I want it to be."

Hana picked up a hidden thread of wistfulness. It was Sheila's dream home, built painstakingly to her and Martin's specifications and sold to her daughter in the mop up of the joint assets. "What's Martin up to now?" she asked, referring to Sheila's adulterous ex-husband.

"Don't know. Don't care," the other woman replied. Sheila seemed happy enough and Hana guessed she'd journeyed through the worst of it. Her appearance had changed in the last year and she was a much trimmer version of her former self. She had always been beautiful, her blonde good looks and pale skin testament to her Swedish heritage, but now she exploited it fully. Her hair was shorter and had acquired copper and brown streaks and her clothes and make up were flawless.

"I don't suppose you'd be able to give me the phone number for Mrs Dobbs?" Hana asked tentatively as Sheila paused for breath. She hurried on, "I had a heart attack in the holidays and needed an operation. Logan missed the funeral - in fact we didn't even find out Alan was dead until it was all over. I feel like I should get in touch with Dora."

Sheila was still stuck on the words, 'heart attack' and didn't dwell on the odd request or its impropriety. Hana no longer had any right to the private list of staff phone numbers and addresses, but fortunately Sheila was more interested in a lively discussion about Hana's holiday, than wondering why the other woman didn't ask her husband for the number.

Deciding after half an hour she should probably go back to the student centre, Sheila left Hana to retrieve her baby from the Year 13 dean. Rory seemed disappointed. "Shame, I was thoroughly enjoying having a legitimate reason to stand around jiggling from side to side whilst reading the newspaper," he grumbled.

Sheila photocopied the staff list and handed it over along with a brief hug as she breezed through the common room on her extremely high heels.

"Thanks," Hana said. "Do you think I should take some baking round?"

"Yes, that would be lovely," Sheila answered and turned to leave. Then her eyes lit up and she imparted a particularly stunning piece of information to Hana's sorry ears. "Oh, I forgot to say, big-mouth-Amanda's been blabbing it around that Logan's the next deputy principal. Apparently she typed up some new contract for him. The stupid woman's even telling everyone what the starting salary is. You should go to Angus about her; she can't seem to help herself. Tell Logan congratulations, anyway."

Hana swallowed and managed only a nod. Feeling excluded and devastated, she left the main building before the bell rang, determined not to run into her overly perceptive husband. His absence all night wasn't completely unexpected, but Hana had no idea what she'd say if she bumped into him. It was hardly the place for hollow congratulations or the beginnings of a divorce. The fissure between them became a canyon as Hana digested the news of Logan's new role and his failure to even discuss it with her.

On the way across the field she used her mobile phone to call the landline on the sheet of paper, disappointed when an answering machine greeted her and Alan Dobbs' disembodied voice asked her to leave a message. Phoenix woke and set up a wail of hungry protest, distracting Hana from her task as she pushed the pram home at speed.

Back at The Gatehouse, Hana put her phone on charge and fed her baby. "That's weird," she said to the child. "My battery hardly lasts any time at all. It used to last all day."

Phoenix paused her suckling to smile and Hana stroked the soft, baby fingers. While winding the baby, Hana tried the number again, finally leaving a message. "Hi, Mrs Dobbs. I'm not sure if you remember me. I'm Hana and I worked with Alan for a long while. I'm sorry to have missed you. I'll call again later."

Hanging up, Hana felt stupid. "I bet she doesn't even remember me," she whispered to her baby. "We went to heaps of social events together but she might just think I'm some crazy; it's not like we were ever friends."

Hana played with Phoenix for a while, crawling around behind her until she was tired, then reading a little cloth book with her. After a hearty lunch and another breastfeed, Phoenix seemed tuckered out and Hana put her upstairs in her cot to nap, bringing the baby monitor downstairs. Her phone looked fully charged but when she unplugged it, the battery light came on. "Yeah, because it's not like I don't have enough problems already," Hana groaned. She plugged it in again and rang Will to see how he was getting on with the artifacts and also because with Phoenix asleep, she realised she was bored. The absence of the diary galled her further.

"Do you think you can keep it under a thousand dollars?" she asked. "I have access to that much quite quickly but if it's any more, I'll need time to get to it."

"It's coming along nicely," Will informed her. "I've repaired the easy ones and cleaned up the frames and glass that were mouldy and dusty. But some of them, I'll need to dismantle and see if I can do anything to safeguard them against further harm. I've had to order some special powder to take off the dust and mould from some of them and that'll be an added cost."

"Ok, thanks." Hana bit her lip and started worrying. If Bodie couldn't sell Amy's house in time to buy Culver's Cottage, she wouldn't be able to afford to pay the old man back. Her other property on Achilles Rise went up for sale during the holidays, but Hana hadn't paid any attention to how it was doing. Tipene came on the phone as Will wheeled himself back out to his shed to continue his work. Hana opened her mouth to ask Will's brother to halt the endeavours, but Tipene's next comment added guilt to the emotional soup of Hana's financial worries.

"Hi, Mrs Du Rose. I just wanted to tell you how grateful I am you gave Will this job to do. It's given him a new lease of life and I can't thank you enough. He talks about nothing else. He can't wait to get the rest of it down here and look over it all. You should see what he's done with those framed photographs of your *whānau*; they're glowing as though they were taken yesterday. He's had his daughter make copies of them down at the printers and I have a disk for you next time you're passing the *marae*. It's an added cost, but my brother's learned from other people's mistakes. There was a *marae* that burned down over near Whangamata last year - they didn't have any copies and it all went up in smoke..."

Hana's mind worried about the money as Tipene chatted and so at first, she didn't understand why he went quiet and then began to apologise. "I'm so sorry, Mrs Du Rose, that was a tactless tale to tell, especially after poor Reuben's death."

"Oh, it's fine. I understand the point you were making," Hana replied. "Don't worry, I'll find a way to get the other boxes from the hotel." As she disconnected the call, a spiteful thought pricked her mind and was out in the open before she could stop it. "If Logan chooses to end our marriage, none of it will be my problem anyway and he'll have to pick up the bill!" The notion caused more misery than release and Hana recognised the level of her increasing investment in his family. She shrugged. "Let it go, Hana," she told herself. "You'd do all this work to restore his family heirlooms and then they still won't accept you. Stop wasting your time."

Hana pottered around the huge house, cleaning things that didn't really need cleaning and generally fiddling about. She tried not to think about her precarious marital situation and the disturbing fact that her husband married her under false pretences. Hana genuinely believed he loved *her* - not some fictitious person he invented in his mind and allocated her body to. *What does he want?* She tortured herself, frustrated. *Some ditzy eighteen year old who cries all day and looks out of train windows with a hopelessness in her eyes, because she's got herself into a whole world of trouble and doesn't know how to get out of it?* That line of thinking brought back terrible memories and Hana chose to push them away. *It turned out all right,* she reassured herself. Her marriage gave her Bodie and Izzie and Vik wasn't always unfaithful. It was unfair of Logan to keep the eighteen year old Hana pinned in that awful place and demonstrated how little he really knew her.

From the attic room Tama claimed and then left in a mess, Hana discovered an unimpeded view of Mount Pirongia. She pressed her splayed fingers against the glass and framed the view, aiming to pluck the mountain from its foundations. A noise behind made her jump and cry out, clapping her hand over her mouth. As Logan's grey eyes watched her, Hana waited for Phoenix to wake up, relieved when the little girl made no sound through the monitor in Hana's pocket. "Go away, Logan," she sighed. "I don't have the energy for your prejudice and rejection this afternoon."

The stand-off between them was tense as he said nothing. Logan's face was impossible to read, the shutters down over his emotions. He was neatly dressed as always, but there were dark circles under his eyes where he hadn't slept. Leaning against the door frame he oozed sex appeal and Hana worked hard at resisting him, instinctively drawn to the natural intimacy between them. She tossed her head and put her hands on her hips, backlit by a setting sun which turned her hair gold. "I'll move out so you can come back here?" she suggested, keeping her tone level and reasonable sounding. "You don't have to spell it out, Logan, I'm not who you thought and probably not what you want. It's better you find out now."

Hana's smile was wooden as she waited, but Logan didn't move, paralysed by some inner demon that held him captive. "Fine!" Her exasperation escaped and she moved towards the door. "I'll leave as soon as Phoe wakes."

"No!" His arm shot out and strong fingers gripped Hana's forearm, clinging on even as she struggled. More than anything, Hana knew she didn't want her marriage to end, not before they'd journeyed further, but resignation told her it wasn't her choice. Logan reeled her in until she stopped just inches from his chest. Her breath moved the fabric of his shirt and she saw the whites of his knuckles over the bone in her arm.

"I hate you," she said, seeing the familiar twitch at the side of her husband's mouth.

"Don't lie."

"I can't be who you want."

"You *are* who I want."

Hana shook her head, cynicism spreading across her beautiful features. "You don't really know me, Logan. Last night made that clear."

"I'm sorry. Hana, I'm sorry. It came out wr...wrong; all of it." Logan's stutter betrayed his stress as his brow furrowed and desperation coursed through his veins.

"I can't keep trying to be someone I was years ago," Hana hissed. "I was never this elfin vision of perfection, but I'm killing myself trying to be her. I'm me and my body is faulty and aging and falling apart. Maybe at eighteen I was beautiful and ethereal and I captured some part of your imagination but Logan, you missed it! I grew up and moved forward. I can't help it if you didn't!"

"It wasn't like that." Logan reached out a shaking hand and stroked his fingers along Hana's jawline, seeing her shiver at his touch. "I love you, Hana. I need you."

Hana's lips parted. "The real me, Logan, or some image of me? Your emotional demands are wearing me out. I can't do this anymore."

"I'm sorry." His voice was a whisper of desperation. "Stay? Let me put this right, please?"

Hana yanked her arm free and ran her fingers down the buttons of Logan's shirt, seeing his pupils dilate. "You won't let me in, Logan and it exhausts me. As soon as I show an interest in your precious family, you expel me like I'm nothing. So keep it all to yourself, I really don't care anymore."

"Hana please, I said I'm sorry." Logan's grey eyes failed to mask his pain in their glittering surface and he reached for her hand again, pulling her into his body. "Forgive me?"

Fearing rejection, Hana moved forward, her breasts barely touching Logan's shirt as she breathed in his familiar scent. It intoxicated her like alcohol, leaving her heady and dizzy. She couldn't bear to look at the pain in his eyes. His skin looked darker in the wintry sunshine and she traced the line of his tattoo through the sleeve of his shirt with her finger, seeing only a faint outline but knowing by instinct each line and twist of its path across his muscular arm. When she looked up, his eyes were on her face, narrowed and expectant but beautifully unsure of himself. It made Hana feel powerful for once.

Logan dipped his head, his fringe brushing her forehead like a feather light stroke. "I keep messing up," he whispered, and his head jittered from the tremble in his body.

"Yes, you do." Hana knew she sounded cruel and unsympathetic and Logan's eyes met hers, amusement creeping into his grey irises. He kissed her gently on her cheek, a tantalising touch from full lips accompanied by the roughness of his bristled cheek. Hana tipped her head back and found Logan's lips close to hers, her heart thudding in her chest like a drummer's beat.

The grazing of her soft lips across his was like the flick of a switch, the giving of permission. Logan's arms fixed around Hana's waist and he hauled her into him, unbalancing her so his kiss became more frenzied than intended. Within seconds, her tee shirt was on the ground next to her and Logan dragged at his tie. He looked in disgust at Tama's half-made bed and the room in disarray. "Come downstairs to bed with me?" he asked tugging Hana's hand. She dug her heels in and her face creased in fear.

"I can't, I don't trust you," she said.

"Hana." Logan's lips turned down in sadness and his eyes narrowed in pain. "You're my equal and you belong in my *whānau*. You're my *pirinihehe*, my princess. I'll earn your trust, I promise, babe."

Hana followed him from the attic, snatching up the baby monitor as she went and hoping she didn't live to regret it.

Chapter Twenty-Seven

Their lovemaking was passionate and frenzied. Logan stripped his wife naked without even bothering with the front curtains facing the soccer pitch. Guilt and confusion made him desperate for her. Hana exploited her advantage, making him suffer for the injustice of their argument, but it only served to make them both unsatisfied and edgy. "I love you. Please don't doubt me?" Logan whispered into the dull light of the cloudy afternoon, pulling her body into his.

Hana narrowed her eyes and pressed her hips against him, enjoying his obvious discomfort. "Then stop making me feel like an outsider."

"I don't mean to."

"But you manage to."

"Forgive me, please?"

"No." The smug smile left Hana's face as her husband flipped her onto her back on the mattress and pressed his strong body onto hers. His grey eyes glittered dangerously and she sighed with resignation. Logan clasped her wrists above her head and kissed her neck, moving his lips sensuously down her body until she groaned with pleasure.

"I know I deserve this," he moaned, unlocking her legs which were deliberately clasped at the ankles. "But I think you've made me suffer enough."

The day disappeared into late afternoon but neither of them took any notice, busying themselves with mending the broken bridges in their fragile marriage.

"Logan?" Hana said quietly later, wondering if he was still awake. "Can I tell you something and you not get mad at me?"

She heard her husband exhale before rolling over onto his side, anticipating some confessed disaster and knowing he couldn't react. Hana lay on her front, her elbows bent and her chin in her hands. Logan pulled his pillow underneath his neck and ran a warm hand down Hana's naked spine, causing her to shiver and wonder if she would be better off engaging him in something other than a declaration of guilt. His dark wavy hair flopped over his eyes and moved with every flick of his eyelashes.

"Sometimes you look so much like Phoenix, or probably she looks the image of you," Hana said, studying Logan's face and biting her lower lip.

"Come on, woman, what have you done?" Logan pressed, running his finger down the side of her mouth and smirking as Hana closed her eyes.

Hana groaned. "It's too difficult having a conversation with you when you're naked and gorgeous. I wish I hadn't started this, especially if you're going to shout." Hana pouted, knowing it would ruin the intimacy they just shared if he got angry.

"Just get on with it." Logan's fingers moved down the side of her bare hip and his interest in conversation waned.

"How long have you got?" Hana asked. "I don't want to get into it if you have to rush off to class half way through. That's how misunderstandings happen."

"Bloody hell, Hana! How long do I need? Have you mortgaged the farm or something?" Logan asked, beginning to sound irritated.

"I've got myself into a bit of a financial mess," Hana admitted, seeing the spark of alarm flit across her husband's eyes. She tried to reassure him, failing miserably. "Not terrible, not gambling or buying expensive shoes or anything. But I went to see someone about the box of family *taonga* from your grandma. He was so excited and I sort of left it with him to repair. He's a Māori restorer and used to manage the artifacts at the *marae* in Ngaruawahia. I asked for a quote but the cost keeps going up and he's such a lovely man, I'll feel guilty taking it away from him. Bodie seems to want Culver's Cottage but isn't in a position to buy yet and I've no idea what's happening with the house on Achilles Rise. I worked out I could pay the first instalment from my current account but after that, I'm pretty much stuffed." Hana gave an exaggerated sigh and pressed her face into her arms, her voice sad. "I wanted to make it all beautiful again and then tell you my idea but I've bankrupted myself instead."

Logan exhaled and rolled onto his back, putting his arms behind his head, a slight smile playing on his lips. "That's about a million miles away from what I thought you were going to say."

"Oh," Hana replied, still not sure if he was cross with her or not. "What did you think I was going to say?"

"I have absolutely no idea. But definitely not that."

Hana pushed her face into his armpit, feeling the dark hair tickle her nose. She smelled his deodorant and the scent that represented Logan Du Rose, warm sunshine and hay. She inhaled deeply, not yet ready to take his good humour for granted. Logan wrapped his arm around her neck and pulled her in close for a smouldering kiss, before pulling Hana's body into his, a look of satisfaction on his face. "You're one hell of a woman, you know that?" he crooned, running his lips along her soft neck. "I know I don't deserve you."

"No, you don't." Hana smirked and pulled away so she could look Logan in the eyes. "You told me I could deal with the treasures and then you decided I couldn't. I'm not sure what to do now."

Logan's face softened and his eyes turned the colour of grit, his pupils black and growing with desire. "Right now, you need to kiss me," he said, his voice husky. His lips on Hana's silenced her pique for the moment as he pushed her underneath him and ran his hand down her inner thigh.

"What's your idea?" he asked as he soaped her slender back in the shower, running his large hands over her spine and up onto her shoulders. Phoenix started to make disturbed noises in the monitor and both parents stopped to listen. The little girl snuffled and then drifted back off to sleep.

"I thought we could make a museum of all the artifacts up at the hotel. There's an empty room behind Leslie's office, right next to reception and if we did it properly, we could charge a couple of dollars for guests to look round. I thought I might use this time while Phoenix is small to document your family's history and then write a pamphlet. I could visit with the *kaumātua* up at the township and ask him for his memories and then there's Leslie - she knows heaps about your family. The man who's repairing the things in the first box knew Rueben from his childhood and..."

Logan became quiet at the mention of his father and his hands on Hana's back stilled. She turned and seized the shower gel from him and put some into her hand, running her fingers over his broad chest and feeling the hard muscle beneath her palms. Logan's eyes had a faraway, absent look and Hana felt annoyed at herself for pushing the point. She wrapped her arms around his torso hard, forcing herself into his space so he almost overbalanced and had to grab onto her to right himself.

The sense of exhaustion and isolation descended on Hana's head, bringing with it a painful loneliness. Logan had shut her out again. Hana let go and took a step back. "I can't do this anymore," she said, her voice strangled.

When Logan said nothing, she left the shower cubicle and snatched up a towel, drying herself in the bedroom alone and feeling pretty stink about everything. She dressed in comfy track pants and an old fleece in an attempt to manufacture comfort of a different kind. Then she depressed herself further by wondering if Logan had come home early because he had a night duty, fed up of her own dire company yet again. Or maybe he came to tell her their marriage was over and she just distracted him. It was foolish to end up in bed with him when the issues were far from resolved.

Logan took ages in the bathroom and the baby stayed asleep, although not deeply. Hana stood in her bedroom doorway wondering whether to wake her up, but deciding against it. Phoenix had inherited her mother's bad temper when woken unexpectedly and Hana was reluctant to endure anyone else's grizzling alongside the sound of her own. Alone in the kitchen, she began to monotonously rustle up an evening meal.

Even that was harder than she thought it would be and acted as another reprimand. "If you spent more time doing what you were supposed to, like food shopping, home-making and bringing up your daughter instead of meddling in things that don't concern you, perhaps you'd be more like the woman in *Proverbs 31*," Hana grumbled at her reflection in the kitchen window. She sighed and leaned over the sink, peering into the bowl of half peeled potatoes. "I hate the *Proverbs 31* woman!" she announced.

Pastors always trotted her out on Mothers' Day to make wives feel inferior. The woman was held up as a model wife and whilst Hana didn't feel capable of hand sewing all Logan's work shirts, she could at least have shopped. Then again, didn't the *Proverbs 31* woman grow her own vegetables and herds? "I'm a bit stuffed all round then," Hana groaned.

The potatoes looked lonely in the microwave, spinning around as they boiled. But the pantry revealed nothing to go with them. Feeling completely inept, Hana made Logan a fairly decent looking omelette and shoved in a packet of microwaved noodles at the last minute. When Logan appeared, Hana was relieved to see him in track pants and an old tee shirt frayed around the edges. "You're not going to work?" she said, her shoulders relaxing and some of the tension leaving her stance.

"Not tonight," he replied and smiled.

"My friend's daughter, Charlotte, calls it a 'nomlette' I think," Hana said, setting the plate in front of him. It contained the entire contents of the pantry and fridge and Hana felt wrong footed and nervous. "There's not much else left. I've done mashed potatoes for Phoe and put the last of the ham and cheese in it."

"This is really nice," Logan said, pointing his fork at the nomlette. "Can you do this again?"

Hana nodded, turning back to the sink to wash up, trying to be the good little housewife. Logan ate in silence and Hana kept herself busy, trying not to let the roomful of awkwardness settle on her shoulders. "What are you eating?" he asked as she laid his cutlery on the plate.

"I'm not hungry," she answered, collecting it up before he sat back in his chair. Hana punished herself as she loaded the dishwasher with the dirty crockery, feeling glum. *You're a fool*, she told herself. *You should never have got so excited about the museum. Or so involved.* The pipe dream was planned out in her head. The room housed the glittering artifacts on shelves and in glass cabinets and Hana saw herself showing guests round and telling the Du Rose story. It fizzled to nothing in her mind's eye. *Fool!* The hotel belonged solely to her husband and she felt like a trespasser. His hotel. His family. His *taonga*.

Phoenix woke up chittering for food and Logan fetched her and changed her nappy. Hana dished up a plastic bowl of the mash and let her feed herself with a spoon. It was a messy business but most of it disappeared into the slot in the child's face, although some of the ham was squished between her increasingly dexterous fingers.

The awkwardness grew to a steady hum in Hana's head and feeling depressed, she donned her outdoor gear and volunteered to do some shopping. "See you later," she called, her voice overly bright, still reaching for the ideal of the 'perfect Hana'. A bigger part of her rebelled as she left father and daughter cuddled up on the sofa in the living room, watching an English soccer game.

"You are so pathetic, Hana McIntyre!" she berated herself, using her maiden name like a hatchet on her own head. "You're such a pushover!"

Hana slunk around the supermarket on Mill Street, filling her shopping trolley and enjoying the chance to shop without a baby taking up room in the cart. Stocking up on healthy things like vegetables to make baby meals and unhealthy things like chocolate and red wine, she arrived back at The Gatehouse as it grew dark, clanking full carrier bags against the front door as she fumbled with her keys.

Phoenix was in her pyjamas, scooting around the wooden floorboards at a fair whack and squealing to herself in pleasure. Logan wordlessly carried the bulk of the shopping inside in two trips. They unpacked in the kitchen, filling the pantry and fridge while Phoenix sat on the floor and tipped items unhelpfully out of the plastic bags. "Phoe! Careful, baby," Hana said, scooping up a carton of dishwashing liquid from the floor as it tipped.

Once all the enticingly rustly bags were removed, Phoenix grew bored and crawled off into the hallway. She sat on the front door mat singing to herself and examining its bristly surface with her hands. Logan watched Hana with a sense of growing nervousness, not sure how to begin a conversation and she crashed around in cupboards, avoiding any lame overtures he made. Conflict resolution in marriage was not a Du Rose skill and Logan sat at the table and examined the scars on his hands. "Hana," he said, blocking her passage past him carrying a tin of beans. "Can we talk?" He reached out his arms and captured her round the waist. "Just stop for a minute, please?"

Hana's body was rigid, standing next to him like a statue, her eyes staring blindly through the dark window. "What's the point?" she asked, her voice wooden. "You let me in and then as soon as I blunder somewhere you don't want me, you expel me like a bad child. I can't live like this."

"I know. The stuff about my father...Reuben, it's still raw. I find it hard to think about, let alone talk about it. I can't help that."

"Maybe," Hana sighed.

"Look, a night alone in the boarding house office made me think about things. I do love you, Hana, that was never in any doubt but you're right - I did create an illusion and tried to trap you inside it. I'm really sorry for that and I want us to move forward, but on a more equal footing."

Logan let go, wary of touching her. Hana seemed distant and hurt and he needed her to understand. "I'm not great at communicating how I feel," he tried, defeat underlying his statement.

"Oh, really?" Hana sidestepped again and Logan saw the warning signs flash behind her green eyes.

"Yes!" Logan snapped. "Yes, I find it hard and you're being unkind for the sake of it now!"

Hana's eyes narrowed in anger and her body was rigid and unyielding as she moved again, finding her husband's tall frame in the way. Logan saw her bring the tins up to chest height and knew she intended to push them into him. He snatched them up, dumping them on the table in one fluid movement and catching her around the waist. "Hana, stop this," he whispered, soothing and cajoling.

Hana glared up into his face as Logan reached behind her and grasped her forearms, careful to avoid the painful scar on her left wrist. He dragged her unwilling arms forward and pulled them around his waist, where he held onto them behind his back. Then he leaned in and kissed her unwilling lips, feeling her resistance. She was pinned and she knew it. Hana's dormant redheaded temper stirred. She struggled and stamped her foot and Logan felt a stab of excitement at his wife's spiritedness, which invited him like an unspoken challenge. "You've still got secrets!" she spat. "You're still freezing me out!"

Logan's ex-fiancé possessed none of Hana's charm. Caroline was wily, spiteful and dishonest. She tried to confound Logan Du Rose with mind games and cruelty and so Hana's simple, honest rage was refreshing and incredibly seductive. "I'm doing my best," Logan whispered. "I'll try harder not to be s…"

"Such a lying pig?" Hana retorted and Logan pursed his lips. Enraged by the smirk in his eyes, Hana tried to withdraw her arms from his iron grip, tilting her head away so his next kiss landed on her neck instead of her lips. "This isn't sorted!" she hissed. "We are *not* ok!"

A sudden hammering on the front door startled them both and Phoenix let out a wail of instant fear from the doormat. With a look which told his wife they had unfinished business, Logan strode into the hallway and snatched his daughter up in his strong arms. "You're fine, ya big egg," he soothed as she nuzzled into him and wrapped her tiny hands around his neck. Hana heard a click as Logan opened the front door and a whoosh of cold air blew in. "You made good time," Logan said as he greeted the visitor.

Chapter Twenty-Eight

Standing outside in the cool night air was David Allen, still wearing his combat pants and air force blue tee shirt. Hana peered through the kitchen door and Phoenix stared at the visitor with her head on one side, resting on her daddy's big safe shoulder. Only Logan seemed unsurprised to see the man, standing back to let the soldier inside the house. "Hey, bro," he said in a gruff greeting. It took David a while to release his feet from the boots which laced above his ankles, but eventually he succeeded and progressed beyond the doormat.

Hana came into the hallway in her socks, looking from one man to the other for explanation. "Is there a problem at the hotel?" she asked. The men looked at her and neither spoke, driving Hana back into the kitchen to finish putting the shopping away, muttering crossly to herself. By the time David arrived at the kitchen table, there was a pot of tea and an opened packet of biscuits waiting. The soldier smiled at Phoenix, still hanging around her father's neck and she frowned and pulled her bottom lip upwards in an upside down fish-face.

"Fine by me, little girl," he chuckled. "I've never been great with kids anyway."

"So what brings you down to Hamilton?" Hana asked again, too curious to leave it alone. She placed a mug in front of the soldier and waited for his answer. He darted a nervous look at his employer.

Hoisting the baby higher up his body, Logan answered for him. "I invited him."

"Oh." Hana gave up at the closed answer and receded inside herself.

The men engaged in small talk. "I've fixed everything mechanical that needed it. I've been riding horses for the last few days," the blond soldier said with a smile. As Hana took a sideways peek at him, he looked tanned and healthy, his light hair having turned almost white in the harsh winter sun. It was longer and tightly curled into his head. He was muscular and a tell-tale bruise and cut on his arm showed at some point, the riding hadn't gone well. Hana heard Nev's name mentioned and tuned back into their conversation, the toast crumb she was rolling on the table suddenly losing its appeal.

"Yeah, we fenced the back sections with the usual and the front with post and rail, like you wanted. It's too rough for the horses at the moment, but Flick moved the calves onto it so they should straighten it out. We left the higher slopes until Toby can spray. He says it's got ragwort real bad so he wouldn't put the mares in there. It's been left in a real mess, more noxious weed than grazing."

Logan grimaced. "The old man lost heart," he said, his voice low. "Nev was powerless to change anything without money or his permission. It'll be good, bringing it all under the same ownership again."

Hana looked at her husband, narrowing her eyes in accusation. Had Neville Du Rose finally made his decision? It sounded as though he had and Logan hadn't bothered to tell her. She felt yet another stab of hurt pierce her chest and it was agony. Logan bounced Phoenix on his knee and she sucked her thumb, making a quiet 'nnnnn' noise and listening to the sound of her voice as it changed with each bump of her father's knee. He sat at right angles to his wife, but she couldn't have felt further away if she'd been on the other side of the Tasman. Their knees touched and Logan felt the tiny movement as Hana decided to get up from the table and walk away from her exclusion. He reached for her hand and crushed it tightly between the strong fingers of his right hand. His face made no outward change and his left leg continued to bounce a regular beat for the benefit of the child.

If David noticed Hana's start of surprise, quickly followed by the flash of naked anger, he said nothing. The men chatted about the farm with Logan refusing to let Hana strop off and she sat and fumed silently in her seat. David's voice cut into her reverie, his question aimed at her. "What shall I do with all the gear in the Range Rover? Should I leave it out there or do you want me to fetch it in?"

"Leave it there," Logan answered. "Hana can show you where to take it tomorrow."

Still burning with annoyance, Hana wondered how on earth she was meant to know where Logan wanted a load of junky stuff to go and for once, kept her own counsel. She knew exactly where she'd like to stick it, the rebellious notion causing a mischievous smile to grace her lips.

Hana managed finally to escape, Phoenix nodding off and providing a ready excuse. She laid the baby in her cot and chose not to go back downstairs, hearing the steady thrum of male voices on the floor below as she got ready for bed and settled herself down for the night. A short time later she heard Logan show David the attic room and his steady footsteps came back down the main staircase for clean sheets and return upstairs. He turned the lights off in the hallway and sat the baby monitor on his bedside table, going to the bathroom for his nightly shower.

Hana drifted off to sleep, a fact which surprised her as misery usually caused her sleeplessness. Even in slumber she exacted her revenge, her body sprawled across the middle of the bed making it difficult for her clean, slightly damp husband to find a space on either side of her. He knew she was mad at him. He seriously contemplated sleeping on the sofa downstairs but the sight of her glossy hair on his pillow, shimmering in the moonlight from the gap in the curtains, drove him to climb in next to her.

Logan stroked Hana's hair, painfully aware how close he came to losing her a few weeks ago. In his mind's eye, he saw Mark's long surgeon's fingers compress her breastbone so hard Logan thought it would snap under the pressure. "I'm not wasting another night apart from you over a misunderstanding." Logan whispered as he brushed his lips against her cheek. "Especially one that my own stupidity caused."

Logan pushed closer against his wife's body, smelling toothpaste on her breath as she sighed in her sleep. Sliding his hand gently up her body, he accidentally-on-purpose rucked up her nightdress, exposing her slender legs under the covers. She drove him crazy, especially when he felt offside with her. He pulled her into his body, waking her gently with soft kisses, tasting the peppermint and eucalyptus left around her lips. Hana stirred and responded, which warned him she wasn't properly awake.

His wife felt warm and fluffy and her skin was so soft, Logan got quite carried away with loving her. By the time Hana collected herself enough to remember she actually didn't like her husband at the moment, it was far too late to do anything about it. Logan felt the sudden rigidity in her body underneath him and stroked her cheek in the darkness. "You are one stroppy mare," he whispered and felt her struggle, part of her wanting to hate him and make him suffer, while the rest of her enjoyed it too much to stop. Logan didn't allow her chance to release the ready retort, covering her lips with his and distracting her.

Hana was breathless and fed up with her husband when he finally allowed her to sit up and pull herself back against the pillows. The room was freezing cold and she had no idea where her nightie was. She made Logan get out of bed naked and hunt around for it in the dark. "You're so bloody demanding, *wahine!*" he grumbled. He annoyed her further by getting back into bed shivering and wafting the sheets.

Hana pulled her head through the neck of her nightie and slapped him as he sidled closer to get warm. Logan laughed softly and pulled her down into the bed. "You're incorrigible," Hana squeaked, irritated at him.

"Bet you can't spell that," Logan snuffled into her hair.

"Bet I can!" she replied, "But you can't spell diarrhoea!"

"I can but right now, I'd prefer not to," Logan chuckled. "It's not something that's uppermost in my mind."

"No, your pea-brain is full of admiration for your own ego!" Hana snapped. "There's no room for anything else."

"Harsh!" Logan murmured, feigning hurt.

When he didn't say anything else, Hana relented, feeling stupid for passing up an opportunity to make things right with him. "Sorry," she whispered. "It's your hotel and your *taonga*. I should learn to stop meddling in your affairs. It's up to you what you do with your grandma's things. It was a dumb idea and I can see that now." Hana sighed and snuggled down the bed, feeling on the outside of his world. She cuddled into Logan's hard chest and breathed in and out, feeling the hairs move underneath her nose. It was soporific and when her husband still didn't reply, she felt herself twitch and realised she was falling asleep. His soft voice came to her through the first fog of slumber.

"Hey, *Circle-Line-girl*, what's mine is yours. Including my screwed up *whānau* and all my worries."

"Not all of them," Hana's addled brain slurred. *Not your new job.* Hana felt Logan's gentle fingers stroke her face, but peace called and she leapt eagerly off the cliff and embraced it.

Logan lay awake for ages in the huge, empty house, one of Hana's long curls tumbling over and over his left index and middle fingers. He thought about the dirty tube train he first met Hana on, so many years ago. Had he ever truly believed one day he would be lying in bed with her, feeling so utterly fortunate? It was a dream for as long as he could remember, to be with the girl from the Circle Line train. He wanted to dry her weeping eyes and stop the world ever hurting her again. Every time he thought he might have managed it, some other curved ball spun their way and down they went like imbalanced skittles, crashing to the deck with abandon.

Logan squeezed Hana into him. Sometimes he wished he could gather her up and stuff her into one of his pockets for safekeeping. He knew she would only escape, causing mayhem wherever she ran to. He spoke the truth. Hana wasn't the person he thought she was. She was much, much more.

Eventually, the Māori drifted off to sleep himself, feeling the burden that was his love for Hana and Phoenix weighing comfortably in his broad chest. He temporarily pushed aside the information Odering had imparted to him that morning. "Are you serious?" Logan had challenged and the detective nodded. "So you found the tennis player's car near the staff units and it was registered in whose name?"

"Alan Dobbs," Odering replied. "Weird aye?"

Chapter Twenty-Nine

Hana sat bolt upright as the alarm sounded on Logan's cell phone next to the bed; her hair a woolly mop of tangled red. Logan sighed and stretched his arms above his head, rubbing his eyes in the dim winter morning light. Then he bounced out of bed, sickeningly awake and ready to go. Hana groaned and turned over, irritated when he turned the light to the ensuite on, scattering the offering from the dim bulb all over her reluctant face. "David's coming to the school gym with me for a workout," Logan informed her, dragging on stubby shorts and a tee shirt. You should probably get dressed while he's out of the way."

Hana felt rebellious, even though she knew he was right. The boss' wife wandering around in a granny nighty probably wasn't appropriate. Creaking floorboards overhead announced David was also up and moving around and Logan shot Hana a warning look. She sighed and sat up again, realising as she looked down that her nightdress was not only on inside out, but also back to front. It accounted for the throttled feeling which disturbed her sleep for most of the night. She pouted. "So after last night you actually think I've got the energy to jump one of your stockmen while you're at work?"

Logan pulled his trainers out of the wardrobe and refused to be drawn, although as he turned away, a smirk crossed his lips.

The men returned sweaty but happy to an impressively cooked breakfast which piled on the fat and calories they painstakingly worked off. "Thanks babe," Logan said, planting a greasy kiss on her lips in the hallway. "But you don't have to try to be my perfect wife, Hana; I love you the way you are. I'm sorry for what I said. Stop letting it hurt you."

Hana frowned at his whispered words and pouted, knowing he was right. He'd apologised numerous times but she still used the angry sentence to birch herself, enjoying the familiar sense of inferiority which cursed her first marriage. She shook herself, not wanting to be *that* Hana again.

Hana stood at the front door and watched her husband's long legs stride across the soccer fields to his tutor group in the main building. Awkwardness descended as she realised that she didn't know why David was there. "Do you have family or friends in Hamilton?" she asked politely as Phoenix gummed on a strip of bacon.

David shook his head casually. "Nope."

Hana cleared up the breakfast things, wondering whether to go out and leave him or if she was responsible for his entertainment for the day. David headed off upstairs for a shower and to get dressed. "Nice one, Logan," Hana sighed. "And you wonder why I get mad at you; you tell me nothing!" She shrugged at her daughter in the high chair and Phoenix grinned back and waved her soggy strip of bacon. Hana chopped vegetables and fried portions of chicken, placing it all into two decent casserole dishes in the oven and setting it to cook. She felt determined to redeem herself as a good wife and mother. Her own ego drove her to shuck failure.

When David reappeared, he looked completely different. His curly blond hair nestled in tight wet ringlets on his head and he donned a pair of smart black jeans which looked as though he borrowed them from a larger man. A tidy grey shirt completed the look. Gone was the rough, scruffy stubble. He had become an extremely presentable man, somewhere in his mid-thirties. Leaning with his backside against the kitchen cupboard saying nothing, he gave off an air of infinite patience. Hana mopped at her daughter's grizzling face and her brow furrowed. *Could he be waiting for me?*

"What are your plans for today?" she asked him, feeling apprehensive. "Are you on leave for a few days?"

David looked confused. "No, ma'am. This is work. I've brought the stuff down. I thought we could take it round now. Mr Du Rose gave me some errands to do in the city with the feed merchants and said it was ok for me to stay tonight. I'll head back up to the hotel tomorrow. I've borrowed Toby's truck and he wants it back then."

Phoenix plucked a lock of Hana's red hair with gentle fingers, making her little face tickle as she rubbed at her eyes with the tresses in her hand. She sneezed. Hana's confusion was evident as her daughter laid her head against her mother's shoulder and closed her eyes. "What stuff?" Hana asked, shaking her head and feeling out gunned.

"Five big boxes of stuff from your room at the hotel. I understood you needed them. Mr Du Rose rang late yesterday and Toby sent me. Everyone else is busy shifting stock around at the moment."

Hana's eyes bugged unattractively and she clamped her top teeth down on her lip. "Boxes?"

Chapter Thirty

"This is amazing! *Ka mau te pai!*" Will's face lit up like a Christmas tree, as David hefted the boxes one at a time into the old man's workroom. Hana stood at the top of a steep ramp, staring at Will's muscular arms and wondering how he managed to wheel himself up and down it. Will sat in his wheelchair watching the steady parade as David and Tipene followed each other in and out of the shed. The boxes were heavy and unwieldy and took considerable manhandling out of the vehicle. They had occupied the large boot space and all available seats, meaning Hana drove ahead of the Range Rover in her car.

"I thought you'd be cross," she said, gulping with emotion at Will's ecstatic grin. She hadn't understood how much it meant to him, being trusted with the treasures.

Will took Hana's hand in his and gave it a decent squeeze, never taking his eyes from the men. "Not on the floor!" Will bellowed at his brother, "Stand them on the pallets." He turned to Hana, "You never store *taonga* on the floor."

Hana bit her lip and looked at the drooping, water-stained box. It showed all the signs of its forty-odd year lifespan in someone's damp garage. "I hope you won't be disappointed at the state of some of the contents," she said, sounding nervous. The smell of mildew wafted past as Tipene tottered by with the sorriest looking box. It was bound to require more of Will's careful treatment and would probably cost more than all the others put together to restore. Hana sighed and wished again she hadn't started this.

Will squeezed her fingers in his gnarled hand. "It's fine, *kōtiro*. Everything will be fine. *Hei aha koa*."

When Hana's brows knitted, he smiled showing his missing teeth. "I mean don't worry, it doesn't matter. I'll take care of everything."

Hana smiled and squeezed his hand back, balancing a curious Phoenix on her hip. Her house in Flagstaff had lain empty after the previous occupant went to prison, leaving his wife without income or support. Hana refused to turn her out and let her stay rent free for a month while she sorted out her affairs and readied her small children to return to the South Island. Hana's phone rang on the drive to Will's house.

"You'll never believe it," the real estate agent chuckled, "but while I was hammering in the 'For Sale' board outside the property yesterday, I was approached by one of your old neighbours. Seems he might want the house for a relative who's back from Australia."

"Gosh, that would be amazing!" Hana agreed.

"I'm showing them round this afternoon. If it's what they want, we can shift it really quickly."

Hana felt cautiously optimistic as Will fudged the question of cost, engrossed in basking in the wonderment of the artifacts. He shouted instructions from the ramp at the men, getting them to move the boxes twice more so he was sure he had room to navigate his wheelchair inside the shed. "It's no bloody good if I can't get to it, is it?" he bawled at them, drawing a snigger from David and an exaggerated eye roll from Tipene.

The workroom was a large, tin double garage with two roll top doors. Inside were sundry tools, all mounted on a shadow board and neatly labelled. The centre of the room was taken up by low work tables and Tipene explained quietly how Will's son painstakingly sawed the legs down so his father could still work at them in his wheelchair. Around the walls were the most incredible landscape paintings, so real Hana was initially fooled into thinking they were photographs. "My brother painted them all," Tipene proudly informed her. "It passed the time when he lost both legs and helped with the agony after his wife died a few months ago."

Hana walked around the workroom, marvelling at the skill that went into creating the realistic scenes before her. Easily recognisable were the mountains of the North Island, the three peaks of Mount Pirongia, the snow dappled faces of Ruapehu with Ngauruhoe in the background, all in beautiful tone and shade. The stratovolcano, Mount Taranaki rose from lush green surroundings, dusted with white on its peak, icing on a craggy, undulating cake. The foreground was dominated by an aged, lichen encrusted farm gate and the perspective was stunningly accurate. The painting had something about it which pulled at Hana's insides and made her desire to own it. The prospect of selling Achilles Rise made her rash and before she had considered her words, she asked Will to sell it to her. Phoenix snuffled in the car seat, the unintentional reprimand lying heavily on Hana's heart. Will's price was not exorbitant but inwardly Hana panicked. "I want to give it to Logan," she said shyly, hoping that her husband would love it as much as she did. Promising to bring a cheque on her next visit, Hana extricated herself and parted ways with David outside the front of the small house.

"Nice guy," David said conversationally and Hana nodded, her conscience getting the better of her. She confessed to Logan just hours ago she had gotten herself into a financial mess and then compounded it. She began to wonder if she had some incredibly destructive need to sabotage herself. "What is all that stuff?" David asked, leaning his neat butt against the truck. "Nobody seemed to want to help me except Rawhiti. They all steered clear of it."

"I think," Hana said, a feeling of doom settling heavily in her chest, "it's a whole heap of trouble actually and I kinda wish I hadn't gotten into this."

The soldier looked at her attractive face, her brow knitted and furrowed. He wisely chose not to ask. It was none of his business. He felt sure that he would be moving on soon anyway. All the farm vehicles were fixed and he was just waiting for the local township garage to get him a part for the plough. Then he would be surplus to requirements. David Allen was philosophical. He had been well fed, decently paid and treated with respect. Although his sleep was still disturbed, the deep green of the mountains soothed him and his work wore him out enough to allow the images to relax their haunting. The haggard, hunted look had begun to leave his face, replaced by a tanned, healthy glow.

"You're looking well," Hana commented, desperate to distract herself from her own dilemma. She instantly realised her mistake as the soldier's face slammed shut against her probing. She could almost hear the whirr of the rollers and the clang of metal on metal as everything in him closed. Hana had been there and it made her sad. She remembered only too well the sense of imprisonment, looking out through the dirty windows of her soul at the world carrying on without her, aching to be broken out, but too afraid to scream for help. "Nobody can break you out," she whispered to no one in particular, "because nobody knows you're in there."

David looked at her strangely and Hana felt embarrassed. "Sorry," she said. "I was just thinking aloud...about prisons of our own making. Nobody could help me because I couldn't admit I was in one. The great irony is I just had to try the door handle and pull. It was unlocked the whole time."

David eyed her as though she was a maniac and Hana bit her lip, deciding it was time to leave. She feared he would go back up to the hotel and tell everyone she was a loony. She looked again into his deep blue eyes and knew he wouldn't. Belting Phoenix's heavy car seat back into place, Hana sent up an arrow prayer that God would undo her stupid words and make David forget. She also prayed God would make her lose her voice at relevant moments and sort out her financial concerns. Heaven sniggered fondly at her randomness and the angels present smiled, as they forced the impact of her wisdom harder into the soldier's damaged heart, compounding and not lessening the effect.

"Thanks for your help," Hana said, climbing into the Honda. "I've made dinner but if you get a better offer, I'll understand."

David watched her without expression and Hana gave up and started the engine. Tipene waved happily from the front door of the tired little house before going inside. Only David remained in the quiet street, his backside against the door of the Range Rover and his mind elsewhere. He couldn't seem to shake off Hana's words. *'I just had to try the door handle and pull. It was unlocked the whole time.'* Now why did that sentence affect him so damn much?

Hana pulled over to answer her mobile phone. The lay by was directly opposite her favourite coffee shop on Peachgrove Road. A full fat latte called to her from underneath the sign, and she turned her face away. She couldn't just nip anywhere anymore.

The phone call was from Mrs Dobbs, replying to her message of the previous day. "I'll be round just before three o'clock today then," Hana said. She didn't get to say goodbye as the phone mysteriously cut out on her. Peering at the screen in expectation of a depletion in signal, she was astounded to see the battery light flashing. *Again.* "You only lasted an hour!" she said crossly to it, throwing it back into her bag.

Hana glanced down at her baby sleeping next to her in the passenger seat. Her little head tilted sideways, looking like it was held on only by the car seat strap. Not for the first time, Hana wondered how she never seemed to wake up with neck ache. As if in response, the lips tightened around the crinkly thumb and her eyelids fluttered gently against her olive skin. Dark hair peeked out of the knitted hat, curling back against the pink woolly hem. Her daddy's did that when it got longer, curled away from his face in great shiny waves. "Phoenix Du

Rose, you're going to be a stunner," Hana breathed, wondering if there were any photos of Logan's grandmother in the boxes. It would be a fascinating comparison to make, especially as Tipene had recognised the genealogy in the child so quickly.

At home, Phoenix was wide awake and wired after her nap. She crawled around the kitchen floor getting underfoot, crying a couple of times in anger as she pushed herself back onto her bottom and bowled over flat onto her back.

"You really need to master that whole 'sitting back' thing baby," Hana murmured soothingly to her as she kissed the sore spot on the back of the little girl's head and rubbed it. She plugged her phone back onto charge in disgust, wondering how she was going to tell Logan the expensive gift was already broken. One-handed, with the baby on her hip, she turned up the heat on the casseroles, one for them and one for Dora Dobbs and went to change her child's nappy.

Hana walked around the house with Phoenix, exploring properly and imagining the house used as a school in the early days. The walls and floors oozed their history from every knot and mark and it was fascinating. Phoenix was happy in her mother's arms, content to look out of the high windows at the things Hana pointed out. "Look Phoe," Hana said, "that ridge of mountains surrounding Hamilton makes it one of the most geologically sound places to live in the whole of the North Island."

Phoenix screwed her face up without understanding and pushed her nose against Hana's shoulder. "Ok, maybe a bit advanced for now, then," Hana said.

In the baby's bedroom as Hana wandered around, Phoenix pointed hopefully towards her cot and her mother laughed. "You're such a sloth! You only woke up an hour ago, girlie. It's nearly lunch time." Hana retrieved the fluffy horse Tama bought the child and Phoenix cuddled it in tightly to her body, squeezing it hard around the neck and looking as though she was trying to stuff it under her armpit one-handed. She burbled something lovingly at its dangling form and then faced a dilemma of epic proportions. One tiny hand rested around Hana's back like it always did, fiddling with the red curls and the other, gripped the cuddly horse. The pink lips pursed in dismay as she realised she didn't have a free thumb to suck. Hana kissed her on the cheek and set off downstairs to make lunch before the little girl grizzled. "No matter how hard I try, Phoe, I can't sort that one out for you."

Phoenix sat in the high chair and tore a hastily made cheese sandwich to shreds, pushing tiny chunks into her mouth. At the end of half an hour, there was nothing left to see, apart from a smear of grease on the tray. Hana wondered if the child was having a growth spurt as she devoured a bowl of pureed casserole. "Maybe you're going to be tall like Daddy," Hana mused as the spoon went in and out of the little face like a supermarket conveyor belt.

The baby was showing all the signs of wanting to go to sleep, despite Hana's best efforts to keep her awake. "I wanted you to sleep at Dora's," Hana grumbled. "She'll have all these expensive ornaments and I'm bound to say the wrong thing if I'm trying to stop you crawling all over exploring." It was futile. The obligatory breastfeed was the final straw and the baby ended up in the car seat out in the hallway, as Hana reasoned she needed to get the duty call over with earlier.

David appeared with a packet of blue airmail envelopes and after borrowing a biro, sat down at the kitchen table and bit the end of the pen. Hana indicated the casserole dish in the oven. "It's ready now if you want it early. Just leave half for Logan."

David nodded and turned his eyes to the blank blue page before him. He scratched his head and bit the pen a bit more, still writing nothing.

"Er, sorry for interrupting again. But please would you apologise to Logan for me?"

David's eyes widened and he raised an eyebrow.

Hana bit her lip. "He promised to come home to do his paperwork instead of doing it in the office. Just tell him I had to go out." Logan also promised they would talk, although Hana didn't believe he knew how. She wrote him a note and left it on the side, apologising for her absence but not telling him where she went, her destination seeming irrelevant.

David watched her wrap tea towels around the hot casserole dish and juggle with it because it was still too hot. Hana felt embarrassed. "I'm taking it round to someone who recently lost her husband in an accident. But I'm a dreadful cook, so it's probably inedible anyway." She glanced across at its twin nestled on the draining board and cringed as David glanced at his dinner nervously. But he didn't ask and so she didn't expand on the topic, leaving him to his blank paper and maudlin thoughts.

Fortunately, the dish sat firmly on the tea towel underneath it, without spreading its contents on the carpeted floor of the Honda. Phoenix snored in her car seat. "If I get this casserole to Mrs Dobbs in one piece, it'll be a miracle," Hana groaned as it tipped dangerously pulling off the driveway.

"Hello." The voice sounded disjointed and at first, Hana couldn't work out where it came from. She looked around, noticing the dark saloon car pulled over on the school driveway. Winding her window down, Hana smiled at Detective Inspector Odering and he smiled back in his clipped, uptight way. It was apparent he wanted to speak to her. "I'm just nipping out," Hana called, feeling her shoulders slump as he crooked his finger and beckoned her over.

"It won't take a minute," he said with authority.

Feeling huffy and irritated, Hana got out and walked the few metres over to him, waiting next to his open window like a naughty teenager caught vandalising a bus stop. "I do have a baby in my vehicle!" she said crossly. "You could have walked across to me."

Odering ignored her barbed comment and waited. "How's your day going?" he said, smiling pleasantly as Hana grew nervous.

"Good, thanks. Until some cop made me stop what I was doing."

"Awesome," he said and looking down, put his gear lever back into drive.

Hana was surprised. The detective wasn't one for small talk and eyed the Du Roses in general with mild distain. Why on earth would he care how her day was going? "How's the investigation going?" she allowed herself to ask.

"Which one?" he replied, facetiously.

"I wondered if you'd caught Lachie's killer yet," Hana asked, tossing her red hair and showing her annoyance.

"Who?" Odering screwed up his face in confusion, rubbing his hand over a smoothly shaven chin. Looking at her, he struggled to achieve some level of professionalism. "Oh, fine thanks. We'll get to the bottom of it. Is that son of yours not keeping you informed?"

"No!" Hana's reply was indignant, aware the senior officer was trying to catch his lackey out for disclosing confidential information.

Odering waved his hand dismissively, knowing he had gotten on the wrong side of her. "Tell me," he asked, seeming uncharacteristically nervous. "Do you get fed up when your husband works long hours and does night duties over at the boarding house?"

"Yeees," Hana replied slowly, wondering if he was insinuating something about Logan. Her emotions began to work overtime. "Why?" She'd been here before with Vik, not realising he was having an affair until after his death, by which time saying her piece became irrelevant.

"So if it got too much for you...would you...do you think...?" Odering's cheeks flushed and his usually steady hand gripped the rim of the open window with an unexpected tremor. "Well, would you call it quits and divorce him?"

It was a weird question to ask a comparative stranger. Hana wasn't quite sure how to answer. "I hope I'd talk to him first," she replied with a smile, trying not to betray the cracks in her own marital armour.

Odering looked hard at her, as though trying to read something unseen in her face. "What if you'd already done that, but he hadn't realised how serious it was?"

His face was so earnest Hana felt pity for him. "If it was because I was struggling with Phoenix and couldn't cope alone, divorcing Logan wouldn't help, would it? Because then instead of being alone a lot, I'd be alone all the time. So there would have to be other factors. We'd probably try couples' counselling first."

Odering's face broke into a broad grin at the thought of the tall Māori sitting in a counsellor's office, talking about his 'inner feelings.' It cheered him up left him with a snigger on his lips. With a nod of acknowledgement, he put the car in gear and sped off towards the main office and his meeting with the principal.

Hana wandered back to her vehicle, feeling fairly sure the policeman had marriage problems. She remembered how she coped with Bo and Izzie while Vik worked exceedingly long hours after they first arrived in New Zealand. It was important to him and there was always someone new to impress. She ran around after work with this club and that group, baking for shared lunches like a maniac whilst trying to hold down a job of her own. Vik's job always took precedence. It became part of his makeup - the workaholic image. There was no wonder Hana missed the indicators when he had his affair. *Although*, she chastised herself, *until then, he had been better after becoming a Christian and he did keep coaching the tennis club*. With a sigh, she turned back to the Honda and climbed in. Phoenix sniffed and blew out a snort as Hana put her seat belt back on. The hysterical giggle began in Hana's chest and burst out through her lips, making the baby jump in her sleep. "Couples' counselling!" she sniggered. "Whatever possessed me to say it? Like Logan would ever agree to *that!*"

The journey across town was uneventful and despite some obtuse angles, the casserole stayed in the dish. Deciding she would pull onto Dora's driveway so she could keep her child in view and drop the meal off, Hana felt damned. She didn't really want to hold a lengthy conversation with the grieving widow, certain the woman must know she and Alan Dobbs never got along. But nor did she want to seem shallow and unfeeling either. When Vik died, people were kind to her and it was a way of paying it forward.

Hana found the Dobbs' house and pulled carefully onto the driveway, one eye on the slopping liquid as she traversed the kerb. The driveway was steep and long and she stopped half way down, next to the steps up to the house. To her dismay, another car pulled in behind her, forcing her down towards the red garage doors below. The Honda came to rest at a jaunty angle and gravity pulled the liquid in the dish towards the lidded rim. Hana sighed. "Nothing's going right for me today!" Even her phone refused to charge and she left it sitting on the work surface in the kitchen, sucking in electricity that seemed to have no effect as soon as the device was unplugged.

A tiny woman about Hana's age plunged from the cockpit of the huge SUV which forced Hana down the driveway. She was miniscule. She practically abseiled from the driver's seat and hefted a large pie tin out with her, bustling up the front steps in a business-like manner. Hana sat in her seat, contemplating her next move. It seemed she was destined to drop and run and the idea was appealing, despite the guilt. She waited a while in case the little lady came out. Morbid curiosity made her want to see how the woman climbed back into the huge truck. When she didn't reappear, Hana chided herself for her misplaced nosiness, surmising the other visitor was staying and would allow her to escape. She reached into the passenger side for the casserole, almost upending it totally as she overbalanced whilst trying not to wake the baby. Clicking the door closed with her hip she lumped crossly up the steep steps, finding herself on a porch next to the front door.

Here goes. After knocking, Hana tried to prepare her face appropriately to greet Alan Dobbs' widow, despite the urge to hand over the dinner and run away. But it wasn't Dora Dobbs who opened the door but the tiny lady. Up close, she was very attractive, a mop of curly dark hair around an open face. "Come in, come in," she cried merrily, waving her arms behind her to indicate a long hallway with various rooms either side. Hana felt like a party guest, rather than a sombre visitor following a traumatic death. A little spaniel appeared from the kitchen door and wagged his flag-like tail at her hopefully.

"My baby's in the car," Hana smiled apologetically, her nerve finally abandoning her. She pushed the dish at the woman, who neatly sidestepped it.

"I need to go too. Bye Dora," she called over her shoulder and leapt down the steps as fast as her little legs could carry her. Hana stood in the open doorway, a winter wind attacking her jeans and a hot casserole dish balanced between two tea towels. *Awkward.*

The SUV roared to life in a haze of exhaust fumes that threatened the ozone layer a bit more and backed up the driveway. When Hana looked back, the tired face of Dora Dobbs arrested her from the end of the hallway. The skin on her face was pale and ashen, betraying a woman who hadn't slept for weeks. Her blonde hair was scraped back from her face into a bun, severe and school ma'am like. The smiling happy face of the woman who seemed like such an incongruous match for the stern Alan Dobbs, was gone. Hana relented. "Would you like me to stay?" she asked and Dora nodded.

Phoenix snoozed in the car seat on the kitchen floor and the casserole joined the other food items on the table. "I forgot it was like this," Hana commented sadly. "It's the kiwi-way isn't it? Bring a meal and a platitude and hope it makes everything better. After Vik died we didn't need to shop for a month. The first thing we ran out of was toilet rolls." She chuckled, but Dora didn't. "It's a way of showing love," Hana concluded and finally Dora nodded. Hana continued making noise for the sake of it. "I had hungry teenagers, so I was actually really grateful. When I went back to work, everyone assumed I was 'over it' so it's good that people are still thinking about you a few weeks on."

Shut up! Hana told herself as she ground to a sudden halt. The atmosphere crackled with black depression as Dora sat opposite her at the kitchen table, peering over the mountain of cake, cookies, pies and casseroles. A woman on her own was never going to eat it all. Hana looked around, noticing another door in the kitchen leading through to a lounge. Huge, well stuffed chintz sofas and armchairs peeked back at her from their set places. It looked like a pretty room, sideways on to the rest of the house and gathering the last rays of a watery sun.

"Have you seen him?" Dora asked and her voice came as a plea. Hana shook her head, wanting to say she only saw the vertically challenged person on the doormat but it sounded rude so she clamped her jaw closed. Dora looked sad and dazed. It was surely only to be expected. "I've been looking for him at the school," she said. "That's where he said he was going. Nobody's seen him since." A sob escaped her, causing her chest to heave and Hana's eyes widened in fear.

It was possible the woman was heavily medicated. It was common to prescribe 'a little something' to people suffering from shock. But for Dora to be scouring the school grounds for her dead husband was more than weird. It smacked of a deeper problem. Hana didn't know what to do and wracked her brains for someone suitable to call, groaning inwardly as she remembered her mobile phone endlessly charging in the kitchen at home.

Hana glanced down at Phoenix, hoping for once she would wake up and then they could make their excuses and leave. *You're so selfish*, she chided herself. Hana shook her head at the internal argument. *No, perhaps I can summon help once I'm home. Angus would know what to do.*

Dora followed her gaze and sighed. "She's like Logan," she said softly. "Alan thought the world of him. He was scathing when Angus recommended him so highly, but then he was suspicious of everything Angus said or did." Dora stopped herself abruptly and Hana got the feeling the woman thought she already said too much. It was the first indication she ever heard of an issue between the principal and his deputy. Whatever it was, they had kept it well hidden.

Hana worked to keep her inappropriate curiosity under control. "How's your son coping?" she asked gently, remembering a blond boy a few years younger than Bodie.

Dora leaned forward in her seat and her face became hopeful. "*Have* you seen him?" she asked again.

Hana shook her head and the other woman visibly slumped in her seat. "I don't know what to do," she began to weep. "I'm getting really worried. He was devastated by Alan's death but he seemed ok in himself. It's been over a week. I just don't understand."

"Oh," Hana breathed with sudden realisation. The woman's haggard appearance and sleepless nights became quickly obvious. She was talking about her son, not her husband. "Do you mean you've been looking for your *son* at school?" Hana asked. "Why would he be there?"

"He went there all the time. You *know* he did!" Dora spat, plucking at a button on her cardigan with frenzied fingers. Hana wondered again if she was losing the plot and wished the small person had remained behind with her; for moral support. That woman seemed capable and practical; she would have known what to do. Hana didn't.

"I don't really know your son," she ventured, speaking to the overwrought woman opposite as though she had made a completely understandable error.

"Of course you do!" Dora retorted, her eyes flashing in anger. "He was so excited when he met you - he adored your husband."

"Logan?" Hana asked, feeling thick. Odd Logan never mentioned it.

"NO!" Dora was on her feet, yelling across the abandoned food. Hana felt afraid, leaning back in her chair to put distance between them and feeling trapped. "The other one! The Indian man. He coached him at tennis club. He told me. You practiced with him in the tennis courts. Renton said so!" Dora put her hands up to her ears and sank into the kitchen chair, the high pitched keening filling the kitchen. "Where is he? Where's my Renton?" she wailed.

Chapter Thirty-One

Hana felt physically sick. The blond tennis player was Renton Dobbs. The tennis player was dead. Renton Dobbs was dead. He wasn't coming home ever again. Who was it who decided the body belonged to Lachlan Reynolds? Obviously they were wrong.

It wasn't Hana's place to tell this poor woman her son was dead. It was a job for the cops. Hana's heart began to pound in her chest, giving her a sensation of light-headedness. Knowing she needed to get out of the woman's company, she rose shakily to her feet and indicated towards the baby. "I need to get Phoe home. Logan's waiting for me," she lied. *He didn't even know where she was.* Dora rose in her seat too, looking desperate, wringing her hands together as though furiously washing them under burning hot water. "I'm sorry...about Alan and everything," Hana said with futility, cursing her own ineptitude and knowing she was out of her depth. She shouldn't have come. She definitely shouldn't have brought Phoenix with her.

Hana bent down next to the car seat, lifting the carrying handle and locking it into place. Phoenix slept on, blissfully unaware of the trouble her mother had gotten herself into.

Dora plonked herself back down at the kitchen table behind the food mountain. Its surface was stripped pine, but only the sides were visible. Hana was reminded of childhood images of mountains of milk powder and grains, when the European Common Market went through a stage of enthusiastically stock piling. African families had starved, but the food mountains grew to the size of football pitches, filmed in shaky black and white footage for news items. Poor Dora. Hana knew from experience there was nothing she could do to help. She needed to get home, ring Bodie and let him deal with it. The double grief would be far too much for Dora to handle on her own.

Hana turned to leave, pausing at the door to bid goodbye to the broken woman in the kitchen chair. "I'm sorry for your loss, Mrs Dobbs. I'll leave you in peace now."

Dora looked exhausted and met Hana's gaze with eyes glossed by defeat. "You won't be able to leave," the older woman said quietly.

Hana contemplated the steep driveway and the horrid reverse manoeuvre to get back up it and sighed. It would have to be ok. She wasn't that bad a driver. "I'll be fine. It can't be that hard."

Dora's words took on a whole new clarity when turning towards the door into the hallway, Hana came face to face with the dead man himself.

Whereas Renton Dobbs had changed completely, growing up and outwards into a handsome, blond, muscular man, Lachlan Reynolds hadn't changed at all. He was still the proud owner of the nondescript sandy red hair and the same freckled face. He wasn't good looking, but nor was he ugly. He was simply forgettable, just like he always had been. His body shape was thin with very little muscle tone and his face held a look of cruelty and deceit. Hana gasped and took a step backwards, shaking her head to clear the image of the ghost in front of her, but he didn't go.

Vik hadn't liked the child and Hana remembered his words as a rush of realisation. "He puts the other boys down and they don't like him. I overheard him bullying Renton Dobbs. I've spoken to Angus about it; hopefully he'll punish him."

Lachlan held his hand out for the car seat and Hana swung away from him in an instant maternal reaction. *No way was he getting Phoenix.* A nauseating sense of evil had entered the room with him. "Goodbye," Hana said confidently, trying to push past him. His deceptively fragile frame didn't shift against her and panic lit a fuse in her heart. He indicated the kitchen table, as though inviting her to partake in the feast and one look at his closed face showed Hana he wasn't messing around. She moved towards her seat and stuck her backside to the chintzy pad, nursing the car seat on her knees.

Lachlan didn't sit. He leaned against the doorframe and pulled a pistol from the front of his jeans. He stared at Hana but it didn't produce the desired reaction. "You don't scare me," she said with a sneer. My brother had a gun licence growing up and my husband has a gun cupboard bigger than your wardrobe." Hana didn't like guns, but there were always different weapons lying on her mother's kitchen table in various states of dismantling. Black powder on the carpet was a common point of argument in their house. There were guns up at Logan's hotel, literally all over the place. The stockmen wandered around with them slung across their backs, dirty great shotguns which they used to keep down the possum population. Logan bought Hana a pistol last summer and taught her how to use it.

Even to Hana's inexperienced eye, she could see the safety catch was on, rendering ineffective Lachlan's frantic brandishing of it in her face. He was a pitiful boy and he had grown into a pathetic man. Dora Dobbs reacted differently. She panicked, a woman on the edge of a nervous breakdown. She put her head in her hands with her elbows resting on the table and huge wrenching sobs escaped her, seeming to come straight from her stomach. "How long have you been here, terrorising her?" Hana asked Lachlan and he smirked.

"Just since yesterday. All these years she's had to see me in secret and now we can meet out in the open, she doesn't want to know."

"I wonder why," Hana mused sarcastically to herself, just loud enough for him to hear.

"Please don't antagonise him?" Dora Dobbs begged and Hana silenced herself, purely for the other woman's benefit.

The little King Charles Cavalier pit-patted into the kitchen and began to slurp water from a terracotta bowl in the corner. Its huge brown eyes watched Lachlan nervously and the little dog's presence seemed to make Dora even more upset. Hana saw why when Lachlan lifted the pistol and aimed it at the dog's furry little bottom and swaying tail. "No, no!" Dora screamed and stood up. Lachlan switched the gun's open mouth onto her and she stilled.

"I need to separate you from that baby, I think," Lachlan mused out loud, turning the gun on Hana.

False bravado burned in her veins as she struggled to keep herself calm. The last thing she needed was her pacemaker to detect a spike or dip in her heart rate and give her a shock. She fixed Lachlan with a determined stare. "Go on," she egged, "try it. That's only a rabbit gun and will leave a nasty bruise. After which, I will rip your damn head off and make sure when my husband gets here, he kicks it into next week."

Two things occurred to Hana in quick succession as Lachlan peered at the pistol with a look of confusion. The first was that he had obviously raided Alan Dobbs' gun cupboard and grabbed what he thought would be an intimidating weapon. Hana with her big mouth and brave talk just alerted him to the fact it wasn't. Downstairs would be an array of hunting guns, according to Logan, who hunted with Dobbs numerous times, as recently as the previous month. If Lachlan fetched one of those, it might not go well for her or her baby.

The second issue was Lachlan had no idea how to use the gun. Whilst an incompetent gun-wielder could be a good thing, Logan had drummed into Hana it was actually a very bad thing.

Because it led to fatal accidents. Hana held her breath and wished her husband were there. She imagined him telling her to shut up. The gun might not kill her but if it hit the baby in the wrong place, it could do serious damage.

Hana eyed the man warily sideways and spun the car seat so Phoenix's feet rested against her stomach, presenting the hard body of the car seat towards him. Hearing her husband's wisdom in her head, she dutifully shut up. Lachlan seemed happy with the change in his captive and relaxed, shoving the gun down the front of his jeans again. Hana prayed hard the safety slipped and blew his nuts off. It was nothing less than he deserved, threatening her baby and the cute little dog.

"Get me something to eat, Mother," the man demanded, indicating the food on the table with an outstretched hand. As Hana watched in amazement, the proverbial penny dropped into place in her slow brain. Dora rose like a spectre from the table and began mechanically assembling a plate of the various goodies for the man with the gun.

Chapter Thirty-Two

Logan was consumed with fear and misery. David gunned the elderly Range Rover through the streets of Hamilton, seeking directions for the unfamiliar turns and intersections. On the dual carriageway part of Cobham Drive heading south of the city, Logan pointed emphatically towards a right turn into a residential street. After a number of frenzied turns onto other smaller roads, Logan indicated a low, white, single storey house, set back against a dark stand of trees which backed onto a gully. He undid his seatbelt and seized the door handle, ready to surge from the vehicle and race onto the property. To his surprise and frustration, David didn't slow down but kept driving past.

"Stop the bloody car, now!" Logan's panic masqueraded as dead calm, acid and dangerous when unleashed.

David shook his head confidently. "That's not how we're going to do this," he replied. "I'll pull over up here and swap places with you. I want you to drive slowly past the house and I'll assess it. Then I'll get out and you'll wait in the car while I go and knock on the front door."

David stopped the Range Rover by a grassed area, put on the handbrake and took the car out of gear. He turned sideways in his seat and Logan watched as the man ceased to be his employee and morphed into a capable and commanding soldier. The Māori struggled inwardly, used to being the decision-maker. He'd been his own boss since the age of eleven, when he worked out nobody else gave a damn about him and it was the only way to guarantee his survival in the twisted Du Rose family. But there was something about David Allen which forced him to obey. "I have to get them out," Logan said, his grey eyes wide and glittering.

"We will."

As the other man spun out of the driver's seat, Logan shifted himself across the divide and settled, adjusting the seat position so his long legs could fit underneath the steering column. "I'll do what you say for now," Logan said, through gritted teeth. "But there's no way I'm staying in this vehicle indefinitely."

"Yeah, yeah, but you'll trust me for now." David simultaneously slammed the door and put the seatbelt around himself, although he didn't do it up. "It's just for appearances, in case a passing cop shows an interest," he said, raising his blond eyebrow at Logan. "Are you driving then, or what?"

Logan did a messy 'u' turn on the wide deserted street and drove slowly past the Dobbs' residence. The white house looked single storey, but had a deep basement housing a garage and a rumpus room below. It meant the driveway sloped sharply down towards a bright red garage door. Logan knew from memory there was also a gun cupboard down there. He dared to drive across the centre line and spotted Hana's Honda nestled at the bottom of the driveway. It filled him with angst. "She's there! Bloody hell, I knew she would be."

David exclaimed as Logan went too far over the centre line in his distraction and glared at him. "Obvious much?" he asked sarcastically and Logan bridled, barely controlling his anger at the situation. "Go up the road a bit and turn again and this time drive more carefully. Then pull up a few houses past and I'll get out. Let me walk around to the trunk so I can get that bag out, like I'm going to stay for a few days. Then wave and drive off real natural."

"No way!" Logan shouted. "My girls are in that damn house. *Bloody Hana!* Why does she always walk into trouble like this? I'm going to flamin' well kill her when I get her out of there!"

"Well, that'll be productive then!" David replied, too calmly. "Just do as I tell you and it'll work out fine!"

"I'm not driving off," Logan said stubbornly through gritted teeth. "Stuff that!"

"Park in the next street and walk back real calmly, like you're on your way to somewhere. Don't raise any alarm. And while you're doing that, call the cops."

The men were silent while Logan drove back past the house and David looked at the frontage. When the vehicle stopped a few houses along, David turned to Logan. "I know it's hard but you have to trust me. We have no idea what's going on in there. So I'm playing it real cool. What's the woman's name who lives here?"

"Dora, Dora Dobbs," Logan answered sullenly. "But unless I'm completely wrong about her, there's no way she'd hurt my wife and baby!"

David nodded and wisely kept his own counsel. In Afghanistan, he saw many people behave in completely out-of-character ways. It was one of the reasons he stuck two fingers up to Britain and walked away. Nobody listened to the things they didn't want to hear. Sometimes their own atrocities equalled that of the enemy in wartime and it was sick-making. He fought the bile which rose up into his gullet and centred himself, rooting his backside firmly into the car seat while he solidified his plan. He didn't share it with his companion. "Remember," he said, "park, call the cops and walk back."

Logan nodded. He didn't ask what David expected of him once he walked back to the house. Because the soldier knew as well as he did, he would break the door down and start hitting people until he got what he wanted. Nobody messed with Logan Du Rose's wife. David got out of the Range Rover, retrieved his rucksack from the trunk and waved as he slung it casually over his shoulder. With gritted teeth, Logan waved back and pulled away from the kerb, making the turn into the next street to grudgingly fulfil his part of the bargain.

David sauntered up to the front of the house as though he had all the time in the world. The sun was warm on the top of his head and made his curly blond hair glint strangely as the curls captured the shadows it caused. He went up the front steps, his observations skills heightened by adrenaline. By the time he reached the front door, he had already estimated the square footage of the property, worked out roughly where all the rooms might be and decided exactly how he would gain entry. He knocked on the door, a confident hearty rap, like a salesman or Jehovah's Witness.

He assumed the thin terrified woman who opened the door a crack, was Dora Dobbs. "No thank you!" she said aggressively and tried to shut the door in his face.

David used the door-stepping technique, keeping his steel toe capped boot in the gap. Then he dropped his bag to the porch floor, holding out his arms. "Aunty Dora! Don't say you forgot! I'm Ellen's son remember? She wrote and told you I'd call on my way through New Zealand." His English accent foxed her for a moment, enough for him to push the door and shift her easily out of the way. Her mouth was slightly open as she put her fingers to her lips.

"I might have forgotten," she blathered, doubting her ability to remember something that important in the living hell of the last three weeks of her life.

David embraced her gently in his muscular arms and leaned in towards her ear. It didn't take an expert to judge she was as much a victim in this as Hana. "Where are they?" he whispered and her eyes widened, watery and hopeful. Dora pointed a shaking finger towards a room off to the left of the hallway. David nodded quickly, then continued his charade. "Oh, Aunty, is my car ok parked out there or would you like me to move it?" Completely taken in, Dora moved towards the balustrade and

David gave her a firm shove. "*Go!* Turn left and keep walking," he hissed.

Dora looked down at her slippered feet and found her own front door shutting in her face. David's bag was on the porch and she propped it up neatly against the side of the house, before walking slowly down the steps and out onto her sloping driveway. Once safely on the flagged pavement of the street, she stood still as though lost and began to cry.

David banked on whoever was inside thinking Dora and the visitor were outside on the porch discussing parking. The woman would be under instruction to get rid of the caller. The soldier crept stealthily through the hallway, keeping to the walls without knocking into them. Every few steps, he stopped and listened. Dora indicated a room at the end of the hall but David didn't completely trust her not to set him up. He silently checked through each of the open doors as he passed. His finely tuned instincts were reliable when they told him the sense of tension emanated from the final door on the left and he moved towards it. David stopped again outside the room, listening with a soldier's patience. He wasn't disappointed.

The unmistakable sound of a baby's delicate sneeze came to his ears and the suggestion of a whimper, quickly silenced by a desperate mother's quiet 'sssh.' David tensed his body once and then relaxed. He centred himself, planted his feet, breathed in, breathed out and then took off at speed from his standing start. He knew exactly where the enemy would be and so he wasted no time seeking him out.

Lachlan Reynolds was behind the door, which was hinged on its left-hand side. The man was keeping a woman and baby against their will, which defined him as a coward. An enemy like that had no sense of decency and his own self-preservation was stronger than anything else. It stood to reason he would be in hiding. Lachlan peered through the gap in the door jamb but David moved so quickly past his vision, he actually thought the dark shape was his mother returning. "You took your time!" he snapped spitefully, realising too late the dark shape was too tall and too wide, as the full force of the door met him in the side of the head and he reeled backwards. David was on him in less time than it took Lachlan to blink in surprise and the soldier hit him, full in the face with a huge square fist. The younger man heard the cartilage in his nose snap under the pressure and felt a painful pop inside his head.

In David's mind, Lachlan morphed into the child he killed a year ago. A skinny, dark skinned boy wearing child sized jeans and a tee-shirt with a Nike logo. His head was partly covered by the familiar white cloth, ready to protect his mouth and nose in the sand storms which blew out of nowhere. His gun was a 7.62 calibre AK47. In western civilisation such a thing would never be in a child's hand; in Afghanistan, it was more commonplace than a McDonald's Happy Meal toy. It was a routine house search in a zero threat area, thought to be free of insurgents and it changed David Allen's life forever.

David's section broke the door off its hinges. Sleep and water-deprived, the soldier in front of David momentarily stumbled on debris underfoot, leaving him in danger. The men crisscrossed into the fatal funnel, stacked up either side of the door. The child stood there in the shadows; a target. David instantly batted the soldier who had hesitated to the ground, catching the hostile movement in his peripheral vision as he continued to execute the room clearance through the red zone target area. He instinctively fired the silenced double tap into the boy's chest without a second thought.

It was only after the area was successfully secured, he had time to inspect the body. In death, the child's face still held the same expression, ignorance, naivety and delusional self-enlightenment. The memory sickened David, alongside that maniac brand of selfless and needless heroism he encountered over and over. In wartime, everyone was a hero, especially the dead. The child died instantly, his body blurred by the soldier's training. *Shoot-to-kill.* But the boy's silent face appeared regularly after that in moments of great stress and violence. It finally drove the man insane with an emotion that had the taste of guilt.

Remembering the pistol in his right hand and sensing David's momentary distraction, Lachlan tried to raise it. Certain the gun would defend him in his naivety, he aimed it at David, his oppression of the two women giving him confidence. But the weapon was useless against a man drilled in close quarter combat, with much stronger and more desperate opponents. As Lachlan brought the pistol level with David's stomach and began to pull the trigger, he found his hand batted easily upwards and the shot went off loudly and buried itself into the ceiling, leaving a round, neat dent. He gripped the pistol hard in his hand, aiming to get off another round. But by the time his index finger found its way back to the trigger, his arm was braced against a hard thigh and the bone arched backwards painfully. His forearm ached and then went dead and Lachlan let the pistol fall to the carpet. "Men like you make me sick!" David snapped the bone anyway, as though casually breaking up kindling over his thigh for a fire. Lachlan screamed a sickening, awful noise into the now silent house.

The soldier kicked the gun away with a snort of disgust. It would never have killed him, even at close quarters. It was for hunting rabbits and birds. It would have hurt, but he suffered worse in Afghanistan. His opponent was a mess though, his famed tennis arm displaying a gory open wound where the two ragged pieces of bone emerged through the flesh. Lachlan Reynolds lay on the floor, whimpering in agony.

David looked across at Hana for the first time since entering the room. She sat stunned, sunk into an oversized squashy armchair by the window, her eyes locked on his face in horror. On her knee sat Logan's precious daughter. The baby faced David, casually laying with her back leaned against her mother's stomach and chest, her grey eyes peeking from under Hana's protective fingers. The brown eyes of the terrified Afghany boy flickered in David's mind's eye and then went out, replaced with the wisdom and understanding of the penetrating grey irises.

Phoenix gave the broken man a beatific smile and pointed a tiny finger towards him. "Daba," she said clearly, speaking his name.

David felt the weight of the world slide off his tortured shoulders as that one nonsensical word infused him with courage, forgiveness and grace.

It wasn't the child. She couldn't give him any of those things. But she did offer hope to a man who travelled home to the land of his forefathers looking for absolution. Peace settled on the ex-soldier and he smiled. His whole being lit up and rendered the contours of his face into the handsome, gentle man he always was underneath. Lachlan grovelled on the floor groaning as David stepped over his prone body and went to check out the other occupants of the room.

Hana cried silently with her hand over her face, huge tears dripping onto her baby's soft head like rain drops. Phoenix kept putting her pudgy fingers into her hair in confusion, unable to reach the rain with her short little arms. Unconcerned, she made it into a new game. '*Drip - grab - miss.*'

David knelt down next to Hana's chair and pulled her arm gently to remove the shaking hand from her eyes. "It's ok," he whispered softly, "it's over."

"I tried to cover her eyes," Hana sobbed. "I didn't want her to see him hurt anyone."

"I know," David soothed. "Your husband will be here any..."

The door flew back against the expensive china cupboard behind it with an enormous crash, causing the female occupants of the room to jump and the prone male on the floor to let out a wail. The door caught Lachlan on the forehead before using the rest of its force on the poor china cupboard. David didn't flinch as Logan's tall frame lurched through the doorway.

Hana's husband bent so as not to clout the top of his head on the doorframe. He quickly registered the man on the ground; his wife and daughter in the armchair and the soldier squatted next to her. He felt fleetingly torn between wanting to hurt Lachlan badly and needing to comfort his wife. He chose the latter and saw approval in David's eyes as he moved out of the way.

Logan enfolded Hana in his long, muscular arms, including Phoenix in the wrap around embrace. His daughter squealed and tugged at his jumper excitedly, liking this game of 'hidey boo.' But Hana cried silently and struggled to make herself understood.

Chapter Thirty-Three

David stood over Lachlan until the cops arrived. The occupants of the room heard the sirens pour down the road long before they arrived, turning the quiet suburban street into a fiesta of lights and action. Residents, formerly invisible, appeared in the street to partake of the excitement and offer evidence which was part conjecture and mainly invented.

Lachlan Reynolds was taken away in an ambulance to have his arm dealt with but Hana and Phoenix were detained by ambulance staff and police. "I just want to go home," Hana begged over and over until finally they listened. Logan summoned Angus to deal with the distraught Dora Dobbs

"I'll take her back to mine," Angus said, his complexion paler than usual. There was an uncharacteristic tremor in his fingers and Logan watched him with curiosity.

"Two female officers will accompany you," Odering said as the principal led Dora away by the arm. Angus stuffed the frail Dora into his mid-life-crisis car parked on the driveway, his arm firmly around her shoulders. He caught Logan's eye and the younger man gave him a nod of acknowledgement. But there was something else in Logan's eyes and Angus quickly looked away, his shoulders slumping in defeat.

"Take your wife home for now," Odering told Logan. "She's not making much sense so I'll pop round in a while and take her statement. I'm sure she'll give me the convoluted version, as always." He waggled his eyebrows and Logan glared at him.

"Yeah, well if you weren't such a useless detective, she wouldn't have to give you a statement, would she?"

"Because of my psychic powers?" Odering asked and Logan balled his fists. "Careful, Logan," Odering hissed. "You know how much I'd love to arrest you."

Back at The Gatehouse, a shocked Hana dealt with the physical needs of her daughter as an antidote from the deep shock that seemed to surge unchecked through her arteries. She felt muddled and at the same time intensely numb. When the zip of the change bag caught on itself and refused to budge, Hana yanked it with too much force, disconnecting the zipper on one side and detaching the metal catch from the surface. It was sharp and the tiny piece of twisted metal stabbed into the pad of her middle finger as she tugged and it gave up the fight.

Hana sat back on her heels, her daughter's bare legs kicking into the air, riding an invisible bicycle. Phoenix sucked her thumb and looked around her, her grey eyes flicking from one object to another in the cavernous bathroom. Feeling detached still, Hana stared at the cut on her finger, watching as the blood rose to the surface and then stalled. It wasn't deep enough to properly weep and the blood got on with its job, clotting and blocking the inner layers from the air and sealing the gash over with its specially designed formula of natural chemicals.

Hana felt disappointed. She expected it to bleed. She *wanted* it to bleed. Not prolifically, but perhaps just enough to drag her from the 'nothing' place she felt her mind had gone. She squeezed the end of her finger, hoping she might be able to persuade it to blood-let some more. A tiny bobble of red rose up to the surface but disappeared back to its work as soon as she released the pressure. *You can't even bleed properly, idiot! You can't do anything properly!* Hana cruelly admonished herself, feeling only disappointment.

A memory of another time rose unbidden and looking down at her left wrist, Hana saw the blood gushing in a rainbow arc of red and scarlet from the open wound. It splatted on the neat driveway, making the same noise as water wrung from a soaking wet cloth. Hana shuddered and closed her eyes, forcing the image to disperse and wishing she hadn't invited it. She gripped the scar with her right hand, closing her fingers over it roughly. The pain sparked to life, the suspect shard of glass inside the vein causing damage again with its microscopic points. With a gasp Hana let go. But it worked. She was back in the bathroom, on her aching knees with her daughter wriggling on the mat. "Oh God," she prayed. "Why me?"

Hana fitted the tiny leggings back over Phoenix's gangly legs and watched as the little girl flipped awkwardly over onto her front. The child set off on a big adventure to examine the sink pedestal, the bottom of the toilet and the side of the bath.

Hana watched her, the numbness dissipating. For Phoenix, everything was intriguing and new. Every surface was to be explored and touched - reaching for a greater understanding of her surroundings like an insatiable thirst for knowledge. Hana woodenly packed the detritus from the change bag back inside its folds. The zipper dangled sadly from one side of the opening, the contents rolling around unchecked inside like something half disembowelled. As the baby tottered up onto her knees in order to grab at the toilet seat, Hana shook herself and stood up, retrieving the child and bag in one swift movement.

Outside in the corridor, she almost fell headlong over her husband's legs. Logan sat outside the bathroom door on the split level landing, his back against the wall and his legs stretched out in front of him. He heard the door opening but didn't retract his feet fast enough as Hana bowled out of the room. "Whoa, steady." Logan jumped up, righting Hana by seizing her wrists in his strong hands. She hissed in pain and dropped the bag, managing to keep hold of Phoenix who wrapped her legs around her mother's waist. There it was again - the sharp feeling of reality which came with the stabbing reminder. Hana clung to it, trying desperately to stay in the here and now and not let her mind begin its dreadful wandering. "Sorry, sorry," Logan said, wincing in sympathy as Hana automatically looked down at the site of the pain.

"It's ok," she replied softly, dragging her gaze away from the livid scar as her husband hefted the baby onto his hip. "It's helping."

Logan looked at his wife warily, not really understanding but afraid for her. "Hana," he began, "about before. About the diary and stuff. I..."

Hana cringed visibly and held her hand up in front of her face. Her eyes closed and she shook her head. "I can't do this now, Logan."

He reached out for the bag feeling chastened, noticing it was wide open and the contents rolled around inside haphazardly. Wisely he made no comment. "Let's chuck the bag in the bedroom and then we need to go downstairs. Your best mate wants a word with you."

"Anka?" Hana said, the hope in her voice pitiful.

"No babe, I meant Odering. He's downstairs." Logan tried to mask his disdain for the detective.

Hana's shoulders visibly slumped. "I need a plaster," she stalled.

"In the kitchen cupboard, I'll get one." Logan nudged her with his hand as he hurried down to the bedroom to dump the bag inside the door. Hana didn't move. "Let's get it over with," he urged.

Odering sat at the kitchen table sipping a very dark brown cup of tea. "This tea's bloody awful," he complained to David. "It tastes a bit...spicy."

The liquid looked incredibly bitter, as though the tea bag had been thrashed to within an inch of its life to yield a colour as vivid as that. David looked smug and Logan smirked as he sat at the table. "Don't make me one like that," he said to him.

The soldier turned back to the sink and began clattering around with more cups. Hana fiddled with the plaster Logan gave her and wondered whether to decline a drink, if that was the calibre of tea making the British Air force produced. In a fit of clumsiness, she dropped the paper packaging from the plaster and began to grovel around under the table, retrieving the pieces.

When her mug of tea appeared on the table, Hana stared at it. So did Inspector Odering. Hana's looked drinkable for a start, a decent shade of rimu brown with a goodly helping of milk. Odering peered across at Hana's cup and then back at his own, a disappointed sigh escaping his lips. Behind his back, David lifted his right eyebrow in a quizzical, humorous manner and Logan looked away to avoid laughing out loud. In the twenty minutes since Logan left the pair alone, Odering had managed to upset David already.

Hana exhaled loudly as Odering's pocket book appeared from his suit jacket and everyone looked at her. "Oh," she said, pointing, "you've got a new one."

Odering humphed and flipped the blue cover open, staring at Hana and growling, "Yes, Mrs Du Rose. I used up the last one on you!"

Hana glanced at her husband in time to see him grit his teeth and look away. She saw him look at David and it was clear they shared some private joke at the policeman's discomfort. Odering took another swig of his tea, pulling a face as he instantly regretted it. He pushed the mug away in distaste. As Hana began laboriously relating her story for him to write down in his book, David replaced the tea bags in the pantry cupboard.

As Logan watched, a jar appeared in David's hand. It was only a view of the lid and part of the label, but it was enough to make Logan's eyes widen and the snort become harder to keep in. The label said Curry Paste and the jar disappeared back into the pantry as David's shoulders heaved with suppressed laughter. Logan peered at Odering's mug and saw the beginnings of a greasy film on the rim around the edges of the liquid. David leaned back against the work surface; his combat pants looking frayed and worn around the knees. He folded his muscular arms and fixed his face into a neutral stare, as though not plugged into anything. As Logan stole a last look at him, the soldier made an offensive gesture with his hand, instantly turning it into a two fingered scratch either side of his nose as Odering turned and shot him a hard look. "When the children are quite finished!" the detective snapped and Logan snorted and then swore.

"Sorry, sorry," he said, clasping Hana's hand in his. "Keep going. You're doing great."

"You're not even listening." Hana's voice contained a whine and Logan glared at David and then wished he hadn't. The soldier's face was blank and it made it somehow funnier.

Logan tried to focus on his wife as he let Phoenix down onto the floor, registering the heated debate beginning between Hana and Odering. "But you know it all, you just said so," Hana argued. "So I don't need to tell you then, do I?"

"Yes you do need to tell me, Hana!" Odering's frustration made him speak to her with familiarity. "Why do we always have to do this? Will you tell me the bloody facts?"

The policeman's hand banged heavily on the dining table and Phoenix stopped crawling and looked at him, her lips turning down into a pout. Logan's eyes narrowed and his face hardened, ready to defend his wife. "Don't talk to her like that," he threatened.

Odering fought for control, his jaw bone snaking under the skin of his face as he gritted his teeth together. "Please. Just. Tell. Me. From the beginning. It's been a long day. I'm supposed to be at my daughter's birthday party in under an hour's time and I need to get your statement." He didn't add, '*Before my wife divorces me,*' but it hung in the air nonetheless. He was a man on the precipice of disaster.

Hana's mouth clamped shut on her ridiculous protest, feeling instant guilt. Vik routinely missed birthday parties for Bodie and Izzie. Humbled, she related her tale succinctly and without debate, while Logan made the man another drink. Phoenix found a little green pea on the floor of the kitchen and Hana started in alarm as the little girl raised it to her mouth.

David got there first, hoisting Phoenix into his strong arms and rattling a packet of biscuits in her face. Excitedly she dropped the pea without hesitation. David stuffed her into the high chair and buckled her in, handing her the chocolate biscuit while her father rammed a bib over her head and rolled up her sleeves. Her eyes were wide with anticipation as the biscuit rose up on clumsy fingers, slotted into the hole in her face. She sucked it with her eyes tightly shut, savouring the new flavours.

Hana tried to concentrate on Odering's slow scribble, wondering where the pea came from. "We haven't had peas yet," she said out loud, seeing the detective's face squeeze into a scowl.

"So, what happened when you got to the house?" Odering asked.

Hana dragged herself back to him. "Another visitor let me in, a tiny lady but then Dora saw me and I gave her the casserole. Maybe that was where the pea came from."

"What pea?" Odering banged his hand on the table. His ears twitched backwards in a fear reaction as Logan swore in a low grow behind him.

Hana tried to continue. "Dora invited me in and I went because she seemed so sad and I know what that's like. Whenever I saw her at school, she looked at me like she wanted to talk to me. I thought it was because I was a widow."

David looked interested. It was a fact he hadn't known about Hana Du Rose and it put her earlier perplexing statement into context for him. She knew loss.

"What happened when you entered the property?" Odering asked, trying to force Hana to stick to the facts. Conjecture and surmising would be of little use in the witness stand.

"Nothing really," Hana said, to everyone's surprise. "Phoenix was asleep in the car seat and Mrs Dobbs thanked me for the casserole and for coming. She did seem odd, but I thought she might be medicated; I was medicated after my husband died. I realised when she mentioned Renton was missing and that he was the man I played tennis with, that I knew something quite important and decided I should leave. I didn't realise Lachlan was listening behind the door between the kitchen and the lounge." Hana stopped and bit her lip. "Lachlan appeared and stopped me leaving. I had felt uneasy but thought perhaps it was the awkwardness of the situation. Grieving people do tend to make me nervous because I'm always sure I'll say the wrong thing - which is easy to do. Lachlan just stood there, leaned against the door frame casually at first. I remembered him as soon as I saw him. He still had the sandy hair and the same gangly body. It's odd because when I saw him, the first thing I thought of was that really skilled backhand he did. It's what won him that stupid trophy. He had a pistol in his jeans and he threatened Dora and I with it. He tried to get Phoe away from me but I wouldn't let him take her." Hana's gaze roved to the chocolate coated baby and her eyes narrowed with relived horror.

"Eventually, he made me go into the lounge with him and he took the missing trophy off the mantelpiece. *'Remember this?'* he said, as though it was a harmless ornament. But I saw the blood on the wooden base. He hadn't even bothered to clean it off. I knew then what he'd done."

"What had he done, Hana?" Odering pressed her.

Tears began to run down Hana's face. It was as though a dam burst somewhere inside her head and she leaked profusely, without sound or control. Logan rested a hand gently on her thigh under the table and she sought it out with her fingers and gripped it. The tears fell, but she continued on, concentrating on breathing and getting it all out. It wasn't just sadness which cascaded down, but anger, pure livid anger.

"He killed him, the tennis player. Renton was so gentle, such a kind, lovely man. I didn't recognise him from the school tennis club, but I should have. That's why he knew me. Vik coached the teams for a good few years while we were playing doubles. They change so much as they grow up sometimes, but he was always white blond. I remembered him as soon as I saw Lachie and that's when I realised."

"Realised what, Hana?" Odering asked. Logan struggled to sit still and even Phoenix stopped licking her bare biscuit. Only David looked impassive, leaned against the work surface, arms and legs crossed, his body inclined gently backwards.

"The tennis player was Alan Dobbs' son. That's how he had the keys to everything. The cops looked for a 'random guy' but he wasn't. That's why nobody knew who they were looking for. Because he wasn't just some stranger. He was Renton Dobbs, the deputy principal's son and an Old Boy of the school. Lachlan was his half-brother. He killed him with that damn trophy!"

"But we found the car you described on site. It had the ball serving machine in the boot and the racquets you mentioned a few weeks ago. One of them had 'Lachlan' written on it in black ink - just like you described."

"Yes but you knew it wasn't Lachlan!" Hana exclaimed.

Odering looked warily at her, shaking his head. "How do you know that?" he snapped, instantly alert but not expecting the answer he got.

"You told me," Hana replied. "When I was going out the front gates this morning, you pulled up alongside me and I asked how you were getting on finding out who killed Lachlan Reynolds and you said, *'Who?'* You'd already moved on to knowing it was someone else. At first I was relieved, thinking maybe it wasn't the tennis player who died, but then I got to wondering and realised I knew something. Only I didn't understand what it was at the time."

"I must be slipping," Odering said under his breath, at the same time relieved it wasn't Bodie who gave the game away.

"It had to be the tennis player who died, because you emphasised how blond the dead person's hair was. His build, his clothing everything, sounded like him. So if he wasn't Lachlan, then who was he? The men were half-brothers, because Lachlan called Dora, 'Mother'. The police wouldn't have let Dora know Renton was dead, because they had no idea who he was. Poor

Dora." Hana looked crestfallen. "She's lost her husband and her son. All she has left is a killer. No wonder she was so distraught."

Logan leaned in and wrapped his arm around his wife's shoulder. Phoenix squeezed her eyes tight shut and pointed what was left of the manky biscuit at them, saying, "Ahhhhh," in the cutesy voice they used for her.

"Can we go back to what happened when Lachlan Reynolds showed you the trophy?" Odering dragged Hana back almost to the beginning, much to her frustration.

"Dora saw the blood on the trophy at the same time as I did. She dropped her cup and it smashed on the floor. She lunged for Lachlan and he pushed the trophy at her. He said, *'Here you go, Mother Dear, take it. Have what's left of your perfect son.'* It was dreadful. Dora stood looking at it, tears rolling down her face." Hana gulped. "She cuddled it to her and it was so sad. Lachie laughed. He seemed to think it was funny. I could see how desperate Dora felt, but didn't know what to do. I needed to keep Phoe safe and my heart was pounding so hard." Hana put her right hand up to her chest and then looked at her husband. "It didn't go off though," she said smiling gently at him. "I'm think I'm all better now."

"Bloody hell, Hana!" Logan pulled his wife into his shoulder and rested his face in her hair. He felt strangely overcome by emotion and didn't want the other men in the room to notice, turning his head away from their gaze. Hana stroked his cheek with the back of her hand. Out the corner of her eye, she noticed Odering looking surreptitiously at his watch and bit her lip.

Phoenix leaned forward and fingered the soldier's trousers with her dirty fingers, looking hopefully up at him. It worked. The packet rustled and another biscuit made its way into her sticky, chocolate encrusted fingers. She looked at it, suddenly not sure she wanted it. But she flattened out her tongue and laid it against the side of the biscuit. The taste of chocolate assailed her taste buds and the wave of nausea bubbled up in her chest and then subsided. Phoenix screwed up her face at the rotten taste of bile in her mouth and laid the biscuit flat on her tray, pushing it around in the dribble and making little chocolate tracks on its white surface.

Hana took a deep breath. "Dora asked Lachlan, *'Why,'* and he replied, *'You know why.'* I didn't understand but I knew I had to keep still for Phoe's sake. It made it impossible for me to run or fight or do anything with her there. Lachie seemed crazy. I didn't want to draw attention to myself. It didn't matter in the end. Phoenix woke up and I had to feed her to keep her quiet. She laid on my lap and seemed to know she had to keep still. Lachlan left me alone but he made Dora run around fetching us drinks and food. I had to sit in the chair and not move, otherwise he waved the gun at me. I wasn't scared for myself but he was so unpredictable, I couldn't be certain he wouldn't hurt the baby or Dora. He let me go to the bathroom once and I said I had to take Phoe so that I could change her nappy. There was no way I was leaving her. They all came and waited outside the door. *Oh no,*" Hana looked ashen. "The dirty nappy's still in the bathroom. It'll stink the place out."

She looked appealingly at Odering, but he shook his head. "It's the least of my problems right now, retrieving a Code Brown from a hostage house."

Hana was made to run through her story a number of times until she grew sick of the sound of her own voice. She recalled vividly the bright floral print on the seat covers and the chintzy wallpaper which dated the owners. Lachlan was both calm and terrifying. His blue eyes were hard and unyielding, refusing to listen to the pleadings of his birth mother and he made them wait and wait, for something, or someone.

"It's really weird," Hana commented. "I know Lachie already killed Renton and possibly Alan Dobbs but there was this odd sense that he was waiting for someone else. He was happy to sit there with us. I don't know how long his patience would have lasted, but he seemed convinced that something else needed to happen in order for it to all be over."

"Did he say, or do anything that led you to believe that?" Odering asked sharply and Hana racked her brains. She and

Dora were made to sit, but Lachie moved freely around the room, simply telling his mother to *'shut up'* whenever her pleadings and tears became too much for him. He waved the pistol a few times and threatened them. Hana shut her eyes and thought about him standing in the doorway. It was an odd place to stand unless he was expecting someone to burst in on him and wanted to be ready. Lachlan was ready for David, only he hadn't been as ready as he thought he was for the soldier. Hana shook her head. "That's because it wasn't David he was expecting. It was someone else."

"What?" Odering asked, narrowing his eyes in confusion.

"I could see the red in his hair glinting in the sunlight. I knew he couldn't ever have been the tennis player. Nobody could dye out a colour like that, not without having obvious regrowth at the roots. The lounge faced towards the back of the house, but Lachlan kept going out into the hallway. He stood so he could still see us both but he was watching out of the windows either side of the front door. Dora spent most of the time crying but a couple of times I heard her praying. She kept saying, *'God forgive me, God forgive me.'* I felt so sorry for her. Once she said under her breath, *'I should never have told him,'* but I had no idea what she was talking about. Eventually, it became really difficult keeping hold of Phoe, because she wanted to get down and crawl around and I couldn't let her do that. I fed her and fed her until I thought she might explode, because it makes her want to sleep."

"What did Lachlan do when Mr Allen knocked on the front door?" Odering asked, glancing backwards at the soldier who hadn't moved a muscle since he handed the biscuit over to the baby. "Did he become upset or agitated?"

"Excited," Hana said without hesitation. "Very excited. It was like 'game on' - like the thing he waited all afternoon for was about to happen. He couldn't seem to contain himself. He made sure the gun was loaded and went behind the door. He instructed Dora to 'let him in' as though he knew who it was and she went off to do it."

"How could he have known it was me?" David piped up abruptly. "*I* didn't even know it was going to be me, until about ten minutes before I walked up the steps."

"He couldn't," Odering answered shortly, his daughter's birthday party disappearing before his eyes. "It was someone else, a male. The big question is, who?"

He got to his feet and went down the hall into the huge lobby to make a phone call. Returning to the kitchen, Odering collected his notebook and pen together and slipped them back into his pocket with a tired sigh. "Thanks for your statement, Mrs Du Rose. It's been enlightening. Someone will call you tomorrow to come in and sign it. I should go now."

"To the birthday party?" Hana asked, rising to her feet and following the tall police inspector back outside. To her dismay, he shook his head.

"No, I need to go and interview Mrs Dobbs now. She must know who Lachlan was waiting for."

"Don't do that, please don't." Hana reached out and touched the policeman's arm gently. Logan appeared in the kitchen doorway and watched his wife, resenting her momentary physical contact with the other man. As though she sensed his presence, Hana let go and dropped her hand to her side. Odering turned slowly back from the front door and looked straight at her with a question in his eyes. "Go home," Hana implored him. "The party will be a couple of hours at most. Do that first. Delegate the rest to someone else and pick it up again later. Explain to your wife you'll have to go back to work after the party, but please go. It's probably the most important thing you'll ever do - support your children. We don't get to go round again, to make up for the lost moments. And they never forget."

Odering's face was full of his internal wrangling. Hana pushed her advantage, on behalf of the children who hardly knew their father and the wife who was manoeuvring for divorce on the basis of neglect and irreconcilable differences. "Go home!" she told him forcefully - and he went, closing the door quietly after him.

Chapter Thirty-Four

"So what made you both come looking for me?" Hana asked as she stood with her hands on her hips in challenge. Her tears had dried on her cheeks, leaving dull tracks on her skin and she looked formidable. David shrugged easily and pointed at Logan, who looked conflicted. Looking to the other man for help, he got none, as the soldier high-tailed it back into the kitchen.

"I had a conversation with someone and things fell into place," Logan began tentatively. "I came home for lunch and David said you'd gone out. When you weren't back by tea-time, he mentioned you took food to a widow. It was obvious something was wrong."

"Why was it obvious?" Hana asked, noticing the warning stress vein in her husband's neck begin to tick.

"Because of where you'd gone," Logan replied, his face shutting down and his body language growing tense and uncomfortable.

"What was the conversation?" Hana asked and Logan blanched.

"*Someone* received a text from Dora Dobbs. At the time he seemed very upset. When you didn't come back, I rang him and asked what the message said. He read it to me and it said her son knew who his father was and that she was sorry. Her son was demanding to see this person and would hurt Dora if they didn't turn up. As soon as I realised where you were, I knew you were in trouble."

"So whoever he was didn't go then? He was happy to let Lachlan hurt Dora?"

"Looks like it." Logan spoke through gritted teeth.

"So Dora really is Lachlan's mother then? He called her 'Mother' so I guessed that much. But who were you talking to? Who's his father?"

Logan exhaled and visibly struggled. He ran a nervous tongue over his lips and focussed on a spot above Hana's head. He kept lots of people's secrets and was loyal and trustworthy. As his grey eyes fixed hard on Hana's green ones, she saw how much he wanted to tell her, but also what it would cost him to do so. They had been here before and Hana ended up feeling like an outsider. Logan's brow knitted and his jaw worked furiously through his cheeks. "You don't want to tell me, do you?" she said, her voice sounding sad.

"It's not that." Logan wrestled with an inner demon. "I don't want you to think badly of someone you really like. I want to tell you, but I know it will destroy something."

Hana knew she had to release him. She raised her hands in a universal stop sign, shaking her head slowly. "It's ok, don't tell me, Loge. I don't think it would help me to know somehow. Lachlan Reynolds is one very sick individual and I pity the person who has to admit to being his father."

Logan looked confused for a moment, but it quickly turned to relief as his body relaxed. "You genuinely don't want to know?" he asked. "You trust me?"

Hana nodded and he held his strong arms out towards her. With a sigh, she welcomed the comfort of being wrapped in his safe embrace.

"Ahhhh," came their baby's cute voice from the doorway as she pushed herself successfully back from a crawl into a sitting position. Her parents watched with pride as she beamed and squeezed her eyes tight shut with pleasure at her own hard-won skills.

"Phoe, you did it!" Hana exclaimed, smiling at her daughter. Phoenix Du Rose clapped her tiny hands but tilting back too confidently, the inevitable happened and gravity seized the little girl's head, hauling her backwards into the doorframe. There was a hiccough, a pause and then a shrill, angry wail of pain.

As Logan snatched Phoenix up in his arms, she snuggled her face into his neck and let him rub the back of her head with his fingers. "All better," he crooned. But as he swung away from Hana and went through the kitchen door, Hana's face was level with her daughter's. Tears stained the olive cheeks but the child smirked with her eyes as her father bore her away for medical treatment. Hana heard Logan and David running a tea towel under the cold tap and debating how best to treat the bump.

Hana shook her head and wondered if Logan knew what he was up against over the next few years. She narrowed her eyes through the doorway at Phoenix and the little girl did a fake whimper and grinned over Logan's shoulder, pushing her button nose into his shirt.

It was Bodie who appeared the next day with a neatly typed statement for his mother to sign. Hana was desperate to ask if Odering made it to his daughter's party, but decided it was no longer any of her business. "So did Lachlan kill Alan Dobbs as well?" she asked her son as he hovered over her with a black biro. He shrugged.

"We'll never know. He says not, but how can you tell? Dobbs died from his injuries as a result of tumbling down the stairs. It could have been a genuine accident. But there's no doubt Lachlan lured him back to school. The forensics guys spent ages on the crappy security video recordings and managed to get a good enough likeness, once they knew who to look for. The evidence won't be good enough for the court, but his DNA was all over the letters we found. Dobbs hid them in a locked drawer in his office and it was confusing at first because they had a Singapore postmark. We knew Lachlan Reynolds had been abroad for the last ten years coaching tennis to rich oriental families, but we found that out when we thought he was dead. There had to be a connection; it just didn't make sense."

"What did the letters say?" Hana asked, finally signing the statement with a flourishing signature. Bodie visibly relaxed.

"Just that he hated Dobbs. He was coming to get him. He wished him dead. That kind of stuff. Dora's told us Dobbs forced her to have him adopted. Then he also stopped her seeing him. It seems Lachlan was adopted by alcoholic parents, which was why he ended up in the boarding house. Dora worked out a deal with Angus whereby she covered the fees secretly. Dobbs had no idea who the kid was until he started making trouble for the younger boy, Renton. Then when Dobbs tackled it as a routine bullying issue, out it all came and the trophy incident was born. The last letter stated he was coming home to get what was rightfully his."

"Oh," Hana said sadly. "What a mess. Did Renton know Lachlan was his half-brother?"

"According to Dora Dobbs, that was a recent development. Lachlan's return to New Zealand was not exactly triumphant and he turned up at the house to see Dora. Alan and Renton were both home. They threw him out and it got out of hand. The proverbial beans were spilled and it came out that Dora had been in touch with Lachlan the whole time. She tracked him down when he was a little boy and it went from there. Lachlan wanted to know who his father was and nobody would tell him. So he set Alan Dobbs up. We're guessing it was to somehow force him to tell him, but Dobbs wound up dead."

Hana sighed. Phoenix Du Rose's strange statement drifted back into her mind, unbidden.

'The women are the curse of this family. But the men will be its ruin.'

Perhaps it wasn't just the Du Roses. Maybe it related to families everywhere.

"So what did Dora say about who Lachlan was waiting for? Obviously it was his father."

Bodie looked embarrassed. "Actually, Mum, she's denying all of that. She says she has no idea what you're talking about. Odering put it to her and she said it wasn't the truth. Sorry, Mum, but it's your word against hers."

Hana's jaw had dropped open in amazement. "*Really*? The woman's still playing games after losing a son and a husband? That's ludicrous!"

Bodie raised a hand in placation. "It doesn't matter. Odering says it's conjecture anyway and won't have any bearing on the case. If it comes up in court, our brief will deal with it. There's enough evidence to put Lachlan inside without it mattering why he was there or who he was actually waiting for."

Hana tutted, irritated. Then she remembered something that bothered her. "Why was Renton killed in our unit? I don't understand that."

"That's something else we don't really know," Bodie sighed. "But from what Dora said, Renton knew you and talked to her about meeting up with you again. He was two years behind me at school and possibly learned I was a cop. We think he knew Lachlan killed his father and wanted your help sorting it out. Your mail would all go into the school's private bag at the post office, so he needed a better way of getting your attention. There was a piece of paper found underneath the sofa when we moved your furniture out. It possibly blew there off the coffee table and we initially thought it was something of yours. We don't have any recent examples of his handwriting, but the note started with, *'I hope you don't mind me asking, but I need help with a problem that I've got and you...'*"

"That's it?" Hana asked, a little scathingly. "It doesn't sound much like evidence to me."

"Odering showed Logan a few days ago and he said it wasn't your handwriting or his or Tama's, so it could only have been someone else who was in the unit. Possibly someone disturbed him half-way through writing it. It had what we now know to be

Renton's DNA on it but not Lachlan's, so it must have blown off without him seeing - perhaps as Lachlan pushed the front door open. Obviously there were links in the DNA of close familial relationship but the different fathers confused things. It's what sent us looking at the identity of the dead man again; something didn't add up.

"Renton had a master key to absolutely bloody everything, by the way. Literally the keys to the kingdom. He must have got a copy of Alan's, which is bad. Anyone in town cutting those keys is supposed to contact the school in order to verify they're meant to have it. It's a bummer."

"It had to have been cut fairly recently then," Hana conjectured, "because all the unit locks were changed earlier this year when the units were renovated."

Bodie shook his head. "No, the key was old. It seems there's a range of locks that can be accessed by that particular master. The locksmith just made sure all the new units had locks related to that one."

Hana looked unnerved. "So do you think everyone who has a master key can get in here?" she asked, looking around the old building.

"Probably," Bodie nodded. "Sorry."

"*Fantastic!*" she replied," stamping her foot.

Chapter Thirty-Five

"Wow!" Logan Du Rose said, with genuine appreciation. Will rolled his wheelchair back and forth a couple of inches in anticipation, as though the big wheels were unable to contain his excitement. Logan touched the large jade club with a forefinger, feeling the smoothness under his skin. It had been polished until it reflected the light like a mirror. He hefted it in his hand as though about to wield it in anger, looking like a Māori warrior of old.

Displayed around the enormous table were the artifacts, no longer just items in a rotting box, but beautiful treasures, shining and clean. Free from mildew and silverfish, the photographs beamed out of new or repaired frames, the sepia faces alive and real.

Logan stood for a long moment over a wooden framed, black and white picture of a woman. She wore her hair pulled back from her face but hanging long down her back. It looked dark and wavy in the frame, shafts of light glinting off the tresses as though her hair was alive, her traditional feathered cloak smooth around her shoulders. "*Kia ora, Kuia,*" Logan whispered. "*Tahuti mai.*" His brow knitted with a look of pain and it caused Hana to falter with concern as she moved towards him.

"Welcome indeed," Hana heard Will whisper behind her. She knew without asking the woman in the photograph was Logan's grandmother, the original Phoenix Du Rose. *Ta moko* tattoos covered her regal chin and her head showed a defiant lift in the way she held it; the same look of authority which Logan carried. The eyes staring out of the frame were no usual colour, the grey different to any of the other pictures. They bore into Hana, touching her down the ages with a curious knowing look of solidarity.

Phoenix was wide awake in Logan's arms and she stared down at the picture, pointing her little index finger at it and chittering sounds. The likeness between child and grandmother was striking, the same stunning eyes and the classically featured face. Logan looked uncharacteristically emotional and it was so raw and naked it made Hana choke up. To disguise her distress and draw attention away from her husband, Hana turned to Will and complimented him on his labour of love. "It looks absolutely amazing," she said. "I never dreamed you could make it all better."

The old man looked coy under her pretty gaze and fluttered his dark eyelids in bashfulness. "I enjoyed every minute of it," he answered. He rolled his chair forward and back again and stared down at the ground. "Don't suppose there's more? I've gotten intrigued by the Du Rose family; so many twists and turns in the *whakapapa*. I feel like I know them all like my own *whānau*."

Hana laid her hand gently on his shoulder and patted it as though he were a child. His face lit up in a handsome smile and he laughed up at her. Hana pursed her lips. "You might be in luck actually. The housekeeper told me last time we were at the hotel, there's heaps more junk in the attic. Only one of the upstairs wings were made into an apartment, but there are three more. She seemed to think they housed more of the family stuff."

Will looked up at her, his brown eyes filled with hope. "Will you look?" he pleaded. "I'll do you a good rate." He touched the bottom of her sweatshirt, his face pleading. "*Whānau* rates?"

It was an honour, being accepted into his family and Hana took the gnarled fingers in her soft hand and gave them a squeeze. She bit her lip, her heart increasing its beat. "About that," she started. "How do I pay you? You haven't invoiced me yet or given me an idea of what I owe you. The Achilles Rise house has sold now and my son's due to settle on Culver's Cottage any day, thank goodness. I'm happy to give you cash or a cheque, or even do a bank transfer if you'd rather..."

Will held his hand up to halt her halting words. "You've already paid me more than enough." Hana looked confused, knowing she hadn't paid anything yet. Will looked up at her with a smirk in his eyes. "He doesn't talk much does he?"

"Who?" Hana asked, shaking her head to clear the confusion.

"The soldier."

"David?"

"That's him. He brought the cash round last week. It's a lot of money. Enough to do heaps more photos and frames, if you've got them?"

Hana looked sideways at her husband as he moved around the workshop, looking at the artifacts and gently handling the various items on the table. She sighed in exasperation. "He didn't pay for the painting too, did he?"

Will winked at her. "I didn't tell him about your gift, no."

Hana beamed, her red hair catching the light and her eyes narrowing in an ethereal smile. "Thank you, Will. I've got the cash in my purse.

Will shook his head and laughed, pointing an arthritic finger towards Logan's back. "*Tō makau* is a very lucky man. But he's got his hands full with you, *kōtiro*, for sure he has." Will's guttural laughter attracted the attention of Phoenix, who looked at the old man over her father's shoulder. She squeezed her eyes up tight and giggled in response.

Tipene approached Logan and the men engaged in a quiet chat, during which Logan stayed silent. It ended with Tipene clapping Logan heartily on the shoulder and Hana's husband nodding, his face grave and his eyes downcast. Hana ached for the diary, curiosity making her seek the unsolved mysteries within its delicate folds, but Logan hadn't mentioned it since the awful night he confiscated it. Hana felt the pain of exclusion again and wondered if she would ever be free of her outsider label. *Pākehā*. Foreigner.

Logan arranged for the *taonga* to be picked up in the next few weeks and more of the family treasures from the attic to be dropped off. Then he drove his wife and daughter back to The Gatehouse. Hana prattled on aimlessly, getting only nods for her pains. "I'm glad Jas is changing schools now they're moving into Culver's Cottage," she said, watching Logan out of the corner of her eye. He smiled and nodded, but didn't comment.

Pulling up on the driveway, he surprised Hana by turning off the engine but stopped her from getting out, placing his long fingers over hers. "I know you want the diary back," he said quietly. "I've finished with it now. I can give it to you."

Hana wondered, not for the first time if Logan was a secret mind reader. She didn't answer, swallowing and chewing on her bottom lip.

"Tipene will send Reuben's letters over to me. He thinks it might help. It's been hard reading the diary; knowing I'm the product of everything my grandmother *didn't* want. She knew the women were passing haemophilia down the generations and it was killing them. The *rangatira* warned her before his death, so she tried to stop my parents getting together; she didn't want the intermarrying. Reuben was rebellious and did it just to spite her. Phoenix stopped him getting Miriam, so he married her sister and then he took them both anyway. Geez, talk about the sins of the fathers!"

Logan's voice was sad. Hana kept the empty platitudes inside her head, offering physical comfort through a squeeze of her fingers but it seemed inadequate. Her husband's brown skin against her pale hand reminded her of an old poster for the United Nations. *Pākehā*. Foreigner. She pushed the random thought away. Logan was still speaking. "I shouldn't have spoken to you like I did before. You had every right to read the diary because I gave you that right - I wanted you to deal with it all and then at the first sign of trouble, took it back. I'm sorry Hana."

Hana smiled, trying to ignore the freshness of the pain in her heart as Phoenix snored in the car seat behind them, her life blood mingling, Irish, Scots, Māori. What did that make her daughter? *Pākehā*. Foreigner?

Logan's long eyelashes brushed his cheek as he looked down at their joined hands and his thumb rubbed a steady rhythm across Hana's alabaster skin. "Nev's agreed to the land sale. We need to go back up to the hotel this weekend to sign everything. I've put you down as joint owner."

"No, I don't want to joint own anything," Hana began. "I don't feel like I belong. How can I part own something which makes me feel like a foreigner every time I look at it?"

Logan's body seemed to deflate before her, his grey eyes glittering with self-reproach. "I don't want you to feel like that, Hana."

"It's not just you," she acknowledged, leaving her hand in his despite the urge to pull it from his olive fingers. "I don't know who I am anymore. I read the diary and felt such kinship with your grandmother, I understood her struggles and wanted to take care of the artifacts for you and for her. Seeing what Will's done with them just made me feel so disconnected from your past and even more fractured from you. I'll always be the *Pākehā*, the white foreigner."

Logan rubbed his eyes with his other hand, not letting go of Hana's fingers. He sighed and an unexpected smile curved his full lips upwards. "Hana," he said. "It takes time to become part of anything, especially a family. Maybe I like you being my white woman, have you ever considered that? I love that you have a different perspective and you're not enmeshed in all this family mess. *Kuia* Phoenix didn't want her descendants to intermarry and I picked someone from the other side of the world. It's the one thing I've done that would have pleased her, babe; I married you. She would have approved; you stop me being a monumental failure just by wearing my ring and sharing my bed. You and Phoe are all that matter to me, can't you see that?"

Hana snuffed out a small breath. "I try to fit in but..."

"Stop trying," Logan said, his voice determined. "My mountain is your mountain. Anyone who doesn't like it, can leave." With his eyes narrowed and his face set in a powerful grimace, Logan Du Rose looked every bit the tribal chief he was born to be. The *rangatira* strengthened his backbone and drove him on towards claiming back what was his by right. "Please accept it?" he asked, his eyes pleading with naked intensity.

Hana exhaled and nodded, desperate to please him but terrified of the obligation and responsibility. Logan took a deep breath inwards. "There's a few other things. Angus asked me to be his deputy in place of Alan Dobbs. I said 'no' and he asked me to think about it. I've thought about it and today I..."

Logan seemed to be having difficulty with his words as he smashed another stronghold in his life. His role model wasn't the man he thought he was and it hurt. He fought to control the latent stutter, furious at his inner weakness on display. He bit his lip and looked out of the window at the soccer fields beyond, the grass the colour of limes under the burgeoning spring sky. "Today, I quit my job. I don't want to work here anymore and I don't want to be Angus' deputy. I can't for reasons you'll have to trust me on. We leave at the end of the year."

He looked at his wife's stunned face, guilt etched into his own. "I know I should have talked to you first. I hoped you'd understand."

Hana looked up at the attractive building before her, the white panels and the old fashioned beams. The Gate House seemed to smile down sadly on her. She saw the school buildings behind them, winking at her in the side mirrors of the Honda and the sports fields laid out to the right and the left. She felt a curious detachment register in her soul, as though having been cut off without her realising. "What will you do?" she asked her husband softly, surprised by the sudden light in his eyes.

"That's the other thing I wanted to talk to you about. I spoke to your dad. I thought we could spend Christmas with him and Elaine in the UK and then just do whatever we wanted for six months - like we talked about."

"Wow," Hana whispered. It seemed like such a lot to take in. "What about after that?"

Logan smiled and his face looked beatific. "If it's alright with you, I think I'd like to go home."

Hana thought about the house on top of the hill. The 'new' house Phoenix Du Rose demanded he build, not made from bricks and mortar but honesty, integrity and new blood mixed in with the Du Roses. She nodded slowly, her enthusiasm growing as she contemplated their future together, cutting all ties with the troubles of the past. Logan looked ecstatic and leaned across and kissed her. A group of passing boys whooped loudly as they spotted them necking in the car. Logan glared at them and then laughed as they scurried away. He ran his forefinger gently over Hana's soft lips and whispered, "He called me '*Nama*'- my father. That was his special name for me. Tipene told me."

Hana's face fell, isolation flooding her eyes once again at the unfamiliar word.

"It means, 'borrowed' in Māori," Logan translated and smiled.

Epilogue

The Circle Line on the London Underground was busy, even though rush hour was still a while away. Tube trains buzzed in and out of stations, wheezing their strange electrical noise as they hissed and fled down dark tunnels. Commuters hung around in the doorways of moving trains. They swayed calmly in the motion, ready just to leap onto the platform and continue their familiar journey on another train, or make their way up to the fresh winter air above. The metal rails were coloured yellow and the seats and fittings were bright and fresh looking. Gone was the tired carriage of a quarter of a century ago, where two confused and lonely teenagers momentarily connected in a single glance.

The pretty redhead sat serenely in her seat, gazing calmly at the other travellers in the carriage. Her hair hung long down her back and shoulders, curling in the humidity of the train. Her striking green eyes raked the faces of strangers around her and she wondered who they were and where they were going. Once, she wished she could swap places with them and carry on in someone else's less complicated life. Now, she felt glad of the denied wish.

Feeling his eyes on her face, Hana stared across at her husband, acknowledging the grey irises riveted on her, despite the distractions around him. She smiled and enjoyed their shared memory. Logan was transported back in time to another day on this same tube line, when the tearful green eyes settled on him and Hana smiled. He fell in love and fell hard.

The train popped out of the tunnel and into the station, re-joining the hustle and bustle of humanity and the carriage emptied and then filled again. Logan Du Rose left the ghost of his fourteen-year-old self on the seat and joined his soul mate on hers. He settled his daughter back on his knee just in time, as the train moved again with a hiccoughing start. The little girl was transfixed by the sights and sounds of everything; wide-eyed and fully awake as her father leaned sideways and kissed his wife. Hana smiled contentedly and leaned her head against his shoulder.

Despite the freezing roads outside and the Arctic blast which entered the carriage every time the train doors opened to admit newcomers, Phoenix Du Rose went into battle with her little shoes and socks again. Hana made a lurch for the cloth shoe as it shot down the carriage. "There goes another one!" she complained and Logan laughed.

With a beaming smile of success, Phoenix waved the other one in front of her mother's face and twinkled her naked toes in the cold air. The children of *Aotearoa* always had bare feet - it was in their genes.

High up on a mountain in her homeland, *tangata whenua*, the people of the land were stirring. Recent summer rains had exposed the tender roots of an ancient kauri tree which sat proudly atop a high mountain range, guarding the land. The soil was raw beneath it. A rotted cloth bag stared up blindly at the engravings in the bark depicting the Du Rose *whakapapa-*. The bag's string neck sagged and its contents glimpsed the light of a New Zealand dawn, flecked and glimmering in the canopy's silver ferns. The bone pin was smooth and white and the greenstone inlay, priceless.

The baby's pretty olive toes flexed under the harsh strip lights of the London tube train as she fought against the refitting of the shoe. Then without warning, her brow knitted as she felt the powerful tug of the *whenua*, like a dull ache in her chest. The land of her forefathers called her back to ash-black sand, lush green grass and an endless blue sky.

Like her father and the soldier she was permitted to wander, but the leash grew taut and painful. Like an elastic band stretched beyond Hook's Law, the child felt the tug again and understood. Her grey eyes flicked to her father's and she saw he felt it too, as their *tāngata* cried from *Aotearoa* and ordered them home.

Du Rose Sons

SAMPLE CHAPTER

Nothing rivalled the sight of breaking glass; a crashing, glittering parade of beautiful prisms; each one lethally charged with death. The transparent panes of the French doors were aged, placed into the wooden frames by hands long since dead by the time the rugged, red brick passed through their mottled surface. The clay missile fractured the wooden struts and caused two of the panes to hang like a torn curtain. The third shattered spectacularly, showering the room's single occupant with spiteful shards of glass.

"What was that?" The first ear-splitting sound was followed by a deafening second as the hotel's elderly housekeeper burst into the family room, her eyes wide and frightened and her ample breasts wobbling under her work shirt. "I was next door. What was that crash?"

The dark skinned Māori approached the woman on the sofa, who sat with her hands over her head as though pinned to the cushions. The housekeeper halted at the sight of the speckling of glass littered in the curly auburn hair and blood on the shaking hands. "Oh my goodness, oh no! Get Mr Logan," she cried to a waitress who appeared at the heavy door and propped it open with her foot. "Tell him the missus is hurt!"

The face and the foot disappeared. "Hana?" The housekeeper, *ngā hāwini*, touched the redhead, disturbing the glass which tinkled down onto the sofa cushions and pinged off the wooden rimu floor. "Did you see who did it?"

Auburn hair bounced and the glittering glass shone like diamond dust, beautiful and deadly. "No, it happened too fast."

The redhead put her right hand up to her face and winced as she contacted a series of tiny open wounds, bleeding steadily and dripping stains onto her white blouse. The elderly book on her knee fell to the floor with a clunk - yet another damaging moment in its long suffering existence. The cover fell over the pages of guilty secrets, hiding them from view.

Another face appeared at the door. "Sal says she's radioed Mr Logan. He's on his way. Shall we bring the vacuum cleaner to get up the small bits of glass? Or do you want us to call the cops again?"

The housekeeper pursed her brown lips and gave the matter much thought. "Wait for the boss to get here. He'll decide. Find me a comb. There's glass in the missus' hair. You should bring me the first aid kit from the kitchen too; she's bleeding."

"Look, Leslie, I'm fine really. Let's just clear it all up. There's no need to bother Logan." Hana attempted to stand and glass cascaded down like a snow storm. Some of the substantial pieces hit the floor with a tinkle.

The waitress arrived in the doorway with a comb and handed it over to her superior, who took it without thanks. Hana protested futilely as Leslie bustled around her, raking savagely through the coils and ringlets with a small black comb. "Whose comb is it?" Hana protested. "That's gross!"

"Stop your complaining," the old woman tutted as numerous tiny shards pierced her fingers in her efforts. Finally she stood back and admired her handiwork. "I think it's all out," she announced, her brow creased in concentration and annoyance. "But we'll need to get your clothes off. Best do it here and we'll clear up in one go, otherwise youse might track the glass all through the house and then my *moko* will cut her bare feet."

Hana sighed and bit her pretty lip as she considered her daughter. At barely eighteen months old, Phoenix Du Rose refused to wear shoes and toddled around the hotel corridors with barefoot enthusiasm. "Fine!" Hana groaned. "But I'm only doing this for Phoe!" Her cheeks pinked with embarrassment as she stripped down to her bra and knickers in the middle of the family room, aware of the hotel full of people nearby.

Leslie slapped Hana's bottom with a flat palm and chuckled. "Youse still a gorgeous girlie for your years. No wonder that boy can't keep his hands off you. My Alfie would love me to look like that."

Hana turned and screwed up her face. "That's just weird," she said. "You can't say things like that about my father-in-law." Knitted brows communicated Hana's distaste and Leslie gave a belly laugh, her ample bosom wobbling with glee.

"Youse way too serious, girlie. Now, stop shifting yer feet or there'll be more cuts to mop up."

By the time her husband arrived, the slender redhead was wrapped in a large black tablecloth from the dining room, mopping at painful cuts on her cheek and hands with a scratchy corner of the starched fabric. "Geez, Hana!" Logan said in dismay.

"Don't come in!" Hana turned towards her husband, releasing one porcelain toned hand from the tablecloth to ward him off. "There's glass everywhere. You'll walk it out into the hall."

Logan Du Rose shifted awkwardly in the doorway, the heels of his cowboy boots grinding the glass shards which had spread that far. His olive skinned face betrayed agony at not being able to reach his wife and Hana sensed him reading the distress in her face. She was coping just fine until she saw him, but fought the urge to cry as relief flooded over her. Logan's six foot four inch frame tensed as he made his decision. "Sod it!" he exclaimed and strode over to his slender wife, bending at the knees as he scooped her up into his arms, tablecloth and all. "Take her socks off," he ordered the housekeeper, who gently peeled them off Hana's delicate toes. Glass tinkled everywhere and Hana giggled as Leslie patted gently at her bare feet.

"Where's Phoe?" Logan asked and the housekeeper replied in Māori. Hana caught the word *kai* and realised her child was eating without her.

"You should have told me. I didn't know she'd woken up."

Leslie smiled. "Little *moko* is fine. Thank the good Lord you didn't push her pram down here to choose your book. She would have been hurt." Leslie formed the sign of the cross on her breast with great reverence.

"I was only going to be a minute." Guilt flooded through Hana, compounded by maternalism. She left the baby with Leslie in the family dining room, next to the hotel's enormous industrial kitchen. The wall clock told her it was over half an hour ago. Hana bit her lip, tears prickling behind her eyes. She hadn't been choosing a book, but trying to find somewhere safe to read the old brown journal in peace. One minute she was engrossed in the crabbed handwriting and the next, woken by glass showering her face. Hana rubbed the back of her hand across her eye and felt the sting as small particles ground in the cuts. She hissed under her breath.

"Shower," Logan spun on his heels and crunched across the floor with determined steps. He shouldered the fire door open and turned back to Leslie. "Leave the glass and lock the door. Get the cops again. My daughter could have been in here too."

"My book!" Hana held her hand out, green eyes widening in her face. "I should probably read it after all this trouble."

Leslie placed the worn journal into her palm, eyeing the tattered fabric cover with fleeting curiosity.

The shower in Logan's childhood room took a while to warm up as the cold spring water surged through the pipes to the heating element. The hotel was full and the guests had used much of the copious supply earlier, not to mention the post-breakfast washing up in the kitchen. Logan balanced Hana one-armed on his hip in the ensuite, his biceps bulging through his shirt while he ran water over his hand and nodded once, satisfied. He flicked the handle and the water ceased so he could lower his wife and her shroud into the cubicle. Hana kept her arms wrapped tightly round his neck, resisting as Logan tried to release her onto her feet. She nuzzled at the skin under his jaw. "Mmnn, you smell of horse."

Logan laughed, a deep, gorgeous sound that reminded Hana of the mountains and she sighed, noticing the tiny fragments of glass on his shirt. "You're covered now!" She smiled with mischief in her eyes, putting her feet down and hauling her husband into the shower. "You have to get undressed in here too."

Logan narrowed his grey eyes and gave his wife a sultry look. "I was actually in the middle of something important."

"Drenching horses isn't as important as me." Hana bit her lip, tears of shock threatening again in her pretence at bravado. Logan saw and took his cowboy boots off in the wet shower tray, rubbing the soles on his jeans to release the clinging shards. Then he threw them out of the cubicle and closed the glass door, trapping his body close to Hana's.

"Drenching's important if you're the horse."

He peeled the tablecloth gently away from Hana's body and let it drop, running his fingers over her cold shoulders and up underneath the fiery coils of hair at the back of her neck. Hana shuddered with relief as he bent to kiss her, tasting the remnants of chewing gum on his lips and allowing herself to feel safe.

***

"You saw and heard nothing, Mrs Du Rose? You didn't hear anyone run up to the doors and throw the brick, or see anything out of the corner of your eye? You were sitting side-on to the doors, you said, which is how the cuts are all on the right side of your body?"

Hana sighed audibly. She felt under interrogation. The South Auckland policemen were battle weary, suspicious of everyone and everything and she began to think they didn't believe her. "I sat down with the book and got distracted. I think I nodded off," she began, interrupted instantly by the jaded blond cop.

"You nodded off! But the call came at just after ten o'clock this morning."

Hana glanced fearfully across at Leslie, whom Logan drafted in to sit with his wife during her statement taking. His head stockman had called him with another problem and he left with an apology, nominating the housekeeper as his replacement. The wise old lady's eyes bore knowingly into Hana's and she quailed and heard herself gulp. "I didn't sleep too well last night," she ventured, watching Leslie out of the corner of her eye. "I think I'm probably still out of sync after our trip home from Europe. With all the worry about what's been happening around the property lately, it's affected my sleep patterns."

Hana picked at a knot on the massive wooden dining table, which generations of Du Roses had eaten over, argued over and smacked the snot out of each other over. It had probably seen its fair share of the other kind of passion too and Hana put her cut hands back underneath the table. She heard the clank of metal pans in the kitchen next door. Phoenix sat in her high chair, still eating and learning to make an art form out of it. Her father's grey eyes fixed on her mother's face and twinkled as she beamed, displaying her tiny, pearly teeth. The little girl waved her third piece of Marmite splattered toast at her mother and giggled. Hana focussed on the brown streaks on the child's lips and face and felt bile rising up into her gullet, accompanied by the familiar surge in her stomach. Phoenix's teeth look like marbled stalagmites. Hana kept her breathing shallow and smiled back at her daughter, whilst deliberately distracting herself with the sound of cars crunching in the gravel at the front of the hotel as guests came and went. The policeman's eyes were on her and she blanched. "Sorry, was there another question?"

Hana glanced across at Leslie, finding the older woman studying her, much as a butterfly collector inspects his pinned bugs. Leslie's once black hair was white at the front, receding into grey towards the tight bun which she restrained her long tresses in. Her olive skin had wrinkled over time and her body spread into an A-line shape like a Christmas tree. But her hazel eyes held all the sparkle of youth, revived through her recent marriage to Logan's elderly father, Alfred. Hana smirked at the memory of Logan's disgusted face when the old folk's coupling was mentioned. She wiped it quickly off when Leslie narrowed her eyes and jerked her head towards the policeman. "Sorry, what did you say?" Hana struggled to recover and turned her body towards the policeman's growing annoyance.

"I asked if you thought whoever threw the brick, knew you were in the room."

Marmite. Brown, streaky Marmite.

"I honestly don't know."

Bored with her late snack, Phoenix entertained herself making finger pictures on the surface of the high chair. Hana's senses went on red alert as the scent of the awful brown stuff invaded her nostrils and Leslie watched with curiosity, as Hana's face went from white to pink and back to white again.

Hana just made it to the dustbin in the corner, ripping the lid off and sticking her face into the massive black bin bag inside. The remnants of the stockmen's breakfast; bacon, eggs and fried bread, stared back at her and finished the last of her resolve. She threw up spectacularly - mimicked by her daughter who copied the noise - and watched by two policemen and her mother-in-law.

The next novel in this series is Du Rose Sons.

Dear Reader,

I would love it if you could leave a review at your usual retailer.

I find the opinions of readers helpful and constructive. Reviews are the Holy Grail to an author as they cause our work to sink or swim. It is the bench mark for other readers and can determine whether our work will be successful and reach many or none. It doesn't have to be an essay or a literary criticism. A few words about what you liked would be most appreciated. The shortest review I ever received for my work was, 'Great,' accompanied by five stars and the longest was a whole video from a gorgeous woman in the USA. My favourite to date has to be the lady who said, '*I read until my eyes fell out.*' I keep looking at that one because it makes me laugh.

You can review on my website, ktbowes.com. Go to the book's buy page where you can follow through to your own retailer and leave a review for me.

And hey, let me know when you've done it. I'd love to hear from you.

About the Author

K T Bowes is a bestselling teen and women's author.
Her novel, *A Trail of Lies*, was the winner of the genre award for Author's Cave in 2014.

Phoenix Du Rose was considered for the prestigious Ngaio Marsh awards for 2021 and *Her Quiet Legacy* in 2022.

K T Bowes is an Englishwoman in exile in New Zealand, swapping rugged cosmopolitan for mountain ranges and terrifying rivers. She loves Māori culture and has learned to weave flax using traditional methods. Her other passion is Rongoa Māori, which involves creating medicines from native plants. She is a student of Te Reo Māori.

You can find her hanging out on social media in the following places.

Check in and say hello. Maybe suggest she gets back to writing and stops watching cat videos.

FACEBOOK
https://www.facebook.com/NZauthorKTBowes/
TWITTER
https://twitter.com/ktboweswrites
INSTAGRAM
https://www.instagram.com/k_t_bowes

Also by this Author

The Hana Du Rose Mysteries Series:
Logan Du Rose
About Hana
Hana Du Rose
Du Rose Legacy
The New Du Rose Matriarch
One Heartbeat
The Du Rose Prophecy
Du Rose Sons
Du Rose Family Ties
Du Rose Vendetta
Phoenix Du Rose
Wiremu Du Rose

The Calculated Risk Series:
The Actuary
The Actuary's Wife
The Actuary in Trouble
The Heart of The Actuary

Troubled series for teens:
Free from the Tracks
Sophia's Dilemma
A Trail of Lies
Gone Phishing

Escaping the Back Country NZ Series:
Pirongia's Secret
Deleilah

Standalone novels:
Artifact
Demons on Her Shoulder
All Saints
Her Quiet Legacy

Humorous Cozy Mystery Series from New Zealand
Dead Straight
Bad Hair Day
Side Parting

www.ingramcontent.com/pod-product-compliance
Lightning Source LLC
LaVergne TN
LVHW030323250326
834688LV00047B/1715